"The perfect mix of funny, hot and heartwarming. I enjoyed it immensely!"

—Mia Sheridan, *New York Times* bestselling author

"Consider yourself warned: *Four Letter Word* will grab you from page one and won't let you go! It was deliciously sexy, and achingly beautiful. Completely and utterly brilliant, I loved every word!"

—Tara Sue Me, *New York Times* bestselling author

"*Four Letter Word* is the perfect blend of heat, emotion and humor. J. Daniels does an excellent job pulling you in with relatable characters, solid writing and a beautiful story about finding love when you least expect it and forgiveness. I can't wait to see where she takes us next with Tori and Jamie!"

—Tara Sivec, *USA Today* bestselling author

Also by J. Daniels

The Dirty Deeds series

Four Letter Word

Hit the Spot

PRAISE FOR J. DANIELS'S DIRTY DEEDS SERIES

BAD FOR YOU

"If you're a fan of tortured bad boy heroes with hearts of gold who fall head over heels for their one true love, then you are going to absolutely adore this book!!! I read this book in one sitting and loved the story, loved the writing, and loved the romance. This is definitely a new favorite!"

—Aestas Book Blog

"*Bad for You* is a distinctive blend of passionate romance, heartrending story, and hopeful message, and it left me a satisfied mess with a big smile on my face.... A beautiful romance that is a testament to acceptance, love, and second chances."

—*USA Today*, Happy Ever After

HIT THE SPOT

"An intense, passionate game of wills that will have you speeding through the pages to find out what happens next!"

—S. C. Stephens, #1 *New York Times* bestselling author

"So sexy, so heart-tugging and heart-melting, *Hit the Spot* definitely pushed all the right buttons for me! A must read!"

—Katy Evans, *New York Times* bestselling author

"Sinfully sexy and surprisingly sweet, from the first page you will fall in love with Jamie and Tori's story."

—Jay Crownover, *New York Times* bestselling author

"*Hit the Spot* is off the charts sexy. Cocky playboy? Check. Professional surfer? Check. I promise Jamie McCade will dirty talk his way into your heart."

—R. S. Grey, *USA Today* bestselling author

"Steamy and seductive, ereaders everywhere will burst into flames. With playful dialogue and a passionate conclusion, *Hit the Spot* is a five-star read!"

—J. B. Salsbury, *New York Times* and *USA Today* bestselling author

"*Hit the Spot* is a slow, delicious burn that hit me in ALL the right spots!"

—Harper Sloan, *New York Times* bestselling author

"A perfect balance of laugh out loud funny and crazy sexy, *Hit the Spot* is an alpha romance brimming with sassy banter that you won't want to miss!"

—Meghan March, *USA Today* bestselling author

FOUR LETTER WORD

"Daniels turns up the heat in the first book in the sexy new Dirty Deeds series. Fans of alpha males will devour Daniels' spicy new-adult romance."

—*Booklist*

"Love! That's the four-letter word to describe how I felt about this unique, sexy story. J. Daniels' hottest book to date."

—Penelope Ward, *New York Times* bestselling author

BAD FOR YOU

A Dirty Deeds Novel

J. DANIELS

FOREVER
New York Boston

Forever
Hachette Book Group
1290 Avenue of the Americas, New York, NY 10104

forever-romance.com
twitter.com/foreverromance

Originally published as an ebook in January 2018.

First Trade Paperback Edition: July 2018

Forever is an imprint of Grand Central Publishing. The Forever name and logo are trademarks of Hachette Book Group, Inc.

The publisher is not responsible for websites (or their content) that are not owned by the publisher.

The Hachette Speakers Bureau provides a wide range of authors for speaking events. To find out more, go to www.hachettespeakersbureau.com or call (866) 376-6591.

Library of Congress Cataloging-in-Publication Data has been applied for.

ISBNs: 978-1-5387-4345-4 (trade paperback), 978-1-5387-4343-0 (ebook)

Printed in the United States of America

LSC-C

10 9 8 7 6 5 4 3 2 1

To Bobby.

I'm sorry we didn't do more for you. You were loved and are loved still.

R.I.P.

And to my brother, J. R.

You got this.

BAD FOR YOU

Prologue

SEAN

"I need new clothes for school. Can we go to the store?"

Mom kept her eyes ahead, going back and forth between the show she was watching and the toenail she was painting as I stood beside the sofa.

She didn't look at me. She never looked at me.

I didn't know why I still got sad over that.

"No. I'm busy, you little shit," she snapped, causing the cigarette stuck between her lips to bob and drop ash on the carpet.

"But school starts tomorrow."

"So?"

"My shoes are too small, and they got holes. My big toes are sticking out."

And they hurt my feet, I didn't say. I didn't want to sound like a baby. She'd yell at me for that.

Mom dipped the nail brush back in the red, gloopy polish and kept painting, kept watching her show, kept refusing to look at me.

"Sew up the holes. You don't need new shoes," she said.

I bit my lip and turned away.

I was going to be stuck wearing the same clothes I wore last year to school. Same shoes. Same book bag. Everyone else would have new things, and they'd notice when I don't. There's no way they wouldn't notice that.

Third graders notice everything.

"Can I just get a new shirt or something?" I asked.

"No."

"Just *one*?"

She stopped painting then and peeled her gaze away from her show. Keeping hold of the nail brush, she pinched the cigarette between two fingers of her other hand and pulled it away from her mouth to bark, "I ain't made of money! You want new clothes, go out and get a damn job. It's about time you started pitching in around here anyway, since you don't do fuck-all else. What the fuck are you good for? Huh? *Nothing!* Just taking up space."

"I can't get a job. I'm only eight," I told her.

I didn't think other moms needed to be reminded how old their kids were. But I was constantly having to do it.

She waved me off with her hand holding the cigarette, ash dropping onto the sofa in the process. "Not my problem. Now, go do something before I get mad and smack the shit outta you. You're making me miss my show."

Tears stinging my eyes, I turned and left the room.

I knew asking for anything was a long shot, but it didn't stop me from asking. It never did.

I wanted nice things. Newer things. I wanted what other kids had.

I wanted a different life. I hated this one. I hated everything about it.

I walked past Mom's bedroom and saw the guy she'd brought home last night passed out on the floor. I didn't know his name. I never knew any of their names. They never spoke to me. And I stayed clear of them.

I learned that lesson when the one pushed me into the wall so hard, I threw up and had a headache for days.

I hated throwing up, but I just couldn't help it sometimes.

I stopped in the doorway and looked at the guy. He was hunched over, his back against the bed and his head hanging down. A needle stuck out of his arm.

Mom said she wasn't made of money, but she always had enough for those needles with the stuff in them that made everyone so sleepy. I found those needles all over the place.

The guy's wallet was open on the bed next to trash and empty bottles. I walked over to it, keeping my steps light so I wouldn't wake him up, and flipped open the soft leather.

There were three one-dollar bills inside.

I thought about what my teacher had said about taking stuff that wasn't yours, but then I thought about how much my shoes hurt my feet, so I took the money, tossed the wallet where I'd found it, and ran.

I shut the door to my room and moved quickly to the dresser. I kept my money hidden there—cash I found lying around the house.

My hand curled around the crinkled bills tucked behind my socks. I added them up with the money from the wallet. Total, I had eight dollars.

Maybe that would be enough for shoes and a new shirt. I could just wipe off my pants real good. Kids might not notice how old they were if I did that.

This plan felt like a good one. I actually smiled a little, and I never did that. Not here.

Keeping quiet, I snuck out the window instead of using the front door, worried I'd get caught, and ran as fast as I could down the street.

The closest store was a Payless Shoes. I walked inside and looked at what they had, picking out my favorite pair. They were all black with red stripes. I thought they looked so cool.

I took them up to the front where the woman was standing behind a tall counter, slid my box up beside the register, and dug my money out of my pocket. I flattened out the bills and handed them over.

The woman looked at the money, then at the shoes, and then back down at me. She was wearing a strange look, like she was a little sad about something. I didn't understand why.

I was buying new shoes. That wasn't sad.

"Um, this isn't enough money, sweetheart," she said, placing the bills down on the counter and sliding them closer to me.

I looked at the money and then back up at her. "What?"

"These shoes cost fifteen dollars. You only have eight."

I frowned. "But I don't have any more money," I said.

She was frowning now too. "I'm sorry. You'll just have to wait until you have enough."

The phone behind her started ringing. She turned away to answer it. I looked at the money again and at the shoes I wanted.

No. Not wanted. Needed.

I needed those shoes. My feet hurt so bad from that run.

Again, I thought about what my teacher always said. Stealing was bad, but she was talking about people who took stuff when they had other choices, and I didn't have other choices. My toes were bleeding now through my socks. I could feel it.

I wiped harshly at my face when I felt tears, and then, making sure no one was watching me, I did it.

I grabbed my money and the box of shoes, and I ran until I couldn't anymore, because it hurt too bad.

Hiding behind a car, I pulled off my old shoes and put on my new ones. They fit so good. They didn't hurt me at all. I thought I'd feel bad for taking them, but I didn't. I needed these shoes.

The run home felt so much better.

Mom never noticed me, so I never got into trouble. But I would get into trouble eventually.

My teacher said stealing was wrong, but sometimes people needed to do things that were wrong, because they didn't have another choice.

I was nothing to nobody.

I never had another choice.

Chapter One

SHAYLA

I wanted to tell her no. I wanted to lie to Gladys or Dorothy, whatever this sweet old lady's name was seated in my section, and say we were fresh out of ranch dressing, and the little cup of it that came with her large garden salad was the last drop. If I didn't and obliged her request, it would mean walking back over to the kitchen window I avoided like the plague and speaking to *him*—Sean "Stitch" Molina. The keeper of the dressings. The cook at Whitecaps Restaurant. He hoarded the ranch back there, and the only way to get more of it was with words.

And we didn't do words anymore. Not as of eight months ago.

So, instead of doing my job as a waitress, I contemplated the dishonest route, which could very well get me fired.

Was I willing to roll those dice? Maybe. It might be worth a shot. My boss, Nate, could overlook my wrongdoing. He was understanding enough.

We're fresh out of ranch, I could tell the lady. *And all other dressings, for that matter. I am so sorry. Could I maybe get you another refill? Or something else not located in the kitchen?*

I thought on this plan—it could work. Maybe she would believe me. Or maybe she would rethink her request and decide she no longer needed more dressing.

Help a fellow woman out here, Millie. Christ.

"I just need a little bit more," the lady requested with a gentle smile. "Would you be a dear? I won't trouble you for anything else, I promise."

"Of course," I replied, the response compulsively leaving my tongue. I couldn't fight it. I couldn't lie. I'd feel terrible.

Besides, this was my job. If someone requested more ranch dressing, I got them more ranch dressing, even if it meant speaking to the man I was completely and pathetically infatuated with, no matter how badly it hurt me to do so.

I gave the lady a smile in return before moving away.

My steps were slow as I weaved between tables and headed toward the kitchen. I tried to keep my head down, to focus on the tile floor disappearing beneath my feet, but I couldn't.

I had to look.

Who was I kidding? I *wanted* to look.

As I approached, Tori was leaning close to the window that separated Sean's domain from everyone else's. She slid two plates of food off the ledge, commenting, "Looks good. Thanks, Stitch," before walking off to deliver her orders, winking at me as she passed.

Sean only went by Stitch when he was here, I was assuming. I wouldn't know for sure since I'd never spent any time with him outside of work. It was a nickname Tori and I had given him when he'd cut himself a bunch of times during his first week on the job, and he didn't seem to mind being called that.

Back then, he didn't seem to mind a lot of things, like listening to me talk and talk about anything and everything, putting my problems on him in between waiting tables, my stresses, my fears, needing a person to vent to and him being the only person I wanted to vent to because of the way he listened and looked at me.

No one had ever seemed so interested in what I had to say before. Like what I was saying meant everything to them. Like it was a privilege just to listen.

And no one had *ever* looked at me the way Sean did—glances that only ever lasted a few seconds at a time, but those few seconds of eye contact—holy crap. I thought my skin was going to combust it would tingle and heat up so quickly. The man had a stare unlike any stare. Equal parts intense and intimidating. But his eyes, sweet mother of God, his eyes were unreal, this rich, golden copper color. And when they were on you, you didn't just see that beauty—you felt it.

It was a two-punch combo that turned me into a puddle. No man had ever affected me that way before.

And that effect wasn't going away. I was still feeling it.

Even now with us not speaking to each other, or rather, with me not speaking and him not listening, I still couldn't get Sean out of my head. I missed what we used to have, yes, but it was more than that. It was so much more.

A man I barely knew, who seldom spoke, and who had never showed interest in me *in that way* had somehow taken hold of my heart and twisted it all up. I didn't understand how it had happened, I just knew it happened.

Pathetic, right?

I reached the counter silently, which was a miracle considering how loud my heart sounded in my ears. Keeping my breathing quiet, I looked through that window and peered into the kitchen.

Sean had his back to me as he flipped burgers and stirred something in a pot. I allowed my eyes to travel the length of him, something I hardly ever let myself do anymore. We shared quick glances now, that was it.

Sean was well over six feet tall—way taller than me. His back was broad. His hair was long, a beautiful caramel color, and almost always pulled back; his arms were covered in tattoos and roped in muscle; and he had a thick, short beard that hid what I just knew was a strong jaw.

Sean was beautiful. And he was intimidating. Not just how he looked, but how he acted too.

He smoked. He drove a motorcycle. He never smiled. He rarely said a word. Everything about Sean said *leave me alone*, but eight months ago I couldn't.

And eight months ago, I didn't think he wanted me to.

I thought that was why he looked at me the way he did and listened so well. I wasn't even nervous when I finally asked him out after hearing about a local party. I was excited.

I wanted Sean. I wanted to kiss him and touch him and *God*, hear his voice more. I had gotten so little of it. I wanted to do everything with him. And I thought we would. I thought we'd go to that party together as friends and leave as something more.

But Sean wasn't interested in the more I'd been after. He wasn't interested in me at all.

Now, that was perfectly clear.

Sensing me, or maybe he was finished minding the burgers and whatever he was stirring in the pot—I didn't know for sure, since I was still letting my eyes wander—Sean spun around and stepped forward, snapping my gaze off his body in a panic. Our eyes met.

Mine widened.

His narrowed angrily, like I'd pissed him off and he hated me for it, and further hated me for catching him pissed off about it.

I didn't understand that look, but no way was I asking about it. I was doing what I came over here to do, and then, hopefully, staying far away from this window the rest of the day.

Maybe I could convince Tori to put in my orders.

"My lady needs more ranch," I informed Sean, swallowing thickly when my voice came out sounding stressed and distorted. "Could I get a little more for her?"

Sean's gaze lowered to my mouth like he was waiting for more words, which didn't make sense to me, until I considered the one word I left off he was most likely waiting for.

"Please?" I added.

His eyes lifted to mine and stayed narrowed. His nostrils flared. His jaw set.

I almost apologized for being polite and for not lying to that woman about our condiment supply. Things were so awkward now, I couldn't stand it. I missed how easy this used to be.

Memories flooded my mind in an onslaught as I stood there waiting, and my back stiffened. I pictured Sean watching me with care and concern. I remembered the smiles behind his beard I used to catch, and the way his eyes would follow me through the restaurant and brighten when I would wave. We were friends. I wanted to scream at him for ruining that. I wanted to scream at myself for still caring. What was wrong with me? He had completely shut me out. We were nothing now. We were *this*.

But with a quick hand, Sean snatched a dressing cup off the shelf and ladled some ranch into it before I spoke another word. He sat the cup on the ledge, removing his hand before our fingers touched, and briskly turned back to the grill without giving me another glance.

"Thank you," I mumbled at his back, turning before I lingered another second.

He shut me out. I needed to do the same to him.

I delivered the cup of ranch to the sweet old lady, picked up a check for a table who didn't wait for change, and took care of their tab at the register. Then because I didn't have any other tables needing anything from me at the moment, I moved to a vacant booth far away from that window and busied myself filling ketchup bottles.

The next time anyone needed extra dressing, I'd send Tori.

Three Days Later

I am getting one of everything.

Twisting the dial on the radio, I quieted the music I was listening to when the truck ahead of me pulled forward, allowing room for my Civic to squeeze up next to the speaker.

Mouth already salivating, I rolled my window down.

"Welcome to Taco Bell. Can I take your order?"

My stomach growled as I surveyed my choices.

I eyed the fiesta taco salad. The quesarito. The never-ending list of combos and the specialty options. Everything intrigued my taste buds.

I stuck my head out the window and directed my order at the speaker. "Can I have a number six, please? Chicken supreme with a soft taco? And a Mountain Dew."

"That'll be six fifty-seven at the second window, please."

I couldn't pull forward yet, so I kept my foot on the brake, and just as I was about to roll up my window to keep the cool March air from filling up my car any more, a song I knew and loved began playing low through the speakers.

I had no idea what the name of the song was or who sang it, but I knew every single word. And this was not a song you didn't crank up and sing along to with your windows down.

Fingers twisting the dial until music poured out of my car, I started moving my hips in time with the beat and smacking the steering wheel, eyes closing and fingers snapping as the lyrics left my mouth.

"Oh oh oh oh oh oh,
You don't have to go, oh oh oh oh oh
You don't have to go, oh oh oh oh oh
You don't have to gooo."

The drum kicked up. I shook my head and felt pieces of my short, dark hair lash against my cheeks.

The girl giggled through the speaker.

Smiling and not feeling one bit shy about the audience I was entertaining, I leaned halfway out the window and sang to her as loud as I could, reaching and pointing like she was front row at my concert.

"Ay ay ay ay ay ay
All those tears I cry, ay ay ay ay
All those tears I cry, oh oh ah ay
Baby, please don't goooo."

She laughed harder this time, whooping and cheering me on.

"How's that?" I asked. "Think I got a career in singing if all my other options fall through?"

"You bet!" the girl yelled. "That was sick!"

Giggling at myself, I sat back in the seat and turned the volume down halfway, noticing through the windshield the space between the truck in front of me and the car in front of it.

My eyes narrowed. I beeped twice. I was starving, and this was not the time to be messing around. What was this person doing?

The truck jerked forward, gears grinding over the music, loud enough I actually cringed. It was an old, beat-up Chevy, covered in dirt and rusted all along the back, with most of the paint chipped off and the muffler barely hanging on by a thread. The well loved and *very* well used vehicle was probably on its last leg, as was the worn smiley-face sticker half peeled from the bumper, leaving only one eye and half a mouth showing.

That thing had definitely seen better days.

Staring at all that rust, I had a moment of panic when I imagined the truck dying on its owner and blocking my path. Come hell or high water, I'd get my chalupas. Though I really didn't feel like stepping out of my car and walking inside where the lunch rush sat. I was wearing sweats covered in bleach stains, a baggy sweatshirt, zero makeup, and not a lick of dry shampoo. No way was I presentable for the public yet.

This was why God invented drive-throughs and curbside service—so women like me could sleep in on their days off and rush out the door when a hankering hit without even bothering to glance at themselves in a mirror.

But when the truck made it up to the window to pay without a hitch or stall, most of that panic left me.

And when the driver pulled away after collecting their order and turned out onto the highway, *all* of that panic left me.

I rubbed my hands together. *Come to Momma.*

"Hello!" I greeted the young girl with a smile and a wave, feeling like we had one of those lifelong friendship connections since I'd just serenaded her.

Grabbing my bag off the floor in front of the passenger seat, I dug around for my wallet.

"No need for that!" she said, turning my head and pausing my search. "That guy just totally paid for you. God . . . I *love it* when that happens. It doesn't happen enough. It's such a treat!"

I sat up and looked at her more fully. "What? What guy?"

"The guy in the truck."

"Really?"

Nobody had ever done that for me before, and I used drive-throughs a lot. *Well, shit on my head.* My first random act of kindness, and I had rushed the poor thing along.

I suddenly felt bad for beeping.

"Yep," the girl said, smacking her gloss-covered lips. "He asked me how much your order was and gave me enough to cover you both. And he wasn't bad looking either."

I leaned closer to the window, my interest in this mystery man spiking off the charts. "Yeah?"

"Oh, yeah. He had that dark, smoldering look about him. Real sexy."

Nice.

"Did he say anything? Leave his number on a napkin or something?"

"No." She shrugged. "Just paid for you and left. He acted in a rush." The girl turned to pack up my order.

Huh.

If he was interested, he would've gone beyond just paying for my food. I would think he would've at least waited before speeding out of here—at least pulled over and given me the opportunity to thank him.

Maybe he was just doing a good deed?

Letting myself think on that, I smiled and took my drink. "I'd like to pay it forward. How much is the person's order behind me? I'll take care of them," I said while blindly digging my wallet out of my bag.

"*Really?*" The girl clapped her hands together and squealed. "This is awesome! And they say there's no good people left in the world."

I laughed and made a face like I was agreeing with her, though I really didn't. I knew a lot of good people. Dogwood Beach was full of them.

And I was blessed to have a lot of those people in my tribe, supporting me, giving me friendship and love, and others, not necessarily in my tribe, but around me enough I got to see their good.

Still, I understood this girl's excitement. It wasn't every day a complete stranger did something out of sheer generosity. And selfless to boot. Who didn't stick around to take credit when credit was due? That was practically unheard of.

It's funny how a simple gesture can affect you. But kindness was powerful that way. It not only had the ability to alter moods, but it was also infectious. People wanted to spread that good around once they got it put on themselves.

Hell, I was doing it. Maybe the person behind me would do it too, and so on. We could all pay it forward.

Smiling, I thought about that mystery man in the beat-up truck, wondering if he knew just how inspiring he was. How *good* he was. I hoped someone was telling him.

After safely securing my bag of deliciousness in the front seat, I got the total of the order from the car behind me, paid, got my change, cranked up my stereo again, and sped off, leaving my window cracked so I could serenade Highway 355.

Even though I lived in a beach town, my two-bedroom, one-bath apartment wasn't even within walking distance of the beach. But just being within a half-hour drive of the ocean made me happy. And I swear, you could still smell the sand and saltwater from the parking lot surrounding Pebble Dune Apartments.

When the wind picked up...

Bottom line, it worked for me.

It was old; the building and the apartments themselves could use a remodel, new plumbing, and some fresh carpet. It was tiny—the bedrooms, the kitchen/living room/entryway, which combined, could fit inside my parents' two-car garage. But I truly loved it.

It had promise. It held history. And most of all, it had the spare bedroom I needed to kick-start my career.

Hair styling was my passion, and for the past three years, I'd been living that passion and loving every second of it.

Until three months ago, I'd been a stylist and color specialist at an upscale boutique in Dogwood. The atmosphere was sleek and edgy. The other stylists were pleasant. I got along great with my boss. All in all, it was an amazing learning experience for me, but it wasn't *mine*, and within a few months of working there, I realized I had bigger dreams:

Hair by Shay, with that kickass little trademark symbol next to it.

Or *Hair by Shayla*. I couldn't seem to decide.

Which was why I was using both #hairbyshay and #hairbyshayla across all social media platforms, posting at least three times a day and making sure it was included in my signoff.

I had hope one of the hashtags would eventually reach trending status.

I wanted to work for myself and build something from the beginning, something I could be proud of knowing how it all began—a quiet idea I couldn't shake that blossomed into a living, breathing passion. And staying in the one-bedroom studio I had been occupying for the past five years wasn't going to give me the room I needed to shape and create this new life.

I would've felt weird cutting hair in the middle of my living room/kitchen/bedroom.

I was anticipating keeping male clientele. Aside from the level of unprofessionalism, I really didn't want people seeing where I slept. I was not a bed-maker.

So, I started picking up as many extra shifts at Whitecaps as possible, socking away as much money as I could, and when I found an apartment I could afford with the room I needed to shape and create, I signed the lease, quit my job at Salon 24, and began the journey leading me in the direction of my dream.

It was scary.

It was stressful as a *mother*.

But it was exciting.

So, even though Pebble Dune Apartments sucked when it came to views, mine being nothing more than dirt and blades of grass, since I was on the bottom level, it was perfect to me.

I didn't need a view. I needed that second bedroom for my dream.

Sucking ice-cold Mountain Dew through my straw, I hit the lock button on my key fob after parking in front of my building and took to the stairs, carrying my lunch and, depending on how full those chalupas were stuffed, my dinner.

I was hoping to get two meals out of this. Hair by Shay (or Shayla) was on a budget.

Descending the three concrete steps, I paused when I hit the landing, having spotted the large, rectangular cardboard box that was perched in front of my door and the man leaning his elbow against it, playfully looking bored.

"*Finally.*" Patrick, the manager's son, dropped his head back with a heavy sigh. He was tall, nearly lanky, with skinny limbs and strong, angular features. "I've been freezing my nuts off out here. I thought you said you'd be home when this thing was delivered."

My eyes fell to his unzipped hoodie and the thermals he'd layered underneath. "Freezing your nuts off? You have on, like, four shirts. And it's not even that cold out."

It really wasn't. The air was cool, not cold, this time of day. Mornings called for coats and hats, but by lunchtime, the temperature typically hung out in the low sixties.

When Patrick looked at me again, his dark brown hair flopped over his right eye, the way it always did lately since he'd committed to growing it out.

Patrick was only a couple years older than me, and basically ran the front office at Pebble Dune. He was good at it too. Everyone living here was grateful to be dealing with him when they needed someone to deal with.

Even though I'd only seen him a couple of times, Pat Senior was stricter about certain things, such as paying rent in a timely fashion and abiding by certain pet policies.

Patrick just didn't give a fuck, as long as you *paid* your rent before the next round was due, cleaned up after yourself and any roommates with fur, and didn't cause any trouble.

Pulling the straw out of my mouth, I stepped closer to the box, head tilting slightly, and noticed the stamped logo running along one long side. "I ran out for food," I explained. My eyes widened. "Is that my chair?"

"That or a fucking elephant. This thing's huge. You should've seen me and the guy getting it off the truck. I almost dropped it."

My face split into a grin. "This is the best day of my *life*!" I shrieked, raising both arms straight above me, careful of the precious items in my hands. "First free tacos and now my beautiful baby is here? Shit, yeah!"

Patrick snorted and stepped back, shuffling the box back with him to allow me space to get to the door. "How'd you get free tacos?"

"The guy in front of me. I got up to the window, and my order was paid for." I slid my key into the lock and twisted, pushing the door open.

"That's fucking baller," Patrick commented. "I need to start doing that. I don't think to do shit like that."

"Ooh, for *Angela*. I bet she likes free tacos."

Angela lived at Pebble Dune too, in one of the other buildings, and Patrick was totally infatuated with her. I liked giving him a hard time about it. It was all in fun.

I propped my heavy, wrought-iron umbrella holder stand in front of the door so it wouldn't close and dropped my food off in the kitchen before rushing back outside to help.

Patrick bent down to grip one side of the box while I awkwardly gripped the other. It was too heavy for me to lift off the ground, so I slid my end inside, stopping at the carpeted living area.

"Where do you want it?" he asked.

I moved around Patrick and the box and closed the door.

"Second bedroom. Let's break it down here, though. I don't think the box is going to fit through the doorway." I glanced toward my tiny kitchen and squinted between the counter and the cabinet space, trying to see the knife holder beside the toaster. "Scissors..."

"Like a Boy Scout." Patrick pulled a switchblade out of his jeans pocket and flicked it open, then proceeded to cut down the tape holding the seams of the box together.

I watched with excitement quickening my breaths as my beautiful black leather styling chair was removed from the box and cut out of the plastic surrounding it.

Never before in my life had I ever been this excited over a piece of furniture. But this thing had a flared back, cushioned arms, a footrest, and a fancy hydraulic pump.

You'd have to be mental not to get excited over something this stunning.

Under my direction, Patrick carried the chair into the second bedroom for me and sat it in front of the large, rectangular mirror and floating shelves I had already set up, displaying an array of products waiting to be used.

"This place is starting to look legit," he said, hands on his hips as he glanced around the small room.

I looked away from the chair and gorgeous styling area to take in the space. My second bedroom didn't look anything like a second bedroom anymore.

The futon I'd originally been using as a living room sofa before I purchased a legit living room sofa was the perfect waiting area for clients. If, no... *when* I had back-to-back appointments, they would need a comfy place to sit.

In the corner next to the futon was my sleek black leather dryer chair I had saved up for. And on the walls, just like any salon, were framed beauty-inspired art pieces I'd found on Etsy.

The closet, had it been used as a closet, could've kept this place looking like a bedroom, but I had popped the doors off and stored roll-away carts in there that held my brushes, clips, bobby pins, and combs.

Even without my styling chair, this room looked pretty legit. But now? I couldn't have agreed more with Patrick.

Hair by Shay (or Shayla) was officially open for business.

"Hey, you don't mind if I go around and stick flyers under people's doors offering one free haircut, do you?" I asked him.

I needed to get the word out somehow, and I knew the term *FREE* had major draw. I was hoping if I had twenty takers, ten of them would return for another service. And maybe five out of those ten would mention me to a friend. Or even three out of the ten. That would still be amazing. Plus, there was also the appeal of doing a good deed by offering this. Maybe someone living at Pebble Dune was up for a job interview or had some big, important event they needed to look presentable for. That free haircut could be my first random act of kindness.

Patrick pushed his hair out of his face and turned away from the mirror. "Go for it," he said. "And if Angela takes the bite, let me know, and I'll stop over when she's here to *fix* your thermostat or whatever else we can pretend is broken."

I smirked. "Why don't you just ask her out already?"

"I'm getting there. I'm just waiting for the perfect moment."

"Create the perfect moment yourself and just do it," I said, stepping forward and poking him in the chest. "Man up, dude."

He quirked an eyebrow. "That guy, Scar or Needle or whatever the fuck you named him, did he man up yet?"

I scowled and turned away, folded my arms underneath my chest, and admired my new chair again.

I didn't want to talk about Sean. Talking about him led to thinking about him, and I did that enough without talking about him.

Working with someone you were trying to get over was basically the equivalent to having a room stocked with fabulous hair dye, at your convenience at all hours of the day, and not using any on yourself.

Currently, I was sporting a pretty shade of pink on the bottom half of my head, which looked amazing with the short, choppy bob I kept, loving this cut for its edginess and versatility. Even when I didn't bother styling my hair, like today, it still looked perfect with messy waves. And having a bright color underneath really popped against the deep brown framing my face.

Last month, I had gone with purple.

I was certain I'd continue changing it up, since it was impossible not to experiment when I had color this brilliant on hand.

"What's that?" Patrick chuckled from behind me. "Sorry. I didn't hear you."

I spun back around and shoved at his chest, moving him out of the bedroom and toward the front door. "I have work to do, such as delivering flyers before it gets too cold and too dark outside, and unless you'd like to help with that, it's time for you to go. I'm running out of daylight."

"It's not even two o'clock yet."

I ignored his solid point, not having a comeback for it, and stopped shoving him when we reached the tiny tiled entryway. "As a thank-you for the chair lifting, you get free haircuts for a year."

"Figures you offer that when I'm growing this shit out," he mumbled.

I tipped my chin up and narrowed my eyes.

He smiled, thinking my irritation was amusing, like always, then turned and pulled the door open, calling out a "Later" on his way out.

Stomach growling, I grabbed my food out of the kitchen and planted myself in the middle of the living room floor in front of the sofa, along with the printer paper I was using for the flyers and a few different colored markers.

I ate while I sketched up an appealing advertisement. I was offering haircuts as a walk-in service but recommended people call or text if they wanted color, putting my apartment and cell phone number on the paper. The ad looked good. It was bright and eye-catching, thanks to my colors—hot pink, purple, and black. In the very center in large, block lettering, I wrote *Hair by Shay*. And just below it, *or Shayla*, in parentheses. I really needed to make up my mind already.

After eating both chalupas, I walked around the apartment complex, knocking on doors before I slid the flyers underneath.

A couple people who happened to be home answered, but mostly everyone was working or out, or refusing to answer, so I didn't get a lot of face-to-face time. But the ones I did get to speak to seemed interested enough. Or they were at least being polite. I was too happy to care either way.

This was happening. Finally. And, my *God*, this chair was fantastic!

The second I got back from distributing the flyers, I shared my news. I couldn't wait another second.

"Guys! Check it out!" I turned the phone screen and showed my Snapchat followers my sick setup. "You know what this means, right? Hair by Shay, or Shayla, is open for business! Whoo!"

Taking a seat in my new chair, I added to my story and kept the filter giving me a pretty headband of flowers. I liked that one so much.

God bless the inventor of filters. It didn't even matter I wasn't wearing any makeup. No one could tell.

"I am so, so excited, you guys. Seriously, this is my dream. You know how I've been dying waiting for this room to get set up, and it's finally set up and I'm just...I don't know. I'm just so damn happy. I can't stop looking at everything and touching everything. I never want to leave this room."

I added my snap and switched to the cat filter, loving how this one made my voice sound.

"Follow your dreams, people. Follow them! Whoo! Just look at this chair! And it's comfy too." I slouched in it and spun around, smiling at the camera.

Once that snap was added, I switched to the life filter, the one that made you look flawless and needed to be installed on every iPhone, Android, Nikon, whatever the fuck camera you were using. All of them. This filter was life, hence the name I'd given it.

"Thank you all so much for following me and all of your sweet, encouraging messages while I waited for this. I am so beyond ready and excited. And I hope you guys are too. Dogwood Beach peeps and anybody living close, if you would like to set something up with me, a cut or a color or whatever, shoot me a message and we'll talk. Okay? You guys are the best! Bye!"

I blew a kiss and waved, adding the snap to my story.

Standing from the chair, I took one more quick video showing the entire room, and then a still shot of the Hair by Shay sign hanging on the bedroom door, which I edited with a note that read *or Shayla, still deciding*, and a smiley face next to it.

My phone started ringing.

"Hey, Mom! Guess what?" I answered.

"Shayla, I'm sorry to have to tell you Nana died."

My breath left me.

My nana had been fighting a battle with lung cancer for several years. Every time we thought she was over the worst of it, the disease would come back on, full force. It never let go of her.

I leaned against the wall and slid to the floor. "Oh, no. When?"

"About an hour ago," she said, her voice tight with emotion. "It was a long time coming. She's been sick and suffering for so long, but it's still a blow. She loved you so much. She loved all of us so much. Your dad is pretty upset."

I bit the tremble in my lip. "How is he doing lately?"

"He's the same, sweetheart."

I didn't like hearing that, but I knew that was the answer I'd always hear unless things changed, and when they did, it wouldn't be for the better. Parkinson's was a progressive disease. Dad would be the same, until he was worse.

I didn't know which response I feared more.

"How's Pop?" I asked.

"He's been preparing for this, I think." She sniffled and blew her nose. "But there's a lot to take care of, and I don't think he's up for it. Nana didn't want a funeral or any fuss whatsoever. That's one less thing. But she had so much stuff in that house, Shay. And Pop can't mess with all that."

I brushed the tears slipping down my cheeks. My poor nana. And my sweet pop. They were two of the best people I'd ever known.

"Your dad and I need to go out to Ohio to make arrangements," Mom said. "I think Pop wants to stay there after she's cremated. I don't think he wants to leave the home they shared. Your dad wants to make sure he's settled and okay before coming back. Do you think you could watch the boys for us while we're gone? This might take a couple weeks, and I don't want them missing that much school. Dominic's already behind in math, and Eli can't be missing therapy. They always have so much homework, and making all that up... *God*, I just can't deal with all this right now..." Her sad, small voice trailed off. "They're just going to have to miss school. I don't see any other way around it."

"No. I can do it," I answered, not liking the level of worry in my mother's voice. "I'll take care of them, Mom. I can handle everything. I promise."

"Shay, they have a ton going on. It's going to be a lot on you. And with your job—"

"I can talk to Nate tomorrow about it. He's understanding, Mom. He is. He'll let me work around them."

I wasn't worried about Nate. And I knew if I needed entire shifts covered, I had my girls to help me with that. Tori, Kali, and Syd would pitch in. We always had each other's backs.

"He won't mind, Mom. I promise."

I wanted to assure her. My mom had so much on her plate already, and how she managed it all while keeping herself together, I would never know. I was sure she could handle anything. But I wouldn't let this add to her stress when I had the ability to prevent that.

I could do this.

"Okay," she said, sounding a little better. "That's great. That really helps us out a lot, sweetheart. We're leaving tomorrow after we take them to school, so you'll need to pick them up. Dominic gets out at three-fifteen and Eli gets out at three-forty-five. Is that okay?"

I was supposed to work tomorrow until three, but again, I knew Nate would be cool with this. "Yeah, that's fine. That's no problem."

"I'm going to make a list of everything you'll need to know. I need to pack still. I think I'll have time to make a calendar or something. What's going on tomorrow? *God, what day is this?* Oh, right. Monday. Tomorrow..."

Mom's voice softened until I couldn't make anything out, and I knew she was speaking more to herself now than to me, going over everything she still needed to do and stressing herself out further.

"It'll be fine, Mom. I got this," I said. "Everything with the boys will be taken care of."

She breathed a sigh of relief. "I am so lucky to have you. Thank you, sweetheart."

"Tell Dad I love him and give Pop hugs for me, okay?"

"Okay, baby. I love you."

"I love you too."

I ended the call and noticed twelve notifications from Snapchat on my screen. I'd get to them later. Dropping my head against the wall and resting my arms on my knees, I looked over at the chocolate-brown futon.

Waiting area/bed it is.

Chapter Two

SEAN

I pulled my bike behind Whitecaps, parked it, and cut the engine. Closing my eyes, I let my head hang between my shoulders.

I felt dead.

Barely two hours of sleep last night. My muscles ached. The skin on my hands felt stretched, burned, and broken. My back was fucked up, courtesy of the floor I'd passed out on like a dumbass, knowing I should've quit and gotten some shut-eye when I noticed the time creeping up on four a.m., but also knowing I couldn't quit.

I *wouldn't*.

Not until that shit-hole, dump I was now the owner of was good enough.

I thought it would mean something, signing all those fucking papers yesterday, getting my name on the deed, walking out with the keys in my pocket, I thought I would feel...something. Anything.

I'd done it right. Saved up and sacrificed. I fucking *did it*, the way I was supposed to. The way you're supposed to do it.

So how come I didn't feel a fucking thing?

Maybe because the house didn't look worth jack shit, had more holes in the wall than actual fucking wall space, carpet that was stained and ripped, a roof that leaked, jacked up plumbing, a shoddy heater. The room sizes were shit. The yard was shit. The kitchen was shit.

The house? Yeah, you guessed it. Fucking *shit*.

But it was all I could afford, and I couldn't wait any longer.

Lucky for me, I could fix it up. I knew how to do everything that needed to be done, and what I didn't know, I'd figure out. I'd learn. But it was a lot of fucking work, and I couldn't have this taking a while. It had been long enough. Too fucking long. Meaning this wasn't going to be the last time I rolled up to Whitecaps feeling like ass. I had a lot of long nights ahead of me. I'd give up sleep entirely if I could.

Fuck it. That house was more important.

I rolled my neck from side to side, stretching it, as I headed for the back door. Fourteen hours on my feet was going to be a bitch after last night.

No way was I passing on another shift, though. I couldn't do that.

The restaurant lights were on inside, bright fluorescent and unforgiving, but it was quiet. Nobody was here yet. Nobody except Nate, my boss. Sometimes I thought the poor bastard never left.

I rapped my knuckles against his closed office door, noticing the dried compound still caked on my fingers and the back of my hand. Scowling, I picked it off.

Real fucking sanitary, dick.

"Yeah?"

I opened the door and walked inside.

Nate sat at his desk with a shitload of papers scattered in front of him, dressed in a shirt and tie like usual, his head down while he studied some order or whatever the fuck as his fingers dug into his temples.

Not once had I ever walked in here not seeing damn near close to the exact same scene in front of me. I didn't think there could've been that much shit to do when you stayed on top of it the way he did, but what the fuck did I know? I didn't own a business.

I had a feeling part of it had to do with keeping his mind off his dead wife.

Nate was a good guy. I had mad respect for him, for a lot of reasons, but most of that respect stemmed from our first meeting and the shot he gave me when he didn't have to. When nobody had to.

And when I didn't think anybody would.

* * *

December 2015

Arms pulled across my chest and jaw tight, I breathed deep through my nose as I waited for the question I knew was coming.

The guy, Nate—the owner of Whitecaps Restaurant—was reviewing my application. Currently on the second page and scanning the bottom of it. Lingering there. Not flipping to the third page.

Which fucking sucked for me. I was hoping this guy was the type to check work history and experience only.

But now? I should've known before I even walked in here.

I didn't deserve this job. I didn't deserve shit.

Never did. Never will.

So what the fuck was I even doing standing here? I was wasting my time. Nobody was going to hire me.

"I'm gonna go out on a limb here and say you purposely skipped over this question for a reason?" Nate's eyes came up and leveled me.

We had to be around the same age. I wouldn't peg this guy for much older than thirty, but he looked beat the fuck up, like he'd lived twice as many years as I had. And worse ones too, which was pretty fucking impossible.

"You got a record?" he asked curtly.

Lie. Lie. Lie.

The word *no* danced on my tongue.

The truth wasn't in my best interest. Maybe this guy wouldn't verify. Maybe I'd get away with it for a few months and make a little money before I had to split.

"I'll check," he added, like the bastard could read my fucking mind.

Shit.

I inhaled a deep breath through my nose and nodded once.

"This a recent thing?" he asked, resting his elbow on the desk.

I hesitated to share, but thought... fuck it. Didn't matter one way or the other now if he knew my history. No way was I getting hired.

"Just got out yesterday," I told him. "Can't really get much more recent than that."

"What were you in for?"

Suddenly restless, I shifted my weight on my feet. "Is that something you gotta know?" I asked, speaking louder. "It's not like you left space on there for me to write it down. You just asked if I'd ever been convicted of a felony. I answered that."

"It's something I need to know if I'm going to hire you," Nate shot back.

My head jerked. "You're still looking to hire me?"

Nate leaned back in his chair, letting the application drop to the desk, and cocked his head. "I got Miguel in the kitchen and only Miguel, and he's leaving Friday," he shared. "This job has been posted for two months, and you're the first person to come in here asking about it. You got experience. You seem to know what you're doing. Okay, so you have a record. We all make mistakes or got something in our lives we aren't proud of. I'm not excusing whatever it is you did. But I'm also not trying to close this place down while I wait for somebody else to come in here asking to get hired. That can't happen. So, unless you tell me something I really can't look past in order to give you a chance, yes, I'm still looking to hire you. Job's yours if you want it."

I blinked at the man.

Honest, I didn't know what the fuck to say to that. I was pretty sure I was hearing things.

I hadn't been offered many chances in my life. Not from people I knew who should've given a shit about me. Not from strangers who could've. If I wanted something, or if I needed something, which was typically the case, I took it. If I couldn't get something I needed, I found a way to get it. Either way, nobody did me any favors or gave me any handouts. It didn't fucking happen.

There were people who deserved good. I learned early on, I was not one of those people.

Still, I wasn't stupid. I knew I might not get a break like this again. Even though I was risking telling him something he might not be able to look past, I had to take that chance.

Bottom line: I might not deserve shit, but I needed this job.

At twenty-seven years old, I was going straight. I'd work hard for everything I got from here on out. I'd change my path.

I had to.

Not because I earned this or anything better than what I got dealt. This wasn't for me. Nothing was for me. Not anymore.

I wasn't worth dick. And I wouldn't let myself forget it. That was my penance.

Nate brought his hand up to scratch at his chin. His brows lifted. He was waiting.

I pulled in a deep breath. Yeah...fuck it. Time to confess. I needed this fucking job.

I wasn't sure what classified as excusable behavior or not. After I gave him the run-down of everything I'd done, figuring it'd be best to be up front about all of it and not leave anything out, I expected him to toss me out.

So when he took less than a minute to think his decision over and asked me, "When can you start?" I thought for sure I'd gotten hit one too many times in the head and was just now feeling the effects of those blows.

A weight I didn't realize I was carrying slid off my chest.

Again, I just blinked at the guy, not knowing what to say.

"Shit," he mumbled. "My girls are going to eat you alive. That silent treatment thing doesn't really work with them. Trust me."

I didn't know what he meant by that. Didn't really care either. I was still wondering if he realized he'd just offered me a job.

Me. Fucking *me*.

"Is tomorrow good? Or Friday? I was hoping you could train a day with Miguel..."

"Don't need to train. I know what I'm doin'."

He nodded in appreciation.

"I'll be here tomorrow, though. I wanna get started," I said, keeping to myself how desperate I was feeling. If I could've started today, I would've. But he wasn't suggesting that.

"Sounds good. Be here at eight. We open at ten." Nate stood and offered his hand to me. I stepped forward and shook it. "I'm not going to regret hiring you, am I?"

I shook my head. "I'm done with that life."

"Good."

"Plus, there ain't nothing here I wanna steal."

He stared at me.

Shit.

"You won't regret it," I uttered quickly, stepping back.

Jesus. I was one dumbass comment away from holding the record for world's shortest length of employment. Just shut the fuck up and leave.

Nate lifted his chin once more as he smoothed out his tie. "All right, Sean. Thanks for coming in. I'll see you tomorrow."

I stalked to the door and turned the knob, glancing back once more before I opened it. "Appreciate this. A lot," I said, my throat suddenly feeling tight. "I wasn't expecting... just, thanks. I mean that."

Nate dropped his head into a nod.

I walked out of the office and crossed the restaurant, pushing through the double doors that led outside.

* * *

Starting over wasn't easy, but I didn't want easy. I just wanted a chance to make it happen, and Nate gave me that.

I owed the guy.

But now I needed to make sure he knew that just 'cause I owed him and probably would for the rest of my fucking life, that didn't mean I could be pushed around. And I wasn't leaving this office until he got that point.

Whitecaps had two cooks now. Me, and this kid Nate hired last week.

I worked with J.R. for a day and a half while he was training. He seemed all right enough. Knew what he was doing. Talked a little too fucking much, but I was used to that kind of shit around here. And yeah, it was damn good luck he started when he did, seeing as I needed the day off yesterday for settlement, but every motherfucker here had another thing coming if they thought I'd just sit back and watch my job get taken from me. No fucking way.

Nate glanced up when I stopped on the other side of his desk. "Hey. How'd it go with the house yesterday?" he asked, sounding genuinely interested. "Everything work out?"

"Yeah." I crossed my arms over my chest, thinking about how I wanted to approach this. "Gotta talk to you about something, though."

"What's that?"

"I'm not stepping down so that little prick can take my shifts."

Nate's brows lifted. He sat back in his chair and removed his glasses, dropping them on the desk, and studied me, saying nothing.

Fuck. I gritted my teeth, thinking maybe I should've approached this differently. I wouldn't have shifts to fight for if I got my ass fired.

"Are you referring to J.R.?" Nate asked.

I nodded.

"He handled it well yesterday. No major issues. No complaints."

"Yeah? Good for him," I growled. "Ain't like it's brain surgery."

Nate tilted his head, asking, "What's the problem, Sean? You needed the day off, and he covered it."

I breathed deep through my nose, wanting to keep my anger out of this but finding that hard when I was feeling threatened. But tearing into Nate? What fucking good would that do? I couldn't mess this up.

And I always messed everything up, fucked it all when it was going good.

Don't blow this, asshole.

"Appreciated that," I said calmly. "I don't remember saying anything to you about it Sunday, but just know I'm grateful. That shit yesterday was important."

Nate said nothing. So I kept going.

"That being said, I need the hours. I need the money. I need my fuckin' shifts. I can run that kitchen by myself. You know I can. So, I'm not seeing a reason for that kid sticking around. You need to cut him loose. If he handled things yesterday as well as you say he did, he'll have no problems finding work. You don't even need to feel bad about it." I shrugged. "Shit, I'll tell him if you want. I got no problems doing it."

Might even enjoy it a little too. Payback for talking my fucking ear off.

Nate's mouth lifted into a half smile. "I think that kid might shit his pants if you fired him," he said, then his face grew serious as he sat forward, looming over his desk. "I hired J.R. to help," he shared. "To take some of the workload off you. I know you can handle that kitchen, but Jesus, man, everyone needs a break. You open and close for me every day."

"Am I complainin'?" I asked.

"No, but I doubt you would. You and I both know there are days and times when we're busier than others. There's no reason why there can't be two of you back there."

"Full season, I can handle it. I'm not askin' for help."

"And I'm not asking your permission to give you help, am I?"

Nostrils flaring, I clenched my jaw to keep from saying something I couldn't take back.

"Look." Nate raised his hand to halt me from speech. "Let me say this before you flip my desk over and knock me out, since you look ready to do that. You and J.R. are going to be splitting up the shifts. That's not up for discussion."

Cursing, I turned and headed for the door.

Fuck this. Fuck this fucking job and every motherfucking asshole working here. I am done.

"And I'm giving you a raise."

I froze, blinking at the wall. *What the…*

"And just so we're clear on this—it'll cover the cut in hours you'll be taking and then some."

I slowly turned my head, meeting his eyes. "Why?" I asked, voice tight.

Nate gave me a look like he knew that question was coming. "How long have you been working for me?" he asked.

"Fourteen months."

"And how many times have you been late in those fourteen months?"

"None."

"Sick? Called out for whatever reason? How many times?"

"None."

"Complained about hours?" He smirked. "Complained about *anything*?"

I turned to face him again. "So I don't bitch? So what?"

"You come in here, you do your job, and you do it well, Sean," he said. "You're the best damn cook I've had in here, and I appreciate the fact that you don't give me shit or cause drama. You wanna know why I'm giving you a raise? Because you earned it. You've also earned a break, so take it. Split up the shifts with J.R. Work together. Let him take some of the load. Just figure it out. I don't want to see you when I get here and when I'm leaving at night. Take some days off, man. Christ. Nobody needs to be here as much as me."

I stood there unable to speak, just processing everything Nate just said, which was a fucking lot, more than he'd ever said to me at once before. But mostly, I was focusing on the fact that I was going to be making more money and working less, which meant I would have time to fix up that dump.

I wouldn't need to be pulling late hours and giving up sleep entirely. Hell, I might even be able to get it ready sooner than I thought.

This was a *good* thing. I didn't understand why, but I was getting an opportunity, another break, and there was no fucking way I wasn't going to take it.

"Are we good?" Nate asked when I still hadn't said anything back to him. "Or do you want to try and talk me out of this, and maybe still punch me?"

I stuck my hands in my pockets. "I'm not gonna punch you."

"Do you still have a problem with J.R.?"

"No."

"Good." He shook his head, the corner of his mouth lifting. "You need to ease up a little, Sean. Give yourself some credit. If you work hard for me, I'm not going to ignore that. Keep it up, all right?"

Nodding, I turned away from Nate and got the hell out of that office, feeling strange as shit.

Good, yeah, I felt good about the changes, now that I knew how this was going to play out for me, but I still didn't know how to feel when I was handed something. Especially when I knew I didn't deserve it.

Treat me like garbage. Be a complete dick to me. That I could understand. But Christ, anything else was confusing as hell.

After shrugging off my coat, tying my hair back at the base of my skull, and washing the rest of the compound off my hands, I went to the walk-in and started taking inventory.

Work kept me busy and my mind off shit I still couldn't wrap my head around, no matter how hard I tried. For an hour, I had silence.

Prep done, I was working on the soup of the day when J.R. came in through the back.

"What's up, man?" he asked, sounding pleased as fuck to be here and see me, like we were close or something. This kid was weird. "Hey, did Nate talk to you about how we're gonna split up the shifts?"

I jerked my chin, keeping my eyes on the pot I was stirring.

"'Cause I just wanna let you know, I'm down with whatever," he continued as he moved around the kitchen. "So if there's days when you want me to cover early, I got that. Or if you wanna roll out of here before close, cool. My shit is flexible."

That ache in my neck continued to throb. "Wouldn't mind getting out of here before too late tonight," I said, meeting his eyes then. "You sayin' you got this covered?"

J.R. smiled, tugging off his beanie and running his hand through his blond hair, spiking it up. "Brother, I got you. No problem. Hey, man, this is gonna work out. I know you seemed a little... *unsure* about me getting hired on, and I got that. I'm young. I got this new style about me. It's intimidating. I feel you. But you'll see. We'll probably be best friends by next month."

I stared at him. It's *intimidating*? Jesus Christ. What the fuck was this kid on? And why the hell was he calling me *brother*?

His smile grew, stretching his lips wide. "You're serious as fuck back here, man. You need to lighten up a little." He laughed at himself, then looked toward the window separating us from the restaurant.

I was just about to get back to what I was doing, considering I had nothing else to fucking say to this kid, when his next words stopped me.

"Morning, ladies! Who else froze their balls off driving over here? Just me?"

I didn't give a shit what he was talking about. That's not what had me turning more and looking through that damn window myself.

I had to know *who* he was talking to.

Kali stopped in front of the window first, giggling as she tugged off her wool hat.

She was one of the waitresses. Young, like the rest of them, but had a kid I knew she was raising on her own, considering how much all of them fucking talked around that window. She didn't say much to me, though, never did, and unlike two of the others, didn't get up in my shit every other second like they were getting paid to do it. I didn't mind her too much.

"Don't you have heat?" she asked J.R.

"Not heat that'll shoot up to my balls," he replied. "Why hasn't someone invented that yet? There needs to be one of those vents below the wheel, shooting straight at my junk."

"How lovely." She chuckled.

"My balls are fine!"

Hearing that voice, my shoulders pulled back and I sucked in a breath. I watched Shayla smile and laugh as she walked toward Nate's office.

Our eyes locked—hers so fucking big. Almost too big for her face; it should've looked weird, but it didn't.

They were one solid color—a rich brown, shiny like wet soil, and *Christ*, they were beautiful. I'd never seen eyes like that before. I could look all fucking day at a pair of eyes like that.

But, like usual lately, my time for looking was limited.

Shayla immediately turned away, her cheeks a shade redder, which I'd put money on having absolutely nothing to do with the cold, and knocked on Nate's door. He called out, and she disappeared behind it.

Gritting my teeth, I turned back to the stove and kept stirring my pot of crab soup, reminding myself how fucked up it was to be wanting attention from someone I had no business getting attention from.

This was the way it needed to be. She should be turning away. She should be avoiding me and keeping all those sweet words to herself now. So what if I felt like a giant piece of shit for doing her the way I did. I had to do it. She shouldn't be wanting anything from me anyway. She deserved better.

I had no idea why she took to me in the first place. I sure as fuck didn't ask for it.

I wasn't particularly nice to her. I didn't go out of my way to talk to her or even so much as look at her back when I first got hired on. I kept to myself and worked. That's what I got hired on to do, so why the fuck would I do anything else? I didn't give a shit about anyone here. And they shouldn't give a shit about me.

But for some reason, that girl felt inclined to push her way in, like talking to me was something she not only wanted to do, but enjoyed doing. And I couldn't keep ignoring her. I tried. *Motherfucker*,

I tried. I didn't give her anything in return those first couple of days, not even making eye contact with her when she'd drop off a damn ticket. Just let her ramble on and on. She told me about everything. Everything she was thinking, feeling, wishing for, and wanting more than anything. I kept my focus on my work and nothing else, until I slipped up and looked up after hearing something in her voice, something I didn't like that sounded an awful lot like fear, and for the first time I saw who the fuck was talking to me like they were in some sort of competition for most words spoken in a minute.

I saw her eyes first. That stopped my breathing.

Then I looked over the rest of her face, taking in all those sweet features—pale flawless skin, cute little nose, and full pink lips. Her hair was dark and stopped just below her chin, cut choppy, and held out of her face with a skull bandana. She looked young as fuck, couldn't have been much older than twenty. She looked tiny as fuck too. I could see most of her, since she was sitting up on the counter and peering at me through the window, but I didn't get to check out much more than her face before I watched those pretty lips stretch into a smile, shutting my brain down completely from further functioning.

It wasn't just the fact that she had a good smile, a fucking great smile, actually. One that somehow made that mouth even prettier. She had a smile that lit up her whole damn face like she was standing in a spotlight, making her shine from the inside out.

It was the fact that she was giving it to me and giving it good, like she'd been waiting for me to look at her and couldn't have been happier about that wait ending. And then she further fucked me up when she opened her mouth and spoke, saying something I shouldn't have heard and further, shouldn't have given a shit about.

Too bad I did.

"There you are," she'd said, holding on to that smile while she jumped down, staying turned to face me. "I thought I was going to have to set myself on fire to get your attention. That would've sucked." She giggled.

And that laugh was fucking pretty too. Don't ask me how, but it was.

I watched her cross the restaurant and tend to some dickheads who got seated in a booth.

She was joking, obviously; I'm not an idiot. She wouldn't have set herself on fire, but I suddenly felt like the world's biggest asshole for putting those words in her mouth.

Maybe I should've been giving her attention…

What? No. Fuck, no.

Shaking my head, I got back to work, doing what I should've been doing all along for about two seconds before I was stopped again.

"I'm Shayla, by the way."

I quit working and looked up.

She was back to sitting on the counter as she finished scribbling on a ticket, smiling softer now, like she was thinking about something funny but didn't want to share it.

That pissed me off.

And then it pissed me off further because *why the fuck did that piss me off*? What did I care what she was thinking about?

And why the fuck was I still looking at her?

I watched as she ripped the ticket off her book and slid the paper across the lip of the window, pushing her body closer and giving me a view of her uniform top.

My eyes fell to her name tag. "You go by Shay?" I asked.

Her mouth dropped open as she stared at me for several seconds, gaze lingering on my beard. "Uh…y-yes?" She cleared her throat and her cheeks pinked up. "Sometimes. I go by both."

"You like one better?"

"I don't know."

My eyebrow lifted. "You don't know?"

She stared at me for a breath before responding. "I guess I like whatever people want to call me. I like both. I answer to Shay or Shayla. What do you like?"

"Shayla."

My response shocked the shit out of me and threw her off too. Me because *what the fuck was I even saying*? Why was I telling her what I liked? Why did I even like it? And why the fuck was she even asking? What did she care?

I didn't get this girl, but I knew my response meant something to her. I could see it.

Shayla blinked those big, brown eyes, mouth slack, my answer clearly stunning her, which I'm guessing had to do with me giving her one so quickly, then she started smiling at me again, and muttered a "Cool" before hopping back down and busying herself getting drinks.

I didn't want her busying herself getting drinks. I wanted her to plant her cute little ass back on that counter, and keep talking to me, and I wanted her to do it while I looked.

Something was seriously fucking wrong with me.

I got back to work and tried not giving her any more attention for the rest of the day, which I fucking sucked at. I didn't say much else to her, but I looked. I fucking looked a lot. I looked forgetting I shouldn't *be* looking, and when that realization hit me later that night when I got back to my shit-hole trailer, and I remembered why I didn't deserve to be looking at someone like that, seeing as I wasn't ever going to be better than the filth surrounding me, I vowed to put an end to it. The next time we worked together, I wouldn't give her shit. I'd ignore her. And she'd eventually get the hint and leave me the fuck alone.

Yeah... That didn't happen. I didn't ignore a damn thing. And she didn't sway either.

We kept at it for months. *Months.* Her talking. Me listening and looking.

And although I liked it more than I could remember liking a lot of things, I needed it to stop. I wasn't ever going to be worth what this girl wanted to give. I knew that, and I needed her to know it too, but I couldn't say anything. I couldn't do a damn thing to stop what was going on between us. I had to look at her. I had to listen to everything she was telling me, knowing that it could and would end and wanting it to just as badly as I didn't. I couldn't fight it. I needed *her* to fight it. Something had to get this girl away from me.

And when an opportunity came for me to fuck it all up, I saw my out and I took it.

Her invite to some bullshit party sounded friendly, but I knew it wasn't. I could tell by the way she was looking at me, smiling, licking her lips, and telling me with those eyes how badly she wanted this—us—to happen. And I stared right on back, wanting it just as bad, wanting *everything* with this girl, maybe more than she did, but not letting that on. Not letting anything on, not even how I had no intention of going with her.

She found that out on her own, when instead of walking to her car come closing time, I got on my bike and took off, not even giving her so much as a glance. And I knew she was watching me, expecting at least an explanation.

I couldn't give her that. This was my way out, and fucking her over was the only way she'd leave me alone.

All of this was my doing. I wanted to break her. I did it so she'd pull away.

So if someone could please explain to me why the fuck it pissed me off every time she *did* pull away, that would be great. 'Cause I sure as hell didn't get it.

"Dude, the soup is boiling."

J.R.'s warning jarred my focus. Cursing, I quickly turned down the heat and stirred the thick broth, grateful it hadn't burned.

Fucking women. Nate couldn't hire a bunch of men to wait tables? What the fuck was wrong with him?

"I'm gonna get started on the marinara," J.R. said, grabbing a pot off the shelf above me.

I jerked my chin.

"You're such a go-getter, J.R. Good for you," he mumbled, laughing at himself.

I turned my head and glared. He took a step back, his one hand raised defensively, and moved his pot to the other set of burners on the other side of the grill.

Christ, I was going to be sharing a kitchen with this idiot. My days were going to feel a helluva lot longer now. I just knew it.

"I loved your story yesterday, Shay," Kali said.

"Really? Thanks! I always wonder if people think they're stupid or not. I go a little nuts on there."

Grabbing the tray of chicken I'd already prepped and seasoned, I moved to the worktop in front of the window and started dumping extra seasoning on the breasts, which I had no fucking reason for doing, except that doing it put me closer to that window, which put me closer to *her*.

I glanced up, saw Shayla standing on the other side of the bar where Kali stood making drinks, got those eyes I couldn't get enough of for a full fucking second, and then watched her turn away, looking uneasy.

Goddamn it. She shouldn't be turning away and looking uneasy.

What the fuck? Yes, she should.

"No, it was great! I'm so excited for you," Kali said, filling another cup with water after passing one to Shayla. "Your stories are always so cute and funny. Mine suck."

"They do not. You're crazy." Shayla took a sip of her drink, met my eyes again because I sure as fuck wasn't paying attention to chicken that didn't need any more seasoning, and was only watching her, then took those eyes away from me as she moved away. "I'm gonna go wipe down the tables," she called out.

"I'll help. Hold on." Kali turned toward the window, sipping her water.

"What story is she talking about? Is she a writer or something?" I asked, keeping my voice low.

It pissed me off I was even having to ask this question. I should've known this. She had told me everything else about her life. Why the fuck wouldn't she tell me this?

Kali looked up at me and slowly lowered her glass. Her eyes were round. "Are you talking to me?" she whispered, staring at me like I'd just appeared in front of her out of thin air.

Jesus Christ. "Is anyone else standing there where I'm lookin'?" I growled. "What do you think?"

"Well... it's just, you *never* talk to me," she said, leaning closer. "Like ever. Are you feeling okay? Is something happening? Are we under attack right now?"

"Are you gonna answer my fuckin' question or not?"

"*Sorry.* This is just weird." She quickly leaned back. "It's, uh, Snapchat. Her Snapchat story. That's what we were talking about."

"What the fuck is Snapchat?"

"Dude." J.R. came to stand beside me, looking amused. "Even my grandmother knows what Snapchat is. Have you been living under a rock or something?" He gestured at the tray. "Pretty sure that chicken has enough seasoning now."

Motherfucker. "Did I fuckin' ask what you thought about the chicken?" I gritted out through clenched teeth. "Go work on your fuckin' marinara."

J.R. chuckled and kept standing there.

Great.

"It's an app," Kali said hurriedly. "You know, the little icons on your phone. You can download them. It's another social media thing. Like Instagram, but it started the filter craze. Now everyone is biting off Snapchat. Even Facebook. Wait . . . um, you know what social media is, right? Do you have an iPhone? Do you even know what that is?"

I glared at her.

She pointed at me. "I'm going to take that as a yes. Anyway, Shay adds snaps to her story and anyone who follows her can watch them. She snaps all the time."

Snaps? What the fuck is she talking about?

"If you have your phone, I can show you," she offered, smiling kindly at me.

I hesitated for the briefest second, not knowing what the fuck I was doing asking about this or why I even cared, but then I quit wanting to hesitate, cursed and wiped my hands off to dig the phone out of my back pocket.

There was just some shit not worth fighting against.

"I guess I'm wiping off tables *alone*!" Shayla yelled out from the front of the restaurant.

"Shoot. Sorry." Kali grabbed a rag from underneath the counter, then rolled up on her toes to get closer, holding on to the lip of the window for balance. "Her username is *HairbyShay*. One word," she whispered before hurrying off.

I looked down at the phone, not knowing what the fuck to do, then feeling eyes on me, turned my head and saw Annoying As Fuck grinning like an idiot while he motioned for me to hand it over.

"I got you," he said. "Watch the master work."

"Whatever." I gave up my phone and looked out into the restaurant, watching Shayla smile at something Kali was saying.

"Dude, your shit isn't password protected? Are you insane?"

"Who the fuck is gettin' into that phone besides me?" I bit out.

"Unless I give permission, nobody's touchin' my shit. What the fuck do I need a password for?"

J.R. thought for a second, then nodded his head. "Good point. You're scary. Okay. Quick run-down." He held the phone out and showed me what he was doing. "Here's the app. You need a username to get started. Once you lock one in, and don't try taking *badass-motherfuckincook* 'cause that's mine, you go up here to *Add Friends by Username*, and voilà. Enter that shit."

I took my phone from him and jerked my chin, moved fast out of the kitchen, and kicked the back door open, yelling, "I'm stepping out for a smoke!"

"Ah! And by *that*, you mean—"

The back door shut behind me, cutting off bullshit I didn't need pointed out to me right now.

I knew what the fuck I was doing. I was taking a smoke. And I was looking at Snapchap stories or whatever the fuck they were called.

Leaning back against the building, I lit up, filled my lungs with smoke, and then clicked on the app, typing in the first username that came to mind so I could hurry this shit up.

Username.

Yeah. That would do just fine.

Remembering J.R.'s instructions, I swiped up and clicked on *Add Friends by Username*, typed in *HairbyShay*, found her, *fuck yeah*, and hit *add*. Then I just stared at the fucking thing. I didn't know what to do. He didn't tell me.

Shit. Why didn't he tell me what to do next? What the fuck? I seriously hate that kid.

There was a square thing in the bottom left corner. I clicked that, then got out of it because that didn't do a damn thing. I tried the three dots in the right corner, and there, *right the fuck there*, there she was.

I smoked and watched her sweet, heart-shaped face fill my screen.

She had flowers on her head and she was showing off her place and looking right at me, like she was talking to *me*, just like she used to. Then the video ended, and I almost smashed my phone, wanting it back and not knowing how to get it, but another one began.

I watched her like I'd never watched anything before in my life. I never felt this focused.

She had stupid shit on her face in one video, making her look like a goddamn cat, and her voice sounded weird, but who gave a fuck? She was talking, and she was smiling. And then it was her, nothing on her face and no change to her voice, just her, so fucking sweet and cute.

Those big brown eyes staring right at me. She waved and blew me a kiss.

I choked on smoke and felt my dick jerk against my zipper. *Fuck.*

Coughing, I flicked ash onto the pavement and pressed my knuckles to the front of my jeans. Then I took another inhale and leaned back, eyes pinching shut as I rested my head on the building and blew smoke out above me. I needed to calm down.

Goddamn it. What the fuck was I even doing with this shit?

When I looked at the screen again, it was over, and she was gone. She wasn't talking to me anymore, and I thought *good*, because I knew I didn't deserve to be watching her the way I was doing and thinking this was for me and nobody else.

Then my thumb slid on the screen, pushing past advertisements, and there she was again.

I clicked on *HairbyShay*, not knowing what it would do and wondering why she settled on that name instead of Shayla, but her videos started up, and I stopped wondering.

Fuck it. Fuck it all.

I took another hit and watched her videos again, pretending they were only for me.

Chapter Three

SHAYLA

My brothers went to school in Hyde, the county just outside of Dogwood Beach, so the drive wasn't bad. From my apartment, it was thirty minutes away, and only a forty-five-minute drive from Whitecaps.

I grew up in Hyde, for the most part. My parents moved there when I was in fourth grade after Dad got a job transfer, taking us out of the small Ohio town we'd been living in.

At the time, I hadn't wanted to move. I didn't want to leave my friends or my grandparents, and everything else that was familiar to me. But then I'd found out how close we'd be living to the beach and quickly changed my tune.

I'd never seen the ocean before.

And the second I saw it, I'd fallen in love. That very first feel of sand beneath my feet and the water on my toes, the smell of the air, the sun, and how different it felt and looked, reflecting off the water. We lived close to paradise, but I couldn't wait to live closer, and as soon as I turned eighteen, I packed up my things and moved to Dogwood.

I loved it here for so many reasons, but I liked visiting home too. I was grateful to be close enough to do that anytime I wanted.

Since the buses were filling the pickup circle in front of Hyde County Middle, I pulled up along the side so I could still see the front entrance where the kids were walking out, and threw the gear into park.

I still had fifteen minutes to kill, so I tugged my phone out of my bag and pulled up Snapchat.

I had a few more notifications from followers, people congratulating me or requesting information for an appointment. That made me crazy happy. I'd be lying if I said I wasn't nervous about this whole thing, so knowing people were interested gave me a rush of relief.

I took ten of the fifteen minutes to respond to everyone, even the followers just congratulating me, and then switched to video mode, selecting the filter that gave me killer lashes and a halo of gold leaves.

"You guys, *seriously*, thank you so much for all the sweet messages! I'm so grateful to have followers like you. You guys are the best!"

I added the snap and took a quick photo with the life filter, blowing a kiss at the camera. After sending that one through, I typed my hashtag and *DM me for info!* on a black screen, and added that to my story just as someone knocked on my back window.

Dominic was standing by the car.

I unlocked the doors and put my phone away as he climbed in behind the passenger's seat. His book bag hit the floor with a thump.

I turned halfway. "What up? How was school?"

"Fine," he grumbled. He pushed his hood down and rubbed at his short, dark hair while fishing the phone out of his jacket pocket, then he slumped back against the seat and started typing.

"Just fine?" I asked. "Anything cool happen today?"

"No."

"Did you have any tests or anything?"

"Can we just *go?*" he snapped, gaze still fixated on his screen. "Why are we still sitting here?"

I narrowed my eyes, but I didn't get on him about giving me an attitude. For two reasons.

One, I was used to it, seeing as he was thirteen now and basically hated everyone who wasn't one of his friends from school. So it wasn't personal.

And two, I knew he was having a hard time with Dad's diagnosis, and I figured Dom had a right to be angry at the world, if that was part of his process of coming to terms with it.

The situation sucked. We were all having difficulty dealing.

I could put up with a little attitude.

The drive to Hyde County Elementary was made in silence.

Dominic stayed glued to his phone, and I kept the radio off, just in case he wanted to initiate conversation. When he didn't, again, I didn't take it personally. Still, I wanted him to know he *could* talk to me, if he wanted, so I made sure to look back at him and smile every chance I got, those times happening when I was forced to stop at a light.

Dominic thought me smiling at him was weird, I could tell, given the looks he'd given me in return. Maybe I was overdoing it.

After parking at the curb in the designated parent pickup lane at Hyde County Elementary, I waited on the sidewalk for Eli, giving Dom the space I figured he wanted.

When my eight-year-old brother walked out with a crowd of kids surrounding him, I smiled and waved.

He didn't wave back, but he did smile, big and bright, before breaking into a run and pushing past the other kids. When he reached me, his head hit my chest, his arms wrapped tight around my middle, and he gave me a squeeze.

"Hey, E," I said against the top of his head. "Did you have a good day?"

He pulled away and nodded.

"Getting straight A's?"

He shrugged.

"Girlfriends? How many? I see a couple cute ones over there..."

Red-faced, he quickly looked left and then right. "*S-Shay.*"

I smiled and ruffled his dark hair, which he always kept longer so it reached past his ears and fell a little in his eyes, something I always thought he did to hide when his voice drew him attention.

"Come on. Let's get going," I said, ushering him around the car and opening the back door for him.

I tossed his book bag on the passenger seat and climbed in the driver's side.

"Okay, so here's the plan," I announced, pulling away from the school. "We're going to swing by the house and get everything you guys need for the week, and then we'll—"

"Why are we grabbing our stuff?" Dominic asked curtly. "Why aren't we staying there?"

I glanced in the rearview mirror, expecting to see the top of Dom's head since I was sure he was messing with his phone still, but he wasn't messing with his phone. He was glaring at me.

I sighed. "Because I'm working out of my apartment, and I need to be there as much as I can right now," I explained. "People might stop over to get a haircut or something. It'll just be easier to stay at my place instead of going back and forth."

"I thought you were a waitress," he returned.

"I'm a hair stylist, who just so happens to also wait tables, 'cause I'm badass like that."

Eli chuckled. I met his eyes in the mirror and winked.

"Whatever," Dominic grumbled. "I don't want to stay at your stupid apartment."

"Think of it as an adventure, Dominic. Like a mini vacation."

"A shitty vacation," he mumbled.

"*Hey*," I snapped. "My apartment isn't shitty, *or* stupid. And don't say shitty."

"*You're* saying it."

"I'm ten years older than you. I'm allowed to say it." *Jeez, I get having a little attitude, but what is his problem?* I turned us onto the highway, picking up speed so I could merge. "It'll be fun. You guys can even go to work with me at Whitecaps and hang out."

"Oh, that sounds like a lot of fun," Dominic mocked.

My hands wrapped tighter around the wheel. *Why do people even have teenagers? What's the appeal? I'm not seeing it.*

"Well, I'm excited to be spending time with you guys," I said, swallowing my annoyance and sticking with the whole *kill them with kindness* routine. I'd wear Dominic down eventually with it. "You're excited, right, Eli?"

He nodded fast in the mirror. I seriously loved that kid.

Shifting my eyes, I watched Dominic scowl and shake his head before putting his attention back on his phone.

It was nearly five o'clock by the time we got all their stuff and made it back to my apartment.

As I crossed the room, I slipped off my coat and draped it on the back of a kitchen chair. "You guys are staying in the bigger bedroom, so if you want, go ahead and put your stuff in there. I'm going to figure out what we're having for dinner."

"We're sharing a room?"

I lifted my head and met Dominic's eyes. "Yes. What's wrong with that? It's a full-size bed."

"I'm thirteen," he said. "I should have my own space."

Exasperated, I held up both my hands and told him, "Well, I'm twenty-three, Dom, and when I was your age, I thought I'd be married to Justin Timberlake by now. Obviously, he's moved on, and I'm having to deal with that. Just like you're going to have to deal with sharing a room with Eli, unless you would like to sleep on the futon in my salon."

"What's a *futon*?" he asked, brow tight and already disapproving.

"It's like a couch-bed thing. I don't know. Go check it out." I motioned at the door to the second bedroom, and he quickly stalked in that direction.

"You don't mind sharing a room, do you?" I asked Eli when we were alone. "I really don't want you guys sleeping on the couch. You should be in a room."

"I'm g-good," he said, smiling.

"You're also my favorite," I whispered.

His smile grew into a grin.

"I'm not sleeping on that," Dominic griped, storming back out into the living room and hooking his thumb behind him. "That room smells like straight-up chemicals. I'll probably wake up choking on my own puke."

I sighed and dropped my head back.

Who knew thirteen-year-old boys could be this dramatic?

"I'm not telling you to sleep in there, Dom," I said, moving into the kitchen and surveying meal choices in the fridge. "I was just giving you the option. Either take my bedroom or choke on your own puke. It's your call." I pulled out the butter, ham, and sliced cheddar cheese. When I turned around to grab the bread off the counter, I flinched, startled by the slamming of my bedroom door.

Bending down to peer below the hanging cabinets, I smiled at an uneasy-looking Eli.

"Hungry?"

By the time I coaxed Dominic out of the bedroom, promising to give up my wi-fi password if he ate with us—a card I really didn't want to play yet, but I was desperate and out of options that didn't involve smoking him out by starting a fire—I already had an idea how dinner was going to play out.

And when he finally *did* emerge, brow furrowed, mouth tight, and footsteps heavy, looking ready to eat me instead of the meal I'd prepared, that idea blossomed into full-blown reality.

Still, I wasn't giving up yet.

"Glad you could join us," I said, smiling when Dominic reached the table.

He scoffed and kicked out the chair next to Eli, slumping into it. "Password?" he asked.

"After dinner."

His face burned with rage. "That wasn't the deal, Shay."

"Well, unless you'd like to explain to Mom and Dad why you're running up their bill, it's the *only* deal." I pointed my spoon at him. "You're lucky I don't make you wait until the end of the week."

His eyes widened, and he visibly tensed. I'd be lying if I said a little part of me didn't enjoy seeing that.

"I won't do that, though, because I'm an awesome sister," I said, relieving his anxiety. I looked to Eli. "Right, E?"

He nodded and slurped up his soup.

"Eat, Dom. Then I'll give you the password."

Dominic scooted closer to the table and looked down at his food. "Grilled cheese and tomato soup?" he asked, sounding unimpressed.

"It was chilly today," I replied. "This is the perfect meal for chilly weather."

"Whatever," he grumbled, dunking his sandwich and biting into it.

"There's ham in some of them." I scooted the plate of extras closer to the boys.

"I don't like ham," Dominic said, mouth stuffed full as he shoved in another bite.

I narrowed my eyes and watched him eat, realizing he was doing it fast and risking choking himself just to get that damn wi-fi password, which would get him away from this table, and thus, away from me.

Crap.

I didn't have much time. If this meal was going to somehow bring us together, I had to act quickly.

"Do you want to talk about Nana?" I asked, looking between my brothers.

They hadn't been as close to my grandparents as I had been, but that didn't mean they weren't affected by this. Their grief mattered too. I wanted them to know that.

Dominic shrugged and kept eating. Looking to Eli, I watched his gaze lift from the table.

"You okay?" I asked him.

He nodded.

"Do you guys have any homework?"

"No," Dominic said.

Eli nodded again.

"After dinner, we're getting on that." I watched my perfect youngest brother comply, just like he seemed to do with everything. "What kind of dinners would you guys like this week?" I dunked one half of my sandwich into the soup. "I'm going to go grocery shopping tomorrow. I can pick up whatever you want. Do you want to do pasta or something tomorrow night? Like spaghetti?"

Eli lifted his head. "With g-garlic bread?"

I grinned. "Hell, yes. Is there any other way to eat spaghetti?" Getting approval from Eli, I looked to Dominic. "Does that sound good, Dom?"

He lifted the bowl to his mouth and tipped it back, draining every last drop of soup. Then setting the bowl on his empty plate, he wiped his mouth off with the back of his hand and shoved the dishes to the center of the table before getting to his feet. "Password?"

I exhaled a defeated breath, ready to give it up because I refused to go back on my word and risk losing Dominic's trust, no matter how badly I wanted to deny him, but just as my mouth opened, my cell phone rang from the kitchen.

"One sec," I said, getting to my feet.

Dominic, making all kinds of hate noises at me, slumped back into his chair and brought his arms across his chest.

I was happy to see him seated again and debated dragging out this phone call all night, no matter who it was.

"Hello?" I answered, retrieving my phone off the counter. I didn't recognize the number.

"Hi, Ms. Perkins. This is Erin Kennedy, Dominic's math teacher. Your mother gave the office your contact info."

"Oh, hi. How are you?"

"I'm just calling to let you know Dominic missed his tutoring session today. Were you aware he stayed after school for that?"

I turned my head and glared across the table, keeping my voice smooth and pleasant. "No, I had no idea he was *tutored*." I watched my brother sink lower into his seat, avoiding my eyes. "It was today?"

"Yes. It's every Tuesday and Friday. We're really trying to get his grade up, so it's really important he makes these sessions."

I closed my eyes, feeling so pissed off I could scream. "I had no idea he was supposed to stay after today. I'm so sorry. My mom forgot to mention it."

"Well, I'm sure she has a lot on her mind. She informed the office of your grandmother's passing. I'm sorry to hear that."

"Thank you. That's nice of you to say." Grabbing a notepad and pen out of the kitchen drawer, I sat back down at the table and scribbled that information down so I wouldn't forget it. "My brother will definitely be there Friday. I'll make sure of that," I said, keeping my eyes on Dominic, who was refusing to look at me.

"Okay. That sounds great. Have a good night, Ms. Perkins."

"You too." Disconnecting the call, I dropped my phone on the table and sat back, staring hard as silence filled the apartment. "Is there a reason you didn't tell me you had tutoring today?" I asked Dominic.

He shrugged and kept looking at the table. "You were there to pick me up."

"So?" I sat forward, the movement lifting his eyes. "You could've told me you had to stay after, Dom. I would've just gone to get Eli and waited for you. Why didn't you just say something?"

"Why didn't you *know*?" he asked, voice growing louder. "Shouldn't Mom have told you?"

My lips pressed together.

I understood my brother's argument. I couldn't fault him for it.

For the briefest moment during that phone call, I had allowed myself to wonder the same thing, shamefully putting blame on my mother, but then the reality of the situation made it obvious.

"I don't know," I said. "Maybe she just forgot, Dom, since she has so much going on right now. What with Nana dying and everything happening with Dad. Maybe she expected you to say something to me, since it's *your* life."

His jaw started clenching the moment I mentioned our father. "Whatever. This isn't my fault. It's *his* fault," he spat. "I wouldn't even need tutoring if it wasn't for him. Nobody helps me anymore. If I'm stuck, it's on me. Mom doesn't care I'm failing. *Nobody* cares! And you know what? I don't even want your stupid fucking password anymore. I'll run up their bill. I want to." Dominic shoved back from the table and stood with such force, he knocked the chair over. Then he turned and stalked away.

"Hey!" I yelled after him. "Don't say things like that! What's the matter with you?"

The bedroom door slamming was his only response.

I sat back, feeling angry but also completely understanding where my brother was coming from. And that was why I stayed in that chair.

I'd never wanted to simultaneously shake and hug someone to death before, and I wasn't sure which urge would dominate if I went after him.

Looking to Eli, I watched him pick at the corner of his crust.

"Hey. You okay?" I asked, reaching across the table and putting my hand on top of his.

"H-He's mad about D-Dad," Eli said. "H-He g-gets s-so m-mad at h-home, S-Shay. H-He's…s-s-s-" Eli shook his head, his face growing red with frustration.

I squeezed his hand, hating the pain and embarrassment he was feeling and wanting more than anything to take that away. "I know. That's just how he's dealing with it," I said. "If he acts mean or gets mad at you, he doesn't mean it, okay?"

Eli nodded and looked into my face with the one eye not covered by his hair. "Is D-Dad g-gonna get b-better?"

"I don't know, E. I hope so."

My stomach tightened into a knot.

I didn't know which was worse, saying those words or being on the receiving end of them. I felt terrible. I hated adding to Eli's worry. And Dom—I didn't want him thinking I didn't care. I just wanted to do everything I could to make this easier on everyone, especially my brothers.

And I was off to a shitty start with it, that was for damn sure.

"I'm f-full," Eli said, pushing away his plate gently.

"Okay. Get started on your homework. I'm here if you need any help, okay?"

He smiled softly before leaving the table.

Okay, so dinner hadn't turned out the way I had hoped. But I wasn't discouraged. I had a plan. I could help with homework. I could make sure Dom got to his tutoring. And I could do everything in my power to make this easier on them.

Tearing off a piece of notebook paper, I scribbled the wi-fi password down, crossed the apartment, and stuck the paper halfway under the bedroom door.

Eight seconds later, I watched that paper disappear, and I turned away, smiling.

Chapter Four

SEAN

The cold metal of the cuffs pinched my skin as they tightened to the point of pain.

"Please," I rasped, breathing erratically, my cheek pressed to the hood of the squad car as I got searched and read my rights.

I couldn't hear a damn thing the cop was saying. I could only hear the high-pitched, terrified screaming coming from the car my body had just been dragged out of.

They were wailing—my girls. Both of them. Scared and needing me, not knowing what was happening. Their terror filled my ears.

I blinked, feeling wetness run down my face and drip onto the hood. Struggling to see clearly, I kept looking through that windshield at the back seat. My gaze fixated as I panted heavy breaths.

Every time one of them moved, I got a glimpse.

Blonde heads whipping about, red faces streaked with tears, and tiny hands reaching, seeking comfort and safety. Seeking me, and I couldn't go to them. They needed to be told it was going to be okay. Somebody needed to tell them.

"Daddy! Daddy!"

A violent shudder tore through me.

I'd been cooperative up until this point, but now, fuck that. I thrashed against the hood, bucking back and cursing, spit flying out of my mouth as I tried with all my strength to get this prick off me so I could get up, because I needed to go. I needed to get to them and tell them I was sorry. They needed to know it was going to be okay. It was all going to be okay and they were safe, and I was never, ever going to hurt them like this again. I was never going to let anything hurt them. And I'd fucking kill anyone who tried.

The cop shoved me down, pressing on the back of my head and gripping my hair so tight, I sucked in a breath. He was saying stuff to me, but I couldn't hear him.

"Daddy! Daddy! Daddy!"

The screams grew louder and more desperate.

Rage blurred and spotted my vision. I fought harder, nothing stopping me, not even when I felt the blood dripping down my hands from the cuffs as they started tearing my skin off.

I fought knowing I shouldn't be fighting, and not caring. I was getting to my girls.

"DADDY!"

"Fuck! Let me the fuck up!" I roared, struggling in his unrelenting grip. "Get off me! GET THE FUCK OFF ME!"

Pain shot up my side when I was struck below my ribs. I groaned, and my knees buckled, momentarily halting my efforts to get away. But the cop was sick of my shit and knew I wasn't done. He threw his weight on top of me and slammed me forward, crushing me against the hood and draining the air from my lungs. I struggled to breathe.

"Please," I croaked. "I gotta see them. They're scared."

The cuffs tightened, and my hands went numb.

I kept my eyes on that windshield as I was dragged off the car and thrown in the back seat. The cop said something to me before slamming the door shut. I didn't hear him.

I heard their screams. Or maybe it was my own.

* * *

Gasping awake, I pitched forward and knocked over the can of soda by my leg, spilling it onto the wood floor I'd discovered after pulling up the carpet.

"*Fuck!*" I pulled off my shirt, not having a rag near me, and used that to clean up the mess before it soaked in and ruined the wood. Then I balled up the wet tee and tossed it across the room, rubbing at my face as I slumped against the wall.

I was used to the nightmares. Hell, I welcomed them. They were a good reminder of what I'd done and what I deserved to feel for the rest of my life. That regret was never leaving me. I wouldn't let it.

My girls scared and screaming was the last memory I deserved to have of them.

But it wasn't what they deserved.

I'd give them better. I'd make up for what I did. I'd give my girls everything I never had, and this time, I'd do it right.

Getting to my feet, I walked over to the tall lamp I'd stuck in the corner of the room and turned it on, giving me enough light to work.

It was pitch black outside. I knew it was late. I knew I could've stopped and called it a night. My shoulders and back ached, begging for relief, and that burning pain in my neck was still there, but I ignored it. I ignored everything. Even though I'd gotten a lot done already after getting home from work, there was still too much left to do. I needed to keep going.

I tied my hair back, grabbed the fraying edge of the carpet and pulled, ripping it clear off the floor.

I worked for hours, not sitting down again because I knew I'd fall asleep, and I hadn't meant to the first time. Once I got all the carpet up in the living room, I moved on to something else. I patched holes in the drywall, then I got to work on the kitchen, taking out cabinets that were busted up or on the verge of breaking once you sat one fucking dish in them. I worked until I would catch my eyes closing and jerk awake while holding power tools, finally stopping then because I knew I was risking injury doing some of the shit I was doing without focus.

If I got hurt, I'd have to stop, and I didn't have time for that.

It was after three when I finally called it a night.

After cleaning up and showering, I went to my room. All the furniture I owned was in there: a mattress that sat on the floor and one of those old military trunks I kept all my clothes in. That was it. I didn't even have a fucking bed.

Pulling on a pair of boxers, I sat on the edge of the mattress and pulled up the contacts on my phone. There were two.

Nate and my ex, Val.

I hit dial, pushed my wet hair back, and pressed the phone to my ear, waiting for the greeting I always got no matter what fucking time I called her.

I understood why she never picked up. I was just hoping she was listening.

"Hey, it's me," I said, clearing the sleep from my voice. "Just wanted to let you know I got a place. A house. It ain't much, but it's better than the trailer. The girls will have a room and shit here, so…Look, it's a fuckin' dump now, but I'm fixing it up, and when it's ready, I'd like the girls to see it. I'm really trying to do right by them this time. I want them to have what I didn't. I want that more than I ever wanted anything, you know that, but I'm doin' it right. It's fuckin' killing me, but I'm doing it, Val. Just think about letting me see them. *Please.* I'll call when I have it ready. Just hear me out. That's all I'm askin'." I shook my head, nostrils flaring, so fucking angry with myself. "Christ, I know I don't have any right to be askin' shit from you, but I'm askin' for *them*. I'm not doin' this for me. I don't deserve nothin' anymore, I know that, just let me make this right. I'll call when it's ready. Please, just hear me out. I'm sorry. I'm so fuckin' sorry."

Ending the call, I fell back on the mattress and gripped the phone against my bare chest.

I could feel my heart slamming in suffering against my rib cage. I was panting, my skin breaking out in a sweat, my stomach rolling and twisting.

I worried she wouldn't listen. I worried I'd never get the opportunity to fix my mistakes. I worried this was all for nothing. And I had no fucking *right* to worry about anything.

Feel like shit, because that's what you are, and that's all you're ever going to be.

I could taste the sick creeping up the back of my throat. I tried swallowing it down. I tried not hearing the voice that never left my head, but it was all I could hear.

You think you're special? she screamed. *You ain't nothing, boy! Just a stinking, piece of shit taking up space in my goddamned house! You ain't nothing! You ain't never gonna be nothing either! You hear me?*

I hadn't gotten around to pulling up the old carpet yet in my room. That was a good thing, since I never made it to the toilet.

Rolling over, I hung my head over the edge of the mattress and vomited on the floor.

Chapter Five

SHAYLA

They say a great day begins with breakfast.

Maybe that was why the next day was turning out to be so terrible.

When you miss breakfast due to oversleeping, this blame landing solely on me since I'd forgotten to set my alarm according to school time, it starts your day off on the wrong foot.

The boys weren't too happy with me when I made them late, rushing them out the door after shoving Nutrigrain bars at them. Dominic's annoyance was obvious. Aside from tossing the bar in the dumpster before getting in the car, I was convinced he only knew how to look pissed off, and, lucky for me, he wasn't shy about letting me see it. Eli, on the other hand, was more subtle with his disappointment. He ate and kept his head down on the drive to school, and barely smiled at me when I would crack a joke.

It sucked. I hated letting them down, and even though I knew an apology wouldn't go far, I still gave them several.

Neither said a word to me on the way to school.

I knew I had to do better. Not just for them, but for my mom too. She was relying on me to handle this and I wouldn't let her down.

After setting the alarm on my phone so we wouldn't be rushed again, and then setting a backup alarm, I stopped at my parents' house to pick up something that would make my apartment a little more...fun.

Feeling good about my efforts, I had a smile on my face that afternoon when I drove to Dominic's school to drop off his gear for practice.

That smile felt good. Too bad it didn't last.

You see, Dominic played lacrosse, not baseball. And I'd unfortunately either forgotten that information or been too preoccupied running around trying to do *better* to check which sports bag I'd grabbed before leaving my apartment.

After looking in the trunk and discovering my error, Dominic was pissed. I'm talking *pissed.* He yelled. He screamed. He slammed my trunk and cursed, telling me how stupid I was and how much he hated me.

I wanted to argue that he could maybe borrow some equipment, or at least sit and watch, but that didn't seem like the right thing to say at the moment or an option Dominic wanted to hear.

He looked defeated. He climbed in the car, shaking, face beet red and tears in his eyes.

I couldn't remember how many sorries I gave him on our way to pick up Eli, but I knew it was a lot.

I also knew it wasn't enough.

When we got back to the apartment, Eli homed in on the Xbox I'd taken from the house and immediately started up a game. He thanked me three times for setting it up for them.

Dominic joined him after dropping off his stuff in the bedroom, grabbing the other remote, and plopping down next to Eli on the couch.

He didn't thank me. He didn't even look at me.

Again, I deserved his anger, so I didn't get on him about it.

When Mom called later that night to check on things, I kept the conversation on Nana, Pop, and Dad, figuring if I did that, I wouldn't have to share my monumental mess-ups and risk upsetting her. When she asked how the boys were doing, I told her they were okay. *Okay* seemed like an appropriate word.

Not great. Not terrible.

My response seemed expected. With Dad's disease progressing the way it was doing, I had a feeling she was used to them being just *okay*.

I wanted to do everything I could to help with that, and after I finished speaking with her, I went ahead and set a *second* backup alarm on my phone. I wasn't leaving any room for error.

The next day started out so much better than the previous.

We got up on time. The boys got a good breakfast in them. There wasn't any rushing around, and Dominic didn't seem to hate me as much as he did the night before, at least making eye contact with me when I'd ask him a question. I had high hopes. Today was going to be a good day.

I even had my first appointment in my brand-new, spectacular chair while the boys were at school. The lady who lived across the hall in 6B went from drab to fab when I put some blonde with rose gold peekaboo highlights in her hair.

Her husband was returning from deployment soon, and she wanted to surprise him. I was stoked she was giving me the honor. That made the experience even more special.

She hugged *me* after the blow dry, loving how her hair turned out, booked her next appointment, *and* asked about bringing her kids over for fresh cuts.

I couldn't help myself. I was just so happy. I had to hug her again.

After that, I took to Snapchat and posted a pic of the before and after.

It was difficult waiting for 6B to leave before I danced all around my apartment, but I fought the urge. Then, once that door closed behind her, I really let loose.

I shimmied my hips from room to room. I even posted a little video of my celebration with the hashtag *thankful*.

Tori, Syd, and Kali all commented on my video, telling me how much ass I was kicking. That made me feel good.

I was determined to start kicking ass at everything.

School pickups went by without a hitch that afternoon. Once I got the boys home, I heated up the leftovers and set the table for dinner while they worked on their homework.

Eli was happy. Dominic cracked a smile when I stubbed my toe on a chair, which I typically wouldn't appreciate, but at least he was smiling. I thought we were over the bad. Especially when the boys actually ate dinner with me and didn't request more game time.

I wore a smile during that entire meal. I didn't even care how weird I looked, chewing and smiling at the same time. Everything was going to work out. I wouldn't let the boys down anymore, and I wouldn't disappoint my mom.

My phone rang just as I was washing up the dishes.

I dried off my hands while leaning over the counter, looking at the number flashing on the screen.

Again, it was one I didn't recognize, but I just figured it was someone looking to get their hair done, so I didn't get an uneasy feeling.

"Hi, Shay, this is Rachel, Eli's speech therapist..."

As soon as I heard her greeting, I *knew* in my gut, this was not going to be a good phone call. My pulse quickened with worry, and that uneasy feeling filled me up inside. I slumped into the nearest chair.

"I know your parents are out of town right now," she continued, "but Eli missed his therapy today. It was at five o'clock. Were you aware?"

"No," I replied, voice cracking. I turned away from where the boys were sitting in the living room and blinked at the wall. "I mean, I knew he had therapy, I just didn't know what day it was. I'm sorry." I cupped my hand over my eyes. "Can he make it up? Do you have time tomorrow, or maybe this weekend? I can bring him whenever."

I knew how important Eli's speech therapy was. I couldn't believe I'd forgotten to ask him about it. *Why wasn't I thinking?*

"Unfortunately, I don't have any open slots for makeups. He sees me on Mondays and Thursdays, though. Those are his set appointments. Always at five o'clock."

I grabbed the pen and scribbled that information down on the notebook paper I was quickly filling. "Okay. Um, could you maybe bill me instead of my parents for that one? It was my fault. I should've found out when his therapy was."

"That can be arranged. That's fine."

"I'm so sorry. My mother is superwoman. I'm not sure how she does all this."

I wrote the word *STUPID* in bold black ink at the bottom of the page and pointed an arrow at myself.

The woman laughed softly in my ear. "Probably because she has to. Don't be too hard on yourself. It happens."

Her words were kind, but they didn't penetrate.

"Okay, I'll have him there Monday. Thank you for calling."

"You're welcome. I'm sorry to hear about your grandmother."

"Thank you."

"Take care."

Disconnecting the call, I set the phone down on the notebook paper and dropped my head into my hand, groaning. "Eli?"

"Yeah?"

"We forgot about your therapy today, buddy." I slowly looked up, meeting his wide eyes over the back of the couch.

"Oops," he said, wincing. "I f-forgot."

"Me too. I didn't even think about it." I shook my head and sat back, tossing the pen across the table and watching it roll onto the floor. "I'm not thinking about anything. This is my fault. Not yours."

Suddenly, Eli got to his feet and turned to face me. His shaky hands cupped his cheeks.

I sat up tall and asked him, "What is it? What's wrong?"

"D-don't be m-mad at m-me, S-Shay."

"Buddy, I'm not mad at you. I just said this is my fault."

He shook his head and quickly rounded the couch, stopping at his book bag on the floor against the wall, and bent down to dig through it. When he straightened again and walked toward me, his feet dragging the carpet like he was fighting against some force making him move, he was holding a bright red folder.

"I w-was s-s-supposed to g-give you this. I f-f-forgot." Eli handed me the folder over top of the table, then shoved his hands in his pants pockets and lowered his head.

I opened the folder and saw papers inside with my mother's careful handwriting.

There was a list of contact numbers, the boys' school agendas, and a calendar of activities.

Everything I needed to know was in here.

Dominic's tutoring schedule, practice days and times, and Eli's therapy days. Everything was listed and detailed. Times, places, directions, she included everything. And at the bottom was a note to me, thanking me for all my help.

I bit my lip to keep from crying and looked up at Eli. "Hey."

He kept looking at the carpet.

"E, hey, look at me," I said, getting his eyes that time. There was so much sadness there, it was difficult to take, but I somehow managed to give him an easy smile in return. "Thank you so, so much for giving me this. I forgot to ask you for it. Mom told me you had it, and I just completely forgot. I'm sorry."

His eyes flickered wider, and he sucked in a breath. "S-She did?"

I nodded. There was no way I was letting him take the blame for this. That look on his face was killing me.

"I-I . . . it w-wasn't my f-f-fault?" he asked.

I stood then, dropping the folder on the table and pulling him into a hug. "No, it was my fault," I said against his hair. "You reminded me. If you wouldn't have done that, I don't know what would've happened. You totally saved the day."

His little body sagged with relief, then he hugged me back with the strongest arms of any eight-year-old boy, I was sure of it.

I kissed the top of his head. "Thank you."

"Y-You're welcome."

After giving me a smile, Eli walked away, his steps lighter now since he wasn't carrying the weight of that worry anymore. He sat down on the couch, laughed at something Dominic said, and resumed playing his game.

I made sure the kitchen was cleaned up, then I carried the folder to my salon room and closed the door behind me.

The futon was back to its waiting room position, looking more like a couch than a bed. Sighing, I plopped down on one end, tucked my feet underneath my hip, and flipped open the folder in my lap.

Even though I had everything written down, I still took the rest of the night and studied the contents of that folder as if someone were taking it away from me at any second. I wouldn't mess anything else up. I wouldn't forget. I wouldn't make any more mistakes.

I went over that calendar until the dates blurred into each other, and then I made some coffee and went over it again.

Tomorrow was Friday. Dominic had math, which I knew now, but there it was, written right in front of me. Eli had a field trip to the botanical gardens in the morning and baseball practice after school.

I wasn't sure how I was going to pick up Dominic while Eli was at practice, since I didn't want to leave him there by himself, but I would figure it out.

I had to.

It didn't matter how much I could kick ass at hair. It didn't matter how awesome of a start Hair by Shay was off to. I needed to kick ass at this. *This* was what mattered—those two boys needed me, and I wouldn't let them down anymore.

"It's Friday!" I sang, pulling out of the apartment complex the next morning. "Are you guys excited for today?"

Dominic mumbled an annoyed "whatever," as he played on his phone, while Eli sat forward, gripped the back of my seat and smiled at me in the rearview.

I giggled at him. "I know why you're so excited. It's field trip day, right?"

"Y-Yes! I get to m-miss math and r-reading!"

"Sweet." I held my hand over my shoulder and got a high-five. "Speaking of math, Dom, I'll be picking you up today after your tutoring. Don't forget."

"How could I? You've reminded me ten times already since I got up."

I ignored Dom.

Death stares and attitudes weren't penetrating my happy mood today. I felt prepared and even a little excited with the arsenal of information I was carrying in that bright red folder sitting on the passenger seat. Even all the looking I *knew* I'd be doing while working my shift at Whitecaps today wasn't getting me down.

My pathetic heart aside, I was feeling pretty powerful.

Waiting for the traffic to clear, I pulled us out onto the main highway, got about a mile up the road, and then came to a stop when the cars in front of me slowed.

"W-What's going on?" Eli asked.

"Just a little traffic." I gave him a reassuring smile in the mirror. "Fridays are always like this. It'll be fine. We'll start moving soon."

He nodded, finding comfort in that, and settled back against the seat to look out the window.

I slid my hands around the wheel as a quiet concern began to circle inside my head.

Maybe we should've left earlier to prepare for this. It's what Mom would've done.

No.

We are not getting stuck in traffic. We will not be late. This is not happening.

Resilient to anything bringing us down today, I twisted the knob on the radio and filled the car with music, silencing that pesky worry I couldn't listen to for another second.

The cars moved ahead, and we inched forward. Then we sat still for a solid thirteen minutes and eleven seconds.

"I c-can't be l-late, S-Shay!" Eli whined from the back seat.

"Buddy, you won't be late. I promise," I said, not having the right *to* promise him something like that, but they were the only words I could think to say at the moment. I didn't want him worrying. God, his sweet little voice was the saddest thing I'd ever heard, it was so panicked.

"Look. Here we go."

We started moving again, slowly, but it was a steady crawl.

"I swear to God, if it's just people rubbernecking up here, I'm gonna knock someone the *fuck* out."

"S-Shay!" Eli giggled. "You s-said the f w-word!"

Dominic chuckled under his breath.

I sat up straight. "Oh, uh, ignore what I just said," I told them both, cringing.

When we got about a mile up the road, the flow of traffic finally began to pick up, and I floored it, knowing it would take a miracle not to be late at this point.

There were nine red lights between the highway and Dominic's school.

We hit every.

Single.

One.

"*Shay*," Eli whined, his legs bouncing against the seat so hard I could feel it in my back.

I skidded to stop at the curb in front of the entrance of the middle school.

"Jesus. Drive much," Dominic snickered.

Feeling murderous, I whipped my head around and snapped, "*You are not helping.* Now get your ass out of the car."

"I need a note."

Shit. Of course he needed a note. HE WAS LATE.

After frantically looking around the front seat in search for some loose-leaf and coming up empty-handed, I flattened out a crumpled Taco Bell receipt and scribbled on the back.

"Here," I said, shoving it into his hand. "Now go. Hurry."

He looked at the receipt and then at me like I was crazy for giving that to him, mumbled something under his breath while grabbing his book bag off the floor, and finally exited the car.

The door slammed. I was about to pull away from the curb when sniffling turned my head.

Big, fat tears poured down Eli's face as he stared at the window. "M-My f-field trip. I'm g-gonna m-miss it."

Fuckfuckfuckfuckfuck.

Whipping back around and shifting the gear into drive, I sped away from Hyde County Middle while whispering every prayer I could think of.

"We'll get there. It'll be okay, E," I said as I drove safely but still well over the speed limit.

Eli kept crying and bouncing his legs.

I was gripping the steering wheel so tight, my fingers were going numb. *Please. Oh, God. Please.*

I let out a sigh of relief when I saw a couple buses still parked in front of the school. After stopping at the curb, I got out with Eli, keeping my car running, and sprinted with him inside.

"Hi! He's here. He's here," I said, rushing into the front office with him. "We aren't too late, are we?"

An older black woman dressed in a pantsuit was standing at the counter. She looked at me, smiled, then lowered her gaze to Eli. "Not *too* too late," she said, tilting her head as she studied him. "Whose homeroom are you in, sweetie?"

"Ms. Coleman's," Eli answered.

Her lips pressed together. "Oh, you just missed the bus. They just left to go to the botanical gardens."

"No!" Eli cried, looking back at me. "S-Shay!"

I gripped his shoulders. "It's okay," I said, trying to summon a smile. "I'll just take him on my way to work, and he can meet up with his class there."

The woman stepped forward, shaking her head while motioning for Eli to come to her. "No, he would've had to have ridden the bus. I'm sorry, but it's school policy. He'll just have to stay here and wait for his class. Come on, sweetheart. What's your name?"

I kept my grip on his shoulders so Eli couldn't move. "This is ridiculous! Why are you punishing him? He should get to go on the field trip with his class. Can't you see how much he wants to go?"

She glanced at Eli, who I knew was still crying—I could feel his little body shake and hear his quiet sniffles. Then the woman locked eyes with me and said in a firm voice, "He'll have to stay here. I'm sorry."

Closing my eyes through a harsh breath and fighting against the strongest urge I'd ever had to punch someone right in the mouth, I stepped to Eli's side and looked down, my heart breaking into a million pieces when I saw the steady stream of tears running down his face.

"Hey," I whispered, bending down so we were eye level. "I'm going to take you to the botanical gardens, okay? We can go tonight, or tomorrow."

"I have b-baseball."

"We'll go after baseball. Or we'll do whatever you want to do. We'll go somewhere really special, okay? Wherever you want. I promise."

Eli kept his eyes on the floor. He wouldn't look at me.

My promises probably meant jack shit to him now. I could promise him the world, and it wouldn't matter.

"I am so sorry, E," I said, giving his arms a squeeze.

Head down, Eli walked away when Ms. Unwilling-to-Be-Understanding-in-Her-Stupid-Ass-Pantsuit beckoned him forward again, and the two of them disappeared behind a door.

I felt like a complete failure.

Pissing Dominic off was one thing. That hurt. But disappointing Eli? That pain was unbearable.

After signing him in as late so it wouldn't get marked unexcused, I walked out to my car, barely pulling away from the school before I started crying.

I'd held it together up until that point, but I just couldn't fight it anymore. I kept picturing Eli's face while I drove.

This was all my fault.

I wasn't thinking. I wasn't helping out my Mom. I wasn't making anyone's life easier. I was fucking *everything up*.

Sniffling, I pulled around the side of Whitecaps and backed into a space. I had exactly twelve minutes before my shift started.

I was using those twelve minutes.

With my hands free now, I buried my face in them and sobbed.

Chapter Six

SEAN

Go back inside. This ain't your business. You got what you wanted by pushing her away. Don't fuck it up by walking over there.

I stared at the back door, one hand on the wall beside it and the other on the knob, stilled, not twisting it the way I should've been doing. Panting heavy breaths through my nostrils, I tried forgetting what I just saw and staying out of shit I didn't need to be getting involved in, but just like that stupid fucking app I couldn't keep deleted off my phone, there was no fighting this.

There was no fighting anything when it came to her.

Cursing, I spun around and stalked across the lot.

It was my own fucking fault, really. I was out here watching videos and looking at pictures I'd already looked at a million times. If I had just stayed inside, I wouldn't have watched Shayla pull around back, park, and then bury her face in her hands. I wouldn't know she was upset, and I sure as fuck wouldn't be pressing her for information like I was about to do. I'd be staying clear of her.

But then she'd be out here crying by herself and thinking she was alone, and I didn't know what pissed me off more—that understanding or the fact I knew I had options that didn't involve me, and I wasn't taking them.

Tori was here. I could go inside and tell her to handle this, knowing that was the smarter thing to do, but was I doing that? Was I even *considering* doing that?

Nope.

I was a fucking idiot when it came to this girl. One look at my phone, and anyone would see that. That stupid app was still open.

There was also Nate. I could go to him. Jesus Christ, I could even get J.R. out here. Anyone. This didn't need to be me.

Except it did.

I had to do this. It was either me or no one, and I wouldn't let it be no one.

Stopping at the driver's side door, I rapped my knuckles against the window and watched Shayla jerk her head out of her hands and turn to me with wide, tear-filled eyes.

She had streaks of black running down her cheeks, and her pretty pink lips were parted. She looked confused. She looked sad as fuck. She looked a little scared.

I got the confused—I didn't understand what the hell I was doing over here either. I had an idea what was getting her so sad. But the scared shit? What the fuck?

Was she scared of me?

When she didn't move, I motioned for her to roll the window down.

Shayla hesitated, then slowly reached over while keeping her eyes locked with mine and pressed the button on the door.

"Your dad?" I asked her when the window was lowered.

Back when she was planting her ass on that counter and speaking to me throughout her shifts, her dad had been diagnosed with Parkinson's disease. She worried about him all the time—she told me she did, and even if she hadn't, I would've known how worried she was just going off the fear in her voice every time she spoke about him.

I figured this was what had her so upset.

She was slow to respond, just kept staring at me and looking more confused by the second, then finally, my words penetrated.

"*What?*" she whispered.

Or maybe they didn't.

"Your dad," I repeated. "Did somethin' happen? Is he worse?"

"You remember about my dad?"

"Wasn't that long ago you told me about it. Why wouldn't I remember?"

"I…I don't know. I just." She quickly shook her head, as if to clear thoughts away she didn't want to hear. "Never mind. Um, no, he's the same. Nothing happened." Shayla sniffled while rubbing the back of her fingers against her cheek to catch a tear, then noticing the black on her knuckles, she cursed and proceeded to wipe aggressively at her cheeks with both hands, cleaning the mess off her face.

I watched her do this while waiting for her to share what was bothering her, but then decided she probably wouldn't offer that information up without me asking her for it, and that was the *last fucking thing* I needed to be doing.

So here it was—my out. This was when I needed to walk away.

And I could. Shayla seemed to be calming down. She wasn't steadily crying anymore, meaning there was no fucking reason for me to be standing here. It was time for me to go.

"If it ain't about your dad, what is it?" I asked instead of heading inside, realizing that was the last fucking thing I *wanted* to do, not needed. I wasn't thinking about what needed to happen anymore. I was doing what I wanted. Fuck it.

There was a lot wrong with me, but this might've been the dumbest fucking move of my life. I might've regretted this forever.

Or…

Shayla pressed her head back against the seat, closed her eyes through a breath, and then opened them to look at me with an expression I never expected to see from anyone: gratitude. She *wanted* me to pry, because she couldn't share what was going on with her if I didn't.

We didn't do this. Not anymore. We didn't talk.

I'd made sure of that the day I fucked her over.

But now, I was changing that. I was asking for more, and maybe she wanted me knowing just as badly as I wanted her telling. And if that was the case, I'd keep asking her. I knew I would. And I wouldn't regret anything. Not with that look she was giving me.

"Um, well, to start, my nana died," Shayla said, biting the tremble in her lip as her eyes watered again. "Which I don't think I've processed yet, so that's kind of hitting me full on right now. My parents had to go out to Ohio to take care of things for my pop, so I've been left in charge of my brothers while they're gone. I think I told you about them, right?"

I lifted my chin.

I knew she had brothers. Two of them, both younger.

"Well, I'm basically ruining their lives," she informed me. "And this is not me being dramatic either. I keep messing up. I'm pretty sure Dominic hates me, and Eli . . . he's too sweet to hate me, but if he could, he would. I keep forgetting things. Dominic had to miss his practice because I brought him the wrong equipment. Eli missed his therapy. Dom gets tutored after school—I didn't even know about that, and I'm pretty sure he's failing in math. I felt like an asshole when his teacher called me about it, and Dom . . . he doesn't think anybody cares, which isn't true, but I'm not doing anything to make that better. I'm oversleeping and making them late because I'm not thinking about stupid Friday traffic. And today was the absolute *worst*. Eli had a field trip this morning he couldn't go on because we were late, and his face, God, he was so sad. So upset with me. So disappointed. Everyone is. I'm overwhelmed and I'm scared to tell my mom how badly I've messed up, because she has so much going on, you know? With my dad and Pop. I don't want to let her down, but I can't do this. I can't." She whimpered and shook her head. "And I miss my nana. I feel like everything is falling apart, and I'm just making things worse."

She squeezed her eyes shut, and I watched fresh tears fall past her cheeks.

"Seems like a lot for one person to handle," I said, drawing her eyes to me again.

"My mom handles it."

"She's also probably used to handling it. And it ain't like your brothers just need you to take them to school and pick them up. It sounds like they got a lot goin' on."

Her shoulders jerked as she wiped at her face. Shayla wasn't hearing me, and I needed her to hear me. I didn't want her feeling this.

"You ever take care of anyone before?" I asked her.

She shook her head. "Just myself. And I had a fish once, but I killed it."

My brows lifted.

"Accidentally," she offered shyly. "He, uh, didn't survive my last move. I'm pretty sure the cause of death was stress."

"Good to know you ain't a murderer, but I'm not talkin' about pets."

"Pets are people to some. Didn't you ever have a pet before?"

"No."

"Never?"

I shook my head.

"Well, that's just sad," she said. "Everyone should at least have a fish."

"Not everyone," I muttered, referring to me but watching Shayla's eyes widen and light up a second before her mouth started twitching,

I realized she thought I was referring to her, and instead of taking offense to what I'd just said, she was finding it amusing.

Her mouth was threatening a full-blown smile, and I knew once that happened, I'd forget my point and spend the rest of my time out here staring, leaving Shayla to feel that guilt and continue feeling it.

I didn't want that, so I kept my focus, meeting her eyes again and repeating, "I wasn't talkin' about pets. You ever take care of another person before?"

"No," she answered, smile no longer threatening. "Just me."

"There you go."

"That doesn't matter. I should be able to handle this. I'm not a kid."

"I didn't say you were. But when you go from only lookin' after yourself to lookin' after other people overnight, that change can be a lot. It'd be a lot on anyone. Not just you."

"I don't know," she whispered, closing her eyes through a breath.

"Look, I'm sure your mom knows what all she's askin' of you. I'm bettin' if you said something about it bein' too much, she'd understand that."

"I really don't want to do that, though," she said softly, peering up at me.

I planted my forearm on the roof of the car, bent closer, and told her, "Sounds to me like you ain't got a choice."

I knew I was only speaking the truth, but hearing those words come out of my mouth, tasting them, something felt…off. I didn't like this being her reality. I didn't like what this was doing to her. If Shayla didn't want to tell her mom, I didn't want her making that call either. Not if it meant feeling like a failure, which was the vibe I was getting from her right now.

Fuck.

I wasn't just getting up in her business, I was staying up in it. I was getting involved.

This might've been the dumbest fucking move of my life. Only time would tell.

"What do they got goin' on today?" I asked her, watching Shayla's eyebrows tick up.

"What do you mean?"

"They got school. What else?"

"Oh, um..." Her lips pressed together as she thought. "Eli has baseball practice, and Dominic has his tutoring."

"You able to handle both of those?"

She hesitated, briefly looking like she might puke all over herself, before rushing out an "I have to."

That was all I needed to know.

"Right. I'm thinkin' the younger one will want to be with you, so I got the older kid. Which one's that?"

Now Shayla didn't just look like she might puke. She looked like she might puke, then pass out, then pass out again after coming to.

"You all right?" I asked her.

"I...I'm not sure," she whispered. "What are you saying? Are you offering to help me?"

I jerked my chin.

"Why?"

Straightening off the car, I shoved my hands into my pockets, breathed deep, and just stared at her.

I had no fucking idea how to answer that question.

What could I say? I was over here because I couldn't ignore her? That no matter how hard I fought it, I couldn't mind my own fucking business when it came to her? Oh yeah, sure. I might as well also fess up to watching her videos every free chance I got, staring at her when she didn't know it, thinking about her when I was alone...yeah. I'd get right on that.

I didn't understand what the fuck I was doing any more, I just knew I had to do it. And if I didn't understand this, how could she?

I figured Shayla would accept my help without needing an explanation, just fucking take what I was offering since she was needing it so bad, but then she started rolling up her window and shutting me out.

I narrowed my eyes. *What the fuck?*

"Hold on," she said quickly when she noticed the vein in my forehead about to burst.

I stepped back when Shayla threw the door open after cutting the engine.

"I need to clock in before I'm late," she explained, hitting the button on her key fob and locking up the car. She turned and looked up at me, holding a bright red folder in her hand. We were a foot apart.

We never stood like this before—not this close. Not without a barrier.

I knew Shayla was a tiny fucking thing, but I didn't realize how much I'd tower over her.

I was six foot three. I'd guess she was five foot two, *maybe*, the top of her head hitting several inches below my chin. And she was little everywhere. I could tell even with her thick coat covering her.

She wouldn't even need to wrap her legs around me and hold on. I could carry her all fucking day, no problem.

My jaw clenched.

Shit. What the fuck? What the fuck was I doing? Why was I thinking about her legs wrapping around me and any part of her holding on? Jesus Christ. I did not need to be thinking about shit like that.

Shayla cleared her throat, drawing my eyes off her body—*you're a motherfucking dick for looking*—and motioned at the building with her head. "Can we talk inside?" she asked.

I nodded, letting her lead the way.

The time clock was in the lounge, so I knew that was where she was headed. After entering through the back door, I stayed straight and made for the kitchen while Shayla veered off.

"You coming?" she called out.

I froze just outside the kitchen, looking up and seeing interest in J.R.'s eyes where he stood at the stove, stirring something in a saucepan. Brows lifted, a grin quickly spread across his face.

Ignoring him, I turned my head and slid my gaze to Shayla.

She gave me a timid smile over her shoulder before taking the remaining steps to the lounge and disappearing behind the door.

Okay. *Huh.* She wanted me to follow her. I figured we'd have our conversation with me in the kitchen and her perched on the counter, the way I was used to having our conversations. The way I *liked* having them. But maybe she didn't want to air her business with all ears listening. She just wanted me to hear it.

Just me.

Fuck, why did that feel so good?

"Well? You going or what?" J.R. asked with laughter in his voice.

Cutting my eyes to him, I barked, "Get to work!" before turning heel and heading in Shayla's direction.

"I *am* working!"

He was still laughing. I could hear it.

"Then get to work some more!" I shot back.

Whitecaps wasn't open yet, so I didn't give a fuck how loud I was being.

I also didn't give a fuck about the look Tori was giving me from her stance at the bar as I moved out into the restaurant.

She was curious about what was going on, but she was also looking suspicious as fuck. Her hand was stuck on her cocked hip, her gaze was hard and moving with me, and her mouth was tight, like she was fighting the urge to comment.

Big fucking surprise there. She was always wanting to comment.

And knowing Tori, her comment would be heavy on the attitude and one I wouldn't want to hear.

I liked her just about as much as I liked Kali or the redheaded one who worked occasionally. They were all sweet, but Tori could be mouthy as fuck. If she had an opinion on something, she shared it, and it didn't matter how many fucking times I told her I didn't want her giving said opinion. She still gave it. Especially if it involved someone she cared about.

If it had to do with one of her girls, Tori was getting involved.

Well, fuck her suspicions. This wasn't Tori's business. It wasn't J.R.'s business either. It was mine and Shayla's. She was asking *me* to follow her, not them.

And everyone who wasn't involved could butt the fuck out.

Scowling to convey that opinion, I watched Tori's eyes narrow in challenge before I looked away, yanking the door open to the lounge.

I stepped inside and locked that shit behind me, and wouldn't you know...

The door rattled, then a knock sounded with a heavy fist. "Shay!" Tori yelled, still yanking on the door. "You say the word, and I'm grabbing the ax we keep hidden and busting in there!"

Shayla finished shoving her coat in a locker before slowly turning her head, curiously looking from the door to me.

"Didn't know if you wanted privacy or not," I explained, gesturing at the lock before drawing my arms across my chest. "Your girl likes getting up in my shit, so..." I shrugged.

Nothing else more to say about that. Facts were facts.

Shayla's mouth twitched before she hollered out, "I'm fine, Tori! And...I don't think we have an ax, do we?"

I heard a growl through the door. "You aren't supposed to tell *him* that. What's the matter with you?"

"Shit. Sorry!" Shayla laughed.

"You're good?"

"I'm good, T."

"All right, well, I won't be far, so if you need me, I'll be sharpening that ax we absolutely *do* have. You just forgot about it."

I glared at the door, then turned away when I heard the slam of a locker.

"We don't really have an ax. She's just playing," Shayla told me, smiling a little as she tied on her waitress apron.

"And she wouldn't really be gettin' in here. Not unless you wanted her to," I shot back.

Shayla blinked and stood taller, losing her smile but looking like what I'd just said meant something big and important to her, then she took a seat on the bench, opened the red folder in her lap, and glanced over at me like she was expecting something.

My brows furrowed. Expecting *what*? What did she want me to do? I'd followed her in here, didn't I?

Shayla smiled, then patted the spot beside her.

Oh.

She wanted to talk. That's why we were in here. But she didn't just want to talk. She wanted to talk with us sitting close.

Not sure that was the best idea, but nobody was telling my feet that.

Huffing out a breath, I moved around the bench and sat down, leaving about an inch of space between our hips. I gripped my thighs, digging my fingers in so I wouldn't move.

My muscles were locked stiff.

We had stood close outside but not this close. I wasn't used to this. Even when Shayla would lean into that kitchen window and drop her voice, telling me something she didn't want anyone else to hear, there was still a good amount of space there. And being surrounded by the food I was cooking, I had no fucking idea what she smelled like.

That was not the case now. I knew exactly what she smelled like.

Honey.

She smelled like sweet fucking honey. Her hair. Her skin. Both, I wasn't sure. And no fucking way was I getting any closer to make that distinction.

"So, um, here's their schedule," she said, holding the folder between us so I could see the calendar she was pointing to. "Dominic, that's the older one, has his tutoring today, like I said. It's at his school. Um, Hyde County Middle...do you know where that is?"

I didn't, but she didn't need to know that. She'd worry I wouldn't find it, and I'd find it.

I jerked my chin.

"Okay, great. His tutoring should be done around four-thirty, so if you could be there a little before, just in case he gets done early, and bring him to, uh..." She flipped the calendar over and read off the back. "Patterson Field. That's where I'll be with Eli for his practice. I have directions here, if you need them."

I didn't. I'd find it.

"You keep those. I got it."

"It's not going to be an issue with work? You can leave?"

I met her eyes when she pulled them off the paper, and noted the worry there. "With J.R. here, it ain't a big deal. I can step out," I said, squashing that worry.

"Okay." She gave me a soft smile, one that felt fucking *good* to be on the receiving end of, then closed the folder and lowered it to her lap, suddenly looking uneasy. "I do have a concern," she said. "About him going with you..."

I watched her tongue wet her lips before her teeth caught hold of the full bottom one.

"You don't want him on a bike?" I asked, figuring this might've been the thing giving her discomfort.

Not that I had experience with parents or anyone giving a shit about safety, but Shayla seemed the type to give a shit. And this was her brother.

Her brows lifted. "No! No, that's not it at all," she said, shaking her head. "My dad rides…um, well, he used to ride. He can't now. But we've all been on the back of his bike. We're used to it."

"So, what's the problem?"

"He doesn't know you. And Dominic basically hates everyone right now, so I'm not sure how open he'll be to this plan. He might refuse to leave with you."

"He'll leave with me," I told her, standing then since I figured this was settled and I needed to be getting to work.

"I'm not so sure…"

"Worry about the other one. I'll handle him."

"Wait!"

I stopped halfway to the door and turned back.

"You don't even know what he looks like," she said, a soft giggle escaping her as she stood. "I can text you a picture of him, if you want to give me your number…" Shayla pulled her phone out of the back pocket of her uniform pants, and waited, holding it out to me.

Right. I did need to know what this kid looked like. And if something happened, I would need a way of getting in touch with Shayla.

Not that I was anticipating something happening, but I didn't want to be shit out of luck if it did.

I walked back over, keeping her eyes, until I had to look away to take the phone.

"Wait. Here," she said, punching in the four-digit passcode she didn't even bother hiding from me. "Oh, I'm still in Snapchat. Let me just close that out." She laughed under her breath. "You probably don't even know what that is…"

My mouth twitched, then hardened immediately, because I'd forgotten what that felt like.

When the fuck was the last time I'd smiled?

"There you go," she said, handing it over again.

Refocusing, I pulled up the keypad and typed in my number.

She took the phone back when I was finished, slowly dragging her fingers across mine, then held the phone against her chest and looked up at me, breathing slow and heavy.

I wasn't breathing at all, just looking down into her face, at all of it, wondering if her mouth tasted like honey too, or if it was just her lips and the soft skin around them.

Yeah... Time to fucking get to work.

"Send me the picture and whatever else I need to know," I ordered, getting to the door and sliding the lock over. "And quit worryin'."

"Okay. Um, thank you! I really appreciate this!"

I walked out before I turned around again, saw the smile I knew she was wearing, and officially fucked myself. I was already well on my way without even looking back.

The door to the lounge swung shut behind me.

Tori paused whatever the fuck she was doing at the bar to kill time before she could get up in my shit, then proceeded to get up in my shit when her eyes slid from the closed door to me and narrowed.

Cursing, I cut a right and moved through the restaurant in the direction I had come, just as Tori made for the lounge.

"I'm watching you," she hissed at my back.

"Yeah? Big fuckin' surprise," I bit out, turning the corner into the kitchen.

Jesus.

Knowing I had work to do, I pushed up the sleeves of my thermal and washed up at the sink, then I got the shit together I needed to make the daily special—crab cakes—and carried the ingredients over to the counter.

"Chicks. Am I right?" J.R. commented at my back.

I ignored him and kept at the crab cakes. I was working on my third when the lounge door swung open again.

Tori emerged first, eyes sparkling and mouth smiling at me in a way I'd never seen from her before as she moved quickly in my direction.

Looking past her, I watched Shayla step out of the lounge next.

She'd put on more makeup. Her eyes were black-lined again, and her lashes were darker. That was all I got to notice before Tori stopped in front of the window and leaned over the ledge, blocking my view.

"Those crab cakes look amazing, sweetie," she commented. "Super yummy. I can't wait to try one."

I locked eyes with her, and when I did, that smile she was wearing became a grin, one of absolute beauty.

Tori had looks you'd have to be blind not to notice. She was a tall, blonde knockout, who had it even when she wasn't smiling. Even when she was running her mouth, she fucking had it. But add the grin, and dickheads she'd wait on practically threw their wallets at her.

The grin I was getting was natural and came easy, I could tell. Just like the *sweetie* shit. Wasn't the first time she'd used that on me. But the grin was also the kind you'd give a person you were appreciating. It held meaning.

Shayla had filled her in on what was going on and what I was offering to do. That was clear. And Tori was letting me know how she felt about all of it.

So that shit wasn't private after all. Shayla was telling everyone, not just me.

Feeling like an asshole for thinking different, I glared at Tori.

Seeing that, a laugh burst out of her mouth. "Oh, my God," she cackled. "I think you have more attitude than me, you know that?"

"Now that's fuckin' funny," I muttered.

"Keep it up, Stitch. We all know you got a squishy little heart of gold under all that edge. You ain't fooling us." Tori winked at me before stepping away, leaving space for Shayla to slide in.

But she didn't just stand in front of that window. Shayla hopped up onto that counter and leaned over that steel ledge, getting as close to me as she could get without actually climbing through that window.

Just like she used to.

"Yo," she said, smiling, elbow propped on the ledge and chin resting in her hand.

I liked her sitting up there more than she'd ever know. I liked her cute little greeting too. Wasn't sure why, but I did.

And liking everything I liked, I gave her my attention. Just like I used to.

Her lips were shiny now and peach colored, and she'd braided the front pieces of her hair and tucked those strands behind her ears.

I liked all of that too.

Focusing on Shayla's smile and remembering Tori's appreciating one, I quit listing shit in my head I liked and said what I needed to say. "You got her helping you now, or am I still doin' it?" I asked.

If she'd rather Tori, then fuck it. Probably for the best anyway.

Shayla lost the smile and pushed off her hand, sitting back. "Uh, I didn't...she's not helping me. I just told her you are."

"Is that what you want?"

"Yes," she replied, no hesitation. "Unless you can't now..."

I shook my head. "Didn't say that. Just figured I'd ask since you told her what all's goin' on. That's your girl. I'm sure she'd help you out."

And maybe Tori should. It would keep me out of this.

"I didn't tell her everything," Shayla said. "Just that my nana passed away and I had some family stuff going on that was getting hectic, and you'd offered to help me out with it. That's it. That's all I said."

"That's all you said," I repeated, disbelief heavy in my voice. "You didn't go into specifics?"

"No."

"Why not?"

"I . . ." She tilted her head, thinking on this. "I don't know. I just didn't."

"You wanted me knowing and not her. Explain that."

Shayla sat up taller and stared at me. "No."

"No?"

"You're offering to help me, but won't tell me why. Explain *that*," she countered.

I blinked. *What the fuck?* "That's not what we're talkin' about."

This was some brain ninja shit. Mind games. Well, fuck that. I wasn't falling for it.

Shayla looked at her nails. "You explain, I'll explain," she mumbled.

I shook my head, then got back to work on forming the crab cakes, holding tight to my ground. No way was I revealing a damn thing. I'd sound like a fucking idiot.

"Maybe there's just no way to explain something you don't understand," she whispered, seconds later.

It wasn't just the volume of her voice that made me stop and lift my head again, it was the words she'd said, mainly to herself but also as an offering to me, for me to take and use as my own.

And I did. I took them, because she was right.

"Yeah," I muttered, seeing understanding in her eyes, and something else. Relief, maybe.

"So, we leave it at that," she suggested.

"Works for me."

"Good." Shayla smiled again, then slid off the counter and joined Tori over by the tables to distribute silverware.

"Dude. That's the most I've heard you say. Like *ever*," J.R. said, stepping up beside me and looking through the window. "You staking claim to that one? She's cute. Like a little pixie you could carry around with you. She'd probably fit in your pocket. *Pants pocket*, you know what I'm . . . " His voice trailed off when he turned and met my glare, head tipping back since I stood taller than him. "You know, I think I'll go ahead and wash some dishes. Or your bike. Whatever. I'm down for anything."

"You down for shuttin' the fuck up the rest of the day?"

"Normally I'd say no, but since you're so chatty, I'll give you the floor." He slapped my back, grinning big before turning away and stepping up to the rack of dishes.

Chatty? I wasn't fucking chatty.

I got back to work on the crab cakes, and the next time Shayla planted her ass on that counter again, I listened. I did not fucking chat.

That much.

Chapter Seven

SHAYLA

I had absolutely no idea what was going on.

Twice I'd checked to see if there was going to be a full moon tonight. There wasn't. I'd also Googled weird weather occurrences that caused extreme atmospheric shifts, like *The Day After Tomorrow* kind of stuff, convinced something of biblical proportions was about to go down, and that was the explanation for Sean's sudden change of heart.

No dice on that either.

I had zero explanation for why Sean was offering to help me out. I just knew he was, and I was grateful.

I also had zero explanation for why I was falling back into old habits I'd quit cold turkey when Sean made it clear how *not interested* he was in me.

Sitting up on that counter wasn't something I did anymore. Neither was speaking to him, and I was doing both. *Really* well. Like we hadn't had months of distance, and this was just what we did during our day-to-day.

We didn't. We didn't even have a day-to-day. There was nothing routine about us. Not anymore.

But seeing as Sean was offering to help me out, had actually engaged *me* in conversation when he walked up to my car, and had said more words to me in one day than he'd ever spoken total in all of our past interactions, I thought, what the hell? The least I can do to show my appreciation is be friendly with the man.

I'd just ignore how good it felt showing that appreciation. Or I'd at least acknowledge how I *should be* ignoring it.

Maybe it was easier letting go and letting things happen. I wasn't fighting Sean on his offer and forcing distance again. I was accepting it. Just like I was accepting the routine of *us*. Hopping up on that counter and speaking to Sean felt... natural. It was easy and comfortable when, at the moment, nothing else in my life was.

But if I kept wondering, if I kept trying to pick this apart, all of that could change.

Sean probably wasn't struggling for understanding with all of this. So why should I? If he wanted to help me out, awesome. If I wanted to sit up on that counter and talk his ear off, great.

I wasn't going to pick this apart anymore.

I was going with the flow.

"Woo! Go, Eli!" I cheered from the top of the bleachers, getting looks from both my brother and the parents surrounding me.

From Eli because he hadn't done anything to warrant a cheer, unless you counted looking cute covering third base as cheer worthy, which I absolutely counted.

The looks from the other parents had to do with the same thing, I was sure, but I also had a feeling it was because I'd been cheering a lot during this practice, not needing an actual reason to, obviously, and I was standing out doing it, considering none of them had been rooting on their kids *at all*.

I was surrounded by crickets. It was weird.

Crickets who paid more attention to their phones.

Aside from taking a few pics of Eli and sending them to my mom, plus one short video of him up at bat, I hadn't looked at my phone at all until it started ringing halfway through the practice.

Typically, I would've excused myself and stepped away so I wouldn't disturb anyone, but since no one seemed engrossed in anything important, I stayed where I was after digging the device out of my pocket.

Sean's name flashed across the screen.

I noted the time before accepting the call. It was nearly four-thirty. He should've been at the school by now.

"Hey," I answered. "Any problems?"

"Yeah. Do me a solid and confirm I'm not lookin' to kidnap anyone and make a fuckin' dress out of their skin."

"What?"

"Here," Sean grumbled, then not a breath later...

"Did you send some stranger to pick me up?" Dominic's voice was hurried and high-pitched. "Some guy I've never even *seen* before? You actually want me to leave with him?"

"Dominic, calm down," I said. "He's not a stranger. I work with Sean."

"He's a *hair stylist?*"

"Do I look like a fuckin' hair stylist?" Sean griped, sounding close by.

"You look like you want to make a dress out of my skin."

"Okay. Nobody is making a dress out of anyone's skin." Two parents whirled around to look back at me. My eyes narrowed. "Do you mind? Watch your kids," I snapped, gesturing for them to turn around.

"Watch whose kids?" Dominic asked.

"Not you," I told him. *Assholes. Do some parenting.* "Dom, Sean is... a friend. Okay? He's my friend. He's the cook at Whitecaps, and he very kindly offered to pick you up and bring you to me so I don't have to leave Eli's practice."

I began chewing on my cuticle like a maniac, hoping this was all the convincing I would need to do. I didn't know what else to say.

"He's your friend?" Dominic asked incredulously.

"Yes."

"*Just* your friend?"

Oh, my God. "Who are you, Oprah? Just let him give you a ride. And don't act like you haven't been checking out his bike. I know you're into that."

There was a short pause, then Dominic admitted, "It is pretty sweet. Looks like Dad's, but I wasn't really digging the blue on Dad's Harley. I like that black-and-chrome look. Or all black. That's badass."

"You into bikes?" That question came from Sean, and I knew we were all good then.

Smiling, I said into the phone, "Okay, Dom. Go with Sean. I'll see you in a bit."

"Yeah, okay. See ya."

Expecting the call to disconnect, I was pulling the phone away from my ear when I heard a gruff, "Hey."

My stomach clenched. Actually, my entire body clenched. Especially everything near my waist. That was clenching the most.

Not only because this was the first *hey* I'd ever received from Sean—his typical greetings to me consisting of head jerks or other nonverbal cues—but also because of the gruffness in his voice.

Gruff coming from men with deep voices was nice.

Sean's gruff, coming from Sean and *his* voice, was *good*.

Real good.

"Hey!" I chirped, pressing the phone back to my ear.

"He seems convinced I'm not here to do some weird Hannibal Lecter shit to him," Sean said. "We'll be outta here shortly."

"Okay!"

There was a pause, then, "You all right?"

"Yep! Just happy."

Another pause, then, "Right. Gotta go."

"Cool. See ya!"

"Later."

I ended the call, smiling, happy, *really* happy now thanks to that hey, set the phone on the bleacher seat beside me, and looked between the parents, asking "Anybody want to do the wave? I'll start it."

Silence and strange glances were all I received.

"Sheesh. Tough crowd." I looked out onto the diamond and watched Eli bend down and brush dirt off the base. "Woo! Lookin' good, number four!" I yelled.

Eli raised his head and gave me a lopsided smile, which turned into a full-blown grin when I stood, launching into a one-person wave.

I'd do waves by myself for the rest of the practice if it got me grins like that. Not only because I was here to support Eli and cheering him on was how I'd planned on doing that, *take note, parents*, but also because I was determined to make up for that missed field trip.

And I'd make up for it good, too.

"I didn't embarrass you *too bad*, did I?" I asked Eli as we walked across the grass toward the parking lot after practice.

"Nah. M-Mom does that," he said. "Sh-She's always the only one yelling and s-stuff."

I wrapped my arm around his shoulder and pulled him into a side-to-side hug. "So, did you think about what super special thing you wanted to do tonight?" I asked.

When I picked Eli up from school, he didn't seem to be upset anymore, telling me he knew it wasn't my fault we got stuck in traffic (it was, and I'd argued that point), and also sharing how stupid his classmates said the botanical gardens turned out to be (apparently, flowers were boring), but I wasn't going back on my promise. I'd told him we'd do something special, and I meant it.

Walking pressed together, we both stepped over the curb and onto the graveled lot.

"I'm s-still thinking."

"It can be whatever you want," I reminded him. "Just nothing illegal. I don't care how special it is. No dancing girls for you. You're too young."

He giggled.

When we reached my car, I popped the trunk and dumped his baseball equipment inside while Eli took off his cleats, exchanging them for his sneakers he wore to school. Then after setting those in the trunk, along with his hat, which was covered in a thin dusting of dirt, I slammed the trunk closed and turned at the sound of Harley pipes in the distance.

"W-We g-going to get D-Dom now?" Eli asked.

"Nope." I grinned at him, then tipped my head at the bike as it pulled into the lot and made its way down the row of cars, slowing to a stop in front of us.

Eli stepped closer to me as Sean cut the engine and toed the kickstand down. "Sh-Shay, w-who's that?" he asked.

"That's my friend," I told him, no hesitation this time, since I was going with the flow of things.

Dominic swung off the bike and took off the helmet he was wearing, handing it over to Sean.

"How was it?" I asked my brother.

He smiled. He *actually smiled*, without me getting injured.

Pure elation filled me.

"Great," he said. "Sean goes way faster than Dad."

I cut my eyes to Sean, who was slouched over the handlebars and looking directly at me.

I ignored how good he looked positioned like that, which was a difficult task, considering the faded jeans he had on were clinging to his thighs, and the sleeves of his heather-gray thermal were pushed up, revealing magnificent forearms decorated in ink. Plus his hair was styled in one of my favorite ways Sean ever wore his hair—a little messy. Pieces had fallen out of his pony and were hanging in front of his ears, framing his face.

Sean had amazing hair. I wanted to touch it more than I wanted to breathe.

"Not *too* fast, I hope," I said to him.

"He got here, didn't he?" Sean answered.

I cocked my head as most of that elation I'd been feeling left me. *Mm.* Not sure how I felt about that answer.

But he had done me a favor, so I decided not to press, and instead wrapped my arm around Eli, who was staring at that bike and nothing else. "Sean, this is my brother, Eli. Eli, this is Sean."

Sean jerked his chin.

I looked down at Eli and watched him return the gesture.

Holy Lord, that was cute.

"The car unlocked?" Dominic asked.

"Yep," I answered.

He dug the phone out of his pocket and looked back at Sean. "Thanks for the ride, man. It was cool," he said.

"No problem," Sean replied.

Dominic walked to the car, opened the back door, and dumped his book bag inside before climbing in himself.

When I turned back to Sean, he was looking at me again.

"S-Shay."

I put my attention on Eli. "Yeah, buddy?"

"I know w-what I w-want to do now," he said, half of his mouth lifting.

All that admiring he'd been doing, it immediately dawned on me what my brother was referring to.

And although I wanted to give him the world right now, there were certain things that were just out of my control.

"Oh, um, I don't know, E. I think Sean has to get back to work."

"What's the problem?" Sean asked.

I looked at him, mouth open to reply, but Eli stepped forward and spoke first.

"I w-want a r-ride," he told Sean.

Sean's brows lifted. "Yeah?"

Eli nodded his head so fast, I feared it would detach from his body.

"E, Sean has to get going," I said, reaching for my brother.

"I do?"

I quit reaching for my brother and looked back at Sean. "You don't?"

His one shoulder gave a quick jerk. "Gotta be getting back, but I got a minute," he shared.

"Oh. Well, okay!" I stepped up beside Eli and ruffled his hair. "One quick ride around the parking lot. How's that sound?"

Eli tipped his head back and wrinkled his nose. "B-But Dom g-got a long r-ride. I want that t-too."

"E..." I began.

"C-Can you t-take me back to S-Shay's?" Eli asked Sean, cutting me off.

"He's gotta go to work, E," I said. "Just go for a ride around the parking lot. That'll be fun."

"B-But th-that's not special, Shay."

I pinched my lips together. *Well, shit.*

"You live around here, or closer to Whitecaps?" Sean asked, drawing my head up.

Oh, my God. Was he actually considering this?

"Uh...closer to Whitecaps," I said. "I'm at Pebble Dune Apartments."

Sean nodded once, then held out the helmet to Eli, telling me, "Don't know where that is, but I'll follow you."

Oh, my God. He wasn't only considering this. He was doing it.

Helping me out was one thing, but Sean didn't even know my brother. He could've insisted parking lot ride or nothing, but he wasn't.

Wow.

Wow.

"Yes!" Eli punched his fist into the air. "C-Can I go, Sh-Shay? C-Can I?"

I pried my smile off Sean and gave it to Eli. "Heck, yeah, dude. Go for it."

"Yes!" he cried again before breaking into a sprint.

I walked over to the bike as Eli was fastening the helmet, stepped up beside Sean, and quickly admired the jewelry he always wore on his arm—bracelets made of different colored thread. Single pieces. Not three or more strands braided together.

Friendship bracelets. That's what the thread reminded me of—my childhood. I'd made bracelets using thread like that all the time.

Then I bent down and told him with a hushed voice, "Not *too fast*. He's only eight."

Sean smirked behind his short, thick beard. "Sure thing, Mama Bear."

"*Mama Bear?* You cracking another joke? That's twice today."

He stared at me, confused.

"The *not everyone should have pets* comment," I reminded him.

His face hardened, making him look regretful. "I was talkin' about me when I said that."

"Didn't sound that way."

Somehow, his face hardened even more, causing little lines to form in deep, tanned grooves beside his eyes. Now he wasn't only looking regretful. He was looking mildly pissed.

"Relax. It was funny," I told him, smiling.

His gaze lowered to my mouth, and he instantly quit looking

pissed, but that regret was slow to leave him, keeping the tenseness in his jaw until a soft giggle escaped me.

I couldn't help it. I was thinking about that pet comment.

It really was funny.

And even though I missed Ombre, my fish, I still appreciated a good joke.

"I'm r-ready," Eli said at my back.

I spun around and helped him swing up onto the bike. "You remember how you gotta hold on, right?" I asked, guiding his arm around Sean's waist and pressing Eli's hand to Sean's belly. "Like this. Tight."

I felt hardened muscle contract beneath my fingers.

I looked at Sean, breath catching in my throat.

Sean looked at me, his eyes more intense than I'd ever seen before.

Then I looked back at Eli before I passed out, doing this at the same time as he muttered, "I g-got it."

He slid closer to Sean and wrapped his other arm around him, which prompted me to step back since he did, indeed, have it.

The bike roared to life.

Eli's face lit up, and the smile he was wearing rivaled Dominic's, which brought that feeling of elation back on, but this time tenfold, seeing as I was making up for that missed field trip in a good way, the way I had been hoping to make up for it.

And I had Sean to thank for that.

The bike backed up a car length, leaving room for me to pull out of my parking space.

I gave Eli a thumbs up, got one in return, met Sean's eyes and got that head jerk I always found hot in a broody sort of way, but was beginning to find cute too now that I'd seen Eli do it, waved at the both of them, and then got in my car.

"So, how was tutoring?" I asked Dominic once we'd both pulled out of the parking lot, Sean staying close behind me.

"It was tutoring," Dom replied curtly.

Eyes already in the rearview, I looked from Sean to the top of Dominic's head, saw his attention on his phone, and told him, "Hey, you know we all care about how well you do in school, right? Mom and Dad, they love you a lot, Dom. They just have—"

"*God*, I don't care," he interrupted me. "Seriously. We don't have to talk all the time."

Annnnd King Attitude is back. Awesome.

I rolled my eyes away and put them back on the road ahead of me after taking one last glance in the rearview at Sean. I kept my mouth shut and finished the drive in silence, but not because I wanted to.

Part of this whole *going with the flow* thing meant picking my battles with Dominic.

I'd gotten a smile out of him today. A real smile. I wouldn't push my luck.

When we got to Pebble Dune Apartments, I parked in my usual space while Sean pulled up along the curb, allowing Eli to hop off onto the sidewalk.

"My l-legs are sh-shaking!" He giggled, unhooking the strap under his jaw and removing the helmet.

I closed the driver's side door and walked over, asking, "How cool was it?"

"So c-cool!" Eli handed the helmet over to Sean.

I ruffled his hair. "What do you say?" I prompted.

"Th-Thank you."

Sean jerked his chin.

Eli smiled, then returned the gesture in an exaggerated way, so his head tipped way back.

I laughed. "Go get your book bag out of the car," I told him. "Leave your baseball stuff. We'll need it for tomorrow."

"Okay." Eli stepped away and hurried to the car.

"Can I get your house keys?" Dominic asked at my back.

I was going to tell him I'd just be another second, but remembering his smile and how I was picking my battles, I tossed him the keys instead after hitting the lock on the key fob.

Dominic caught them, then he and Eli went inside the apartment.

I turned back to Sean. "Thanks again for getting Dominic for me, and for what you did for Eli. That meant a lot to both of us. You didn't have to do that."

"I didn't do it 'cause I had to," he replied.

He didn't, and I knew that, which was another reason why I was so grateful to him.

Just like the guy who bought my tacos the other day, Sean did a good deed just because he wanted to, and he wasn't expecting anything in return for it.

I thought that said a lot about him.

"Well..." I paused, not sure what to say next, besides a hundred more thank-yous and an invite inside, which I was too terrified to offer for fear he'd shoot me down.

"Gotta get going," Sean muttered, letting me off the hook.

I was grateful for that as well.

"Right. Okay, see ya."

"Later."

I waved as I turned, took the three steps down to the basement level, and paused at the door, looking back toward the sidewalk when the bike engine revved.

Sean and I locked eyes.

Then I watched him pull away.

Before I went to bed that night, I'd decided on writing out a thank-you note to express my gratitude to Sean.

Even though I'd verbally expressed this gratitude already, I believed written words held more meaning. Growing up, my mother instilled in me the importance of writing thank-you notes. It was an older tradition she'd said was becoming nonexistent, thanks to technology. People made phone calls nowadays, or worse, sent texts. (Mom thought texts were the most impersonal.) And I wasn't being raised like that. Not if she could help it. As soon as I *could* write, my mom had me sit down and make out cards for my friends and family the day after birthday parties or any special event where gifts were given.

Now I wrote thank-you notes for different reasons. I didn't have to receive a present from someone. If I felt inclined to send a note of appreciation, I did.

And that night, I was feeling more inclined than I could ever remember feeling, let me tell you.

What Sean did for me meant a lot.

After dinner with the boys, one walk-in haircut, several loads of laundry I not only washed but took the time to fold and put away, and some social media time, I got started. And two rough drafts later, I'd polished up the note I'd written out, proofread it three times, and fancied it up with doodles along the edges of the card.

I also might've sprayed it with my perfume. With a light hand. Nothing crazy.

Then after sealing it in an envelope and addressing it to Sean, I stuck the thank-you note in my purse, made sure the boys were in bed, and turned in myself, considering it was already after one a.m. and we had a busy day tomorrow.

Both Dominic and Eli had sports stuff going on.

Dominic had a scrimmage, and Eli had practice. And both just so happened to be going on at the same time, at two different athletic parks.

Go figure.

It was a lot, but I had a plan. I'd split my time between the two, driving back and forth so I wouldn't be choosing between my brothers, and I figured depending on the length of Dominic's scrimmage,

I could stay for the end of Eli's practice and take him to the other field so we could both watch Dom.

The plan was simple. It was also one that could work.

However, life seemed to have a wild hare up its ass about me lately, so even though I felt good about this plan, I still had a difficult time shutting my brain off and passing out that night. What if there was some weird electrical malfunction where all iPhones shut down for no reason? If that happened, I'd miss the alarm I'd set to allow ample time for consumption of a big, hearty breakfast. The boys needed their fuel. Breakfast bars and cereal just wouldn't do before a morning of sports, so I was relying on that alarm.

Now I figured the chances of this weird electrical malfunction happening were one in a million but again, wild hare. This led to the panicking. And typically when I panicked, I busied myself with a task in hopes I'd get distracted and forget about what I was panicking over.

I had several options, but I settled on alphabetizing my product supply, choosing that because it allowed me to stay in my room and make little to no noise.

It worked too. An hour later, I had systematized my inventory and successfully distracted myself enough to fall asleep.

I wasn't worried about weird electrical malfunctions anymore. I knew the alarm I'd set would wake me up.

So, the next morning, when my eyes slowly fluttered open of their own accord—without an alarm—I was confused. I rolled to my side and pulled the charger cord, dragging my phone across the carpet until it was close enough to press the home button.

My phone lit up and displayed the time: *9:16.*

"Son of a bitch!" I yelled, kicking the blanket off and scrambling off the futon. *My alarm was set for eight-thirty. Why the FUCK is it 9:16?*

"Get up! Get up!" I threw the door open and rushed out of the room, banging on the boys' bedroom door as I continued to yell. "We only have fifteen minutes before we gotta leave! You guys gotta get dressed! Hurry!"

We wouldn't have time for a big, hearty breakfast. The boys would be limited to cereal or a granola bar. I couldn't even offer them something hot and filling, and a morning of sports called for something hot and filling.

Shit!

I was preparing to bust into their room when giggling at my back halted me. Looking over my shoulder, I saw Dominic and Eli seated at the kitchen table, dressed and ready to go.

What the...

"Oh, you guys are up," I said, surprised. Turning completely, I walked over, and getting closer, saw the full plates in front of them, filled with scrambled eggs, pancakes, and sausage links.

Huh? "Dom, did you cook?" I asked.

Mouth stuffed full and syrup dripping from his lips, he mumbled something I couldn't make out.

"What?"

"S-Sean did," Eli answered this time, drawing my eyes to him but not lingering there, and instead, moving to the kitchen entryway when Sean stepped forward and filled it.

My eyes bugged. My mouth dropped open.

Sean Molina was standing in my apartment, wearing his typical chilly-weather uniform of faded jeans and a well-worn thermal, this one midnight blue in color. His hair was tied back at the base of his skull with a few strands hanging in front of his ears, and I would've appreciated that look because it was one I liked appreciating, but I couldn't do that because Sean Molina was standing in my apartment.

"What are you doing here?" I asked him.

He was holding one of the *Blow Me* coffee mugs I'd purchased from Etsy. I'd gotten it because of the hair-styling reference, but it held a double meaning—one I was trying exceptionally hard to ignore right now. I could feel the burn in my cheeks, turning them red.

Sean said nothing, just leaned his shoulder against the door frame and stared at my lower half.

My initial reaction? Flattery.

Was he checking me out right now? Holy shit.

Then reality struck: I never slept in pants.

Gasping, I tugged on the hem of my shirt enough to cover my thong and slowly backed away, saying, "Uh, let me just...put something on. Be back."

More giggles erupted from the table.

I thought I caught a smile behind the coffee mug as Sean took a sip, but I couldn't be sure, since I was retreating fast.

"*Jesus Christ!*" I whispered after reaching the second bedroom and slipping inside. I slammed the door shut and dropped my head against it, groaning.

Sean saw my ass.

My brothers saw my ass.

I didn't really care about my brothers. Yes, it was mildly embarrassing and something I'd probably never live down, but SEAN SAW MY ASS. This was absolutely something I would never live down. I couldn't take this back. I couldn't tell him *Ha! Just kidding! Not my ass!* Because it *was* my ass, and he saw a lot of it. Everything except the crack.

Great.

Most of my clothes were temporarily being stored in the closet I kept supplies in, since my brothers were occupying my bedroom. Hurrying over to the sliding door, I pulled out a pair of jeans and a flannel, quickly got dressed, tugged on a pair of socks, and ran my fingers through my hair before slinking back out into the main living area.

If I'd had the option, I would've stayed hidden away and lived out the rest of my life as a hermit, but I didn't have that option. Furthermore, why the *hell* was Sean in my apartment?

"Hey," I said, walking up to Sean, who was still perched in the doorway of the kitchen, drinking his coffee.

He lifted his chin in greeting. "Your coffee sucks."

"Uh, thanks." I made a mental note about Sean disliking coconut-mocha coffee. Not sure why, but I did. "What are you doing here?"

"Saw on the calendar they had stuff goin' on this mornin'," he began, glancing at my brothers. "Figured you'd have trouble doin' both, so I'm here."

"You're helping me out again?"

"It ain't a big deal."

I stood a little taller, staring back at him and disbelieving the words he'd just uttered, even though I'd heard them loud and clear.

He was helping me out again.

Sean had taken the time to glance over that calendar yesterday when I was merely pointing out a day's worth of activities, and after doing so, came to the conclusion he'd help without me asking him for it, knowing his help would make my life easier.

He was right. This wasn't a big deal. This was a *huge* deal.

"You made them breakfast," I said, pointing out the other part of this amazing act of character. "A hot breakfast. That's so important. I wanted to do that, but I think there's something wrong with my phone. My alarm didn't go off."

"It went off," Sean said.

"I'm sorry?"

"Your alarm. It went off." He tipped his chin at the table. "Already had breakfast going, they were up, so I shut it off and let you sleep. I had it handled."

"You shut my alarm off because you had it handled?"

"That's what I said."

"What time did you get here?"

"'Bout an hour ago."

"And who let you in?"

Sean looked at Eli, then I looked at Eli, who was shoveling bites of pancake into his mouth like this was his last meal on Earth.

I couldn't blame him. Those pancakes looked amazing.

"E, did you let Sean in without letting me know he was here?"

"Obviously," Dominic commented.

I ignored King Attitude and kept my focus on Eli, who finished chewing up his bite, swallowed, and wiped his mouth off with the back of his hand.

"Yes," he answered.

I stepped closer and told him, "I know he's not a stranger or anything, but you really should've woken me up first. Okay? Please, wake me up first next time."

Eli slouched in his chair and nodded.

"What's the problem?" Sean grated at my back.

I turned to him. "Nothing. I just think he should've let me know you were here."

"You got an issue with me helpin' you out?"

"No. Not at all."

"Then what's it matter?"

"Well, for starters, I would've put on *pants*," I snapped, bringing my arms across my chest and cocking my head.

Sean's mouth twitched. Even with his beard, I didn't miss it.

"You know you got a mole on your butt, Shay?" Dominic teased.

"I'm aware, Dom. Thank you."

Eli snickered. Dominic was laughing under his breath. Sean didn't make a sound, but his mouth kept twitching.

"*Anyway*," I continued, wanting to get my ass off the table for discussion, "I didn't need to sleep in. I could've helped you make them breakfast," I told him.

"Didn't need help," he returned. "I can cook this shit in my sleep."

I was sure he could.

This meal was probably nothing for him, and I understood why he was playing it down, but I couldn't do that, and not just because he'd done me another favor either.

I knew what was in my pantry.

"You made pancakes from scratch," I stated, knowing he must have, since I didn't have any pancake mix.

"And?"

"You could've just made eggs and sausage, since I had both on hand, and the boys would've been happy with that. You didn't have to go through the trouble of making pancakes from scratch, but you did. Just like you didn't have to let me sleep in. And you can play that down too all you want, but it's not nothing to me. I like sleeping in, but I would've really liked helping you make them breakfast, whether you needed it or not. Then I could've been thanking you this whole time instead of waiting until right now." I dropped my arms and stepped closer, watching his body straighten off the doorjamb as I got in front of him. Then I tipped my head back and said what I needed him to hear. "Thank you, Sean. Today would've been a little stressful. Possibly a lot stressful, considering my luck lately, and now, because of you, it won't be. Thank you."

He looked from my mouth to my eyes, then nodded his head once.

"I have a feeling I'm gonna need to stock up on stationery," I added.

His brow pulled tight.

I raised my finger to halt him from asking questions, spun around, walked over to the couch and bent over it to dig through my purse, then returned to my spot in front of him with the thank-you note I hadn't been prepared to deliver until my next shift at Whitecaps, but I was more than happy to deliver now.

I held out the card, and Sean took it.

"What's this?" he asked.

"A thank-you note."

"For what?" He lifted his eyes off the card and looked at me. "You already thanked me."

"I know."

I turned around and spotted bites of pancake left over on Dominic's plate. He was finished eating and messing with his phone, so I stabbed two bites with his fork and stuffed the triangles into my mouth.

"Oh, my God," I moaned as the deliciousness of the pancakes slapped my taste buds awake.

Eli giggled, watching me, and licked syrup off his thumb.

"So good, right?" I asked him.

He nodded fast.

I ate two more bites of pancake plus the rest of Dominic's sausage, then straightened up and collected the empty plates. "Okay. Are you guys ready to go?" I asked my brothers.

"Yep," Eli said, standing from his chair.

"My stuff's already in Sean's truck. He's taking me," Dominic informed me as he stood.

"Oh, okay." *Wow. He even came prepared with a vehicle to transport sports equipment. That was incredibly thoughtful.* "I'll probably catch the end of your game. So, good luck! Score some goals or whatever."

Dominic snorted. "I play defense. I don't score."

"Okay, well, good luck defending."

He rolled his eyes.

I was secretly grateful to be on Eli duty today.

"You ready?" Sean asked at my back.

Dominic nodded.

I turned, still carrying the plates, and watched Sean and my brother make their way toward the door.

"We'll see you guys later!" I called out.

Dominic walked through the door, saying nothing.

Sean looked back when he hit the entryway, gave me a "Later," and then pulled the door closed behind him.

My thank-you note was sticking out of his back pocket.

Eli's practice lasted forty-five minutes, which was just enough time for us to catch the end of Dominic's game.

When we arrived at the field, I anticipated Sean being there, but what I hadn't expected to see was him standing along the sideline in the area parents were seated, watching my brother play.

That made me smile, for two reasons.

One, Sean was showing my brother support when he didn't have to, and that meant a lot to me. And two, standing among the preppy lacrosse parents, Sean stood out. In a good way.

There were a lot of polo shirts over there.

After walking Eli over to the playground area where a bunch of other kids were playing, I headed for the field.

"Hey," I said, coming up to stand beside Sean. "How's it going? Are they winning?"

Arms pulled across his chest, Sean looked from the field down to me. "I got no idea what the fuck I'm watchin'," he said.

I laughed. "Yeah, it's a little different. Dom loves it, though."

"He loves beatin' the shit outta people."

"What?"

I looked toward the field then, searched out Dominic's number, and watched him run full speed at another player, drop his helmet to the other kid's back, and level him.

I gasped. "*Dominic!* What are you doing?" I yelled as one of the refs blew a whistle.

"He ain't allowed to do that?" Sean asked.

"Not like that, *no*," I said. "I mean, they can check, but that was crazy."

"He's been doin' that a lot."

I looked up at Sean. "He has?"

Sean nodded, then put his attention back on the field. "Kid's angry," he said. "I don't think he gives a fuck about playin' right now. He's out there to hurt."

I watched Dominic walk up to another kid and knock his helmet into him. The kid wasn't even doing anything.

A heavy breath escaped me. "It's because of my dad," I said. "Dominic's watching that disease just...take him from us. And my dad, he's this mountain. I know you look at me and think my parents are probably little, but Dad's a big guy." I looked up at Sean. "He's so strong. Now, he has trouble tying his shoes and opening a pickle jar. It's so sad to watch. I hate it. But Dom...he can't be angry like this. He can't hurt other people."

A loud crack turned my head, and I watched Dominic stare down at a kid sprawled out on his back.

"Perkins!" one of the coaches yelled. "One more time, and I'm pulling you! You hear me?"

Dominic didn't even look up.

"I just don't know how to help him," I said to Sean. "He won't talk to me."

"Kid needs to let his anger out."

"And how do you suggest he do that?"

I imagined duct-taping the couch cushions to my body and letting Dominic body slam me all over my apartment. I really didn't want to do that.

Sean was silent for a minute, just kept watching the game. Then he rubbed at his mouth and smoothed out his beard before offering, "I got a wall in my house I'm tearing down, plus a few other things that need demolishing. Could use his help, if he's interested."

My brows lifted. "Really?"

There was surprise in my voice, but *God*, there shouldn't have been. Why was I not expecting Sean's help when he was constantly giving it lately?

Maybe it wasn't the offer he was proposing that was so surprising. Maybe it was Sean himself.

He kept catching me off guard. I never expected anything from this man. Not anymore. I didn't even think he liked me enough to be my friend.

"That's . . . so nice of you," I said, drawing his eyes off the field and down to me. "Do you think that'll help him?"

"You ever put a hole in a wall?"

"Can't say I have."

The corner of his mouth lifted. "It'll help. Trust me."

Huh. I was curious how Sean knew so much about this subject matter, but figured there was a better time and place for that discussion, so I didn't inquire.

"He busy tomorrow?" Sean asked.

"No, thank God." I laughed a little. "Sunday is the *one day* neither of my brothers have anything going on. No chance of me screwing anything up."

Sean checked the time on his phone before stuffing it back in his front pocket, doing this while turning to face me. "Right. I gotta get going," he said. "Let me know if he's not feelin' my offer; otherwise, I'll pick him up tomorrow at nine. You gonna be around that afternoon?"

"I work two to close," I told him. "I figured the boys could hang out at Whitecaps. Nate said it was fine."

"I'm headin' in at three, so I'll bring him," Sean offered.

"Okay." I smiled up at him. "I'll talk to Dom after the game and let you know ASAP."

"Let me know whenever. No rush."

"I'd rather give you notice, so I'll let you know ASAP."

Sean stared down at me.

I went from smiling up at him to grinning up at him, watching his expression tighten when I did that. "What?" I asked.

"You all right?"

"Just happy," I answered, because again, thanks to Sean and his thoughtfulness, I was.

So, so happy.

His warm copper eyes moved over my face, then he repeated the need to get going, saying it a little hurried this time, muttered his goodbye, which consisted of his standard "Later," walked between the parents seated in chairs, and sauntered through the grass away from the field.

I watched him disappear over the small hill overlooking the parking lot, then turned back to the game just in time to catch Dominic full-body check another kid.

I winced.

Dominic got pulled from the game with forty-three seconds remaining.

On the bench, he received a lecture from his coach, followed immediately by one helluva lecture from me when I marched over there once the game whistle blew.

Dominic was pissed. Anger was pumping through him so hard, I knew his limbs were shaking from rage and not the typical adrenaline one would feel when playing a sport.

I didn't care. I still lectured him.

Then I informed him of Sean's offer, which seemed to be the equivalent to dangling a fat, juicy steak in front of a starved lion. Dominic's eyes lit up, he smiled, his anger left him, and I would've bet money on him salivating.

He was *very interested* in putting holes in walls.

I was trusting Sean. I had a feeling this would help.

As promised, I shot him a text ASAP, letting him know Dominic was in.

Sean didn't text back, but I wasn't sure he was the texting type. I knew some guys just weren't. They did phone calls or nothing. So I didn't take offense.

Then as I was stocking up on stationery supplies at Michael's half an hour later while the boys moaned in discomfort behind me, my phone beeped.

Be there at nine.

Apparently, he *was* the texting type. I grinned.

People were just full of surprises.

Chapter Eight

SEAN

It was ten to three when I pulled up to Whitecaps the next day with Shayla's brother on the back of my bike.

We'd had a full morning of demolition. A good bit of the afternoon too. Tearing apart shit was a good way of letting off steam, and thanks to the dump I was living in, I had a lot of shit to tear apart. The half wall separating the living room and dining room needed to come down, there was a dead tree out back in the yard threatening to cave my fucking roof in, and I wanted to take out a wall separating the two spare bedrooms to allow for one bigger bedroom.

It was a lot of work. I knew we wouldn't get it all done today, but I kept that to myself. I figured this kid would need some time to get all that anger out of him. I had enough jobs to keep him busy for a few days, at least.

It was a start.

The half wall came down first.

Once I'd handed Dominic the sledgehammer and gave him the go-ahead, he didn't waste any time and swung that thing like there was a face he was putting holes in.

While he did that, I worked on other shit that needed to be

done and gave him some privacy, installing new cabinet doors in the kitchen and fixing the wall socket in the bedroom I was staying in so I could have some light.

Dominic came and found me when he was finished, his shirt soaked through with sweat and his knuckles bloodied, grinning.

I eyed his hands, pausing my work on the outlet, and questioned, "You get tired of swinging?"

"Nah." He smirked. "Just wanted to punch something."

"Yeah? You like that weird-as-shit game you were playin' yesterday?"

"Lax? Fuck, yeah, I like it. It's my life."

"You break your hands, you won't be playin'," I warned him. "Might wanna think about that."

Dominic frowned, looking at his knuckles.

I screwed the outlet cover back on and tested the switch. The overhead light turned on.

"You clean up the mess?" I asked him, tucking the screwdriver into my back pocket.

His brows pulled together. "Mess?"

"You knock down my wall?"

"Yeah."

"Is there wall shit everywhere?"

His mouth twitched. "Basically."

"Go clean it up," I ordered.

Instantly, his mouth quit twitching, and he glared. Then he cursed under his breath and stalked away, and minutes later, I heard all kinds of noise coming from the other room.

He was back to being pissed off. That was good. The whole reason for Dominic being here was to work out his anger, and to do that, I needed him to stay angry. No way was an hour's worth of demolition enough to wear this kid out. He had more in him. A lot more.

So even though I could've helped Dominic clean up, I didn't. And instead, told him where the broom was so he could sweep up the drywall dust when he thought he was finished.

That pissed him off more. Especially when I stood there watching him while taking a soda break.

"Are your arms broken or something?" he griped while scooping up dust into a pan.

"Nope," I returned.

"So why am I doing everything? You can't help?"

"Can help. Just won't."

He scowled and shook his head, dumping the dust into the nearby trash can.

I drained the can of Coke, crushed it, then tossed it into the trash can as I crossed the room, heading for the door. "Finish with that, then meet me outside," I ordered.

"This is child labor!" he yelled at my back. "And thanks for offering *me* something to drink!"

I smirked and stepped outside.

Once Dominic finished up, he walked around to the back of the house where I was tying a rope around the dead tree that needed to come up. It wasn't huge, but it was tall enough it'd do damage if it came down and fell in the wrong direction.

Following my instruction, Dominic tied the other end of the rope to the hitch on my truck, secured it, tested the knot, then stood back as I climbed in the driver's seat and hit the gas. The root pulled out and the tree hit the ground.

"Now what?" Dominic asked, hands to his hips as he stared at the dead branches.

I grabbed the ax out of the bed and carried it over to him, thrusting it into his hand. "Start chopping," I ordered.

He looked at me. "*Seriously?*"

"Yeah."

"And what are you gonna do? Go make a sandwich?"

I smirked, muttering, "Smart kid," before turning and moving away.

I knew when I came back outside, finding Dominic taking a breather was a strong possibility, especially since I didn't just make a sandwich, I ate it and made a second for him.

But when I walked out the door, I could still hear the steady chopping and the crack of the wood. Dominic was showing that tree zero mercy.

"Here," I said, halting Dom from taking the next swing. I held out the sandwich and the Coke I brought out. "Take a break."

"I'm good," he rushed out, panting.

"Take a break," I repeated, holding his eyes until he dropped the ax and took the food and drink from me.

"Thanks," he muttered. Sweat dripped from his brow.

I cleared the branches and carried most of them to the dumpster, then I broke up the thicker ones, stripping them of twigs, and piled up the wood next to the stump in the yard used as a chopping block. I split two logs and stacked the wood along the fence, then I turned back to Dominic, who was shoving the last remaining bite of sandwich into his mouth and chasing it with a drink.

"You need another minute?" I questioned.

"Nope." He wiped his mouth off with the back of his hand, sat the Coke in the grass, and stepped forward. "I'm ready."

"Split the logs, then stack the wood like that." I gestured at the pile. "Got it?"

"Got it," he answered.

I held out the ax.

He tried taking it, but met resistance when I held on, and looked at me. "What?"

"Your dad," I began.

Dominic stiffened. "What about him?"

"You ain't the only one feelin' it, so quit actin' like you are," I said, watching his neck roll with a swallow. "Your mom, Shayla, your brother, they all gotta carry that weight. Only difference is, they're dealin' with it while you're gettin' pissed at every fuckin' person who ain't you. That ain't dealin'. That's throwin' a shit fit, and it's fuckin' stupid."

"What do you know about it?"

"I know because I've done it."

His eyes softened. "Your dad had Parkinson's too?"

"My dad was a fuckin' loser who knocked up my drug-addicted whore of a mother, then split and made a family with someone else. They even had one of those fuckin' in-ground pools with the slide going into it. Ask me how I know that."

"How do you know that?" he whispered.

"'Cause I found him," I said, voice dropping lower. "I found that motherfucker. Saw his perfect house with his perfect fuckin' family, which consisted of a son who wasn't me. A son who was probably a year younger, meanin' my dad didn't waste any fuckin' time once he split to *make* that family. And you know what I did when I saw them?"

"What?"

"I beat the shit outta that kid right in front of his dad, right in front of *my dad*. You wanna talk about fuckin' up, that kid didn't do a damn thing to me. He didn't deserve what I did. And you know what? I was still pissed after I did it. So trust me when I say, throwin' shit fits and actin' out isn't gonna help you, Dom. You're mad. You should be. It fuckin' sucks what's happening, but don't take that out on other people. Especially ones going through the same thing, ones who *get it*. You need to burn out your anger, you come here and I'll put you to work. Or find something else to get it out of you that doesn't involve knockin' other kids around or actin' like a little prick, you got me?"

Eyes wide, he whispered, "I got you."

"Good." I gave up the ax. "Your sister's takin' on a lot lookin' after you and your brother. So how 'bout you ease up on her a little, and I won't stand around when you got a mess to clean up."

Looking remorseful, he nodded.

"You like the sandwich?" I asked.

He stared at me. "Uh, yeah. It was real good."

"You want another?"

"I could eat another."

"Then you'll get it," I said, wanting one more myself.

I headed back inside, made two more sandwiches, and returned with both. After the sandwiches were eaten and the wood was cut and stacked, I got cleaned up, telling Dom we were done for the day.

And when I reminded him of my offer, he confirmed what I already knew.

"Like I said," I began. "You wanna give me a hand with things over here, you're welcome to that. I gotta lot of work that needs to be done."

Dominic stopped at the back of my bike and took the helmet I held out, doing this while smiling. "Yeah, okay, cool," he said. "This was fun. Well, not *fun* fun, but yeah, you know, it was good. Thanks."

It was good.

Meaning, it had worked.

Demolition kicked serious fucking ass.

Toeing the kickstand down, I cut the engine and swung off the bike after Dominic climbed off.

"Are you gonna be helping Shay out until my parents get back?" he asked, handing over the helmet.

I hung it on the handlebars. "If she needs it, yeah."

"How come?"

"What do you mean *how come*? I just said—if she needs it." I stuffed my keys into my pocket and stalked toward the back door.

Dom caught up and filed in beside me. He snorted.

I looked over at him. "What?"

He shook his head.

"*What?*" I repeated.

"Nothing. Just... well, she didn't ask for your help yesterday," he pointed out. "I'm not sure she *really* needed it."

My eyes narrowed into a glare. He was right. I didn't need that shit pointed out to me either. I was aware of it. Still, hearing it out loud was a fucking kick to the balls.

"Shut up," I growled, reaching the back door to Whitecaps and throwing it open.

Dominic snorted again before rushing in ahead of me.

I clocked in and washed up at the sink, then stepped into the kitchen where J.R. was leaning over the worktop, wiping off the edge of a plate.

"I amaze myself sometimes," he muttered, straightening and throwing the rag over his shoulder. "Boom. Look at that." He gestured at the plate.

"It's a burger," I commented, grabbing a ticket off the holder.

"It's a *bomb-ass burger*," J.R. replied. "This thing is fancy as shit. Avocado relish. A little cilantro. I got some alfalfa sprouts on there..."

I quit listening to J.R. list ingredients off a burger we made every fucking day here and looked out into the restaurant.

Dominic and Shayla were talking, and whatever Dominic said to her had Shayla sticking her tongue out at him and ruffling his hair. She looked happy. They both did—they were smiling and laughing. Then Dominic slid into the booth his brother was seated at and picked up a menu. Shayla looked between the two of them, then lifted her head and met my gaze.

I cut my eyes away and looked over at J.R. He was still going.

"...toasted whole wheat bun. Peppered greens. *Come on*. This is a high-class masterpiece right here. This shit will be all over Instagram. You watch." He slid the plate onto the ledge and stuck a ticket beside it, sighing.

"Quit looking at that thing like you wanna fuck it," I said.

J.R.'s eyes lit up. "Hey, that was a joke. You made a joke!" He slapped my shoulder.

"I hear he makes *tons* of jokes."

I looked through the window again and watched Kali smile at me as she slid the plate off the ledge.

I make tons of jokes? Who the fuck would...

Standing at a table now, Shayla was talking to an older couple. She stuck her pen behind her ear, smiled, and pointed at the menu the man was holding as she continued speaking.

Right. She thought I was funny. But I wasn't, so what the fuck?

"This burger looks amazing, J.R. Nice job," Kali said before stepping away with it.

"*See?* Bomb-ass burger made by a bomb-ass cook. Told you," he said. Then he spun around and stepped up to the grill.

"Hey."

Shayla's voice turned my head.

"You got my note, I see," she said, hopping up onto the counter and tacking up the ticket she'd just written out.

"What?"

"The ticket you're holding. I didn't have any stationery with me, so it was either that or a napkin." She gestured at my hand.

That was when I looked at the ticket I'd pulled down, not even having so much as glanced at it before.

In heavily outlined handwriting, my name was written at the top of the ticket in bold black. And below that, a *thank-you*—scripted in purple ink—with Shayla's name at the bottom. That was written in purple too.

"You had this waitin' for me?" I asked, looking up at her.

Another note. She was giving me another note, when all she needed to do was fucking say the words to me. Or don't say them. Whatever. I didn't need Shayla thanking me for shit. I hadn't done what I did expecting anything in return. I never expected a damn thing from anybody.

What was she doing?

"I told J.R. to leave it up there for you," she explained. "But I feel like I should amend it to say way more than just a thank-you, since Dominic is basically a different kid now. Seriously, what did you do to him? He seems...kind of happy. It's awesome."

"You had this waitin' on me," I repeated, reading the ticket again, then lifting my eyes to her. "You didn't need to do that."

"And you didn't need to help me." She cocked her head, then shook it. "It would've bugged me if I hadn't done something. I'm a thank-you note kind of girl. Sorry that one's kind of bland and boring. I was limited without my stationery supplies. I can redo it, if it sucks..."

"No," I mumbled, stuffing the ticket into my back pocket before she took it from me.

Christ. I needed help.

Shayla dropped her elbow to the ledge and smiled. "Mm."

"What?"

"Nothing." She bit her bottom lip, fighting a grin. "So, Dominic...it worked, huh?"

"Putting holes in walls does wonders," I replied, pulling the next ticket down and reading an actual order on that one.

"He told me you said he could keep coming over and helping out. That's really cool of you."

I shrugged. "House needs a lot of work done. It's nothin'."

"It's not nothing," she argued, lifting my gaze off the ticket. "It's not even close to nothing. And we're just going to leave it at that, 'cause this argument could go on for days."

I stared at her. Shayla didn't fight that grin anymore and gave it to me.

And then, I don't know why the fuck I did it, maybe it was because she was grinning and I wanted to keep her that way, or maybe I'd officially lost my mind, but I did it again. I got up in her shit. She wasn't asking a damn thing of me, and it didn't matter. I couldn't stop myself.

"Hey," I barked over my shoulder.

J.R. paused stirring something in a saucepan, and peered behind him. "'Sup?"

"You got nights this week?"

"I got whatever. I told you—my shit is relaxed."

Getting my answer, I turned back to Shayla. "You decide what you need from me," I said. "Who I'm takin' wherever or picking up. I don't care. You take one. I'll take the other. Just tell me what you want me to do. I'll do it."

Shayla blinked, most of that smile already gone from her, and the rest slowly slipping away. "My God. I'm gonna need to make another run to Michael's before the week's up," she said.

I didn't know what the fuck that meant, but she didn't give me time to inquire.

Hopping down, Shayla reached around the soda dispenser and produced the folder she'd shown me the other day. Then she boosted herself back up and flipped the folder open on the window lip.

She showed me the schedule again, pointing out which brother had what going on and where, and we split it up how she wanted it. No questions asked.

Shayla didn't get on me again about why I was helping her, and I didn't ask myself again what the fuck I was doing.

We left it at that.

Chapter Nine

SHAYLA

It was Friday night, and I had a major hankering for pizza.

Though, if I was being honest, I knew it wasn't just the hankering that had me suggesting the idea to the boys after Eli and I picked Dominic up after his math tutoring.

Pizza wasn't just delicious and a huge hit with my brothers, especially pizza from Frank's, who killed it in the crust game. Pizza was also a portable food, and I needed a portable food if I was going to surprise Sean with dinner.

He had helped me out in a major way this week. Not only were the boys' afterschool activities covered without a hitch, thanks to Sean taking Eli for me while I took care of Dom and vice versa, but Dominic had gone over to Sean's house several days to continue working out his anger, and now he was damn near pleasant to be around.

And Sean was to thank for that.

I wanted to do something unexpected for him. What better way was there than showing up with a couple pies from Frank's, some ice-cold beverages, and fresh treats from Duck Donuts?

After confirming with Tori that Sean was not at work and getting affirmative yeses on the pizza and donut plan from the boys, I called in our order and drove us to Frank's.

"Wait here. I'll just be a minute," I told my brothers, leaving the car running and getting out after grabbing money out of my bag.

I headed inside the small pizza shop, which didn't look like much on the outside, but looks were deceiving. Everyone knew Frank's Pizza kicked ass. And since it was Friday night and everyone knew Frank's Pizza kicked ass, the place was mobbed.

After checking on my order and being told it would be another minute, I squeezed between the carryout crowd and stood toward the back so I wouldn't block people coming up to the register.

I was thinking about which donuts we should order when I felt a gentle tapping on the back of my leg.

Looking over my shoulder, I saw a little girl with golden-blonde pigtails smiling up at me. She couldn't have been much older than five, and she had on more pink than I'd ever seen in my entire life.

"Hi," I said.

"Hi," she returned in the sweetest little voice. "I like your hair."

"Oh, well, thank you very much." *How stinking cute was she?* "I like *your* hair. And your shoes. Those are so pretty."

She smiled up at me and toed one of her pink, glittered ballet flats.

"*Caroline*," a woman said, rushing over with a smaller child in her arms, this one also a girl with golden-blonde pigtails. "Sorry." She gave me an apologetic smile. "She gravitates toward pink. In case you didn't pick up on that."

"That's okay. She wasn't bothering me."

The woman, who I'd guess was in her mid to late twenties, had blonde hair like the two girls. She was pretty, with small, delicate features, sapphire eyes, and a brilliant smile. And she had killer taste in clothes. She was wearing a camo jacket and black tattered skinny jeans tucked into combat boots.

"I love the pink," she said, pointing at my hair, then adjusted the child on her hip. "That's really cool."

"Thanks. I like playing around. Habits of a stylist, I guess."

"Oh, you did that yourself?"

I nodded, smiling.

"So, you do hair?"

"Yep."

"In Dogwood? Which salon are you at?"

"I'm actually working out of my apartment right now. I'm starting my own business."

"Oh, that's cool! Good for you."

"Thank you." My chest warmed with pride.

The woman pulled her hair over one shoulder and winced as she played with the ends. "I need to get my hair done so bad," she said. "The girl I was going to moved three months ago, and I'm terrible about just going somewhere and trying someone new. I'm nervous I'll end up with—"

"Pink hair," I cut in, smiling at her.

She chuckled. "A girlfriend of mine had a terrible experience once."

"Oh, well, I wouldn't give you pink hair," I told her. "Unless you asked for it."

"I'm sure someone would *love that*." She looked down at the little girl playing peekaboo behind her leg.

"Seriously, though, if you're looking to get your hair done, I could totally hook you up. First haircuts are free. And I have a variety of colors. Not just pink." I winked at the little princess. She totally looked like a princess in all that pink.

"Really? Okay. Yeah, that would be great."

"Awesome! Let me just . . ." I looked around me, then, spotting the menus up at the counter, I excused myself and slipped up front, snagged a pen and scribbled down my info. "Here. That's my cell. Just call or text me, and I'll get you in." I handed her the menu.

"Thanks. I'm actually really looking forward to this."

"Me too! I'm Shay, by the way. Guess I should mention that."

She giggled. "That's okay. I'm Valerie. And these are my girls, Caroline"—she touched the princess on the head, then bounced the child on her hip—"and Fiona."

I waved at Caroline, then put my attention on Fiona, who looked close in age to her sister.

"Hi, pretty girl. Do you like pink too?" I asked.

Fiona nodded slowly, then buried her face in her mother's neck.

"She's my shy one," Valerie explained.

"Shay! Order to go!" the man at the counter called out.

"That's me," I said. "So, yeah, just hit me up, and I'll totally make all your hair fall out."

Her eyes went wide.

"Kidding! Kidding."

I waited for her to laugh before I moved away, waving back at them, then I stepped up to the counter and informed the man who wasn't Frank—I'd checked—how much I loved Frank's Pizza as I paid for the two pies.

Not only was their crust game on point, but they served patrons with amazing taste in picking a stylist.

Next stop was Duck Donuts.

The boys went inside with me this time so they could pick out their selections. After some debate, we settled on a variety of glazes, toppings, and drizzles to make up our dozen.

I had no idea what Sean would like, so I wanted to cover my bases.

Then Dominic directed me to Sean's house.

I knew the place needed a lot of work and, according to Dominic, it was small, but I could immediately see it had potential. It was on a nice chunk of land, it was decent sized—not big, but I wouldn't say small; average was more like it. It had a cute little wraparound porch and landscape that was overgrown now, but had a good foundation you could build on if you took the time, thanks to the rose bushes and scalloped brick work. Plus, it was close enough to the beach you could make an easy walk out of it, which was *huge*.

Hold the phone. This was practically oceanfront.

"Nice. I like it," I commented after pulling up along the front of the house and parking near the mailbox. "E, can you grab the sodas, buddy?"

"Yep!" Eli was almost as excited as I was to be delivering this surprise. He really liked Sean.

Dominic had the donuts, so I grabbed the two pizza boxes off the back seat and shut the door with my hip.

"It's cool, Eli. Wait 'til you see out back. He's got a tire swing up," Dominic said, he and Eli walking ahead of me.

Huh. *Why would a single guy need a tire swing?* Maybe it had been left by the previous owner.

Both Sean's bike and his truck were in the driveway—a good sign he was home. As I got a close look at his truck for the first time, I saw a half-peeled-away smiley face sticker on the rusty bumper and realized I *had* seen his truck before.

"Holeey shit," I breathed, stopping in the grass. He'd paid for my tacos that day. Sean was the guy. The good deed, doing something for nothing, guy.

And he hadn't said a word to me about it.

I felt my mouth curl up in the corner. *He just couldn't stop surprising me, could he?*

I was beginning to suspect Sean was the most unexpected man in the history of unexpected men. He never wanted anything in return for his actions. He never assumed or anticipated acknowledgment.

He was simply . . . good.

He was a good man.

"Shay, you coming?" Dominic called out.

I turned away from the truck and saw the boys waiting for me on the porch.

"Yep! Just admiring," I explained, which wasn't a lie. I *was* admiring, I just wasn't admiring a vehicle. I was admiring the man who owned it.

Stepping up onto the porch, I balanced the pizza boxes on my forearm so I could knock on the door. I could hear drilling, which stopped the second time I knocked after my first went unnoticed. Then a few seconds later, the door swung open.

Sean stood there wearing his faded jeans and nothing else.

I'm going to repeat that for emphasis—Sean stood there wearing his faded jeans and *nothing else*.

His hair was tied back. He was barefoot. His chest was on display. His hip bones were jutting out nicely. He had fuzz running from his navel to below, and his skin had a light sheen of sweat to it, which was basically the equivalent to icing on a cupcake—the finishing touch that *really* set off the whole package.

These factors, plus others, considering how low his jeans were hanging, had me scrambling to hold those pizza boxes with both hands, for fear I might drop them.

I had never seen Sean without a shirt on before. I figured he had ink on other parts of his body, not just his arms, and he did. His chest was covered in tattoos, as were his shoulders and his ribs, colorful designs that looked to be random, but I was betting they weren't. His abdominals were bare, which, even though I had a major thing for body ink, I was grateful for, considering what his abdominals looked like.

Hell, what *all* of him looked like.

Sean had a body like an Olympian. Like one of those track runners who still had the sculpted upper torso. He wasn't bulky, but the muscles he did have were so finely cut with perfection, you'd think it was God himself who touched Sean after uttering the phrase *Let there be light, plus gorgeous male physiques.*

He was solid. Nothing but taut skin and power underneath.

My eyes lingered on his upper arms, the muscles there, and the ink decorating him. I squinted to study it.

Were those stick figure people?

"S-Surprise!" Eli yelled from behind me.

Startled, I snapped my gaze off Sean's body and looked up. "Hey! Uh, yeah, surprise! Hope you didn't eat yet."

Sean looked at the boxes in my hand. "Frank's," he muttered, smiling a little. "They got good crust."

I sighed. *God, he was just perfect.*

"And Duck Donuts," I pointed out. "Nobody beats Duck."

"I got the s-soda!" Eli said, hoisting the twelve-pack of Coke up to his shoulder.

"Did you eat yet?"

Sean looked from Eli to me after I spoke, a solemn look on his face, and shook his head.

"Great." I smiled, then I stared at him when he didn't move or show hospitality, and giggled. "Uh, are you going to let us in?"

As if he needed the prompt, Sean stepped back then, no hesitation, and held the door open as he rubbed at the back of his neck.

"I like your house," I told him, stepping in. "It's . . . you have no furniture."

I glanced around the empty living room.

There were rags on the floor and a lamp in the corner, plus a few empty soda cans, but other than that, nothing.

"You don't have any furniture?" I asked instead of assuming, turning to look up at Sean.

Maybe he was keeping it in storage until he was finished fixing up the place?

"Got a bed," he uttered, pushing the door shut after the boys stepped inside. "Plus a trunk to keep my clothes in."

"Just a bed and a trunk? You don't have anything else?"

How can he not have furniture? That's crazy.

"Haven't found anything I liked yet," he replied, but something in his voice told me that wasn't true. And when his eyes drifted and I watched him glance around the room, looking both frustrated and disappointed with the house he called a home, I knew he wasn't being picky about furniture.

I decided to change the subject before the mood ruined this surprise.

"Well, I don't know about you guys, but I'm starving," I said, looking at my brothers, who were both nodding in agreement.

We ate in the middle of the room, pizza first, my brothers each devouring three slices and Sean putting away an easy four. I ate two slices of the half ham and pineapple, the other half plain cheese for Eli, then slid the box of donuts in front of me and threw open the lid.

My brothers both nabbed a donut, Dominic's choice being peanut butter glaze with chocolate drizzle, and Eli choosing chocolate on chocolate. I settled on the maple bacon glaze, then gestured at the box, asking Sean, "You want one?"

He shook his head and pulled another slice of green pepper and onion out of the box.

"Wow," I commented. Five slices was impressive.

"Been workin' for hours," he explained, chewing up his bite. "I was about to make a sandwich when you showed up."

"You eat a lot of sandwiches, man," Dominic said.

I looked to Sean, not knowing this about him.

He shrugged. "Sandwiches are cheap. I like cheap."

"I like pizza," Eli replied, chocolate drizzle coating his lips. "And d-donuts."

"Me too," I agreed.

"Same," Dominic added.

Sean folded his pizza in half and took another bite.

He had put on a shirt before we ate, which sucked, in my opinion, but his feet were still bare, and I could not even begin to explain why that was sexy. It just was.

After Dominic and Eli ate their donuts, they asked Sean if they could go out back, leaving the two of us alone.

As the door closed, I sucked glaze off my fingertips and collapsed onto my back, holding my lower stomach. "I have a pizza baby," I said. "He's going to be beautiful. I just know it."

Sean side-eyed me, smirked, then took another bite.

He smirked at me a lot. He smiled at me a little. I liked both.

"Want to play a game?" I asked.

"Nope."

That cracked me up. "You don't even know which game I'm going to suggest," I said, laughing.

"Doesn't matter. I wanna eat."

"You can eat and play it. It's a talking game."

He looked over at me, swallowed his bite, and waited.

"We just take turns telling something about ourselves."

"Hell, no."

"What? Come on."

"Nope." He bit into the pizza, reaching crust.

I could've taken his answer and left well enough alone, but . . . *no*. I really didn't want to do that. Not at all. I wanted to know him. I wanted to know more.

Tori, Syd, and Kali all liked to joke about how Sean looked like he'd been in and out of prison. He definitely had that hard, unapproachable, don't-ask-questions look about him, and if it was true, I needed him to know it wouldn't matter. Not to me. Not when I knew deep down the kind of person he was. So, instead of moving on and changing subjects, I didn't.

I had the ammo. And I was using it.

"You paid for my tacos," I said, pushing up to my hip.

Sean quit chewing and looked over at me.

"You were a stranger who paid for my food," I continued. "Which was a *good* thing. Then you helped me with my brothers when I didn't even ask for it, which was another *good* thing. So, it doesn't matter what you tell me, Sean, because I already know the kind of person you are. What I don't know are facts, aside from you being a cook who's fixing up his house, who drives a kick-ass looking Harley, who works hard doing his job and is great at it—I've tried your food—and who works hard at everything, I'm guessing, considering the appetite you've worked up. I want to know facts. I want to know more."

"You don't know shit," he mumbled.

"Exactly. That's why I want to play this game."

He shook his head and tossed the crust into the box. "You gotta go. I got work to do," he said, getting to his feet.

I got to my feet then too, stood in front of him, and tipped my chin up. "*No*," I snapped.

"No?"

"I'm not leaving until you tell me more. You're my friend. Friends know things about each other."

"I ain't your friend."

Hearing that, I flinched.

Okay, that hurt.

Then I pulled in a breath through my nose, decided he was only saying that to get me to leave, which wasn't going to work, and repeated, "You *are* my friend. And you don't get to back out of this now. I won't let you. Hell, you started it."

His eyes got hard. "I started *what*?"

"You came to *me*." I stabbed at my chest. "You saw me crying and came to me. You offered your help. You bought my fucking tacos. So *you* started it. We're friends now. And you don't get to decide otherwise. It's done."

I was certain, if we had spectators, they would find this standoff amusing, considering the size difference between Sean and me.

I, however, wasn't finding any of this amusing. Neither was he.

Sean looked all over my face. He was breathing loud and heavy, his chest was rising with slow, thick breaths. "Who the fuck are you?" he asked.

"I'm a hair stylist," I answered, because it was true and, well, if he needed examples how this was supposed to play out, I'd give him some. "Who also waitresses to cover bills while she starts her own business," I continued. "I'm twenty-three. I love Taco Bell and would totally have them cater my wedding. I also love Frank's Pizza because of their crust, and Duck Donuts because they're just fucking delicious all around. I have one tattoo. I've never smoked a day in my life. I love being on the back of a bike and miss it terribly. I'm scared about a lot of things, but the big ones being I'll lose my dad and I'll fail at my business. I'm small, but I'm loud. I don't like being told what to do, unless I also want to do those things. I'm bull-headed. I love singing in my car. The beach makes me happy. And I'm good at judging a person's character. I've judged yours. I like it. Now, who are you?"

Sean stared at me, nostrils flaring.

"Well?"

"You've judged my character?" he asked.

I nodded firmly.

"You like it?"

"Yep."

He bent closer, putting his face an inch away from mine, and grated, "That's why you don't know *shit*. You wanna know about me? You want facts? I've been to prison. Not jail. Fuckin' *prison*. Been to jail too. A lot. Got busted on assault, breaking and entering, trespassing, theft. Everything I had growing up, I stole from other people. I stole food. I stole clothes. I stole shit I wanted and wouldn't ever fuckin' get unless I did steal it. Stole cars. Found out I could get money for certain cars, and then stole a lot of fuckin' cars to get that money. I've beaten the shit outta people for being better than me, for havin' what I don't, as payback, and for no fuckin' reason. How you like that character now? Huh? I'm a twenty-nine-year-old *loser*. Those enough facts for you? No? How 'bout this—I got kids. Two girls. Four and five years old. *Little.* Fuckin' *impressionable.* The last time they saw me, I was getting hauled off to jail, right in front of them. I can still hear them screamin' for me 'cause they were scared, and I was the reason for it. *Me.* I'm a fuckup. Nothin' to nobody. That's who I am."

My heart was racing so fast, I could feel its pace throughout my entire body.

"That's not true," I whispered.

"No? Why? You think buying you six-dollar tacos and driving your brothers around makes me what, a fuckin' good Samaritan? You *like* the person I am?"

"Yes."

"Don't," he growled.

My eyes jumped between his.

There was so much going on inside my head. Too much. The first thing being *holy shit, Sean has kids. He's a father.* A father who'd done some bad stuff in his life, yes, but...

"Going off someone's actions isn't the best judge of character sometimes," I told him, verbalizing my next thought.

His eyes narrowed. "*What?*"

"Sometimes people do things because they have to, or for other reasons that are justifiable. If we were to list things we've done in the past and judge each other based solely on those things, you'd think badly of me."

He leaned back, brought his arms across his chest and cocked his head. "Like what?"

"Well,"—I licked my lips, thinking fast since I wasn't at all prepared for this part of the presentation—"I've smoked weed," I blurted out.

He stared at me. "Said you never smoked a day in your life."

"I meant cigarettes. I've gotten high."

"Ooh," he mocked.

I grabbed my hips. "It's still *illegal*. And I've stolen things. I stole a belt one time from Sears. Got caught and had to give it back, which was totally embarrassing since my friends were with me. I've also busted into a car before."

His eyebrow raised.

"See? You're judging me right now. You don't know why I did it," I said, driving home my point. "I'm assuming you stole food because you were hungry?"

Sean's mouth got tight.

"Mm. That's a *terrible reason* to steal. Starving isn't life or death or anything."

He breathed deep and shook his head, mumbling, "This is fuckin' bullshit. You're judging me 'cause of the shit I did for *you*. How's that any different?"

"Good deeds hold more weight, especially when they aren't motivated or asked of a person. They show true character. The person you are deep down. What life can't touch, no matter how bad it can be sometimes." I watched his eyes slowly return to mine. "You saw me crying, Sean, and you could've just walked inside and left me, but you didn't. That's not nothing to nobody. Not even close."

His chest rose slowly, and his lips parted.

"I don't think any different of you."

"You should."

"I won't," I promised.

Sean clenched his jaw and looked away. I knew he was getting frustrated with me, and I didn't want that frustration to turn into anger. So I changed topics while still holding firm to my ground.

"Now, as your friend, I'm going to request a quick tour before I gather up my brothers and leave, since I did believe you when you said you had work to do. But I'm getting that fucking tour. Friends get tours." I smiled up at him after I spoke, then I turned and took three steps in the direction of the hallway, leading to what I assumed were bedrooms, before turning back. "Coming?" I asked.

Sean slowly turned his head, met my eyes, looked distantly at the floor for a brief moment, and then rubbed at his mouth while uttering a curse before moving toward me.

"Why'd you break into a car?" he asked.

"There was a puppy inside, and the asshole owner didn't even crack a window. It was nearly a hundred degrees out," I told him. "That puppy could've died."

Sean stopped in front of me. "You risked goin' to jail to save a dog?" he asked, disbelief in his voice.

"Yep. And I'd do it again too," I replied, smiling up at him.

His eyes lowered to my mouth.

I smiled bigger.

"Now, I'd like that tour please," I requested, gesturing toward the hallway.

Sean lifted his gaze to mine, breathed deep, and then moved around me.

I got my tour.

My parents came home on Sunday.

After exchanging hugs and getting filled in on how Pop was doing, plus hearing stories of Nana and the little packrat she had apparently become, I fessed up to the mistakes I'd made before Sean stepped in to help me out.

Dad didn't hide his disappointment—I should've told them I was having trouble immediately when it started happening. Mom didn't seem disappointed at all—she knew what was being asked of me and expected some difficulty on my end.

They both, however, seemed in agreement on Sean. Especially when Dominic and Eli got to talking about him.

"What kind of bike?" Dad asked after hearing about the rides the boys had taken.

"A Harley. Black and chrome," Dominic answered.

Dad nodded appreciatively. I could tell he respected Sean not only for what he did, but also for his taste in motorcycles.

My parents also noticed the change in Dominic, and then they *really* appreciated Sean, Mom especially.

Using my stationery, she scribbled out a thank-you note and left it to me to pass along.

I couldn't wait to see Sean's reaction to that. He always looked so captivated by those little cards.

My parents stayed for lunch, then I walked with them outside to say my goodbyes.

"So?" Mom whispered, stopping at the front of their car while Dad and the boys filed in. "Is he like, a *friend* friend?"

"*Mom*," I groaned. God. No way was I talking about this with her.

She kissed my cheek. "Well, we would love to meet him sometime. Maybe we'll all go out to dinner one night. How about that?"

I wasn't sure how receptive Sean would be to that idea, or any idea involving my parents. The man wasn't exactly pushing for a connection. But I gave my mom two enthusiastic thumbs up as I backed away.

Smiling, she piled into the car with the rest of the family and they pulled off, waving out the windows.

Now, it was Sunday afternoon, and I was anticipating the arrival of my next client.

Valerie had messaged me yesterday, the sweet woman from Frank's Pizza with the two adorable daughters. She was taking me up on my offer on non-pink hair, and wasn't wasting any time doing it either. She jumped right on my opening today when I gave it to her.

I was really looking forward to this appointment. She seemed cool, and really nice.

"Hey!" I greeted her, propping the door open and gesturing for her to come inside. "Oh, no kiddies today?"

She blew out an exhausted breath. "No, thank God. My sister offered to keep them. Otherwise, *yikes*. They would get into everything. Caroline would find your pink hair color and paint herself from head to toe."

I laughed as I shut the door. "She was so cute in all that pink."

"Always. No other color."

I didn't see any harm in that.

"Well, are we ready to get fabulous?" I asked her. "Because *I'm* ready."

Valerie unzipped her hoodie and shrugged it off, handing it to me when I held out my hand. "Yep! Let's do it."

I showed her to the room.

After getting her gowned up and situated with a cold beverage, I stood behind Valerie and met her eyes in the mirror.

"So, what are we thinking?" I asked, running my fingers through her long hair. It was soft and thick. "You said highlights on the phone. Do you only want highlights? Would you want some contrast in there? A little dark to break it up? And what about your root?"

We breezed through the consultation. Valerie knew what she wanted, for the most part, and loved the suggestions I made in terms of keeping with a more natural look. After mixing up her color, I sectioned off her hair and got to work.

Now, I have always said that if a woman gets her hair done professionally, she's paying for not one but *two* services: hair styling, of course, and therapy.

Women like to talk. Some men do too, especially ones in this industry. And when you're working on someone's appearance for several hours, that's a lot of time to gab. Some clients vent. Some ask advice. Some simply swap personal facts with their stylist.

Valerie didn't waste any time. She shared how long she'd lived in Dogwood Beach—six years—and that she was a fourth-grade teacher who absolutely loved her job, not only because she'd wanted to be a teacher her entire life, but also because it gave her summers off with her girls.

Her girls were her life. Once she got on that topic, she stayed on it.

"So, yeah, my kids are with my sister," she said, pausing to take a drink of her sweet tea. "She's my only sitter. I'm lucky to have her. It's tough sometimes, getting a moment to myself, you know?"

Nodding, I painted another section of her hair, foiled it off, and picked up another. "Mm mm. Time to yourself is so important, though."

"Tell me about it."

"What about their dad? Is he not around?"

She made a sour face in the mirror. "Don't get me started."

I chuckled. "Uh oh."

"You don't even want to know the half of it. My ex...I wasted so much time on him. It was my own fault, though. I knew exactly who he was. I tried to tell myself he could change. Whatever. I just feel bad for my girls. You know, their last memory of their dad is watching him get arrested?"

I stilled my brush.

"Yeah." Catching my eyes, she nodded. "Nice, right? He's not winning Father of the Year, that's for sure. He's out now and wants to see the girls. He must think I'm a fucking idiot. No way."

I finished painting that section of hair and foiled it off, then quickly moved on to the next.

What... were... the odds here? It had to be Sean, right? But do I ask? I don't know. And if it is, do I say I know him?

Shit! Why did people think this was a therapy session? It wasn't. We should be talking hair and hair only.

Valerie took another drink of her tea, watching me work in the mirror.

I had to ask. I had to know.

"So, what does he do now that he's not in jail?"

It was a terrible lead-in, but I couldn't just say, *Hey, what's his name?* That would be too obvious.

"He's a cook. He's always been a cook, but he's never really held a job down. Not really the professional, hardworking type, if you know what I mean. He's a loser."

I bit my tongue.

I really didn't want to hate Valerie, since I was liking her so much and really wanted to keep her as a client, so I kept telling myself she had reason to feel the way she did, and I wouldn't judge her based on that.

"Anyway, he's saying he's kept the same job since he got out. I just don't know if I believe him. Sean's a liar."

Bingo.

"Sean." I met her eyes and stuck my hand on my hip. "You don't mean Sean Molina, do you?" I asked nonchalantly.

Or, at least, *attempted* to ask nonchalantly.

Her eyes flickered wider. "Y-Yes. Do you know him?"

"I work with him."

"You... *what*? What do you mean?"

"I'm a waitress at Whitecaps. That's where he works. I work there too."

"Get out of here!"

I chuckled. "Totally serious. Small world, right?"

"Wow, that's crazy."

I dipped my brush in the color and parted another section. "He's, uh, been there for over a year," I shared, glancing at the mirror.

She lifted her gaze. "He *has*?"

I nodded. "He's really good too. His food kicks ass."

"Sean's always been a good cook. That doesn't surprise me," she said, biting her lip. "That's... he's *really* been there for over a year? Are you sure?"

"He started after I started. I'm sure."

She brought her glass to her mouth, mumbling a "huh" before taking another sip.

Valerie wasn't expecting Sean to be telling the truth, or maybe she just had a hard time believing it herself. I had no idea what all Sean had done to lose that trust from her, assuming it was more than the arrest I was aware of, even though that was probably plenty enough, and even though I wanted to pry more than I wanted her walking out of here with kickass hair, I didn't feel right about doing this behind Sean's back, which was exactly how it felt.

But if Valerie were to *offer up* information, or inquire about stuff I knew about, I supposed that was different.

"How does he seem?" she asked.

"Good. Focused. He was running the kitchen by himself up until very recently, and he didn't have a problem. He just bought a house."

Shit. Maybe I shouldn't have told her that. *What if Sean didn't want her knowing?*

Focus on hair, Shay!

"Sean owning a house," she mumbled, shaking her head a little. "The only thing he ever owned was a trailer. We lived in an apartment with the girls. As soon as we met and got serious, Sean went out and found a place. He refused to stay in that trailer with me. He wouldn't even let me in it. I think he was embarrassed. It was pretty dumpy. He kept it, though. Stored it somewhere, I guess. Good thing too, since he didn't have anywhere to go after he got out. I'd left him."

I listened and focused on my task.

"It's like, you give people so many chances and they just keep blowing it. You have to eventually say, enough is enough, you know? I didn't blame Sean at first. When he'd get into trouble or whatever, it's like, I knew it was all because of his terrible home life. He didn't know any different. But then, I'd think, why am I justifying this? It didn't matter why he was doing the things he was doing, he shouldn't have been doing them. Especially when kids are involved. I mean, my God. I was so unbelievably angry with him when I found out what he did. Even after I knew he was stealing that car to get the money to pay for the hospital bill, I'd had it, you know? The fact that he had the girls with him and he didn't *think*. He didn't stop and worry what that would do to them? *No.* There was no justifying that. My babies were terrified. And when I had to pick them up from the police station, I knew I was done. No more chances."

Valerie paused to take a drink, then licked the sweet tea off her lips and shook her head.

"And now you're telling me he's holding down a job and wasn't lying to me about the house, and I got to be the bad guy and say *no*." She sighed, meeting my gaze in the mirror. "I'm going to need to walk out of here with fabulous hair today. My mood is kind of crappy now."

"*That* I got you covered on," I replied, offering her a smile.

Valerie didn't say any more about Sean after that, but I could tell her mind was heavy and keeping her thoughts hostage. We kept the conversation light throughout the rest of the appointment.

Honestly, I was grateful she was finished sharing for the day. I had a lot to process and work out inside my own head. There were so many questions I wanted answers to, things I was still unclear about.

Who was Sean Molina? Where did he come from? What all had he done, and why? And who was so terrible to him growing up?

I promised Valerie hair no short of fabulous, and I delivered. She was ecstatic with me and the finished product and declared Hair by Shay the hottest spot in Dogwood, swearing she'd refer me to all her friends.

I only had one worry—

I knew I couldn't keep this from Sean.

Chapter Ten

SEAN

Two Days Later

I killed the engine to my bike, swung off, then headed inside Whitecaps.

I'd had to postpone a full day of work on the house after getting called in, which would've pissed me off, but I'd never be pissed about getting paid.

Furniture was my next purchase. I'd drained my accounts getting the house, and even though the raise was helping, any extra shifts I could get I'd take.

I knew Shayla was working today. I'd seen her car, so I was expecting more of what we were doing now: talking. Letting shit play out, which was her idea, and I was grateful she offered it, leaving me not having to explain my actions. So when I stepped out of the hallway and caught Shayla at that exact moment coming out of the lounge, met her eyes, and watched her make a hasty retreat back *inside* that lounge, I didn't understand what the fuck was going on.

But I sure as hell was finding out.

"Give me a minute," I said to J.R., holding him off from

leaving. I prowled out of the kitchen and yanked the door to the lounge open.

Shayla was standing at the lockers, chewing on her nail. She stopped chewing once I stepped inside, and looked at me with worry.

"The fuck was that?" I barked. "You see me and you go runnin'? We're back to this?" I stopped on the other side of the bench seat and stared her down. "Explain," I ordered.

"I didn't think you were working today," she said meekly.

"The kid has something he's gotta do, so I offered to come in. So what?"

"I just... well, I wasn't expecting to have this conversation yet. I'm not prepared."

"*What* conversation?"

"Your ex is my client."

I leaned back. "Say that again."

"Valerie. She's my client. I did her hair on Sunday." Shayla scraped her teeth across her bottom lip. "And I'd never keep something like that from you, but I'd really like to keep her as a client, and I was worried you'd have a problem with that. I knew we were working together tomorrow, so tonight I'd planned on coming up with a list of reasons why her as my client would be a good thing. I'm not prepared with that list, so I retreated in here when I saw you. I panicked."

Pinching my eyes shut, I rubbed at my face. "How the *fuck* do you know Val?"

"I met her Friday night at Frank's Pizza. She was there." Shayla quickly shook her head, as if to read my mind. "But I had no idea who she was to you until Sunday. I swear. This is all just one big coincidence."

I thought on this. Did I care if Shayla kept Val as a client or whatever the fuck? No. That didn't bother me. Was it a little weird? Fuck, yeah. It was weird.

"Um..."

I turned back to Shayla, brows lifted in question. "What?"

"I met your girls," she said, and my chest constricted, making it too fucking hard to breathe. "They were at Frank's too. Caroline and Fiona. I just love those names."

Fuck.

FUCK.

She saw them. She saw my girls. They were at Frank's.

Why the fuck wasn't I at Frank's? I needed to be going there if that's where they went. I'd sleep there if I fucking had to.

"Would you like to see them?" she asked.

I blinked hard, forcing focus. "*See them?*" I questioned.

"Valerie friend-requested me on Facebook after her appointment," Shayla explained as she slowly dug her phone out of her pocket. "She has pictures of the girls on there. I could show you..."

I shook my head in a quick no. I couldn't. Fuck, no. I didn't deserve that.

"You haven't seen them for over a year, right? You should see them, Sean." Shayla said this while hitting buttons on her screen, and then she was grabbing my arm and turning me when I tried to move away. She held the phone out for me to see it. "Look. Look at them," she pleaded.

I swallowed hard with tears burning in my eyes. "I can't."

"Yes, you can. Her profile isn't private. Anybody can see it. Just look." Shayla climbed over the bench, stood beside me, and held the phone out while her other hand stayed wrapped around my arm.

Her thumb pressed on an album labeled *Christmas 2016*.

I could feel myself shaking, my limbs vibrating uncontrollably, and Shayla's gentle touch on my arm growing firmer to comfort me as I looked at pictures of my girls standing beside a tree and opening presents. Eating Christmas morning breakfast. Smiling. Decorating cookies with Val. They looked the same. Slightly taller, and their hair wasn't as curly. But that was the only difference. Shayla clicked on another album. This was one of the beach—last summer in South Carolina. Caroline was standing proudly beside a sandcastle and Fi was filling up buckets with water. There were pictures of them jumping in the pool and at some amusement park riding the carousel. They looked happy. They were so fucking beautiful. Smiling. Always smiling.

"See?" Shayla spoke softly, clicking on more albums. "Aren't you glad you looked? They're so beautiful, Sean."

I wiped harshly at my eyes, clearing wetness away.

"You bought that house for them, didn't you? You're fixing it up and making it perfect for your girls, right?"

I jerked my chin. "Wanted something better than my trailer," I answered. "I'd never keep them there. That house... it was supposed to be what they deserved. It ain't good enough."

"It will be," Shayla whispered, clicking out of the pictures then and tucking her phone away. "Let me help you, Sean. Did you paint the bedrooms yet? I saw the paint cans when you gave me the tour. The pink makes a lot more sense now." She giggled.

I turned my head and looked down at her. "I was planning on starting it today," I disclosed. "Didn't have time before the kid called me."

"So tonight. We'll get started after work. How's that sound?"

"I ain't askin' you to help me."

She tilted her head. "Haven't you realized yet, that is not how we work. Besides, you *want me* helping you. I kick ass at painting. I paint hair for a living, remember?" Her hand on my arm pulsed. "Let me help you. Come on. Let's get that house ready."

I breathed deep, wanting to say no, wanting to pull away from her.

I didn't do either.

I just kept breathing.

* * *

Later that night after I closed up at Whitecaps, Shayla was waiting for me at the house.

She'd gone home and changed into worn, bleach-stained coveralls and secured her hair back out of her face with a plaid bandana.

I swung off my bike and met her on the porch, where she smiled at me under the light.

"I got you something," she said.

I watched her slowly pull her hands out from behind her back and hold up a clear bag between us.

Two goldfish bumped against the plastic.

"The *fuck*?" I asked, squinting at the bag.

"Now you can't say you never had a pet." She giggled and pushed against the plastic. "I named them already—Mac and Cheese. Since you're a cook. This one's...no, he's Cheese...no, wait, uh...you know what? Their names are interchangeable. Here you go."

She shoved the bag at me and forced me to take it.

I looked from Shayla to the fish. *She got me a pet.*

Nobody ever got me anything anymore.

My hand tightened around the plastic. I didn't know what to say to her. I could feel her staring at me, not waiting for anything in return, I was sure, but simply gauging my reaction as I studied the fish.

"They've been cooped up in that bag for a while," she shared. "Don't want the little guys getting claustrophobic..."

I met her eyes after hearing her warning, nodded once, then quickly unlocked the front door and pushed inside.

"I'm excited!" Shayla called out at my back as I went straight for the kitchen, looking around for something I could use as a tank.

I had an old, clear plastic pretzel barrel I kept spare change in sitting on the counter. I dumped the change in an empty drawer, rinsed the barrel a few times, then filled it with water and carefully dropped the fish inside.

"Here." Shayla slipped next to me and placed a jar of fish food on the counter beside the makeshift tank. "Aw, look at Mac and Cheese. They're so happy to be here."

I bent down and studied the fish. I didn't know what the fuck she was seeing. They didn't look happy to me.

"This is for you too." Shayla pulled one of those cards she was always giving me out of the front pocket of her overalls. "It's from my mom. She gets high off stationery, just like me."

I chuckled and took the card, shaking my head. "She didn't need—"

"That's not why she did it," Shayla cut me off.

Holding her gaze, I nodded once and tucked the card into my back pocket. "Right."

Shayla grinned. "Come on. Let's get started. It's late."

She was right—it *was* late. I didn't get home until after ten, and I was fucking tired and felt like I could drop leaving work, but Shayla was here.

Suddenly, I wasn't that tired.

She followed behind me into the large bedroom I was fixing up for the girls. Dominic and I had knocked the wall down days ago. The spots that needed spackling or other repair work were fixed and dried.

It was ready to be painted.

"This is a nice-sized room. My bedroom growing up was tiny," Shayla said, working on the trim on the opposite wall I was working on.

"Won't be that big once I get furniture in here."

"Yeah, I guess that's true. Did you find anything yet?"

I shook my head, dipped the brush in the tray, saturated it with paint, then turned back to the wall, dragging the bristles slowly along the edge down from the ceiling.

"So, you're cool with Valerie staying a client of mine?"

"I don't care. She'll be a good one. Used to get her hair done every other fuckin' minute."

Shayla chuckled. "*Sweet.* She's really nice. I like her."

I didn't say anything to that. My ex had a right to treat me the way she was doing. To keep ignoring me. I didn't blame her, but it was hard keeping my anger out of it.

"She, uh... mentioned a little about the way you grew up."

I stopped going over the pink a second time and looked over my shoulder.

Shayla was peering back at me. "What was so terrible about it?" she asked in a quiet voice.

I didn't talk about this. I *never... fucking...* talked about this.

"Told you I stole food and shit," I said, reminding her—*talking about this*. "I think you can connect those fuckin' dots, yeah?"

Shayla visibly swallowed. "Your parents didn't feed you? They didn't give you clothes?"

"Didn't have parents. Had a woman who didn't want me around. That's it. I took up space."

Her eyes widened. "What?"

"I *took up space*," I repeated, saying it sharply this time as that anger rose up inside me, and as that voice echoed in my head, the one that never went away. "I wasn't no son to her. I was nothin'. She did enough to keep DSS off her back, so she could keep gettin' food stamps and whatever the fuck else I was able to get her, but extras like something to eat and new clothes when I needed it? Fuck, no. I took from her when she wasn't lookin', then I took from other people when she caught on and beat me so bad, I threw up all over myself."

Shayla lowered the brush to her side, turning to face me. "Food and clothes aren't extras, Sean," she said. "She should've been providing for you. She beat you because you were hungry?"

"She beat me 'cause I was alive."

Shayla sucked in a sharp breath. "What?" she whispered.

"I learned to expect nothin'. I went out and took what I needed. Fuck that bitch. I made my own way. It was either that or fuckin' die."

"What about your dad?" she asked.

"Never had one. You wanna know more? Ask your brother."

Shayla blinked. "You told him, you won't tell me?"

"Don't like talkin' about that prick. It's got nothin' to do with you," I said, then I promised her, "But there is shit I will never fuckin' tell you about. Not ever. And that's got to do with me *and* it's got to do with you."

"What shit is that?"

"You'll know when you ask about it. If I tell you that's off limits, or if I just get really fuckin' quiet, do not push me, Shayla. Do you understand?"

She pinched her lips together, looking like a thousand words were trapped inside her mouth, and nodded her head.

Good. I needed her understanding this. She pushed me on a lot of different shit, but I wasn't going there with her.

Then as I was turning back around, she murmured, "You never had a chance."

"What?" I turned back.

Her eyes were glassy.

"You were born into hate. Children are supposed to be born into love. It's unconditional, and you never had that," she said. "What chance did you have? There was no one protecting you. It's a miracle you are who you are, Sean. My *God*. I..." Abruptly, she sat her brush in the pan and started moving toward me.

"What are you doing?" I asked.

Shayla curtly shook her head, her lips pursed in anger, and reaching me, slipped her arms tight around my waist and pressed her body against mine.

I went stiff.

My arms were rigid at my side, and I held my breath as I looked at the top of her head. A second passed. Two seconds... "You done?" I asked.

"Nope." She hugged me tighter. "Friends hug. It's what they do. Deal with it."

"You are the bossiest fuckin' woman I've ever met."

A laugh tore out of her, and she propped her chin on my chest and smiled up at me. "And you can get snippy."

"Snippy?"

"Yep."

"The fuck is *snippy*?"

"What you're doing right now. *The fuck is snippy?*" she mimicked my voice, dropping hers lower and forcing it rough.

My eyes narrowed.

"Uh oh. There he goes again."

"Yeah?" I lifted my brush, still damp with paint, and dragged it down the back of her. "How's that for snippy?"

She gasped, then her eyes went steely as she slowly released me. "You have just declared war. I hope you're prepared for the consequences."

"From a midget? Can you even reach me with that brush?"

Mouth dropping open, Shayla dashed over to the roller with the longer handle and gripped it, challenge raising her brow.

"You're fuckin' on."

"Ha!" she yelled.

Three hours later, the room was finished and nearly dry.

After cleanup, Shayla went home wearing one of my shirts covering her so paint stayed out of her car.

A half hour after she left, I crashed, feeling good about that room. Feeling good in general.

Chapter Eleven

SHAYLA

"I can't believe I'm doing this."

I mixed up the pink toner while smiling back at Valerie, who was nervously tapping the arms of my sleek salon chair.

It had been two weeks since I last saw her, and per Caroline's request, and apparently after going wild on Pinterest and looking up kickass hairstyles, Valerie was back to get some pink in her hair.

I couldn't believe it myself until she showed up.

"This is exciting!" I said. Not only for her, but for me, as well.

Now I had the opportunity to tell more of the good stuff about Sean earlier than I was anticipating.

After our paint night where he revealed his god-awful upbringing, plus a couple more nights I'd gone over to help out where he shared a little bit more, I had become fully, whole-heart committed to talking Sean up in hopes Valerie would let him see his girls.

I was ready with a plan before she arrived.

I'd point out all his good qualities, reassure her of the things I knew to be true, and just simply state my opinion on the man. I was allowed to have an opinion.

I knew one could argue this wasn't any of my business, and I needed to stay out of it. But what kind of person would I be if I kept quiet and passed on an opportunity to help my friend? Not a person I would want to be friends with, that was for damn sure.

I just needed Valerie to bring him up. Or...

I just needed to say the right thing to *encourage* her to bring him up.

"So, what's new?" I asked as I sectioned off her hair, leaving down the pieces underneath she wanted to color pink.

"Not much, really. My life is kind of boring."

"Has Sean reached out to you any more?"

Or, *another option*, I could lose my patience in this matter and simply bring him up myself. *Great.*

I wasn't being obvious at all.

She bit down on an ice cube and swirled her drink. "Yeah, he called last week, telling me how sorry he is again and how he's trying to do right by the girls this time. It's the same ol' speech, basically. All his messages are the same."

"You don't talk to him?"

"I don't want to talk to him."

I nodded with my lips pressed so tightly together, they began to sting.

Shit. I was in way over my head with this. What was I supposed to say? Should I tell her how much *I* liked talking to him? *What the hell good would that do?*

"Do you think I'm doing the right thing?" she asked, with honest concern in her voice.

Holding her hair against a piece of foil, I started applying the color. "What do you mean?"

"By *not* letting him see the girls...They ask about him, and I just—"

"Aw, they *do*?" I met her eyes in the mirror, and she nodded, causing my heart to ache.

"They think he's on *vacation.*" Valerie rolled her eyes. "A vacation lasting over a year, can you imagine? I'd kill for that."

I giggled.

"I think I'm doing the right thing," she said solemnly. "But then, I think I'm doing the wrong thing, and I worry I'm going to regret it as they get older. I worry about it all the time. It would be easier if the court was involved."

My stomach tightened.

"Uh, yeah, but then that's so official," I rebutted, panic filling me as I thought about Sean being *ordered* to stay away from his girls, and what that would do to him. "And would you want that? What if you changed your mind?"

"I know," she agreed. "That's why I haven't done it."

Tension eased from my shoulders.

"What if the girls end up hating me for this, Shay? What if they get older and find out Sean never went on vacation and hate me for keeping them apart?"

Shaking my head, I dropped the brush into the bowl I was dipping out of and closed off the foil around her hair. "They won't hate you," I told her, taking the clips out now that I was finished, then gripping her shoulders and looking into the mirror. "And whatever you decide to do, Sean will understand. This is your call, Valerie. He knows that."

She snorted. "You say that like you know him."

"I do know him. He's my friend."

She frowned.

Shit. Too obvious. Too obvious. Now everything I say, she'll think I'm doing for him.

"I mean, we work together, remember? He's my work friend," I covered, which wasn't a lie. Not at all. We were friends who met at work.

That was exactly what we were.

"Oh, that's right." She waved a dismissive hand. "I keep forgetting that. That is so crazy to me."

I smiled.

Then, as his work friend, I gave in to the urge I was battling something fierce and said what needed to be said.

"He's a really decent guy. More than decent," I told her. "He's helped me out of a few jams, and he seems to really have his shit together. He's done amazing work on that house. It looks great."

"I don't know," she mumbled, her gaze falling away.

"It's your choice. They are your girls, and you will protect them and make the right decision. I know you will."

Valerie reached up and placed her hand on top of one of mine. "Thank you."

"Of course." I winked at her. "Now, it's dryer time. And then, hellllo, Ms. Pink."

Valerie giggled, then followed me over to the dryer so she could cook.

After washing and a quick blow dry, followed by some curls, because I never let any woman leave here without a little something fancy, I spun Valerie in the chair and let her check out her new look.

"Oh, my God. I actually *love it*!" she squealed, fingering the ends of her hair to see the pop of color underneath.

"See? You doubt me. I told you it would look awesome."

Valerie sprung from her chair and wrapped her arms around me. "Thank you," she whispered, leaning back to smile. "For this, and the listening, and just... thank you."

"Anytime," I said, meaning that.

I really, really liked her.

After she paid and made sure her follow-up appointment with me was booked, I walked Valerie to the door, stepping out and waving as she climbed the stairs.

"See ya!" I called out.

"Later, Shay!"

The door across the hall opened as I was turning to head back inside, and Monica (6B) stepped out, directing her son, Thomas, who was carrying a nightstand.

"Hey, Shay!" she said, seeing me, then looking to her son, she said, "Just go stick it at the curb. It's broken."

Thomas carried the small table up the stairs.

"What's going on?" I asked.

"Girl, *tons*. First of all, Victor loved my hair!"

I high-fived her. *Sweet!*

"Of course he did," I said. "You look amazing."

"Thanks."

"What else is happening?"

"Well, he got a transfer."

"No way! So, you guys are moving?"

Bummer. There goes that client.

"Yeah, but, girl, this is a good move. Guess where they're sending him?"

I shrugged.

"Hawaii!" she shrieked.

"*What?* Oh, my God, that's *awesome*!"

"I know! We're so excited," she said, pressing her back against the door to hold it open when Thomas went back inside. "The kids especially. You know, it's just been hard with their dad being gone so much."

"I can imagine. When are you guys leaving?"

"Victor doesn't need to check in until the end of the month, but we're taking the kids on a nice, long vacation before we go. Disney."

"Disney World!" the kids screamed from inside.

I laughed.

"They're *a little* excited," Monica chuckled. "We're planning on leaving right from Disney. It would be a waste to come back here.

We're selling all our furniture now, and what we don't sell, I'm just sticking out by the curb."

"Wait, what?" I stepped closer. "You're not taking your furniture with you?"

Her eyes doubled in size. "Do you have any idea how much it would cost us to ship our furniture to Hawaii, Shay? Like, I don't know, but I'm guessing *a lot*. No way. We'll just start fresh there. It's on-base housing, so that's cheap. And Victor is getting a good chunk of money for transferring. We'll be fine. Most of the stuff we have are hand-me-downs anyway. I'm excited to buy all new stuff."

Thomas stepped out carrying the matching nightstand.

I blocked him.

"Hey," he grumbled.

"How much are you selling everything for?" I asked Monica, keeping my arm around the table so Thomas couldn't move.

"Why? You interested?" She looked perplexed. "Isn't your place fully furnished?"

"Yes, but I have a friend who is needing a lot of stuff. Like basically, everything."

"Really? Well." She shrugged. "For you, Shay, nothing. Just take it."

"Oh, my God, I can't do that!" I gaped. "I at least need to give you *something*."

"You gave me fantastic hair."

"Which you paid for."

"After a discount..."

I cocked my head.

She cocked hers. "Fine. What do you want to pay me?"

I smiled, patted Thomas on the head after dropping my arm away, stepped closer, and keenly suggested, "How about six dollars and fifty-seven cents?"

Monica cracked up. "Well, *that's* a specific amount!"

I nodded, still holding my smile and ready to throw more money on top of my offer if she came to her senses.

But it wasn't needed.

Monica stuck out her hand. "Deal!"

After I paid Monica for her entire apartment full of furniture (six fifty-seven, what a steal!), we discussed when she wanted the furniture out. Anytime this week would be perfect, the sooner the better.

And what was sooner than right now?

Stepping back inside my apartment and shutting the door with my hip, I sent out a group text to Syd and Tori.

Hey! If I can get a hold of a moving truck, can I borrow your man muscle tonight to deliver some furniture? Pretty please?;)

The first response came from Tori: *Where are you delivering furniture to?*

Stitch. I just bought him a shit ton of it for under seven bucks. BOOM!

Syd responded next: *You bought Stitch furniture? Why?*

Because he doesn't have any. Can I borrow your man muscle or not? I gotta make a call.

Tori: *Holy shit. You're in love with him.*

Syd: *I was just typing that. Twins!*

Oh, my God.

He's my FRIEND.

Tori: *So are we. Where's our furniture?*

Syd: *Good one.* :) *Also, I'd like to be filled in on the hows and whys of this new friendship. I feel like we have a lot to discuss.*

Tori: *Sounds like we need a girls' night.*

Syd: *I second that.*

I had zero problem with planning a girls' night, so I shared that, but kept on topic.

Third it. Now FOCUS. Man muscle? Yes? No?

Syd: *Trouble is in. Just say when and where.*

Trouble was her fiancé, Brian. She always called him that.

Awesome. Thank you, Syd!

Tori: *I'm closing tonight, but Jamie can help. Just don't use up all his muscle. I'll want some of it later.*

Yes!

Thank you! Okay, let me call around and I'll let you both know. xoxo

After Googling Budget Rental, calling them, and finding out they were booked until next week, I got the number to Penske and dialed them up. That's where I hit the mother lode. They had a truck big enough for a fully furnished, two-bedroom apartment available *immediately*.

Smiling from ear to ear, I reserved the truck and sent out the text to Tori and Syd.

Then I helped Monica with some packing.

Stomach fluttering and breaths coming quick, I knocked on Sean's door while the boys and Syd waited by the truck.

It was just past six, and the sun was beginning to set low behind the house. The sky glowed orange and dark mustard yellow.

We made it just in time to take care of this with some light out.

The door swung open and Sean stood there, suspicion pinching his brow. To be expected: I hadn't alerted him of my amazing stroke of luck.

"Hey." I smiled at him and took his hand, tugging it gently. "Come here."

"What?" he asked, stepping out onto the porch.

I pointed at the truck and yelled, "Do it!"

Jamie, Tori's boyfriend, flipped the lock on the door and pushed it up, revealing the truckload of home goods.

"Surprise!" I yelled, looking back at Sean. "My neighbor is moving to Hawaii and isn't taking her furniture with her, so it's yours! All of it."

Sean cut his eyes to me. "What?"

"Now you have furniture. My neighbor had a little girl, so there's a pretty sweet pink dresser in there with ladybug designs along the edges. Plus, two twin beds. A couch. A kitchen table—"

"What the fuck are you doing?" he grated, jerking out of my hold. "You got me furniture? Are you fuckin' with me?"

His sharp tone stepped me back.

"What's wrong?" I asked.

Sean stared at me, his chest shuddering, his eyes wider than I'd ever seen. He looked terrified.

Then he turned his attention to the truck, and hollered, "Take it back!"

I gaped at him. "What? Why?" I questioned. I heard murmuring at my back, then the sound of the heavy door sliding. "Wait! Just wait a second!" I yelled, pausing Jamie and Brian, who were both closing it up. I turned back to Sean. "Why can't you take it?"

"What the *fuck*, Shayla?" he half growled, half whispered.

I shook my head, confused.

"You think I can't do this myself? Is that it?" His voice quaked.

"What? No!"

"Then *why*? I didn't ask you for shit! I don't ask you for nothin'. I don't deserve..." He cursed and took a step closer to the edge, bellowing, "Take that fuckin' shit back now!"

"No!" I hollered, pointing at Jamie, who was yanking the door back down. "Don't you move! Keep it open!"

Brian started shaking his head, saying something I couldn't make out at this distance. Syd looked so nervous, I was surprised she wasn't crawling behind that furniture and hiding. Jamie just looked amused, which was typically how he looked, but he took his hand off the door as instructed.

Good.

Then, knowing they weren't closing it up, I planted a firm hand on Sean's chest and pushed him back. "You don't get to decide whether or not someone does something nice for you, do you understand?" I snapped.

He blinked down at me, still looking terrified. Plus, he was panting now. I could feel his heart pounding against my palm.

"You do not *ever* get to decide whether someone treats you with kindness, Sean. Not ever," I told him, holding his stare and speaking with boldness, but also keeping my voice gentled. "You paid six fifty-seven for my tacos. I paid six fifty-seven for your furniture. You did for me. I'm doing for you. But *get this*, even if you hadn't done for me, I'd still be doing for you because you're my friend, because you deserve kindness, because you're a good person who should be having good put back on them, and because I *wanted* to do it. Don't look at this as a favor. Look at it as a gift. And *take it*."

Sean rushed out a breath. Then he swallowed thickly.

"Okay?" I whispered.

Hesitating, he waited for me to wrap my other hand around his wrist before he closed his mouth, inhaled shakily, and jerked his chin.

I smiled and gave his wrist a squeeze in comfort.

"Okay, we're good!" I hollered over my shoulder.

The door slid open, and the boys got to work unloading and hauling stuff in while Syd and I directed them where to put it. Women just knew furniture placement better than men. It was a fact.

Sean stood back at first, just watching everything get carried inside, looking uncomfortable, like he didn't feel like he belonged in his own house anymore, then, as if finally accepting what was happening, the second he saw that ladybug dresser, he jumped in and grabbed an end.

Once everything was carried off the truck, Sean thanked Jamie and Brian for their help, shaking both their hands, which I think was the first time the three of them had ever conversed.

While this happened, Syd tugged on my elbow and whispered in my ear, "He needs to come to family dinner."

I smiled at her. I couldn't have agreed more.

The boys and Syd took off in the truck. I drove separately and got to work on saying my goodbyes.

First, to Mac and Cheese.

"You guys seem to be settled in," I said, bending down in front of the pretzel barrel. The fish swam about, their mouths opening in search for food. "Be good to him," I whispered.

I stepped out of the kitchen.

Sean was glancing around his fully furnished living room, hands on his hips, the shake of his head coming every few seconds.

"Am I more than you bargained for yet?" I asked him.

He turned to me and rubbed at the back of his neck, eyes squinted in confusion. "What?"

"Being my friend," I explained, walking over to him. "I just basically forced a truckload of furniture on you. You already admitted to thinking I'm bossy." I reached his side and smiled up at him. "Just wondering if you're regretting helping me yet, now that you see what all you got yourself into."

Sean looked all over my face. "I don't regret it," he answered, which made my heart skip and beat wildly. "But I ain't used to this."

"Friends doing stuff for you?"

"*That.* And friends..."

I frowned.

Sean looked at my mouth, then shook his head. "Don't feel sorry for me."

"You never had any friends? Not even when you were a kid?"

"I would've been a shitty friend when I was a kid," he answered. "I was lookin' out for me back then. I didn't give a fuck about anyone else."

I tried to picture a younger version of the man standing in front of me—Sean as a child. Alone. Never feeling love. Never knowing how to give it.

He was never shown kindness. He was never taught any morals. He wasn't guided or tended to. He said it before—he took up space.

And still, coming from that, from nothing, Sean had good in him. A lot of it.

I thought that said more about the man he was than anything he could tell me.

"Well, I'm glad you don't regret me, but I wouldn't let you back out now even if you tried," I said, feeling the need to remind him of my bullheadedness, in case he was forgetting about it.

"Can't say that surprises me. It ain't like you ever give me a choice in shit."

I narrowed my eyes at his profile.

He smirked, then slowly looked down at me without moving his head. And because Sean smirking was damn near close to Sean smiling, I smiled back.

Then, side by side, we both got back to admiring all that furniture.

It was Wednesday night, twenty after nine, and I was pampering myself with a rose-infused sheet mask while posting client snapshots on my Instagram and Facebook feed.

To my delight, I was up twenty-some followers on my Facebook page, and over fifty on my Instagram account.

This put me in a fantastic mood.

I had also discovered, when I planted my butt on the couch after applying my mask, that Comcast had put all episodes of *Shameless* On Demand, free for subscribers to watch at no charge.

My fantastic mood elevated to tremendous status. I fucking *loved* *Shameless*.

I was halfway into episode one, season one, and enjoying myself immensely when a knock sounded on my door.

It was late. I wasn't expecting any visitors; however, I was still getting walk-in hair cut appointments from fellow Pebble Dune residents, so the knock didn't surprise me.

In fact, I looked forward to these knocks.

Nevertheless, I had plans this evening involving Lip Gallagher and some pampering, so I was prepared to tell whoever it was to come back around tomorrow, or another day that worked for them.

Pressing close to the door, I peered through the peephole and saw Sean standing on the other side of it.

I gasped.

Not even Lip Gallagher showering me in Korean sheet masks would keep me from opening this door right now.

I hadn't seen Sean in two days. I'd missed him.

As a friend and more.

But Sean never came to visit without the intention to help. And I knew I didn't need any help…

So why *was* he here?

"Hey!" I called through the door, reaching for the deadbolt, then, remembering the current state of my face, I yanked my hand back and gulped. "Uh, just a sec!"

Dashing to my one and only bathroom, which was on the other side of the apartment by the kitchen, I glanced at the timer I'd set on the counter.

I still had two minutes left before my mask reached full oxidizing potential.

You have got to be kidding me.

Sean knocked again.

I looked at myself in the mirror and decided timed masks were stupid. They should start oxidizing the moment they touch your skin and reach full potential a second later.

Immediate gratification.

Ripping the thin sheet off my face, I tossed it into the wastebasket next to the sink, patted the essence into my skin, ran a quick brush through my hair to give it some life, pinched my cheeks, and then ran back across the apartment and unlocked the door.

"Hi!" I rushed out, holding the door open for Sean to enter. "This is a surprise. What's up?"

Sean stopped in the entryway and turned to look at me.

He was wearing dark-wash jeans, his motorcycle boots, and a tight black T-shirt, skipping the thermal, I was assuming, since the weather tonight was on the warmer side.

"Val called," he shared, rubbing both hands down his face, then reaching around to grip his neck so his elbows pointed straight at me.

My eyes widened to the size of baseballs. "She *did*?" I asked, pushing the door closed.

Sean nodded.

"What did she say?"

"That I could see my girls." He looked ready to hit the floor.

"Oh, my God! Sean! That's *great*!" I cried, closing the distance between us in two quick steps.

I wrapped my arms around his middle and squeezed him tight, smiling when I felt his arms drop around me.

His hands gently, almost cautiously, formed to my hips.

Holy God, this was nice. I have lived a full life now.

"Why aren't you jumping up and down? This is good news," I asked, keeping pressed close.

I didn't want to move. Ever.

He smelled so good. Sean didn't wear cologne from what I could tell. And I didn't think it was soap I was smelling. It was just . . . him. He smelled like the outdoors. Like the wind when it filled your car as you were driving past a meadow with the windows down. A little sweet, but all man. Dirt and grass and every other scent you'd catch while you were outside working on something.

"I'm fuckin' scared," he admitted, which immediately had me leaning away to peer up at him.

God, his honesty sometimes...it was shocking. Sean fought me until he didn't.

At all.

"They don't know me anymore," he elaborated. "It's been over a fuckin' year. What if they...they could hate me."

"They won't."

"*I'd* fuckin' hate me."

I shook my head. "Kids don't think like that. Not that young. I promise."

"Well...what about the house? It ain't good enough. I don't got a playground out back for them yet, and the beds don't have anything on them. It's small. It's too fuckin' small, and that fuckin' basement...I still gotta work on that. And some of those walls I patched look like shit...I should've done better. I—"

"Sean, hey." I grabbed his face, forcing him to stop. "Those girls are not going to care about any of that. They just want to spend time with you. It's about *you*. Not stuff. Not your house. And quit selling yourself short, will you? You have done an amazing job getting that house ready. It looks great."

He thought on what I said, nodded his head firmly, once, then I felt his hands slide away from my hips, and he stepped back, forcing us apart.

"You gotta help me," he pleaded, looking desperate. "I need your help."

Now, this was a first... "Of course, I'll help you. What do you need?"

He took the elastic out of his hair and let all those golden strands down.

My hand hit my chest. "Oh, my God, you don't want me to chop off your hair, do you?" I questioned, feeling slightly nauseated at the idea. "I really don't want to do that."

I'd help him another way. There had to be something else.

"Not all of it," Sean specified. "I just don't want my girls not recognizing me. It's gonna be hard enough for them. It's been so fuckin' long. I don't want them scared it ain't me."

"How short do you want it?"

He touched just above his shoulder. "'Bout here?" His brows raised. "That's how it was last time they saw me."

That was three inches, give or take. It would still be longish, which made me happy. Sean's hair was just... wow. It just felt wrong to cut it off.

"Okay. I can do that."

"This too," he said, rubbing his hand over his short, thick beard. "I want them seein' me. Not this."

"Do you want it shaved completely?"

I tried picturing Sean barefaced.

I couldn't do it.

He shook his head. "I had a goatee before I got locked up, plus a little on my jaw." He stroked his fingers there. "Just not this full, you know?"

"Got it." I held my arm out, directing him toward the salon room. "Right this way, sir. Let's get you ready so those beautiful girls recognize you."

His eyes gentled, and I thought I saw a faint smile before he walked in front of me. He stopped at the open door.

"You like goin' by Shay for this?" he asked, pointing at the sign hanging there.

I got beside him. "I don't know. I'm still deciding. I go back and forth." Turning my head and tilting it back, I met his gaze. "What do you like?"

"I think you already know that."

My stomach clenched as I was flooded with the memory of my very first conversation with Sean.

He liked Shayla better. He always did. He never called me Shay.

And because I was on the fence about this decision, not preferring one over the other and possibly waiting for that little shove in the direction I needed to take, I had zero issues changing that sign and all my social media handles *immediately*.

Hair by Shayla sounded more professional anyway.

Or maybe I just *knew* I would really like the way it would sound coming out of Sean's mouth.

"I like Hair by Shayla better too, now that I think about it," I mumbled.

The corner of Sean's mouth twitched. It was the subtlest movement, but I saw it.

Wow.

Yeah, I was totally changing that name.

Sean stepped inside the room.

Happy with my decision and what I was about to do, I followed behind wearing an ear-to-ear grin.

I was finally getting the chance to play with Sean's hair. To say I was excited about it was an understatement.

"Have a seat," I said, and once he did, I draped the cape across him and fastened it at the neck. "Ready?" I smiled at him in the mirror.

Eyes still soft, he nodded.

I got started.

I wet Sean's hair down with a spray bottle, then I clipped up half of it, had him tilt so his chin touched his chest, and snipped three inches off the back.

Neither one of us said a word.

It was weird.

I was *never* quiet doing this, but I just kept picturing Sean's face when I first opened my door, and hearing that unguarded fear in his voice, and I concentrated unlike I had ever concentrated on anything. This suddenly became the most important haircut of my life, because it was so profoundly important to Sean, and I didn't want to risk *anything* distracting me from giving him exactly what he'd asked for.

Lip Gallagher himself could've walked into this room with Justin Timberlake riding him like a pony, and I wouldn't have noticed a damn thing, even if they were throwing sheet masks around like Mardi Gras beads.

Setting my scissors and comb aside, I stood behind Sean and checked symmetry, pulling down the pieces of hair framing his face. I checked a couple more strands. They were even. Then I ran my fingers through the back of his hair and looked in the mirror, smiling at him.

"How's that?" I asked. "It'll dry and shorten a little, so it'll come up to about where you were wanting it."

Sean nodded. "It's good."

"Excellent." I brushed the cape off, then, removing it, I shook off the hair. "Now, the beard. We gotta do that in the bathroom," I said.

Sean stood from the chair, bent down, and checked his hair in the mirror. If I didn't know him, or if it were anyone else, I would've said that was for vanity reasons, but I knew it wasn't. Sean wasn't looking for him.

The chair I used for shampooing was a thrift store purchase I'd found a few months back. It was that squeaky restaurant plastic, and a hideous shade of brown, but it reclined, stood at the height I needed, and it wasn't too much for me to lug in and out of my bathroom.

Until I could afford a shampoo bowl setup, this would have to do.

I pulled the chair into the bathroom and got it in place in front of the sink. Then I motioned for Sean to take a seat.

He plopped down and stretched out his legs until the toes of his booted feet touched the wall.

"Okay, straight razor, or my Venus?" I held up Sean's choices. "Obviously, the Venus would have a fresh blade. But I'm going to warn you, it has a strip of lotion that'll leave your face smelling pretty."

Brow tight, Sean tipped his head at the straight razor.

"No pretty face for you, huh?" I set the blades down and pressed on his shoulder while I angled the chair back, putting Sean's head closer to the sink.

Then I folded a hand towel and stuck it under his head for comfort.

After trimming down his beard to get rid of most of the length, then taking clippers to it, I wet down his cheeks, jaw, and chin with the spray bottle from the bedroom, wiped off any water dripping down to his shirt, and pulled my bottle of conditioner out of the shower caddy.

"I think conditioner does a better job than shaving cream," I explained, squirting a little on my fingertips and then smoothing it over Sean's jaw.

He stiffened.

"What?"

"Jesus Christ," he mumbled between his teeth. "That's you."

"What's me?"

"*That.* What you're puttin' on my face. That's you."

Confused, I quit applying the conditioner to his beard. "Huh?"

Sean closed his eyes. He was breathing heavily through his nostrils. "I didn't know what it was—shampoo, shit you put on your skin, or if it was just *you*, smelling like honey. Now I know." He opened his eyes and looked at me.

I took his heavy breathing and stiffness as my smell not being a good one.

An ache passed under my skin and sunk deep, burning a hole clear through my heart.

Rejection was one of the worst pains one could ever feel. It stuck with you. Scars healed. Bruises went away.

Rejection was lasting. It was a memory you could conjure up at any time and hurt from, over and over again. It never left you.

"Uh, I can... use something else," I stammered, my throat suddenly tight and distorting my voice. "I have other stuff—"

Sean's arm shot out and his hand wrapped around my wrist as I was turning to grab another option out of the shower. He curtly shook his head.

"No?" I questioned softly.

"No." His voice was urgent.

"You don't mind it?"

"I do not fuckin' mind it."

My breath caught. "Okay," I rushed out, licking my dry lips. "Okay, um, that's... I'm glad you don't mind. That's nice of you."

Oh, my God, Sean liked the way I smell.

Or he at least tolerated it enough to wear it on his face.

Either way, *ohmyGodohmyGodohmyGod.*

Be cool, Shay. Be cool.

"It's actually not just this," I informed him. "I have the matching shampoo too. Plus, my body wash is crème brûlée, which basically smells like honey. I like the smell. It's subtle but there, you know? Not too harsh."

Sean didn't say anything in return, but he seemed to be taking in the information I was sharing. He kept his eyes on me.

I took that as a good sign.

Once I finished applying the conditioner and wiped my hands clean, I plugged the sink and filled it with water. Then I picked up the razor.

"I've never shaved another person before. You might lose a lip," I said, leaning over and touching the blade to Sean's skin.

His eyes cut to mine.

"Just kidding," I whispered.

Sean relaxed, exhaling, then looked to the ceiling.

Fighting a grin, I held his face and carefully dragged the blade down his skin.

I took my time. I was careful, not just around the harsh angle of Sean's jaw, but everywhere. I remembered his request—how he kept his beard before—and followed it to a T. Like during the haircut, we didn't converse, which worked for me, considering how close I was to Sean's mouth with my mouth, and how enticed I'd be to lean in and taste his words if he started speaking them. Feeling his breath on my hand was temptation enough. Besides, I needed full concentration for this. Sean's face would be the first thing those girls looked at. And he was trusting me to make this less scary for him, when he was terrified they wouldn't recognize who he was. He worried they'd pull back when they saw him or turn away. He was half convinced they would.

I needed this to be perfect. I wouldn't give him any less than that. Sean had come to my apartment, *asking* for my help, and I wouldn't let him down.

When I had finished up and cleaned off the blade, I took a towel and wiped the excess conditioner off Sean's face. Then I leaned back and smiled.

"All done. Check it out."

Sean pushed out of the chair and stood in front of the mirror. He lifted his chin and stroked his face. He looked left and then right, and then he looked straight on.

"I feel like I'm meeting another you," I said. "The man you were before, I mean. This is what he looked like."

Sean turned to me. "You don't wanna know him," he mumbled.

"No?" I reached up and touched his jaw, which I could see now without hindrance of a full beard.

It was angular, like it was chiseled out of stone. It was a *really good* jaw.

"I like this," I told him, referring to his jaw and the rest of his face I'd just shaven. His damp hair was tucked behind his ears. It grazed the tops of his shoulders. "I liked the beard too. But this... I feel like you aren't hiding from me anymore. This is you."

His muscle beneath my hand twitched.

"When are you seeing your girls?" I asked.

"Tomorrow. Val's bringing them over after work."

"Are you off tomorrow?"

"I switched with J.R. I'm coverin' the morning."

"I'm covering the morning too." I smiled. "Yay."

I loved it when we worked together.

Sean's eyes, which had been holding mine, lowered to my mouth. He swallowed, then pulled back so my hand left him, and uttered, "I gotta go."

Those were not the words I was hoping he'd say, and not just because he was leaving.

A huge part of me wished Sean wanted me with him tomorrow to share this important moment in his life. But he didn't propose it. I wasn't even sure it was on his mind. And it hurt—him not wanting me there or not thinking to offer. But it was a selfish desire, and deep down in my heart, where honest feelings budded and flourished, it was more important to me that Sean was getting this chance for himself than having my own part in it.

So, as I left the bathroom, I didn't allow that disappointment to fester. I thought about what this was going to mean to him instead.

And as I thought about it, feeling good, feeling excited for him, I realized Sean was *booking it* through my apartment, steps fast and heavy, like he was suddenly in a rush to get out of here.

Did I mess something up?

"Hey!" I lunged forward and grasped his elbow, giving it a tug until Sean stopped retreating and turned back, a step away from the door. "What's wrong? You don't like it?" I asked him.

His face was tense, then he registered my meaning and shook his head sharply, once. "I just gotta go," he said.

"Why?"

"Why?"

"Yes, *why*? Do you have plans? Do you need to go do something?"

He stared at me, and I knew his answer without him speaking it.

Maybe he didn't know...

"You don't have to leave, Sean. I'm not asking you to leave. You can stay. We can...I don't know, watch TV or something. Do you want to do that with me?"

Still, he said nothing. Just kept staring.

I begged, *please stay*, inside my head. I almost said the words out loud. I was desperate for him to know he could be here. That he could always be here.

Awareness came on abruptly. My eyes began to sting, because I realized *that was it*. He didn't think he deserved what I was giving. Sean didn't think he was good enough for this, for my company. For spending time with me and hearing me tell him things like *you can stay*, and *this is you, I like it*. He didn't think he was worth it.

"Sean," I whispered.

He tugged out of my hold and pleaded, "Stop," his voice beaten down and broken.

I imagined him, beaten down and broken. A child unloved.

Then he took a step back, turned, and walked out. I touched my fingers to my mouth while I stared at the door. I almost walked away.

But that was not the person I was.

"Sean!" I hollered, twisting the knob and swinging the door open. Then seeing him standing there and not expecting him to be, I doubled back.

Sean was facing the door. His head was down, his chest was moving quickly, and his hands were clenched into fists at his side.

"Hey," I spoke softly and reached for him, but he stepped back.

I wanted to reach out again, even further this time. Fighting that urge was a difficult one, but I managed, and instead waited.

Seconds blurred into minutes, then finally…

"I'm nothin'," he whispered to the ground, with more pain in his voice than I'd ever heard pour out of a person before.

Oh, God.

"Sean…"

He lifted his head. There were tears in his eyes.

"I deserve nothin'," he continued. "Sure as fuck nothin' good anymore. And that's not ever gonna change, no matter what the fuck I do, or what you say or what anybody fuckin' says. I *know that now*. You need to quit lookin' at me like I'm worth lookin' at. I'm not. I'm nobody. I'm nothin' to nobody. A fuckin' fuckup. Tell me to leave." He rushed out a breath. His eyes lost focus on the floor between us, then he whispered this time—he pleaded, "Tell me to leave, Shayla. Tell me I'm nothin', so I can leave."

Breath catching with emotion, I bit the tremble in my lip and shook my head.

He'd said those words to me before—*I'm nothin' to nobody*—and I knew Sean was repeating something he'd heard. Something he was told, over and over, until he believed it himself.

A switch turned on inside me. People I never met and probably would never meet, I hated them. I despised whoever did this to Sean, and I would forever feel this. I knew it.

"Please," he begged.

"I can't."

"Please."

I shook my head faster, telling him, "You're not nothing, Sean. I won't say that. And I won't tell you to leave—I don't want you to."

His eyes came up. He was still and silent, but his breathing…my God, it filled my ears. The sound—it was tortured.

I reached out and took hold of his wrist. "Come inside. *Please.*

Just . . . watch TV with me. Or we can talk. Or we can just sit there, I don't care."

His chest shuddered.

I tugged on his arm ever so slightly, urging him.

I was prepared to drop down on my knees and beg, to not let go of Sean unless he forced me and still, putting up one helluva fight, but he stepped forward when I pulled, then took another on his own.

I held my breath.

Fighting off tears out of pure joy, I moved aside so Sean could enter my apartment.

He walked to the couch and took a seat on the end. I secured the door, then sat on the cushion beside him.

"Talk? TV?" I asked. "I was watching *Shameless* before you came over. Ever watch that?"

Sean shook his head. He looked lost.

"That's okay. All the seasons are on demand right now, so we can start from the beginning." I snagged the remote off the cushion and cued episode one again, starting it over. "The one girl's name is Fiona." I smiled when that grabbed his attention. "If you don't like it, we can watch something else."

"Watch what you want."

"Don't tempt me. I have four episodes of *Shear Genius* saved," I warned, grinning at his furrowed brow. "Relax. I wouldn't do that to you."

"I got no idea what this is."

"It's a reality show focused on hair styling. I never watched it when it originally aired, then I caught some reruns last month. Instantly hooked me. Now I have my DVR set to record them all when they pop on. But it would seriously bore you. *Shameless* is better."

"Put on what you want. I'll sit here."

I sucked in a breath as my nose started stinging.

Sean just wanted to be here. That was all he wanted. He didn't care about anything else.

I fought the urge to hug him again and settled for squeezing his knee.

"Which shows do you like to watch?" I asked.

"Don't know. I never had a TV."

I slowly turned my head and gaped.

Then before Sean could see it and feel embarrassed, or anything that might make him want to bolt again, I quickly looked away.

"It's overrated. I don't even know why I have one. I barely watch it. Most shows are crap." I peeked over at him without moving my head.

I thought, though I couldn't be sure without being obvious and actually turning to look, that his mouth was lifted.

That possibility made me seriously happy.

The show started. Sean watched with focus while I watched with half focus, giving him more attention than the Gallaghers.

Then, before I knew it, my long day of haircuts and colors caught up to me, and I'd dozed off at some point during episode two.

I knew this because, when I finally stirred awake and my lashes fluttered open, I saw the on demand menu pulled up, with episode three cued.

Someone just needed to hit play.

I planted my hand to push off the cushion, but feeling a firm thigh under my palm instead of comfy couch, I froze. That was when I registered the feel of breath moving in Sean's body.

His chest rose under my cheek, slow and steady.

I opened my eyes more.

Sean was still upright, but I wasn't. I had somehow curled up against his side in my sleep, nearly on top of him. My arm was draped around his waist, my leg was thrown over his knee, and my cheek was pressing to his chest.

I was *literally* sleeping on Sean.

Tilting my head back, I peered up and saw his head resting against the cushion. Sean's eyes were closed. He was out cold.

He wasn't holding me or touching me in any way I wasn't encouraging. His one arm was draped over the armrest and his other, as I slowly peeled away, I saw was resting on the back of the couch behind me.

One might interpret that as an invitation to cuddle.

Maybe that was *exactly* what I'd done. Or maybe Sean and I fell asleep simultaneously, and being the natural cuddler I was, I instinctively took the opportunity presented to me.

I couldn't be sure how this had gone down. I just knew I really didn't want to move, ever, and furthermore, I *really* didn't want to do the very thing I did next.

"Sean," I whispered, rousing him awake with my touch on his cheek.

Eyes slipping open, he lifted his head while inhaling through his nose, and looked over at me.

"It's after two in the morning," I informed him, noticing the time when I'd seen which episode was cued up on the TV. "We fell asleep."

He sat up more, brought his arm that was behind me down between us, and scrubbed at his face. "Shit," he muttered, sliding forward. "That show put me out. You were right about TV bein' crap. *Fuck*, that was bad."

My mouth fell open.

He looked over at me and chuckled.

I sighed and melted deeper into the cushion, because Sean laughing inside his chest was a beautiful sound I didn't hear enough, and I didn't even care about him insulting my taste in television anymore. That laugh made up for it.

Then, because my sigh was audible and borderline swoony, I played it off so it wasn't weird by stretching into a yawn.

Sean pushed off from the couch and stood.

"Are you leaving?" I asked, getting to my feet as well.

"Yeah."

"Are you okay to drive? You're not too tired?"

He smirked, asking, "You Mama-Bearin' me?"

"I'm looking *out* for you," I countered, laughing at him. *Mama Bear. That was cute.* "I don't want you wrecking or anything."

"I'll be fine," he said.

"Okay. But, still, can you do me a favor and text me when you get home? Just so I don't worry..."

Sean stared at me, his brows moving slightly lower, his eyes narrowing the tiniest bit, so faintly, I'd have missed it if I wasn't already looking directly at them.

Then he did something I will never, ever forget, no matter how many times he did it again, if I was lucky. I'd remember this first time forever. I just knew I would.

Because he had never done anything like it before.

Sean reached out as he stepped closer, getting beside me at the same time as his hand reached around and settled on the side of my neck. Then, as his head dropped beside mine, his hand gave me a squeeze.

It was gentle, barely any pressure, but I felt it.

It was his version of a hug.

Before I could think to do anything in return or say a word, Sean dropped his hand and moved away.

I watched over my shoulder and followed him to the door, the skin on my neck tingling wonderfully.

As Sean went to leave, that gentle look was back in his eyes, and his mouth was lifted ever so slightly in the corner when he jerked his chin in farewell.

"Later," he called out.

I opened my mouth to speak, but nothing came out.

Friends hug, Shay. You know that. Snap out of it!

"Uh, later," I returned.

The door shut behind him.

Before I turned in for bed that night, I got my text. One word.

Home.

I stared at it, smiling, until I fell asleep.

Chapter Twelve

SEAN

You will never see them again, Sean! You hear me? NEVER! Look what you did to them. Just look! Go ahead! Look at your girls, because it's the last chance you'll ever get. I'm done! You are DONE!

My hands, steepled in front of me, shook as my elbows dug into my knees. I pressed my fingers to my mouth and breathed harshly across my knuckles.

I was sitting on the step outside my house, watching the road. Waiting. I could feel myself trembling. My entire body, not just my hands.

I'd been a fucking wreck like this all day. I cut myself twice at work. I nearly ran off the road coming home.

This is a mistake. I'm not ready. I'll never be ready. I don't deserve—

My phone beeped from the back pocket of my pants. I dug it out, wondering if it was Val telling me she'd changed her mind and *fuck you, you'll never see them again, you piece of shit.*

But it wasn't Val.

Have fun with those beautiful girls and SMILE. You did it, Sean! xx

Shayla.

I took a breath after reading. It felt like my first one in minutes. I immediately felt better.

What the fuck would I have done if Shayla hadn't been working with me today? The whole time, every chance she got, her voice was in my ear, telling me how proud she was of me and how my girls will be proud too. How much they'll love this house and what I've done to it, and seeing me...how happy it'll make them.

I didn't ask her to do that. I didn't tell Shayla I needed to hear what she was saying, she just knew.

Just like now...she just knew what I needed.

This would not be happening if it weren't for her. Not now. I'd still be waiting to get furniture, meaning my girls would not be seeing me today, since Val wasn't allowing them to see me without checking out where I was living. The meet had to be here. She wanted to make sure I was stable—that I didn't lie about the house. I got that. She didn't have any reason to believe me. I had done nothing but lie to her before.

And I wouldn't have allowed my girls here if the house wasn't ready. It was ready now because of Shayla. Because of what she'd done for me.

This was all because of her.

I'd tried staying away from this girl. I knew I had no business being around her. Then I made it my business being around her, because seeing her cry was not something I ever wanted to fucking see again. Now I was in a spot with her I wasn't familiar with—we were friends. She cared about me. She did things for me because she wanted to do them. She did things for me I never expected. She smiled at me. She hugged me. She helped me. She wanted me around.

She did all this without being obligated. She just did it.

I wasn't nothing to her, and I did not fucking understand that, but fighting her, fighting *this*...I couldn't do it.

How the fuck could I stay away? How could I go back to being nothing to everyone when what she was offering felt so fucking good?

You put food in front of a starving man, he's going to eat it. No matter if he thinks he deserves it or not. It was about survival.

And Shayla was keeping me alive.

I didn't respond to her text, but I did read it again, then stowed my phone away just as a black car slowed down in front of the house. It pulled in the driveway behind my bike, parked, and cut the engine.

Breathing heavily, I stood up, watching Val get out of the car first.

She looked at me across the roof, offered a tight smile, appearing hesitant. Then she looked at the house as she opened the back passenger door.

I started regretting not doing anything to the outside yet. The landscape looked like shit. A few of the shingles on the roof had popped off. I could've power-washed the siding.

Why the fuck didn't I do that?

Val bent down for a minute, then straightened up holding Fiona in her arms, and I quit thinking about siding or the fucking landscape as my youngest buried her face in her mother's neck and hid from me.

Fiona was shy and made you work for her affection—but I worried she'd grown out of that, and it was me she was reacting to right now. She was hiding because she didn't want to see *me*.

Sweat broke out at the base of my neck, and my breathing went from heavy to fucking panting.

"Look what you did to them!"

Val closed the door, and I watched Caroline peek out around the back of the car before Val ushered her forward. The three of them stood at the trunk.

Caroline was wearing nothing but pink.

Pink shirt, pink puffy skirt, pink tights going into pink shoes that sparkled. There was a pink clip in her hair on one side, a small pink book bag in her hand, and on her wrist were the bracelets that matched the ones she'd made for me. The threads she'd cut and tied herself, only hers were all pink and mine were different colors. She still wore them.

The only time I took mine off was when I was forced to. Had to get the knots out with my teeth so the motherfuckers holding me wouldn't cut them off. And the second I got out, I put those bracelets right back on. That was the first thing I did.

It meant something to me seeing Caroline still wearing them. I wanted it to mean something to her. I wanted to take it as a good sign, but I couldn't.

Caroline used to rush at me. Anytime she saw me after going some time without, she never walked, she ran. She couldn't get to me fast enough. She was the opposite of Fiona. Caroline loved fast and easy.

She wasn't giving it now, though. She was holding on to Val's leg, looking right at me while she pulled at her lip, appearing cautious.

I told myself to move, to fucking *move to them*, but I couldn't. I stood there frozen, watching Caroline look up at Val and say something to her I couldn't hear. Maybe she was asking her to leave. Maybe she was saying she didn't like it here. Maybe she was asking, *Who is that?* Maybe—

Val told her something back, then Caroline looked at me, got a grin on her face, dropped her book bag, and *fucking rushed*. She took off running across the grass, yelling, "Daddy!" her arms pumping.

My ears burned with a memory.

"Daddy! Daddy!"

Choking on a breath, I darted forward and dropped to my knees in front of Caroline. She hit my chest full force and squealed, yelling, "Daddy! Daddy, you're back!" like she'd missed me so bad, it killed her. My arms wrapped around her little body. I dropped my head and closed my eyes, feeling her hair on my face, smelling it. Baby shampoo—the pink bottle. I remembered that smell. Wetness built on my lashes as I kissed her cheek, her nose, her eyes when she closed them. I held her so tight, I worried I was hurting her, but her little arms around my neck kept squeezing me. She didn't try pulling away.

I told her I was sorry. I told her I loved her. I thanked her for rushing at me. I told her I missed her, over and over again. I kept kissing all over her face until she started laughing, then I went back to just holding her.

"Daddy?"

I leaned away, cupping her cheeks. "Yeah, baby?"

Her little brows pinched together in confusion. "How come we couldn't go on vacation with you?"

"What are you talkin' about?"

"The *vacation* you've been on for the past year and however many months," Val said, stepping up behind Caroline with Fiona still in her arms. "That's where you've been all this time."

Jaw tight, I shook my head.

"*Sean*," Val warned.

"I ain't lying to them," I told her, watched Val shoot me a disapproving glare I was ignoring because I was dead-set on this, then I looked back to Caroline. "Baby girl, Daddy wasn't on vacation. I did somethin' bad, and I had to go away for it. That's why I couldn't see you. I was bein' punished, okay?"

Her head tilted in my hands, and her little nose wrinkled. "What did you do, Daddy?"

"You don't need to worry about that. It's done. I can see you now. That's all that matters."

"You mean you were in time-out?"

"What?"

"You were in time-out," she repeated, saying it as a statement now, like she'd figured it all out herself. She nodded slowly. "I go to time-out at school when I do something bad. I have to sit there *forever*, Daddy. Sometimes I have to miss free play. That's where you've been. You were in time-out."

I wouldn't ever compare where I went to some corner Caroline has to sit in for five minutes for stealing some other kid's crayons, but if that was how she needed to understand this, I'd go with it.

"Yeah, I was in time-out," I agreed.

"Daddy, don't do that anymore," she told me, face serious. "That was the longest time-out ever."

I chuckled and heard Val laugh softly too. "I won't, baby. I won't do that anymore," I promised, then I wrapped my arms around Caroline again when she went in for another hug, and stood with her, putting my attention on Fiona now.

My shy girl. My thinker—she still had her face buried in Val's neck, but she was peeking at me with one eye, and almost... *almost* smiling.

I got closer and closer, leaning in slowly until there was nothing *almost* about it—she was smiling now. Then I kissed her soft cheek, and she reached out for me, both hands seeking purchase around my neck. I gathered her up with one arm, taking her weight on my elbow, and pulled her close. I whispered, "Baby girl," and kissed her again on the forehead while she played with the ends of my hair the way she used to. Caroline was pushing up my sleeve and inspecting her drawing on my arm. She ran her finger over it. I smiled at her, then I looked to Val.

My ex was wiping tears from her eyes.

I stepped closer until she held up her hand, stopping me.

"I'm fine, I'm fine," she said, sniffling, rubbing at her cheek. "God, I knew I would do this... Just, show us the house. You girls want to see the inside, right?" Val forced a smile and blinked away tears.

"Yeah!" Caroline yelled.

Fiona pointed at the door. "I wanna see it."

"Yeah? It ain't much," I told them, hoisting the girls up higher. "Still needs work."

"Sean, just show us the house," Val said, sliding Caroline's book bag up her arm. "They do not care about it needing work. Trust me."

"I wanna see my room!" Caroline squealed.

"Me too, Daddy." Fiona grabbed my face and forced our foreheads together.

I thought about Shayla and what she'd said to me the other night about the girls only caring about seeing me, nothing else. Then I wondered why I didn't ask her to be here. I should've.

"All right, you ready?" I asked, turning toward the door. "Inside first, then I'll show you out back. I got a tire swing out there for you two. Playground is next."

"A tire swing? Awesome!" Caroline punched the air, then wiggled down when I hit the porch and rushed inside, shoving the door open.

Fiona started squirming until I put her down, and ran after her sister, screeching in delight.

Their voices poured out of the house.

I stepped aside so Val could enter next.

She stopped in front of me, eyes soft, and put her hand on my shoulder. Her hair was tied back. There was pink on the ends, like Shayla's. "You look good, Sean," Val said.

"So do you," I replied, meaning that. My ex was a beautiful woman. Sweet face. Pretty smile—she still had it. The hardened life I'd put her through hadn't changed her.

If anything, it made Val more beautiful, just knowing what all she'd survived.

"Well, come on. Give me a tour," she said. Her hand gave me a squeeze, then she dropped it and took a step, getting halted by Caroline, who popped her head out the door.

"Mommy, I have a ladybug dresser!" she screamed in one breath, eyes wide and making her look half crazy. She glanced at me before disappearing back inside in a rush.

Laughing, Val went on inside.

I walked in after her, thinking about Shayla, that pink in her hair, and how she'd be smiling right now and telling me, "I told you so," if she were here.

As promised, I gave a tour of the inside before showing the girls and Val out back.

The tire swing I'd put up was a hit, as was the house, especially the girls' pink bedroom and the fish I hadn't told them about.

"You got fish, Daddy?" Caroline asked, tapping the barrel, while Fiona tried feeding them the entire bottle of food.

Both of the girls were sitting up on the counter. Once they discovered the fish, they couldn't get up there fast enough.

I took the bottle of food from Fiona and dumped some flakes into both of their hands. "Yeah. They got names too—Mac and Cheese."

Caroline started giggling, covering her mouth, while Fiona licked her lips.

"I really love mac and cheese, Daddy," she told me, expression dead serious.

My chest rattled with a laugh. I knew that. It was practically the only thing Fiona ever ate before. I wondered if that had changed much.

"Which one's Cheese?" Fiona asked as she carefully dropped her flakes into the water.

"That one," Caroline answered, pointing at one of the fish. "He's definitely Cheese. Look at him."

Fiona bent down and studied the fish. "Yep. That's him," she said.

The fish were identical.

I looked back at Val, who was observing us by the refrigerator. Her shoulder leaned against it while she still held Caroline's bag in front of her. She was smiling. She looked happy.

"I can't believe you have fish," she said.

I couldn't believe it either, but I didn't tell her that. "Yeah. They were a gift."

Her brows lifted in surprise. I was pretty sure I had that same expression when Shayla gave them to me.

"All right, girls. We gotta get going," Val said, looking at her watch.

"No!" Fiona hollered.

"Mommy, we wanna *stay*!" Caroline punched her thigh. "We still need to take turns again on the swing!"

I grabbed Fiona first and helped her down. Then I put Caroline on her feet.

I didn't want them leaving yet, but I wouldn't argue with Val. She was controlling this. It didn't matter how I felt about it.

Any bitching on my part might lead to pissing her off, which could lead to her keeping the girls from me.

So I said what I could say. I didn't ask for more time.

"When you come back, you can take turns," I told Caroline.

She was pouting and kept hold of that pout when she looked up at me and asked, "Okay. When?"

I looked to Val.

She was unzipping the book bag. "Soon. Your daddy and I have to talk about it. Now, here. Do you want to give him this?" Valerie pulled out a piece of paper and held it out for Caroline.

I didn't like that. *Talk about what?* Did I not pass her test? She's been smiling this entire fucking time.

Gritting my teeth to keep my mouth from going, I watched Caroline take the paper and carry it over to me.

"Here, Daddy. I made you this in school."

I took it, flipping it over to see the drawing she'd done for me.

It was four stick-figure people, the two larger ones on the outside and the kids in the middle. My hair was the length it was now. Our names were written under us—Daddy, Caroline, Fiona, Mommy. We were all holding hands. Caroline was covered in pink.

I bent down and kissed her cheek, saying, "Thank you, baby girl."

Then I stuck her picture on the fridge, securing it with a magnet.

We walked outside. I helped with putting the girls in their car seats, taking care of Fiona and kissing her feet when she took off her shoes. I tickled Caroline. Then I stood back and waited for Val to walk over to me.

"The house looks great, Sean. It really does," she said.

"Thank you."

"I want the girls to be able to see you whenever they want. I don't mind bringing them over after work or on weekends if we aren't busy. I just don't want this to be . . . complicated. They've been through enough."

I nodded in agreement. I couldn't speak.

She was letting them see me whenever they wanted. Holy fuck. What the fuck was happening?

"Your job, you're going to keep it, right?"

"Wanna keep the house, so yeah."

"I'm serious."

I stared at her. "I'm keeping it. I got a good thing going there. I won't fuck it up."

She nodded tensely. "This is your last chance, Sean. I will not say this to you again. If you mess up, you're done." She stepped closer, grabbed my hand, and whispered, "Please. For them, do not mess up."

"I won't," I promised.

Val had tears in her eyes again. She threw her arms around my shoulders and gave me a quick hug, pressing her body so hard to mine, I could feel her heart pounding. Then she turned and walked around the car, climbing in hastily as she wiped at her face.

I waved at the girls as the car backed out of the driveway and pulled off. Then I reached for my phone, wanting to tell Shayla everything about the visit, but I changed my mind.

After locking up the house, I got on my bike and took off.

I wanted to see her face when I told her.

* * *

I parked my bike in the spot beside Shayla's car, cut the engine, and swung off.

I was shaking now for another reason entirely. It was shock. I couldn't fucking believe how that all had gone down.

Jumping the three steps to the basement level, I got to the door and knocked with a heavy fist.

The door swung open not a minute later, and Shayla stood there, still wearing her work uniform and smiling at me around the fork hanging out of her mouth.

She pulled it out to question, "Hey! How'd it go?"

"Good."

"Yeah?"

I nodded and stepped forward, backing her inside and stopping beside her. I put my hand on the side of her neck, squeezed gently, and pressed my mouth to her hair.

"Yeah," I murmured. "Real good."

I breathed her in. Honey. *Fuck, I like that.*

Shayla was still and silent for a breath, then she made a soft, squeaking sound, turned to face me, and wrapped her arms tight around my middle. "That's so good, Sean. I'm so, so happy for you," she said, chin on my chest, beaming up at me. "We should celebrate."

I had an idea in mind for that, but before I could suggest it, Shayla pulled away from me to shut the door, then took hold of my hand and tugged me in the direction of the kitchen.

"Come on. I'm eating dinner. Sit with me and we can talk." She released my hand when we reached the table.

I took a seat across from the plate of food she'd been working on—chicken, brown rice, and vegetables—while she stepped inside the kitchen and opened the fridge.

"What do you want to drink?" she asked.

"Whatever. Coke is fine."

"I have beer."

"Don't drink. Coke or whatever else you got is fine."

Her head popped out of the kitchen, and she studied me. "How come I don't know that about you?"

I shrugged. "You ever seen me drink?"

"No, but...huh." She quit studying me, grabbed something out of the fridge, then emerged out of the kitchen and sat a Coke down in front of me. She took her seat. "So, how come you don't drink?" she asked, forking a bite of chicken and eating it.

I cracked the can open. "Mom drank. Did other stuff too. I never had the urge to try anything she ever touched. Not after seeing what all it did to her."

"You've never done anything before? You never had a drink or smoked weed? Nothing?"

"Nope."

"Wow. That's seriously cool of you."

I took a sip of my Coke and watched her above the can.

Her hair had those braids in it I liked—two in the front, both tucked behind her ears—and the rest of it was in soft waves that stopped just below her chin.

"Sean, do you want to tell me about your mom?"

"Nope." I licked my lips. "I had a good fuckin' day, and she ain't touchin' it."

Shayla's eyes got soft, then she smiled and forked some rice. "Tell me all about it. Tell me everything. Oh, wait." She pointed at her plate. "Do you want something to eat?"

I wasn't hungry, but since she was offering, I snagged her fork—ignoring her quiet little protest—and got a bite of chicken mixed up with the rice and some vegetables. Chewing it, I sat back after setting the fork on the plate.

"You make this?" I asked, keeping disgust from my face as I swallowed.

"Uh, no. Lean Cuisine made it." She blushed a little. "I just like putting it on a plate and pretending I cooked it."

"Don't. That shit is awful."

Shayla laughed, holding her hands up. "Well, *excuse me*. I didn't have some professional cook over here making me dinner. I had to make do." She forked another bite and popped it in her mouth, smiling.

"You want me to cook for you?"

I didn't know if she was just saying that or if she meant it. She never asked me to before.

Shayla paused in her chewing. "Are you serious?" she asked. "Um, *yes*. That would be amazing."

"Say when, and I'll do it."

"When!"

I chuckled.

Shayla laughed at herself, then ate a carrot, which I knew did not taste like a fucking carrot. "Just kidding. You are only allowed to sit there and tell me all about your girls and how happy they were to see you. Did they love the house?"

I nodded.

"Did they give one...fucking...shit about anything you were worrying about?"

I stared at her. She stared back, getting extreme with it and leaning over her plate. Smiling, I shook my head.

"See? I told you so." She bobbed her head from side to side in victory. "Now, tell me everything, from the beginning. From the *moment* you saw them and they saw you."

I leaned back in my seat and stretched my legs, getting comfortable. Then I recounted everything, from the beginning, sharing with her what I was now regretting she hadn't witnessed for herself, firsthand.

But Shayla didn't act disappointed or even mention once how she wished she would've been there. She listened. She kept her eyes on me the entire time, taking everything in, smiling, laughing, doing little dances in excitement when I told her how the girls reacted to the bedroom furniture and the fish.

Her little dances were cute.

How Shayla looked watching me, happy for me, smiling, was not. That wasn't cute at all. It was a lot more. It was a helluva lot more.

I was telling her about Caroline drawing that picture for me when someone knocked at the door.

Shayla was in the kitchen washing off her plate. "Can you get that?" she hollered over the running water.

I stood from the chair and crossed the room, yanking the door open.

Some tall, skinny kid stood there, wearing a pressed dress shirt and holding fucking flowers. His hair covered half his face.

He looked like an asshole.

"Uh, hey," he said awkwardly. "You're not Shay."

My eyes narrowed. *Who the fuck was this?*

"I, hey!"

I snatched the flowers out of the prick's hand and slammed the door in his face. Then I crossed the room, reached the trash can against the wall just outside the kitchen, forced the lid to open with my foot pressing down on the pedal, and dropped the flowers inside.

I closed the lid just as Shayla stepped out.

"Who was that?"

"Nobody."

"What the fuck?" The door swung open and this dead motherfucker actually *walked* into her apartment. "What's your problem, man?"

"Uh, hey, Patrick," Shayla greeted him, looking at me suspiciously.

Patrick. My nostrils flared.

"You walk in here when she *invites* you in. Last I checked, she didn't." My voice was low, murderous.

"I got a key. Technically, I can come in whenever I want," he sassed.

I was in front of him before he could blink, grabbing this little shit up by the collar.

The kid gulped and wrapped his hands around my wrist.

"Sean! Hey! What are you doing?" Shayla slapped at my arm, then started tugging on it. "He's my super! Let him go!"

I looked back at her. "He's your *what?*"

"My *super*! Or whatever you call the people in the manager's office. He's a friend! Quit it!"

Her manager. Managers had keys.

Managers didn't bring tenants fucking flowers, so what the fuck was that about?

I let the prick go.

"Dude, you are psycho." The kid started rebuttoning his shirt. He was breathing heavily. "Shay, you know this guy?"

Shayla still had her eyes on me, full of confusion and questions. Then, shaking her head in discontentment, she looked at the kid. "Patrick, this is Sean, the *cook* I work with. I told you about him..."

She touched my arm, which I liked for several reasons, but the biggest reason being she wasn't touching him, but what I didn't like was her labeling me as just the *cook* she worked with. That pissed me off.

"Sean, this is Patrick. My super, like I said."

"And her friend," he added.

I took a sharp step toward him and backed him up against the door.

"I was saying it like, *just* her friend, you know?" he explained. His hands raised between us. "Christ."

"Sean." Shayla tugged on my arm again.

I looked back at her and glared. "That's all I am? Just the *cook* you work with?"

She sucked in a breath and pressed her lips together, looking like she had no fucking idea how to answer that question.

That pissed me off more.

"I ain't your friend?" I growled.

"Oh." She blinked several times. "Yes! Of course you are. That's not what I meant . . . I, I'm sorry. I just, when I've talked about you before, I would mention how you were the cook there. That's how Patrick would know you. That's all I was saying. It was for reference. I swear."

I steadied my breathing.

"Oh, man, you're Stitches, right?"

I slowly turned back to the kid.

He was smiling, looking between me and Shayla.

"Stitch," she corrected him. Then she reached forward and punched the kid in the chest.

"Ow! What the fuck?"

"Your shirt was wrinkled," she said, glaring at him the way you would do when you were silently communicating something.

I didn't know what the fuck was going on. All I knew was this kid knew about me. Shayla just admitted to talking about me to him. And he was her super. A friend. Nothing else. Not sure why that gave me comfort, but it did.

Wanting my drink and no longer feeling inclined to put this kid through a wall, or standing around to fucking chat, I turned and walked back over to the table.

"Uh, can I get my flowers back?" Patrick called out.

Drink nearly at my mouth, I froze.

Shit.

"What flowers?" Shayla asked.

SHIT.

Before anything else was said, I sat my can down, went over to the trash can, flipped the lid open, dug out the flowers, and stalked back across the apartment. Then I shoved the bundle at the kid and walked away.

"Uh," Shayla began. "Okay. Those are pretty."

"They're for Angela. I'm taking her out. Thought I'd class it up with flowers, which *now* smell like chicken. That's cool."

Shayla giggled.

I could've felt bad about the flowers, but Shayla was laughing, so I did not feel bad. At all.

The two of them talked for another minute before Patrick left. I finished my drink and watched Shayla close the door, turn and smile at me before she started walking over. She stopped in front of where I was standing by the chair and tipped her chin up.

"You're my friend," she said quietly, her smile softening and making her look regretful. "I'm sorry I didn't introduce you as that. I was just—"

"I get it. You already explained," I told her.

Shayla nodded one time. She wasn't back to smiling at me. She stayed regretful. I didn't like her looking that way, and I was hoping my offer would change that.

"Thought about goin' for a ride to celebrate. Is that somethin' you'd wanna do?" I asked.

Her eyes lit up first, then her mouth lifted and stretched into a full grin before she covered it with her hands and made that soft, squeaking noise again. "You're asking me to ride on the back of your bike?" she asked excitedly behind her fingers.

"I sure as fuck ain't riding on the back," I answered.

She looked to the ceiling and burst out laughing.

Nobody laughed like Shayla. It was loud and pretty at the same time. It was too much coming out of someone so little.

It was a noise I liked hearing.

"Get your shoes. Let's go," I told her, picking up my empty can and crushing it.

"Yes, yes, yes!" she chanted before taking off running across the apartment and disappearing behind a door.

She came back wearing shoes and a light jacket over top of her uniform shirt.

I opened the door for her, watched her lock up, then walked beside her to my bike.

I climbed on first, giving her the helmet. She took it, still smiling, looking like she wasn't ever giving it back, she was so happy, and strapped it on, then she swung her leg over and straddled the bike behind me, scooting close.

The engine roared.

Shayla's arms circled my waist, and she held on tight. I looked back at her. She propped her chin on my shoulder and grinned. I grinned too, backing us out. I couldn't help it.

Then we rode.

For a long fucking time.

Chapter Thirteen

SHAYLA

"Babe, you are *delusional*. He's hard up for you. Trust me."

I rolled my eyes for the millionth time tonight and took another sip of my Creamsicle margarita, refusing to agree with Tori, just like I was refusing to agree with the rest of the girls when they'd all said different versions of that exact same sentence at one point or another since we'd arrived at Low Bar.

Well, except for Jenna.

Since she worked at a lawyer's office and didn't waitress at White-caps, she didn't have an opinion on the situation.

My situation.

Ha! I did not *have* a situation, which was why I kept rolling my eyes and giving more attention to my delicious drink than to the crazy going on around me. At this rate, I was likely to be lit before the hour was up. That was fine by me.

Two nights ago, I'd taken the best ride of my entire life, and that included the first ride I ever took on the back of my dad's bike at the ripe age of eleven.

Riding with my dad had been fun. Adventurous. It made me

happy, as did the memories of all our rides together. They were extremely special to me.

But riding with Sean? That was out of this world *amazing*, for many reasons, but the main reason being the feel of his body against mine in places that had never felt parts of Sean's body before.

I was unprepared for how incredible it would be. And our ride was long, meaning I had plenty of time to soak in that incredible feeling.

And I soaked it in.

Now, it was girls' night, which was typically always a good time, and this one was no different, if you didn't count all the conversation focusing on me and my *situation* with Sean.

I never should've told them a damn thing.

Jenna was sitting next to me in the rounded booth we were occupying, wearing a cute little black dress that wasn't as clingy as the one I had on, but still showed major cleavage. Sydney was on the other side of me, also dressed in a little black dress, this one clingy in a halter style. Tori was sitting in a chair at the end, her little black dress putting a whole new meaning to the word *little*. It clung majorly, showed cleavage, *and* had slits going up both sides, showing a peek of skin.

The theme of the night, you guessed it, was little black dresses.

I loved going out with a theme, especially when it didn't require shopping to find something appropriate. I'd had my little black, strapless number I was wearing for years. It was a favorite of mine.

It made my butt look amazing, it somehow gave me curves I knew I did not have, and it stayed up, which was always a delight when dealing with something strapless.

Everyone was looking great. And everyone was here, except for Kali, who was out on her first official date with Cole.

I was hoping she was having fun. Kali deserved it. She was sweet and worked hard for her son, who didn't have much in terms of a father figure. He was a giant, cheating loser.

The only other one of us who had any kids was Jenna. And Brian, Syd's guy, was babysitting them so she could go out with us tonight. I thought that was really cool of him.

"Well, I have to say," Jenna began, "I've never seen you two together, but…it definitely sounds like he's interested in you. He was clearly jealous."

"Clearly. Jealous," Tori echoed, looking at me with knowing eyes, and then sipping her drink.

They were referring to the Patrick–Sean meeting that had taken place in my apartment two nights ago, before my spectacular ride. Really, I just wanted to talk about *that*. I'd like to relive it.

"He was not jealous of Patrick," I argued. "Can't be jealous when you're not interested, and he's not interested."

"Fill me in on why he's not interested again," Jenna requested.

God, this was not what I wanted to discuss. Maybe I'd just subtly change the subject…

"You know what's amazing about riding on the back of a bike?" I asked the table.

Tori stared at me, then smiled at Jenna and informed her, "Jamie had a party last year, Shay invited Stitch, and he blew her off."

I dropped my head back and groaned.

"What?" Tori asked. "*That's what happened.*"

She was not wrong. And I wasn't groaning because she was not wrong. I was groaning because it killed me thinking about this.

And now, I wasn't only going to be thinking about the biggest rejection of my life, but I was also going to be talking about it. This would involve rehashing that nightmare and all the feelings I felt that day, which would lead to me feeling those feelings all over again.

Great.

"Okay, *yes*, that's what happened. Fine. And there's your proof, right there." I looked at Jenna. "You see? He can't be jealous because he isn't interested in me like that. I asked him out and Sean made it really, *really* clear he didn't want to go out with me—I waited for him outside after work, he knew I was waiting for him, and he didn't even look at me when he walked out. He just left. Turned and left. Did not look back. So, trust me when I say, he isn't interested."

Pain circled my heart. Ignoring it was a lost cause, so I didn't even bother. I just felt it.

"Well then, what about throwing away the flowers?" Syd asked.

I looked at her. "I don't know. Maybe he just hates flowers."

It was an honest guess. Sean wasn't exactly the type of guy to have a line of credit going at 1-800-flowers. Maybe he had a bad experience with a florist once. I didn't know.

"Come on, Shay." This plea came from Tori.

"Come on *what*?" I asked, my voice raising and drawing attention from the patrons around us.

I shouldn't have been yelling, but there were a lot of emotions involved here, and I was not one to keep a good hold on my emotions, I never had been, no matter if I was in a public place or not.

"Just admit to the possibility of Sean being jealous," Tori pleaded.

"*He doesn't like me like that*," I snapped. "We're just friends. I'm his buddy, that's it. And you know what? Being his friend means a lot to me, because I can see just how much it means to him. I've come to the conclusion that, aside from his ex, nobody was ever good to him. Ever. I'm talking not even when he was a little kid. Take a second and *think* about that. He thinks he's nothing, because people told him that over and over until it stuck. And I'm doing everything I can and will *continue* doing everything I can to convince him that he is someone who matters and means something, and not just to me. I'll be his friend. I'll be whatever he needs me to be. And if that means I have to bury my feelings for him and never, *ever* act on them, then so be it. Sean's self-worth matters more to me anyway."

I drained my Creamsicle, then pointed at the waitress walking past our booth. "Yo! Can I get another?" I asked her.

The waitress acknowledged me, then gestured around the table with the pen in her hand. "Anyone else ready?"

Nobody said a word.

I glanced around at the three sets of eyes all glued on me—all glassed over with emotion. *That couldn't be right.* I blinked the haze of alcohol away and glanced again.

Still glassy.

"What?" I questioned the table.

Being ignored, the waitress stepped away.

Sydney was the first to speak, and she did it with tears in her eyes. "Um, I just really want him coming to Sunday dinner. He belongs there with us. I want him to know that."

I nodded in agreement. "I'll be sure to mention it to him. I'd like him there too."

"Also, I think what you're doing for him is quite amazing," she added.

"He deserves it," I said. "I'm not doing anything he shouldn't have been getting his entire life."

"May I say something?" Jenna asked.

I looked to her. "Of course, as long as you're *not* going to tell me how interested he is again."

She smiled and pushed her long, dark hair back over her shoulder. "Not that directly, no."

"Even *indirectly*, save it."

"Just hear me out," she requested.

The waitress returned with my drink. I popped the straw in my mouth and narrowed my eyes at Jenna, took a generous sip, then waved her on. "Fine. Go."

She slid her mostly finished drink to the side and angled herself to face me. "Okay, first, I don't even know this man, but I'm telling you right now, when I do meet him for the first time, I will be hugging him."

I smiled at her.

"Yeah, Stitch is definitely getting embraced. *Jesus.*" Tori shook her head. "I hate it when children are dealt shitty parents."

"It's a terrible thing that happens every day, unfortunately," Jenna said, then turning back to me, she continued. "I'm wondering, because of his horrible upbringing and the way he views himself, if maybe he doesn't feel *worthy* of you...and that's why he hasn't made any attempt to take your friendship any further."

Tori began nodding fast, and pointed at me when I looked at her. "Absolutely. That's it. Nail on the head, right there."

"And he's probably felt this way since last year, when you asked him out," Jenna went on. "Which was why he blew you off the way he did. Not that I'm excusing rude behavior, because he could've told you he wasn't planning on going or at least been a little nicer in his rejection, but I'm thinking this is some deep-rooted issue with him. He sees himself as nothing, you said it. And then he sees you as, well...*you*. You're sweet and beautiful and kind to him, Shay, and he doesn't feel deserving of it."

I had stopped sipping my drink, but my fingers were still wrapped around the stem of my glass, and hearing what Jenna had just said, they were now gripping it tightly.

Even in my half-drunk state, I was fully processing what she was saying. I just didn't know whether or not to believe it as a true possibility.

"Oh, my God," Syd whispered.

My head snapped left. "What?"

"Oh, my God," she repeated, still as a whisper as her eyes stayed unfocused on the table.

"What, hon. Spill it!" Tori shouted.

Syd looked over at me. "I can't believe I forgot about this," she said. "I mean, at the time, it was such a passing thing, and I didn't press..."

"What?" I yelled, needing to know what the hell she was talking about already.

"After the party last year, I was working at Whitecaps and Stitch was, you know, *Stitch*. Broody. Making all kinds of noise in that kitchen. He was in such a bad mood back then." She grinned at me. "And look at him now. I almost saw a smile out of him the other day."

"Syd." I leaned closer and snarled, "*Focus.*"

"Right. Anyway, he was glaring at you while you were filling salt shakers or something, and I suggested he just talk to you and quit with the whole silent treatment thing, and he said something about you having this light, and him not being good enough for it."

My eyes widened.

"He said that?" Tori questioned.

"*See*," Jenna said.

Syd nodded in confirmation. "In very few words, yes, that's what he told me. He said you invited him to that party and *what would he do there*? Like he didn't belong, you know? And then he said he had no business being around you. That you had light. He thinks you have light, Shay. And he doesn't think he can touch it. He's not good enough."

"Yes, he is!" I blurted out in anger, which was purely reactional, since Syd wasn't meaning what she'd said as a putdown; she was simply stating how Sean felt about himself. Regretting my outburst, I winced and leaned away. "Um, sorry. I know you're not saying he's not good enough. I just hear that and, well, it pisses me off."

She pulled her lips between her teeth and fought a smile.

"Holy shit. He's *totally* staying in the friend zone with you because he doesn't think he's worthy of more," Tori said. "Holy shit! You gotta make a move, Shay."

"Huh?"

"*Make a move*," Tori repeated. "Stitch won't. He's probably scared to."

"Aw, bless his sweet, little heart," Jenna said, her hand to her chest. "Can we go hug him now?"

"Sure! Shay needs to make her move anyway." Tori picked up her drink and held it out in front of her. "Right, Shay?"

I opened my mouth to respond, then realizing I didn't have the words yet, lifted my drink and downed a generous amount of it. Then I licked cold Creamsicle off my lips and glanced around the table.

The girls were all staring at me, smiling, looking anxious.

I released my drink and touched my cool hand to my neck.

My skin was flushed and hot all over. My heart was pounding. I began breathing faster, thinking about what Syd had revealed and what Tori was suggesting I do, plus, I was definitely half drunk and well on my way to being fully drunk.

Could I go make a move on Sean? Was that even a good idea? What if he rejected me again?

What if they were right, though?

He said I had light. *Me.* And I knew Syd wasn't drunk enough to make up something like that. She was tipsy. All the girls were. Not wasted to the point of inventing some conversation that never took place, though, meaning it *absolutely* took place.

Oh, my God.

There was a very, *very* strong possibility the girls were right about him. He didn't feel worthy. And he was absolutely worthy. Not just of me, but of everything good this world had to offer him. Of love. Of kindness.

And I was going to make sure he knew that for good.

Tonight.

Drinks, and then game on.

* * *

"Jenna, how come you aren't hooked up yet?" Tori asked from the front seat of the Uber we'd hitched after finishing up with our drinks at Low Bar.

We were on our way to Sean's house so I could make my move.

Nerves aside, I couldn't stop smiling.

And giggling. Everything became hilarious to me when I drank.

Like our driver—his name was B.J.

Come on.

"You're gorgeous," Tori went on, turning halfway in her seat and looking back at Jenna, who was seated by the other window, directly behind Tori. Syd was in the middle. "Just look at your cheekbones! Plus, you're sweet. And you still got a killer body after popping out twins." Tori glanced to the driver. "Doesn't she? She's a hot piece, right, B.J.?"

I clapped my hand over my mouth and giggled again.

"Uh, I don't know. I guess," B.J. answered, suddenly looking uneasy behind the wheel.

He reminded me of my old math teacher from high school. Real buttoned up. I wasn't sure he'd ever thought about anyone being a hot piece before.

Tori scowled at him.

"I date here and there," Jenna said. "But most of the guys either aren't good enough to meet my kids and I find that out after one date, or they *hear* about my kids and never call me again."

"That's fucking rude," I snapped, sitting forward to look at her. "Sean has kids, and I love that about him."

Jenna smiled.

Looking to Syd, I saw she was smiling too. And because I knew Tori was most likely grinning, not just smiling, I refused to look at her and kept my eyes down until I could resume looking out my window.

Then I giggled for no apparent reason.

"So, what's the game plan here?" Sydney asked. "I mean, *after* we all shower Stitch in affection."

"Shay is going to make her move on him," Tori informed us.

"*Alone*," I added, glancing around the car. "You hug him and then you leave. I'm not doing this with an audience."

"Oh, come on," Tori pleaded.

"No way."

"I could take pictures!" Syd suggested. "Or a video. Ooh! I could add it to your Snap!"

I loved the idea of having a keepsake of this moment, especially one with a cool filter involved, but still, I shook my head. "No. Blowjob here is going to wait for you to finish with your hugs. Then he's taking you home. Right, Blowjob?" I sat forward, held onto his headrest, and grinned at him in the rearview while the girls burst out laughing.

"Haven't heard that one before," he retorted.

"You haven't heard it from *me*," I said.

"Now I can die a happy man."

"That's the spirit!"

The car slowed to make a turn, and looking out the front window, I saw Sean's house in the distance.

"Oh, my God," I whispered, pressing my back against the seat.

This was it. We were here. I was *actually* going to do this.

"This is so exciting!" Syd exclaimed, bouncing beside me.

I gripped the door handle and looked out my window.

We passed the driveway and slowed to a stop in front of the house. There was a car I didn't recognize parked in front of Sean's bike. A dark four-door.

I worried the girls and Val were here. I couldn't invade during his time with them. That was way more important than my stupid move.

"Um, I don't know if this is a good time," I said.

"What? No way. You are doing this, Shay." Tori was adamant.

I shook my head, looking from the car to the front door as it opened. *Maybe they were leaving?*

"Wait. Look," I said, my finger pressing to the glass.

A woman stepped out of the house.

Not Val. I knew Val.

This woman looked to be around the same age, though. She was wearing a silver sequinned dress that showed a lot of leg and dipped low in the front, her hair was teased out to high heaven, and not in a good way, and she was wearing more makeup than any woman ever should. Even under the porch light, I could tell it was spackled on.

"What the heck?" I whispered.

"Who is that?" Jenna asked.

I didn't know, so I just kept watching while wondering the same thing.

Before she stepped off the porch, the woman shoved money inside a wallet she was gripping.

Money?

"*What the heck?*" I whispered again, more harshly this time.

"Oh, my God, is that…*a lady of the evening*?" Syd questioned.

Tori snorted. "Hon, why would you call her that? Just say hooker. Or prostitute. Because that's *clearly* what she is."

"It is, right?" Syd asked.

"She's definitely dressed for action," Jenna said.

My stomach tightened and rolled at the same time. I felt a pressure build inside my chest, like someone was squeezing the ever-loving shit out of my heart and enjoying every second of it.

A prostitute?

Did Sean *really* just get sex from a *prostitute?*

I watched the woman with eagle eyes.

She walked to her dark, four-door car, which I was betting was not used to haul kids around. Pimps, maybe. She got in, backed out into the street, and peeled out, tires screeching and everything.

Like she was worried she'd get arrested for something *illegal*.

"My grandmother spells whore H-O-R-E," Jenna said. "Isn't that funny?"

"*What the heck!*" I screeched, unable to keep a lid on my reaction to this any longer. I threw my door open and climbed out, then stormed across that lawn as best I could, considering the heels I was wearing and how soft the lawn was due to the rain we'd had yesterday. My cross-body purse bounced wildly against my hip.

"B.J., do not move this car." That order came from Tori.

"Shay, wait!" Syd called out behind me.

I did not wait. I couldn't.

I was angry. I was sad beyond belief. I felt betrayed. But most of all, I was mad at myself for not getting through to Sean in terms of his worth.

All those things I was feeling were tearing me up inside so badly, I could not wait.

With a heavy fist, I beat on Sean's door until it swung open. And when it did, the girls were all gathered behind me, whispering about that woman, about Sean, about me, and about the move I was about to make.

They were rethinking this plan.

Too bad I wasn't.

Sean stood in front of me wearing nothing but those faded, ratty jeans. He was barefoot, shirtless, his hair was damp, meaning he'd just washed that woman off him.

My nose began to sting.

"Hey," Sean greeted us, looking at the girls at my back, and then focusing on me, where his eyes did a slow, sexy travel down my body before returning to my face. "What's up?"

"What's. Up?" I echoed, bringing my arms across my chest and glaring at him. *He did not just "what's up" me after having sex with a hooker.* "Oh, I'll tell you *what's up*. You think you're only worth some dirty, disease-infested, back-alley hood rat, who needs to find a new stylist *immediately*, and that just isn't true. It's not even *close* to being true. You deserve better. The best. You deserve...someone who at least knows how to tease their hair properly. *That's* what's up!"

"Damn," Tori murmured.

"Wow. This is crazy." That comment came from Syd.

Brows raised, Sean didn't say a word. He just kept looking at me.

So I kept going. "How could you pay for sex? How could you think you'd *have to,* Sean?"

"The fuck are you talkin' about?" he questioned.

"That woman! That *skank* who just left! You paid her for sex, didn't you! I saw the money."

"You mean my ex-sister-in-law?"

Someone gasped behind me. *Oh, my God...* They were thinking the same thing as I was.

"Your ex-sister-in-law is a lady of the evening?" I asked.

Sean frowned. "A *what?*"

"A *hooker*. Prostitute. Back-alley hood rat. They have a lot of titles," I answered.

"Good to know," he replied, leaning his shoulder against the door frame and shoving his hands in his pockets, like he was getting comfortable.

Comfortable? Really?

"Um, care to explain why you felt the need to pay your ex-sister-in-law money for sex?" I questioned, hands on my hips now.

"You drunk?" he questioned back.

"No."

"Sound drunk."

"I'm somewhat inebriated."

"Spell *inebriated*."

I glared at him. "I'd rather not, thank you very much."

"That's what I thought—drunk." He looked over my head. "And what the fuck's this? You bring your girls so they can run their mouth at me about shit they don't fuckin' know about too?"

"What the hell does that mean?" I questioned.

"Um, actually, we aren't here to run our mouths at you at all. We're here to give you affection."

Sean stared at Sydney after she finished speaking. "You're here to *what?*"

"Give you affection. Hugs." Jenna shot her arm out over my shoulder. "Stitch, is it? I'm Jenna, Brian's sister. I don't believe we've met."

"This is hardly the time for introductions," I snapped, pushing her arm down.

"Sorry. But I just didn't want it to seem weird when I did this..." Jenna pushed forward to get in front of me, then, stepping up to Sean, she wrapped her arms tight around his middle and gave him a hug.

He stared at the top of her head until she pulled away, then he watched her with suspicion until she pushed her way back behind me, allowing room for Syd and Tori to step up next.

One at a time, they each gave Sean a hug that he did not reciprocate in the slightest—Syd holding on a little bit longer than Jenna, and Tori ending hers with a quick kiss on the cheek.

That would've pissed me off if it wasn't Tori, and if I didn't know the reason behind her doing it. Since it *was* one of my girls and she was merely giving Sean affection that was innocent in nature, I did not make a mental note to beat her ass another day and time.

With everyone back in position behind me, Sean lowered his eyes and met my own.

"You," he said, not sounding angry but not sounding friendly either. "Inside," he gently ordered. "The rest of you, go home. Now."

"Righty-o!" Syd yelled, spinning around and hopping off the porch.

"It was so nice to meet you," Jenna said. She waved at Sean and followed after Syd.

Tori gave me a quick hug and whispered in my ear, "I want major details tomorrow."

I tried to smile when she leaned away, but it was fully hitting me now that I was about to step into Sean's house with him, alone, and confront the shit show I just rolled up on all while making my move. The best I could manage was a half smile while laughing nervously.

"Bye, Stitch!" Tori yelled as she walked across the yard.

I slowly turned around, met Sean's eyes again, and explained, just in case it wasn't obvious already, "It was girls' night. We get a little wild on girls' night, and sometimes come up with a plan that involves a guy in one way or another."

"This plan have to do with givin' me hugs for some strange fuckin' reason?" he asked.

"Yes." I nodded firmly. "They, uh, have all been somewhat informed of your terrible upbringing and wanted to show you the love you've deserved your entire life. They feel you deserve it too. As much as me."

Sean stared at me for a breath. His face held some emotion I was having difficulty comprehending under the low porch light. Then he straightened off the door, rubbed at his mouth, and stepped back, allowing me room for entry.

He did not speak.

I wasn't sure that was a good sign or not, but I didn't inquire. I cleared my throat and moved inside.

The light in the living room was on, but aside from that, the house was dark.

I pulled the linked chain of my cross-body bag over my head and tossed it on the couch. Sean stood at the door three feet away, staring at me. I wanted so, so badly to make my move, but that woman being here was bothering me, and I couldn't get past it.

"I just—I don't understand why you think you'd have to pay someone to—"

"Heard your speech the first time," Sean interrupted. "You don't need to repeat it."

I breathed slowly through my nose and waited, feeling ready to crawl out of my skin, I was so troubled by this.

Sean brought his arms across his chest, took a deep breath, like he was preparing to say a lot, and then shared, "Bridgett, Val's sister, was here tryin' to pay me to stay away from my girls."

My entire body went ramrod straight.

Sean did not, in fact, say a lot.

But what he did say had me flying so fast for that door, I forgot about my heels and nearly face-planted.

"Tell me where that skank-whore lives!" I shrieked. Sean's arm circled my waist as he caught me up. He kept it there and lifted me off my feet, preventing me from reaching the door. "I'm going over there *right now*! She cannot do that to you! She has *no right*!"

"She's got a right, Shayla." Sean spoke in my ear.

"I'm gonna pull out all her stupid, ugly hair and make her eat it!" I kicked the air, reaching over his shoulder for the door, and then allowing his words to penetrate, I quit fighting him, turned my head, and met his eyes. "What do you mean, she's got a right? No, she doesn't."

"She's protectin' my kids," he said. "She's just lookin' out for them and Val. That is not a bad thing for her to be doin', babe."

I sucked in a breath.

Oh, my. Babe felt nice. I liked that.

But I had to keep focus. My argument was solid, and he needed to hear it.

I gripped Sean's shoulders for support. Our fronts were mashed together, and my feet were still dangling in the air. "It is a bad thing if it involves you not seeing them, Sean," I told him. "She can't do that. She can't keep you from your girls."

He shook his head. "She isn't."

"She isn't?"

"Saw the money, didn't you?"

I opened my mouth, then closed it. "Oh. Right." Yeah, I definitely got a good look at that money.

"Bridgett saw the house, saw all the shit I've done to it, and listened while I laid it out for her," he said. "She needed to see this for herself and hear it from me. I've lied a lot in the past, Shayla. A lot. Hurt Val more than once. Bridgett has a right to be comin' up in here and makin' sure I'm not gonna fuck up my kids' lives any more than I already have. She meant good by it."

"I'm having a hard time agreeing with you on that," I told him honestly.

"'Cause you thought I was fuckin' her?"

I flinched and felt blood pooling in certain areas of my body at the same time. That was both a disgusting thought and seriously sexy the way he said the word *fuckin'*.

"Well, can you blame me for thinking that? She was dressed like a two-dollar H-O-R-E."

Sean's mouth twitched. "You are drunk. You can't spell for shit."

"Yes, I can. That's just how Jenna's grandmother spells it." I wiggled until he set me on my feet. "And I'm not drunk. I'm half drunk. There's a difference."

"Yeah?"

"Yes. I have some sense about me still. I saw all the makeup that crusty bitch was wearing and knew it was way too much. If I was drunk, I might've thought differently. How come she was dressed like that anyway?"

"She works at the Dollhouse."

My mouth dropped open. "She's a stripper and she's coming over here judging *you*? Is she insane? Like, I'm seriously asking, because if I *do* see her again, her mental state will determine whether I slap the shit out of her for this stunt tonight. I don't need some psycho chick breaking into my apartment."

Sean grinned. He actually *grinned*. And even though it was one of the most beautiful things I have ever seen in my entire life, it aggravated me slightly because he was doing it out of amusement.

"What?" I asked, hands on my hips and my head cocked to the side. "Don't make fun of me. I'm serious. I don't like how she came up in here looking to pay you off. That hurts me. It hurts me for *you*. You need those girls in your life, Sean, and they need you in theirs. They need their dad. The man you are... their lives would be severely lacking without you in it."

Sean's grin softened when I finished speaking. Then his eyes did this slow appraisal of my face, and just as my breath started picking up under his scrutiny, he reached out and grabbed my neck while stepping forward, pulled me firmly against his chest, circled my upper back with his other arm, and dropped his head so his mouth was in my hair.

We were sealed together. This was a legitimate embrace. Not like the neck squeezes he'd given me before. No, *this* was more.

I forced myself to breathe so I wouldn't pass out and miss this beautiful moment. Then I hugged him back for nearly a full thirty seconds.

I knew this because I was counting.

Cheek pressed to his pec, I inhaled slowly and deeply.

His skin smelled so good. And his body felt amazing against mine. And his mouth in my hair, pushing warm breath across my head, holy crap, that was nice.

I wanted this to last forever. I wanted to go back in time and not drink those Creamsicle margaritas, eliminating the possibility of this moment getting lost in the haze. But more important than that, I really wanted to look at Sean while he embraced me.

Just as I felt his arm loosen its hold, I tipped my chin up, forcing his head back ever so slightly so we could see each other.

His hand was still on my neck, but his thumb had moved to my jaw. This new touch drove me crazy. And considering that, plus the embrace, and the current way Sean was gazing down at me—intensely, like he was feeling something major in this moment—I saw my window.

This was it. Now to do what I came here to do.

But just as I prepared to make my move and kiss him, Sean spoke. "It's late. I should get you home."

I did not want to go home. Not even in the slightest. "Or, I could stay," I suggested bravely.

Alcohol made me giggle *and* it gave me courage. I wasn't sure I would've ever made that suggestion sober.

I was no longer regretting those Creamsicle margaritas.

Sean's brows shot up at my proposal, then his face softened as he subtly shook his head. "Shayla," he began. His voice was strained.

"I just have so much more I want to tell you."

"You've said a lot already."

"Not everything, though." I slid my hands up his arms, past his broad shoulders to his neck, mouth open to say it, *just say it*.

"Not tonight."

The words in my heart died on my tongue.

"What? Why?" I asked.

"You've said a lot, Shayla," he repeated, slowly and firmly.

"I haven't though. Not that much."

"You have," he stressed. "Trust me, you have. I'm still hearin' it, all right?"

My lips pressed together. I understood then what he was saying.

Accepting the things I'd already told him tonight and before wasn't easy, but Sean was trying. He wasn't fighting me or arguing or asking me to call him "nothing." He was hearing me and letting it all sink in.

I had a feeling, a good one, that he'd continue hearing me and everything else I planned on saying. And knowing that and considering how important Sean had become in my life, I'd respect the time he needed. I wouldn't push him.

"Okay," I said. "Not tonight."

Sean's thumb on my jaw moved the tiniest bit. My knees locked.

God, I felt that move *everywhere*.

"You gotta work tomorrow?" he asked.

"Yes. All day. You?"

"Same." He took a deep breath. "This ain't a good idea."

"What?"

"You stayin' here."

"You're right." I leaned closer. "It's a *great* idea."

The corner of his mouth lifted.

I thought about not pushing him, about respecting the time he needed, and made myself clear on one thing.

"If you really don't want me here, you can take me home."

Breathing loud and heavy, he stared deep into my eyes. "I haven't laid with a woman in a long time."

Oh, *God*.

I loved how he said that, and I loved *that* he said that. His honesty sometimes was overwhelming in the best possible way.

"Well, I'm sure it's just like riding a bike," I reassured him.

Deep inside his chest, he chuckled. I knew that was a good sign. I grinned up at him.

"How many drinks you have tonight?" he asked, watching my mouth.

"Three."

"Big ones?"

"Oh, yeah."

"You gonna be hungover tomorrow?"

"It's a possibility. I feel good now, though."

"'Cause you're still drunk." He shook his head, but not in a disapproving way. Then his hand on my neck pulled off so that same hand could find my lower back, where he pressed and turned me in the direction of the hallway.

I took his lead and walked ahead.

My heart was racing. My insides were warming deliciously.

I was spending the night with Sean. I was going to lay with him and possibly cuddle.

This was a big, big deal.

Passing the girls' bedroom first, then the bathroom, I finally made it to the room at the end of the hall, and flipped the light on overhead.

The bedroom was small and hadn't been painted yet, but thanks to Monica, Sean had a bed frame now with a headboard and footboard instead of just a mattress on the floor, plus a wide dresser he could keep all his clothes in, freeing up the trunk he'd been using for storage. That was utilized as a nightstand now.

What he didn't have was a comforter set or any sort of bedding whatsoever. Just a sheet laid out on the mattress, one pillow, and an old, quilted blanket that looked well used. The color was a faded patchwork.

I didn't comment on the appearance of Sean's bed, but I did make a mental note to ask the girls if anyone had any spare bedding they weren't using.

I was also prepared to browse the home section at Target next time I ran out.

"You need anything?" Sean asked, moving ahead of me into the room and looking back.

"Um, just a toothbrush. I still taste like Creamsicle."

He jerked his chin at the door. "Bathroom. I just got the one."

"That works." I smiled at him before turning and heading out, slipping into the bathroom.

I had absolutely zero problems using Sean's toothbrush. Some people might find that gross. I did not. I didn't find anything about him gross.

I quickly brushed my teeth and decided on leaving my makeup as is, since I didn't have face wash or anything besides Dial soap handy, then after relieving myself, I turned off the light and moved back into the bedroom.

Sean was sitting on the edge of the bed, still shirtless and in his jeans, his head lowered, his hair tucked behind his ears, and his hands steepled in front of his face.

When I walked in, he looked up.

"Need anything else?" he asked.

I shook my head and smiled. I was so, so good, he had no idea. Then I walked to the bed, popped off my tall, strappy heels, and climbed on.

Sean stretched out on his back. He'd given me use of the pillow and was using his arm bent up behind him as a cushion.

Even if I had been fully drunk, I wouldn't have allowed that.

I motioned for him to lift his head, stuck half the pillow under there, and then lay on my side with my back to the wall, facing Sean. We shared the pillow.

"You mind if I leave that light on?" he asked, talking about the small lamp on the trunk beside the bed.

The overhead light was off now.

"No. Not at all," I told him, voice breaking with a yawn. "Do you mind if I cuddle you at some point? I'm a natural cuddler."

Sean cut his eyes to me. "I didn't mind it before."

Aha. So he *had* been awake the other night on my couch when I'd done that. Good to know.

"Okay." I closed my eyes on a second yawn. "Good night, Sean."

"Night, Shayla."

Sean dozed immediately.

Forty minutes later, I was still awake and playing with a thread on my dress while watching Sean sleep when the urge to use the bathroom again hit hard.

I carefully climbed over his legs and snuck out of the room.

After doing what I needed to and washing my hands, I grabbed my phone out of my bag and set an alarm for eight a.m., just in case Sean didn't have one set. Then I returned to the bedroom and placed my phone on the trunk.

Standing beside the bed, I looked down at Sean.

He was still on his back, one hand on his abdomen and the other buried under the pillow. His head was turned toward me, lips parted, allowing breath to leave him slowly and quietly.

I let my eyes wander to his ink.

The low light from the lamp cast a glow over his body, illuminating areas of his skin and shadowing others.

Sean's tattoos were still a mystery to me. I'd seen them, but not up close and not like this, where I could stare and study without him knowing.

On his upper chest were images blended beautifully together among a lot of shading. I could make out two baby footprints on one of his pecs, like you'd see on a birth certificate, and the girls' names: *Caroline* and *Fiona* were scripted just below each of his collarbones. Woven throughout the shading were lines that didn't seem to have any rhyme or reason to them. They were thick and dark, looped down to the tops of his ribs, and reached his shoulder, ending there in a bull's-eye swirl pattern. Below the bull's-eye on his left upper arm was that drawing I'd noticed a couple weeks ago. I couldn't see it too well without Sean rolling over, but I could see it enough to know I was right in my observation before—it was a stick-figure person. One like a child would draw. And I knew one of his girls had put that on him.

God, he'd gotten it permanent. That was incredibly sweet.

When my eyes swept back over Sean's chest to study more of the ink, I noticed something. A word written in the background on the skin of his left pec, a word that was mostly hidden by handprints and shadows and the lines weaving, but it was there.

I bent down and got closer.

I saw the word—*Nothing*—tattooed in someone's handwriting. Gasping, my hand flew to my mouth, and my eyes shifted, refocusing on another spot on his chest. I saw another word—*Loser*. Same handwriting. And another—*Worthless*. This one was written around the curve of his ribs.

"Oh, my God," I whispered behind my hand.

The words were everywhere. *Pain. Hate. Pathetic. Undeserving.* They were hidden all over him. On the inside of his arm—the one closest to me that was bent up, and I was sure on the other one as well. I just couldn't see it. Curving around to his back, and in the center of his chest where his heart was. I looked down to the hand resting on his stomach. On the top, spanning to his knuckles, was a tattoo of a skull with roses coming out of its eye sockets, but when I leaned closer and searched, I could see the word hidden in the shading.

Space.

"Didn't have parents. Had a woman who didn't want me around. That's it. I took up space."

I whimpered so loudly, I was shocked I didn't wake him.

Turning away, I clamped my hand over top of my other one and pressed down as wave after wave of agony pulsed beneath my skin and sunk into my bones like a cancer. This pain was rotting, capable of tearing me apart from the inside out. It would destroy all of me, I just knew it.

I rushed out of the room before I made another sound.

The tears were instant, pouring out of me, fast and heavy. There was no stopping them. Pushing the bathroom door closed behind me, I sank to the floor in front of the toilet and sobbed into my hands. I was as far away from the door as I could get without climbing inside the shower.

Maybe I should've done that.

I wasn't in there a minute before the door swung open and I'd been found, and because I didn't want Sean knowing why I was really crying since I wasn't ready to have this conversation with him, being in the current state I was in and feeling the unrelenting weight of my emotions ripping me apart, I lunged at the toilet and hung my head in it.

"The fuck?"

His voice hit me over the sound of my cough/sob, which was the only word I knew to describe what I was doing.

After flushing nothing but toilet water, I wiped at my mouth and lifted my head, blinking away tears so I could see him.

"I just really hate throwing up," I whispered, then immediately began crying again, because he was standing there with those words written on his body and I was mad at myself for not finding Sean sooner so I could've somehow prevented him from doing that to himself.

With worry in his eyes, Sean stepped inside the bathroom and squatted down beside me. He placed his hand on my lower back. "You still got more to get out of you?" he asked.

I stared into his perfect face, belonging to this perfect man, who had overcome so much to be here.

"No, I think that's it," I said, crying more heavily now. "I-I'm done."

Sean stood, grabbed the small towel off the sink and got it damp. He wiped my mouth with it. Then he set the towel aside and lifted me off the floor so I was cradled against his chest.

I buried my face in his neck and sobbed.

"Shit. You really fuckin' hate throwing up, don't you?"

I nodded.

I wasn't lying. I really did hate throwing up. Typically, it didn't upset me like this, but I was okay leading him to believe that.

Feeling the bed underneath me, I opened my eyes as Sean sat me down on the edge. I wiped a few tears away and watched him slide a small bucket out from between the trunk and the bed. He sat it beside my feet.

"Why do you have a bucket in here?" I asked him.

"Nightmares," was all he said.

I pulled my lips between my teeth and trapped a sob inside my mouth.

Oh, God.

Oh, *God*.

He didn't need to say any more. He got sick just from thinking about that awful woman and the childhood he'd had. I just knew he did.

I was softly crying still when Sean lifted my feet into bed and forced me to lie back in the spot he had been asleep in.

He pulled the quilt up and around my body and tucked it in, then he climbed in himself, planting his knee in the bed below my feet and getting up beside me. He lay on his back. He gave me all the covers. He didn't take any for himself.

"You all right?" he asked.

I nodded, swallowing down the emotion thickening my throat. Knowing I wasn't anywhere near finished crying, especially after what Sean had just revealed to me, I turned away from him and faced the door.

So many things filled my head, but one thing was standing out over all the others. I wanted Sean knowing he belonged. That people cared for him, and wanted him around.

"Sundays are family dinner nights at Syd and Brian's house," I began, tears still pouring down my face, but my voice sounding steadier than it had been. "You're invited. It's a standing thing, no matter who can make it or not. Sometimes people bring a dish, but it's not required. You absolutely do not have to bring a dish. Tomorrow, I obviously can't make it and neither can you due to work, but if you're up for it, I would really like it if you'd accompany me to the next one I'm able to attend."

Sean was silent for a moment, then I felt the bed move behind me, and a second later, Sean's chest was pressing up against my back. His arm draped over my waist, and he buried his nose in my hair.

I could feel his warm breath on the back of my scalp.

"Um, is that a yes?" I asked hesitantly.

I felt his head move. *He'd lifted his chin.*

That was a yes.

I closed my eyes and felt my body melt deeper into the mattress.

Hands folded in front of my mouth, I used my fingers to wipe my tears away, then I looked off the bed.

"Sean?"

"Yeah."

"I'm gonna get you to a place where you no longer need that bucket."

His arm around my body tensed. I knew that was him hearing me again.

And since he said no more, that thought was only confirmed, and knowing Sean was accepting my promise, I was able to quietly cry myself to sleep.

The next day at work, I was trying to keep focus on all the positive things that had happened the night before, but I was having difficulty keeping my mind off those words marked into Sean's skin.

I was also wondering while taking down an order how often he used that bucket, not that frequency would matter much to me at this point. Just the fact that Sean had a bucket in his room for when he got sick from nightmares was enough to make me want to go postal.

Never in my life had I daydreamed about torturing people before. It was all I could seem to do today, though. I'm talking *Saw* movie torture. I'd go all out.

"Bastards," I mumbled.

"I'm sorry?"

I looked up from the ticket I was writing on and focused on the man seated at the booth.

Angelo—he was a young guy I'd waited on a couple times before; I recognized him. Italian. Dark hair. Always came in here wearing business attire. He smiled at me a lot and liked chatting me up whenever I came by his table to check on him.

I always got a nice tip too.

"Uh, sorry. Nothing." I gave him a smile. "Would you like fries, coleslaw, or homemade chips with your burger?"

"The chips good?"

"Oh yeah," I answered, and I wasn't just saying that either. Sean's chips were the bomb. "They got a little seasoning on them. Just the right amount of kick. Trust me."

"All right. Chips it is." He handed me his menu and grinned.

I smiled back. "I'll put your order right in. Let me know if you need anything in the meantime."

"I'll do that."

After sticking the menu up at the podium, I tore the ticket off my book and headed for the kitchen window, passing Tori along the way, who was training a new girl—Lauren—and looked ready to gouge her own eyes out.

At least I wasn't the only one struggling to be a people person today.

"Cheesy crab burger and some chips," I announced, sliding my ticket across the window to Sean, and, getting his eyes when he looked up, smiling at him.

I didn't need to be a people person. I was still a Sean person.

"I've decided that when you do make me dinner, I'd like those chips on the menu," I announced.

His eyes brightened, like he was proud of himself, and that made me seriously happy. "That right?"

"Yep. I'll let you decide on everything else. But I'm going to be adamant about the chips. I'd eat them every night if I could." I winked at him before turning away, grabbing a small stack of napkins and carrying it over to Angelo.

"Order's in. It'll be out shortly," I told him.

A slow smile twisted across his mouth. "Thanks, Shay."

"No problem."

"You seeing anyone?"

His question caught me off guard, and I stumbled a little as I was turning away. "Uh..." Our eyes met. "What?"

He laughed. "Dating. Boyfriend. You got one?" Leaning back in his chair, Angelo regarded me with kind eyes, but his mouth was all trouble, and lifted flirtatiously.

I glanced back at the kitchen, saw Sean busy working and concentrating hard, then turned back to Angelo.

How to answer this...

"It's complicated," I settled on. "And new. Very new. Very, very new."

Angelo chuckled. "Bad timing on my part then. I should've said something last month."

I shrugged and offered him a smile.

I didn't know how to respond. Angelo was good looking and always nice to me, but would I have been interested last month?

No. Probably not. I was in love with Sean last month...

"Well, your order will be up soon," I repeated, not knowing what else to say. This was slightly awkward.

Angelo kept the grin he was wearing, revealing not one hint of awkwardness on his part, then he pulled out his phone when it beeped from his pocket.

Just as I turned away, Tori grabbed my elbow and hurriedly pulled me to the back of the restaurant, directly opposite the kitchen.

"What?" I whispered.

"What nothing. You need to fill me in on the details," she said, releasing my elbow and standing to face me. "I've been too busy training Little Miss Zero Personality to get a moment of gossip time. Now, spill it."

I looked over Tori's shoulder and watched Lauren study her nails like there was some big, important, hidden message written all over them. Then I glanced at the kitchen window again.

Sean was looking at me. I waved at him before turning back to Tori.

"Oh, my God, you totally made your move," she said, a big grin on her face. "What happened? Tell me now."

No way was I planning on telling anyone about the words I'd seen tattooed on Sean's skin. Or about the bucket. And since I hadn't really made my move, I wasn't sure there was too much to tell.

Then I remembered all those positive things I was trying to keep focus on. The memory of them filled me up inside. I instantly felt better.

"Well, I didn't exactly get to make my move, but I did spend the night with him."

Tori's eyes widened. "Get out," she whispered.

"Oh, I'm out. And it was amazing."

"Did he hold you?"

"Yep."

"Kiss?"

"No, but I got a legit hug out of him, and it was the best hug of my life, hands down. Plus, he sort of held my face while we were talking. His thumb was definitely on my jaw."

Tori smiled and held up her hand.

I high-fived it.

Then both of us started giggling.

"This is awesome. When are you going to make your move, though?" she asked.

"When the time is right and when he's ready," I told her, and seeing confusion in Tori's eyes, I explained. "He needs time to process. I can't rush him. He's been through so much, T, and it isn't easy for him to accept any goodness put on him. His first reaction is to reject it."

"Well, he has you now, plus he's got his kids back. And I told Jamie to get on board and pull Stitch into the group."

"That's seriously cool of you, T. Thanks."

Tori played it off with a shrug. "Stitch is in with us," she said. "He's got a family for life now, no matter what. We'll take care of him."

They would take care of him.

Hearing that, I threw my arms around her.

Dogwood Beach wasn't full of good people. It was full of the *best* people.

Chapter Fourteen

SEAN

One Week and Four Days Later

I tied my hair back and washed up at the sink, then I stepped inside the kitchen, where J.R. was watching between the fryer and the patty he had searing on the grill.

Turned out the kid wasn't too bad after all. Any shift I needed covered or switched, he handled. I didn't even mind all the talking he did back here anymore. I was used to it.

"Hey," I greeted him.

J.R. lifted his chin. "What's up? Your girl's on the warpath today."

"What?"

He tipped his chin at the window.

Brow pulling tight, I stepped up to the counter and scanned the floor until I spotted Shayla.

She was up at the front stacking menus together in a way it had me wondering what the fuck those menus did to piss her off.

The one guy seated at a table was watching her with suspicion. He was the only person waiting on food.

Typically, this place being dead wasn't a good thing. Right now, I was thinking differently about that.

"She been like this all morning?" I asked, keeping my focus on Shayla.

"Yep. Got here and went straight for Nate's office, then came out of it looking ready to lay the smackdown on somebody. From what I can tell, she's pissed off at everyone. She's even been throwing tickets at me, and I know I didn't do *shit*."

I watched Shayla drop a menu, pick it up, and slam it down on the stack she'd just straightened. Her face was flushed. It looked like she was panting.

I looked at Nate's door.

What the fuck did he say to her?

Knowing Shayla was clearly upset about something pissed me off. And I could've waited until she walked over here and gotten answers out of her, but I went straight to the fucking source instead.

Like an idiot.

"What the fuck is she pissed about?" I demanded, storming into Nate's office without bothering to knock.

Phone pressed to his ear, he stared at me, then muttered, "I gotta call you back."

I waited until the phone hit the desk before I asked again, "Shayla. What the fuck is she pissed about?"

Nate leaned back in his chair. "You wanna rephrase that question, since you're speaking to the man who could fire you?" he asked.

"No, I really don't. She's pissed, and I wanna know why. What'd you say to her?"

"She came in here telling me to give you a raise."

Hearing that, my head jerked back. "She *what*?"

Nate nodded. "*Telling me* to give you one, not asking me, which wouldn't have made a difference. I said it wasn't any of her business what I paid you, and that she was out of line. She didn't like hearing that. I'm assuming that's why she's pissed."

I stood taller and brought my arms across my chest. "I didn't ask her to do that," I said quickly, needing Nate to know this. I didn't want him thinking I'd send Shayla or anyone else in here to speak for me.

"Yeah, I figured." Nate pulled off his glasses to rub at his eyes, breathing heavily, then he slid the frames up his nose and peered at me again. "Any reason why Shayla would come in here demanding I double your paycheck?"

I blinked. "She said *double?*"

Holy fuck. What the fuck?

"Yeah. She also told me I needed to reach out to the local paper and get them to feature you. Then she blasted me for not having a billboard up already with your face on it."

"Jesus," I mumbled, shaking my head.

What the fuck was she thinking? Why would she do that?

"I don't know what's going on, and I don't want to know," Nate said. "Everyone signed the same employee handbook when they got hired on, so they know, personal lives stay out of this building. If that becomes a problem, I'll call people in here. Is it going to be a problem, Sean?"

I looked at him, promising, "No, I'll handle it. She won't do that shit again."

"Good. Because if you're not happy about something here, I expect you to come to *me* about it. I thought I communicated that to you already."

"You did. I don't know why she came in here. I got no clue what her deal is."

I was sure as fuck going to find out, though.

Nate nodded, accepting my response. "So, everything's good then? With J.R., the schedule, *your pay*. The fact that your face *isn't* on a billboard."

"Yeah. Please, don't do that," I rasped.

Jesus. I would hate that fucking shit.

"Wasn't planning on it," he informed me, then he sat forward to pick up the phone. "All right. You done?"

"Yeah."

"You come in here yelling at me like that again, you'll be out of a job."

"Got it."

Getting my cue to leave, I turned and moved out of Nate's office, pulling the door closed behind me and getting Shayla's attention when I did it.

She was standing at the bar filling a cup with ice and immediately went stiff seeing me and the office I was coming from. Her eyes widened.

I shook my head and moved into the kitchen.

"I'm heading out. You got this?" J.R. asked.

"Yeah. Go."

"Cool, man. Later."

"Later."

He moved past me and stepped out.

Nothing was cooking or needing my attention, so I went to the counter and watched Shayla take the drink to the one patron we had. He was eating now. After saying something to him, she turned and locked eyes with me, flattening her hands to her stomach and looking regretful. Then she walked over.

Slow. As. Fuck.

"What's your problem?" I asked when she finally reached the counter. "You went in and told Nate to double my pay? What the *fuck*, Shayla? Did I ask you to do that?"

She shook her head.

"Explain. Now."

"I'm just... not in the best mood today," she said quietly.

"Yeah, I picked up on that when I saw you assaulting the menus like they personally did you wrong or somethin'."

"They just wouldn't line up properly."

I stared at her.

Her shoulders dropped on a sigh. "I went to my parents' house last night to visit, and I finally got to ask Dominic about your dad."

There it was—the reason she was pissed.

"And it just made me so angry," she continued. "Him leaving you with that horrible woman and then going to make another family...how could he not take you away from her? How could he not go and at least check on you? I don't understand that. He's just as much of a monster as she is. He's just as bad." Cheeks burning, she shook her head. "I left my parents' house pissed off, then I went to bed pissed off, I came in here pissed off." Her eyes softened. "I don't know what I was thinking going to Nate, though. I shouldn't have said anything. That isn't my business."

"No, it isn't," I agreed, drawing my arms across my chest.

"I just want you to have the best of everything, Sean, because you deserve it, and that includes this job. I want people knowing how talented you are. I thought the advertisement thing was a good idea."

"You think I'd want that? My face on a fuckin' billboard?"

"I don't know. It might be kinda cool."

I glared at her.

"Okay, okay," she huffed, looking down. "Maybe I went a little overboard in my suggestions. To be honest, though, I only gave him two of the six ideas I had. I was also going to recommend we change the name of this place to Sean's Grill or something equally awesome."

I felt my mouth twitch.

This fucking girl. Christ.

Going to Nate was just another way of her having my back. And I knew Shayla—she would've done that shit even if I had known about it ahead of time and asked her not to. That was just how she was.

And I did not hate that about her.

Still, she didn't need to be doing it again. I wanted to keep working here.

"I got a good setup here, Shayla. I'm good with this job, all right?"

She lifted her head.

"You bringing me food and swapping tacos for furniture is one thing. But going to Nate behind my back when I did not ask you to step in? Don't fuckin' do that."

"I know. I'm sorry." She pressed her hands to the sides of her face. "Please don't be mad at me."

"I ain't mad at you. I'm not sure I know how to be," I told her, and hearing that, she lowered her hands to the counter and began to smile, then lost it. Her nostrils flared, and a second later, her face tightened in rage. "What now?"

"I'm remembering why I was pissed," she muttered.

"I don't think about him. You shouldn't either."

"I can't help it. Today is a lost cause. I'm going to stay aggravated, I just know it."

Seeing the front doors open over her shoulder, I told her, "Maybe this will help," then I met her eyes, gestured with my head, and watched her slowly turn around.

She gasped, then looked back at me and grinned. "Oh, my God," she whispered.

"Daddy! We're here!" Caroline yelled, running past the tables with Val behind her carrying Fiona.

The girls had been to the house a couple times now, but this was the first time they were coming to see me here.

Before I'd had to deal with that shit in Nate's office, I'd been looking forward to this all morning, knowing Val was bringing them in today for a special treat since schools were closed. I wanted them seeing where I worked. And knowing Shayla would get to experience this with me was something else I'd been looking forward to.

I knew she'd love every second of this. Anything that made me happy, she celebrated.

Moving out of the kitchen and into the restaurant, I bent down at the bar and scooped up Caroline when she reached me. "Baby girl," I murmured against her cheek, kissing it as I stood.

Caroline wrapped her arms tight around my neck and squeezed.

I looked down the bar.

Shayla was watching me with emotion shining in her eyes.

"Hey!" Val greeted me, then she put her attention on Shayla. "Hey, girl! It's good to see you." Val set Fiona down so she could get to me, then walked to the end of the bar and gave Shayla a hug.

"You too," Shayla said, still wearing that grin while she reciprocated the embrace. "Your hair looks great."

"Oh, thanks. I have this awesome stylist. She rocks."

"Is that right?"

They both started laughing.

I held Fiona with my other arm, her butt sitting on the inside of my elbow while she tugged at the hair on my chin.

"Daddy, can I get some mac and cheese?" she asked.

"Me too! I want mac and cheese!" Caroline said.

I looked between my girls. "You got it."

"Yes!" Caroline pumped her fist in the air. "Oh, wait, Daddy, we have something to give you." She wiggled so I'd set her down, then ran over to Val and started digging through the bag hanging off her shoulder.

"Here," Val said, stopping Caroline from searching and reaching inside the bag herself. She pulled out a pink ticket and handed it to Caroline, who ran back over to me the second it was in her hand.

"Now you can come to our recital, Daddy," Caroline said, handing me the ticket. "You're coming, right? We're saving you a *seat*!"

I smiled at her.

"It's next Friday," Val said. "We just got the tickets last night. The girls couldn't wait to give you one."

"Daddy, are you coming?" Fiona asked. She was playing with my hair now, her fingers weaving through the ends sticking out of the tie I'd secured it with.

I was already on the schedule to work Friday night, but figured I could get J.R. to switch with me. I didn't think it would be an issue.

"I gotta work somethin' out, but I'll be there," I told Fiona, kissing her smiling cheek.

Caroline started jumping up and down. "We're dancing to *The Lion King* and *Swan Lake*! We're gonna look like princesses, Daddy!"

"Oh, that reminds me." Val turned to Shayla. "Do you think you could do their hair for the recital? I can manage basic ponytails and braids, but beyond that, I'm terrible. And Little Ms. Caroline is requesting something fancy."

"Princess hair!" Caroline shrieked.

Shayla laughed. "Absolutely. I specialize in princess hair. I even have some pink we can put in, if that's okay with everyone." She looked from Val to me.

"Pink? I can get *pink* in my hair?" Caroline clapped a hand over her mouth and started squealing. Her face turned bright red.

"I want pink hair too!" Fiona cried.

"Oh, uh . . . " Val stammered, appearing unsure.

"It washes out right away. It's not permanent," Shayla explained.

Val visibly relaxed. "Okay, yeah. That sounds great. Pink hair for everyone!"

"Even Daddy!" Caroline pointed up at me and giggled.

"No, baby girl. Not me."

"Aw, come on," Shayla teased.

Holding her eyes, I shook my head. She bit her lip and smiled.

"All right, why don't we get a seat?" Val suggested. "Daddy can't cook your mac and cheese if he doesn't get in the kitchen."

"I'll grab some menus. Sit wherever you want," Shayla offered, stepping away.

I watched her walk toward the front, then I followed behind Caroline, who ran ahead. She picked a booth by the window.

"I'm so glad you're coming to the recital. The girls will be so happy," Val said, walking over with me.

"Wouldn't miss it."

She smiled and touched my arm.

"Princess drinks, right?" Shayla asked, sliding menus on the table as Val took a seat on the vacant end.

I let Fiona down and she climbed in next to Caroline, who was leaning over the table and staring at Shayla with wide, curious eyes.

"What's a princess drink?" she asked.

"Well, it's pink, of course," Shayla answered. Then she looked to Val and whispered, "Strawberry milk."

"Ooh, yum!" Val said. She glanced between the girls.

"I want a princess drink!" Fiona cried.

"Me too! I want one so bad, I'm gonna die!" Caroline shouted.

We all laughed.

Knowing what they wanted already, I bent to give the girls both a kiss on the head before I turned and headed for the kitchen so I could get started on their food.

"Two princess drinks coming up," Shayla said behind me. "Mom? What would you like?"

"I'll just have a water."

"You got it."

Quick footsteps brought Shayla to me when I'd gotten halfway to the back of the restaurant. She looped her arm through mine and leaned in close.

"Watching you with your girls is now my favorite thing to do, ever. And that includes hair," she whispered.

Something warm expanded inside my chest.

Shayla being happy for me meant a lot—I knew it would. But it felt bigger today, more important, and I didn't know if it was because my girls were involved or if it had to do with something else.

I just knew I wouldn't have enjoyed this moment so much if she hadn't been a part of it.

I wanted her around all the time now. Here and at my house and wherever the fuck I was going, I wanted her with me. I might've left to go pick her up to bring her here if she hadn't been on the schedule today.

Looking down at her, I smiled, and seeing that, Shayla grinned.

Fuck that might've. *I definitely would've left to bring her here.*

She gave my arm a squeeze, then headed for the bar to make drinks while I stepped inside the kitchen.

I got to work on the mac and cheese and grilled up some burgers to go with it when Val and the girls finished looking at the menu. Then, because we were slow, I got to step out and watch my girls eat.

I missed doing that.

They enjoyed the food. I enjoyed them being here.

And Shayla stood back and enjoyed watching it all happen.

The next day, I opened at Whitecaps, getting off around four and then dealing with bullshit the second I got home.

"Sorry, Sean. I don't know what to tell you. I'm strapped. It is what it is."

Standing in my driveway, arms pulled across my chest and mood in the fucking toilet, I shook my head and stared down Logan, a guy I've known for a long fucking time and who I'd never once wanted to beat the shit out of until this very moment.

Pretty sure it would be a good matchup too. He was my size, my height. Had a good fifteen years on me, but still.

"What the fuck am I supposed to do?" I asked him. "Where am I supposed to keep my trailer? I can't afford to store that shit somewhere. You got any idea how much that'll cost me?"

Too fucking much. I'd already priced it.

Logan glanced from me to the house then back to me. "Uh, how 'bout you sell it? Since you don't need it anymore." He gestured at the house. "What the fuck are you keeping a trailer for when you got a house?"

Jaw tight, I shook my head. "I ain't sellin' it," I growled.

I couldn't. I needed that trailer.

"You know I wouldn't do this unless I had to," he said.

I knew that. Logan was always good to me. If he didn't have reason to do this, he wouldn't.

I was just having a hard time understanding that reason right now.

"Fuck." I dragged both hands down my face. "Fuck!"

"I'm sorry, Sean. I really don't wanna fucking do this."

Shayla's car pulled up in front of the house. I turned my head and met her eyes through the window, then watched her glare at Logan before quickly reaching into her back seat for something. The driver's side door was flung open seconds later. Shayla stepped out with a can of hair spray tight in her grip and marched up the driveway, leaving the door open and the car running.

"What the fuck?" Logan asked.

Shayla's glare intensified the closer she got.

"What are you doin'?" I asked her.

She looked pissed. That I didn't get.

But it was the hair spray that was really throwing me. She was holding that thing like a giant can of pepper spray.

"I'm not doing anything..." Shayla replied. "*Yet.*" She stopped a foot away and kept her gaze trained on Logan. She had one hand on her hip while the other held the can at her side, her trigger finger ready on the nozzle.

"What's your problem?" Logan asked.

"I don't know. You tell me," she countered. "What's going on right now?"

"I don't think that's any of your business."

"It involves him." Shayla tipped her chin at me, but kept looking at Logan. "That makes it my business. You can go ahead and finish up with your conversation. I'll just be right here while you do that. Armed and ready."

My brows lifted.

"Jesus. Is she for real?" Logan muttered at my back.

Going by the looks of her, I'd say yeah, she was for real right now. And I was officially confused as fuck.

"Shayla, what are you doin'?" I asked again, my voice growing rougher and louder, which pried her eyes off Logan and got me her full attention. "Why do you look ready to take out Logan's sight with that shit?" I gestured at the can.

She shrugged. "I wanted to be prepared. You know, just in case."

"Just in case, *what*?"

"Just in case I see you looking angry or upset again, like you did when I pulled up."

I blinked.

She was ready to blind Logan for me?

As if hearing my thoughts, Shayla jerked her chin and announced, "It's cool. I got your back."

My mouth twitched. *Goddamn, this girl.*

"Oh, this is precious," Logan commented with laughter in his voice.

Ignoring Logan, I stepped in front of Shayla, watching those big, doelike eyes dilate as she tipped her head up. "You saw us, saw me pissed off, and thought I needed protectin'?" I asked her.

"Yes," she whispered.

"And instead of calling out first or, fuck, I don't know, walkin' your ass over here and askin' what was goin' on, you grabbed your idea of a weapon and armed yourself?"

"Like that can is gonna take me out," Logan muttered behind me. "I'm a big man, sweetheart."

Shayla leaned to peer around me. "Is that a challenge?" she asked.

I grabbed her shoulders and righted her while Logan kept laughing, thoroughly enjoying this exchange. "Babe, what the fuck?" I looked into Shayla's eyes. "You automatically go into attack mode for me? Why?"

"I don't know any other way to be. Not about you. I can't help it."

My chest expanded with a breath.

Fuck me.

Always doing shit like this, shit I didn't deserve. Caring for me. Looking out. Willing to go up against anyone if it meant having my back.

I bent down to get closer to her, rasping, "*Why?*"

"I can't help it," she repeated on a whisper. "I can't, Sean. I'll protect you first, ask questions later. Always. I'll take on anyone. I don't care."

"*Fuck*," I growled, cupping her face and getting even closer, needing closer. "Shayla..."

She started breathing sharp and hurried. "Sean..."

"Jesus. Let me leave before you do that shit," Logan grated.

I pulled back and looked at him.

He gazed at Shayla, eyes slightly amused, then he looked at me. "Two weeks, Sean. That's all the time I can give you. I'm sorry," he said.

Knowing I couldn't say shit to change his mind, and I was stuck to eat this, I jerked my chin. "Yeah, all right."

"I'll talk to you soon." Logan glanced at Shayla once more, shook his head while laughing low, then walked to his truck parked behind her.

"Two weeks for what?" Shayla asked me as the truck started up.

Logan held his hand out the window and pulled off, disappearing down the street.

"Sean?"

I peered down at Shayla, staring into her eyes as my thumb moved over her cheek.

She went perfectly still. She even quit breathing.

I knew I wasn't good enough to touch her like this. I wasn't good enough to be this close to her either. And I sure as fuck wasn't good enough for the taste I was wanting more than I wanted a lot of things.

I watched as she wet her lips, knowing I wasn't good enough to be watching her do that either, but I didn't care. That was the problem.

Right now, I just did not fucking care.

Fuck it. Fuck it all.

Sliding my hand to the back of her head, I slammed my mouth down on hers.

And finally, *finally*, I got that taste.

Chapter Fifteen

SHAYLA

Oh, God.

Oh, holy God, he was kissing me.

Sean was kissing me.

Sean Molina, the man I was completely insane for and wanted more than I could remember wanting *anything* in all my twenty-three years of life, had his tongue inside my mouth.

I was going to lose my ever-loving mind.

Scratch that. Nope. I lost it.

I lost it right then and there.

That was the only explanation for the way I was reacting to this kiss.

"*Yes*," I moaned while simultaneously climbing up his body and tearing at what we were both wearing. My one hand shoved up his shirt, touching his stomach, his chest, and my other hand worked at the button on my jeans while I hitched my legs around him.

I was crazy. I was trying to strip us right there in the middle of his yard so we could get skin to skin in front of his entire neighborhood.

And I didn't care one bit who saw us or if we both got arrested for indecent exposure.

With his hands full of my ass, Sean backed us up while kissing me with such hunger, I would've thought he'd never kissed a woman before if I didn't know any better.

He was sloppy and rushed and sucked so hard on my lips, it hurt.

It was the best, *the best*, kiss of my life and would forever hold that title. I just knew it.

"Fuck!" His one hand braced us on the side of the house when he nearly stumbled up the porch steps.

I didn't care if we fell. I kept kissing him everywhere.

His mouth. His cheeks. His neck. Kept gasping. Kept moaning. Kept touching him. Gripping and clawing at his muscles. I moved my hands over his back and dipped them beneath the shirt of his I couldn't get off. I grasped at his body like I was starved for it, because I was.

"Hurry," I begged. "Oh, God, please hurry. I need you to touch me."

"Keep sayin' that," he muttered.

"Touch me. I need it. I want this so bad, Sean."

So bad—he had no idea.

Sean got us up onto the porch and kicked the door open. We barely made it inside before he was on his back and I was on top of him.

That was when we went from crazy to fucking *nuts*.

"Shit!" I reached over to push the door closed so no one could watch Sean suck my breast into his mouth. "Oh, fuck...*fuck*!" *Holy Lord, that sensation. His mouth. My body. I was going to explode.* "Sean! Sean, Sean, Sean." I weaved my fingers through his hair and held him to me as he lapped my other breast and tongued my nipple.

My shirt wasn't even over my head yet. It was stuck around my neck. And my bra was still latched but shoved down to my waist.

"A year," he mumbled into my skin. "A fuckin' *year*, I wanted this." He kissed up to my neck and licked there.

Oh, God. The girls had been right. *They were right!*

I shoved my hands between us and fumbled with his belt, getting it loose, then I tried unbuttoning his jeans while Sean grabbed at the pair I was wearing. He attempted getting them over my hips but couldn't with the way I was kneeling.

"Wait. You do you, I'll do me," I told him, flopping back so my ass landed between his legs.

I pulled off my sneakers and ripped off my shirt and bra, then, leaning back, I wiggled out of my pants and panties and tossed them aside as Sean peeled off his shirt, tugged off his boots, and got one leg out of his jeans. He wasn't wearing anything under them.

I barely got a glance at his cock before we were both lunging at each other, kissing, moaning, grasping at every part of the other person we could touch.

This was madness. This was sex without thought, without pause, without question. Letting desire drive and leaving reason and all sense behind. Fuck stopping to think. Fuck wondering, *Should we? Could we? What if we did?* We were just feeling. Feeling and letting it all happen.

It was the most beautiful, chaotic thing I'd ever experienced.

I pulled off his jeans so they weren't stuck around his ankle, then I crawled closer. His hands moved under my thighs and my arms around his back, flew to his shoulders and braced when he slid, hard and heavy between my legs.

Sean's hands shook on my body.

His gaze was wild, beautiful, and terrified.

"Take me," I whispered, staring deep into his eyes and speaking inside his mouth. "Please, Sean, take me."

He fingers tensed. His body grew taut and still.

"*Please*," I begged.

I sank down as he pumped up his hips, filling me in one hard thrust.

"Ah!" Neck arching, I cried out.

A strangled groan tore out of Sean's throat. His breath came out in hot pants on my neck, and his fingers on my skin dug in, then his hands slid to my hips as he stretched out beneath me.

Head lifting, he stared between us.

My body was ready—I was so wet, I could feel it sticking to my thighs—but the fact that I'd gone nearly two years without sex wasn't lost on me in that moment. Sean was so full inside me, and it could've, might've hurt if I didn't want this as much as I did. If I didn't want to move as much as I wanted to move. If I hadn't thought about this moment, obsessed over it, wanting wanting wanting it to happen so badly and never thinking it would.

I didn't feel pain. I felt him—his fingers digging into my hips and his legs beneath my own, the sweat on his skin as I stroked my hands up his body. His heartbeat under my palm.

I felt him, and I wanted more.

When I shifted my hips forward, he groaned, and *God*, that sound, so deep and tortured, it broke out bumps of pleasure along my skin.

Throwing my head back, I moved on top of Sean while he held me and watched me and said words like "fuck" and "please" and "Shayla, God, Shayla." I sped up when he grabbed my breast. I slowed down when his noises grew indecent, because I didn't want this to end, ever. I wanted this man inside me and touching me and begging me to fuck him until I stopped breathing.

"Yes, *yes*," I cried.

Sean shot up, slid his hand through my hair, and kissed me hard, drawing my tongue inside his mouth. He sucked on my lip. He bit it. He groaned against my cheek and then his voice was in my ear.

"A fuckin' *year*," he growled. "Wanted you. Needed you."

Oh, *God*.

I whimpered, head hitting his shoulder, and held onto his neck. I felt his grip on my hip move and tighten.

He took over.

Sean grinded me down. Harder than I'd been doing. Faster than I could go on my own. He built it in me until I gasped and dug my fingers into his skin, and then he flipped me so my back was on the cold wood.

He crawled between my legs, slid his hands against my own, interlocking our fingers above me, and *holy shit*, we were holding hands for the first time and it was everything I dreamed it would be. Then he pushed inside again, driving deep.

"Sean!" I cried out, my body squeezing around him. I shuddered in pleasure. "Oh, God, don't stop, don't stop."

Sean released my hands to lean back and watch me come, his hair falling out of the tie at the base of his skull, his lips parted, his eyes moving all over my face. He stared at me in wonder. He stared at me how I knew I stared at him, not just now but all the time. Then he buried his face in my neck and fucked me against the floor, pumping faster, harder. He grunted into my skin and kept his hand beneath my head so he wouldn't hurt me. He fucked like a man who'd been waiting his entire life to do it. It was frenzied and nearly violent. Then he sat back, grabbed my hips, and yanked me toward him so he sank deep.

Thrusting in quick jerks, Sean stared at my body, staying quiet except for those sexy, impatient noises he'd make while looking between my clit and my breasts. He grew close—the muscles in his arms and abs flexing. His breaths became ragged.

"Sean."

He watched my mouth when I told him, "Come inside me."

His eyes flashed.

I bit my lip and moaned, reaching out so I could touch him. I held his hands on my body. I never wanted them to move.

He jerked wildly now, his fingers digging into my hips and his nostrils flaring as his orgasm took hold.

"Fuck," he groaned. "Ah, fuck *fuck*! Shayla... *Shayla*."

I watched him bare his teeth and the cords in his neck bulge as he finished deep inside me. His body sagged, then he shifted back to pull out his dick. He pushed his hair out of his face and looked down between us. He was panting.

I pushed up to my elbows and stared, getting a good look at Sean for the first time.

His cock was long, thick, wet from us both, and uncut. I watched him with fascination. I knew nothing about uncircumcised penises, but I suddenly wanted to become an expert on the subject. The urge to touch him there and explore him was overwhelming. He was sexy as fuck.

But first...

I sat up and shifted to my knees in front of Sean, taking his face in my hands and forcing him to look at me.

"Talk to me," I said, feeling the severity of this moment at the same time as reality hit hard.

Sean and I just had sex.

Without a condom.

And he came inside me.

Which I totally told him to do.

Sean caught his breath, stared deep into my eyes, and shook his head, sharp and quick. Then just as my heart began to sink and worry filled me, he slid his arms between us, held my face, and kissed me.

Slow.

Soft.

Sweet.

Oh, *God*. This kiss might've trumped the one outside.

Or at least tied it. His lips owned me.

I made little noises of pleasure against his mouth. I held on to his forearms for dear life. I feared I would float away.

Sean kissed me like that for minutes. It was beautiful and everything I'd been hoping for since I started dreaming about kissing him. Then he kissed my cheeks and my forehead. He pressed his lips all over my face, to my closed eyes and the tip of my nose.

I smiled against the tickle of his beard and giggled when he rubbed it into my face.

Then he pulled me against his chest and kissed my hair.

"Sean?" I whispered.

I had so much to say. So much we probably needed to talk about. I also wanted to remain silent and still and simply listen to Sean breathe.

"Think your car's still runnin'," he mumbled.

My eyes shot wide. Okay, plan C then.

Cursing, I got to my feet and started grabbing up my clothes, telling him while I hastily dressed, "Oh, my God. And the door's still open. *Shit!* That's basically an invite."

Sean chuckled, and because he only had jeans to pull on for him to be decent, he stepped out to take care of my car before I even had my shirt on.

Once covered, I walked out and stood on the porch, watching him.

After fetching the can of hair spray I'd dropped and forgotten, Sean pulled my car into the driveway instead of leaving it in the street, then he locked it up and walked across the grass barefoot. When he reached the porch steps, I was laughing.

"Oops," I mumbled behind my fingers.

Oh, well. This neighborhood was safe enough.

Smiling, Sean handed me the keys and climbed the steps. Then he put his hand on my hip and backed me inside the house, closing the door behind us without looking. He stopped us just inside the living room and stared at me.

And since he wasn't smiling anymore, I wasn't either.

"You okay?" I asked.

"I finished in you," he said.

Oh, right. That.

"You did." I placed my hands flat on his chest. "I told you to."

"Why?"

My fingertips pressed in.

Because I've wanted this for so long.

Because you're amazing and this, us together, is amazing, and because I knew that would be amazing too.

Because I'm in love with you and have been since last summer.

I had options, all ready to leave my tongue. It was simple: I just needed to pick one.

"Because you deserved it," I said.

Sean's brow rose.

My God, how stupid did I sound right now? Like Sean had won a prize or something?

Great job on all the fucking, now finish inside me because you've sure earned this pussy!

Ugh!

"Um." I shifted on my feet as nerves prickled low in my belly and the urge to run and hide grew overwhelming. *Explain yourself, Shay!* "You know, aside from there not being any risk of getting me pregnant since I'm on the pill, I just meant, like, you deserved it based on how good you are...as a person. Not at sex. But, well, that too. You were awesome at that. So, so great. Amazing. All the stars."

Sean's mouth twitched.

I could feel heat rising in my cheeks. I wanted to dig myself a hole right there beneath his house and never climb out of it.

"I just mean, you're good enough for sex."

Sean cocked his head.

No. God, fix it!

"All sex. Sex in its completion."

His brow furrowed.

I began speaking at a much faster pace.

"You're good enough for someone who doesn't need to be paid. Someone you can share sex with and have it be meaningful, you know? *Special sex.* You're good enough for special sex, Sean!"

He stared at me.

Sweet Jesus, I sounded like an idiot.

Dropping my head to his chest, I groaned. "Am I making sense at all? I feel like I should just stop talking."

His body shook against mine with a chuckle, then, feeling his hands in my hair, I glanced up.

His lips were curling ever so slightly.

"Do you understand what I'm saying?" I questioned hesitantly.

His eyes got soft and a little sad. "I'm good enough for you," he said, voice quiet.

"*Yes.*" I pressed closer. "That's exactly what I'm saying. That's what I've been saying all along." He tried looking down and away, but I wouldn't let him. I held his face. "You deserve love and kindness because you put out those things, Sean. You deserve to feel wanted. I want you. I want you so much. Let yourself feel that."

He sucked in a breath.

"Okay?" I asked.

He stared at me for a moment, then letting his eyes slip closed, he pressed his forehead against mine, breathing slowly and evenly, and I nearly asked again—I was ready to repeat my entire speech—but Sean's head gave a slight jerk against mine.

Knowing that was his way of saying yes, I clung to him.

Finally.

"Do me a favor?" he asked.

"Anything," I rushed out.

God, I meant that too. I'd do anything for Sean. I wouldn't even question it.

Sean leaned back to look at me. "Don't stop talkin'," he said. "I like hearin' you, Shayla. I always did. I gotta keep hearin' you."

The air went out of my lungs.

Holy fuck. That might've been the sweetest thing anyone had ever said to me. Lord knows, I was a talker. I knew I was. I also knew it annoyed a lot of people. They told me.

And now I knew it did not annoy Sean.

Hot damn.

I grinned at him, stepping closer and curling my hands around his ribs. "Would you like me to tell you *specifically* what all I found to be amazing about our sex? I could go on for hours."

This was not an exaggeration.

His dick alone was deserving of mad props.

Sean bent and pressed a kiss to my forehead. "Tell me whatever you want. Just do it while I make us some dinner. I'm fuckin' starved."

My brows shot up as he pulled away. "Dinner? Ooh, am I getting my *chips?*" I asked excitedly, bouncing on my toes.

Sean smiled over his shoulder as he headed for the kitchen.

Fuck. Yes.

I was getting my chips.

After cleaning up in the bathroom and setting our shoes against the wall so they weren't in the middle of the floor anymore, I walked over to one of the bar stools at the counter overlooking the kitchen and sat down, watching Sean in his element.

He grabbed two skillets out of a cabinet—a cast-iron one and another that was much deeper than the skillets I had at my place—then he went to the refrigerator and pulled out potatoes, some meat wrapped in butcher's paper, two sticks of butter, and some garlic. He poured oil into the deep skillet and got that heating up, along with the cast-iron, then he got to work on the potatoes.

And he did all this wearing nothing but those jeans.

It hit me then, while I was admiring Sean's body, that he did not have any *clue* how I felt about the way he looked, and that bothered me.

"You're really hot," I said.

Sean paused his work on the potatoes and looked up at me. His mouth twitched.

"And sexy," I continued. "I haven't been this attracted to someone my entire life, I don't think. I like everything about you."

Sean stared at me, mouth no longer twitching, but there was an intensity in his eyes now I really liked seeing on him, enough that I opened my mouth to list each and every single quality about Sean's appearance so I could keep seeing it, but then he set down the knife he was holding, stepped over to the sink so he was standing directly in front of me, and leaned forward while grabbing hold of my neck. He pulled me gently, meeting me halfway across the counter, and pressed his mouth firm against mine.

It was a short kiss, but damn, was it hot.

He pushed his tongue inside my mouth. He sucked on my lips. He growled like he wanted to fuck me.

Then Sean leaned away but kept his hand on my neck, our faces close. He stared into my eyes.

"Everything," he said in that deep, gravelly voice. "I feel that too."

Holy crap. Sean liked everything about me. *Everything.*

"Awesome," I whispered.

He chuckled. "Even that—you bein' funny is sexy," he informed me, releasing my neck and moving back over to the cutting board.

"That's good, since I'm hilarious at least five days a week," I told him.

Sean picked up the knife, doing this grinning, then he got back to work while I traced my fingertips around my mouth, still feeling him there.

I watched him start on the chips.

I stared at Sean's hand and his fingers curled under as he chopped at rapid speed. Perfectly uniform thin slices of potato toppled over onto the cutting board.

I'd bet the hair on my head each of those slices measured the exact same size.

Val had said Sean had always been a good cook, and I'd watched Sean plenty of times before do his thing at Whitecaps. I knew he had mad skill, but remembering those first couple days after he got hired, something didn't make sense.

"Whitecaps wasn't your first job as a cook, right?" I asked, chin resting on my hand as I studied him. "You've been a cook for a while?"

Sean kept his focus as he answered. "Working cook, no. I did shit on my own 'cause no one was around to do it for me. Had a handful of jobs before Nate gave me a break, but nothing I kept longer than a couple weeks. I fucked around a lot back then."

"But you've had your skills for a while..."

Sean jerked his shoulder. "Guess so."

"So how come you cut yourself so much when you first started at Whitecaps?"

He stayed silent for a moment, thinking as he prepared the next potato. "I don't know. Nerves, I guess."

"Why were you so nervous?"

"Needed the job," he stated plainly, but his voice sounded tighter. "I was tryin' to be someone for my girls. They deserved it. I couldn't mess up again."

My stomach instantly knotted up.

I sat up taller and watched Sean grab a large bowl out of a cabinet and dump the potato slices in.

"But...the girls at work, we all call you Stitch," I said.

He smirked and began seasoning the potatoes.

I didn't understand his reaction. He should've been angry about that.

"Why do you let us?" I asked. "We were poking a little fun, and you were scared you'd mess up and ruin your chances of seeing your girls again. My God, Sean. Why didn't you tell us not to call you that? Why *don't you?*"

I hated how thoughtless I'd been. I should've realized how nervous he was back then. I should've picked up on that.

For fuck's sake, I stared at him enough. Why didn't I see it?

"Nobody is calling you that again. I'll make sure of it," I promised.

After dinner, I was making some calls.

Sean shook up the potatoes so they were evenly coated, then he sat the bowl down and looked up at me. "You asked," he said. "Anyone else, I might've said somethin'. It was you so I didn't."

I blinked at him.

"You didn't mind it because it was me asking?"

He jerked his chin.

Whoa.

"Do you *like it?*"

"Don't hate it," he answered.

"If you don't like it, Sean, we can stop..."

"Did I say I don't like it?"

"No, but *not hating it* isn't really liking something," I argued. "I feel bad."

He flattened his hands on the counter and leaned closer. "Don't," he ordered, holding my eyes and I swore, it was as if he was begging me not to say anything to anyone. "If I didn't want them callin' me that, I'd say somethin'. Same goes for anything else they do. I don't mind it."

I thought about how often the girls bothered Sean at work while he was cooking, how Tori called him sweetie sometimes, how Syd always smiled at him and tried getting Sean to engage. And last, I thought about all those hugs he'd received the other night, plus the kiss on the cheek, and how he didn't do a damn thing to stop them, when he could've.

Sean didn't mind any of that. And I thought maybe that was because he was getting attention in the form of kindness from a bunch of women who could give it good, when he'd gone most of his life without it. In a way, even the nickname was done with affection. There wasn't any malice intended. Yes, we'd been teasing him a little, but it was all out of love. It was just another way of us welcoming Sean into our work family and letting him know he belonged there.

I changed my mind. I would not be making any calls later.

"Okay," I told him, smiling and going back to resting my chin on my hand. "We'll keep calling you Stitch. I won't say anything. You may resume the important work you're doing."

He chuckled, then reached for the meat he'd set out. "You like steak?"

"Nope. I love it."

Sean unwrapped the two thick cuts and seasoned them up good, then he seared them in the cast-iron with some butter and garlic.

"So, that guy you were talking to outside, who was he?"

"Logan," Sean answered, watching the steaks closely. "We go way back. I met him when I was sixteen. He used to own a Laundromat I stole clothes from. Caught me one day doin' it and could've turned me in. He didn't."

"Why not?"

"Probably felt sorry for me. I was living on the streets then."

"You stole clothes from Laundromats?"

Sean jerked his chin, explaining, "Easier than taking them from a store. You gotta worry about those bullshit security tags."

Huh. Well, that was one way to beat the system.

Sean caught up some of the butter-garlic mixture and spooned it over top of the steaks.

"And the two weeks comment?" I inquired.

"I got my trailer when I was eighteen, but I couldn't afford to keep it anywhere. Rent is no fuckin' joke. Logan let me keep it on his property and didn't charge me. He's got land. I just had to help him tend to it. That was the trade-off."

I smiled.

I immediately liked Logan and set a mental reminder to send him an apology for my behavior ASAP. My stationery would work just fine for that.

"When I got locked up this last time, he kept my trailer there, which was a good fuckin' thing too, since I didn't have anywhere to go when I got out. But now he's gotta sell his land 'cause he needs the money. I got two weeks to find a place for my trailer, and I don't know where the fuck I'm gonna keep it. I don't got enough room here. Plus, the fuckin' HOA wouldn't let me keep it in my yard. I can't afford rent. Not with payin' on the house." Sean shook his head and cursed. "I don't know what the fuck I'm gonna do."

"Can't you just sell it?"

"Fuck, no. I need that trailer."

"Why?"

"It's my backup. I need a backup."

"For what?"

"For when I fuck up."

I stared at Sean. "But... you're not going to fuck up," I told him.

He laughed, but it wasn't a happy one. "I will. I fuck up everything eventually."

Pain circled my heart. How could he think that?

"Sean." I waited for him to look up at me before I continued. "You will not fuck up," I insisted. "Those girls are too important to you.

And you've worked so hard to get them back...you won't mess this up. I know you won't."

Sean was watching me with such intent, I momentarily worried about the steaks.

"Sell the trailer. You don't need it anymore," I said, and then with emphasis, I added, "*You got this.*"

I was referring to his beautiful life with his girls, and also, the steaks.

I didn't know why I'd been so worried. He could probably cook with his eyes closed.

Sean took in a deep breath before resuming his concentration. He didn't argue with me about it anymore. I took that as a good sign—he was hearing me. He'd at least consider selling the trailer.

When the steaks were nearly finished, Sean dropped the potato slices into the oil and fried them up. Within ten minutes or so, I was taste testing one and giving my approval.

"Holy crap, that's good," I mumbled around my bite, moaning and sucking seasoning off my fingertips. "I could eat my weight in these."

Sean smiled and handed me another, which I gobbled up.

After loading up our plates and grabbing drinks, we took our seats at the kitchen table.

Some people liked to sit and enjoy food together while staying silent. I have never been one of those people. You could ask my brothers.

"So, tell me how you met Val."

Sean paused in his eating and looked up from his plate. "You serious?"

"Yes." I giggled at his expression—a fifty-fifty mix of confusion and interest. "I'm curious."

I was. I wanted to know how long they'd been together and at what point in Sean's life she'd entered it. And I wanted this information coming from Sean. I could've asked Val, but I didn't.

Sean eyed me a moment longer. Then he sat back, took a swig of his Coke, and revealed, "I stole her wallet."

My mouth dropped open. "You did not."

"Yeah, I did." He chuckled. "Ask her. She'll confirm it."

"That's crazy! What happened? Did you give it back?"

"After she followed me to the bridge I was living under, yeah. I thought I got away with it at first."

Holy crap. "How old were you?" I asked.

"Eighteen."

"And how long had you been living under that bridge?"

"Don't know. A couple months, maybe. I moved around a lot. I had to."

I tried to push away thoughts I didn't want filling my head right now, but I couldn't. I hated thinking about Sean living on the street. It killed me knowing he was all alone. But what other option did he have?

"When did you move out of your house?" I asked, cutting off another bite of steak and popping it into my mouth. It was juicy and seasoned to perfection. I'd never had a steak this good before.

Sean did the same, except his bite was twice the size of mine.

"Fifteen. I went back when it got so cold I couldn't stand it. Then I couldn't stand being there, so I'd leave again." He popped a chip in his mouth and chewed it. "Went back for the last time when I was eighteen."

"That's when you got your trailer."

"Yeah."

"Val told me she's never been in it."

Sean shook his head while grabbing his Coke. "I wouldn't let her. She was too good for it."

I smiled while he took a drink. Maybe it was strange, but I loved that he said that.

I thought about Sean at fifteen, living on the streets. I tried to picture it. Then I imagined Sean going back to that house one last time and showing off the man he'd become, against all odds. I wondered what that horrible woman thought of him.

"Have you spoken to her at all since the last time you went back?" I asked.

"Who?"

"That woman—your mom—although I don't like calling her that. She wasn't one." Bitch wasn't anything. And if I ever saw her, I'd be sure to tell her that. Using my fist.

Sean eyed me. He was so deadly serious, I lowered the chip I'd been holding and set it back on the plate.

"You okay?" I asked.

Sean looked down while cutting off another bite of steak. He ate it, then followed it up with a chip and another drink of his Coke.

"Sean?"

His eyes came up. "Told you there'd be shit I didn't talk to you about," he said, voice a low rumble. "This is one of those things. Pick another topic."

I shifted in my seat.

Crap. I was terrible about letting things go and not pushing for information. It was a major flaw of mine I lived with.

"Uh..."

No. *No*, I wouldn't do it. I wouldn't push Sean. It didn't matter how badly I wanted to know every little detail about him and hated being told I wouldn't get all those details.

"*Pick another topic*," he repeated, slower and in a harsher tone.

"You're a good man," I blurted out.

It was the first thought that entered my head. It was sometimes the only thought that filled it.

Hearing me, Sean's expression softened.

"You deserve an amazing life," I continued, my voice gentled. "I feel like everyone sees that but you. Your girls don't hate you for what you did, Sean. They love you. Don't you see how loved you are?"

He slumped back in his chair, pushed his hair back, which was completely out of the tie now, and rubbed at his face, giving me full view of his chest and the ink that covered it.

I searched for the words I knew were there. It didn't take me long to find them.

"I'll be right back," I said, getting to my feet and padding across the room in a hurry. I threw the door open and darted outside.

Still barefoot, I jogged across the grass and unlocked my car.

With my lower half hanging out the door, I rummaged around the glove compartment for the black Sharpie I knew was in there. When I closed my hand around it, I smiled.

"*Yes*," I whispered.

Then I grabbed my purse out of the back and returned to the house in the same hurry I'd left it, bursting through the door.

"Come with me," I instructed, meeting Sean's eyes before I dropped my purse on the couch and turned for the hallway.

"Why?"

I gazed back at him over my shoulder. I didn't answer.

Seeing the seriousness in my eyes, Sean pushed his chair back and stood. That was a smart move on his part. I was geared up and ready to drag his body, dead weight and all, if he hadn't gotten up.

I stepped inside his bedroom and waited at the foot of the bed, then, when he entered, I pointed at the mattress with the marker and ordered, "Please sit."

Sean brought his arms across his chest and stared at me. "This important?"

"Yes."

"Important enough we're lettin' the rest of our food get cold?"

I nodded firmly. "It is. And that's saying a lot, since that is the best steak I've ever eaten, and you already know how I feel about those chips. I should've done this already."

"Steak reheated is shit," he informed me.

"Not if you sear it," I shot back, watching his head tilt in appreciation and the corner of his mouth lift.

I knew a thing or two about cooking meat.

"This is urgent, Sean, and I'd rather do it in here. I have a feeling this will lead to something I'd very much like to experience in this bed, considering how many times I've thought about it."

His brows ticked up. "You talkin' about fuckin' or somethin' else?"

I shivered. Lord, his candor was hot as hell. It made my bones turn to jelly.

"Honestly? I'm talking about fucking and the things that typically lead up to fucking we have yet to dabble in."

"Dabble in?"

"Practice. Familiarize ourselves with..."

A slow, sexy smile took shape across his mouth. I shivered again.

"Okay, please sit down before I jump you and bypass the *vital thing* that needs to happen. I'll be pissed if I don't do this now."

"I don't know... I'm kinda wantin' to stall a little."

My lips parted. *Oh, my God, was he...*

"Are you flirting with me?"

"I'm fuckin' trying to."

My heart fluttered.

Holy shit.

I dropped my head back and groaned. "Sean, please come over here and sit down!" I begged, squirming where I stood. "You're *killing me.*"

He really was. Sean flirting was now my kryptonite, right behind Sean shirtless, Sean smiling, Sean doing anything in my general vicinity.

He was grinning still when I lowered my head and looked at him, and he kept that grin walking to the bed and taking a seat.

"I had no idea you had such mad flirting skills," I said, motioning for him to scoot back so he was leaning against the headboard. I straddled his lap.

"Mm." He caught my hips and held me there. "They ain't that good if you had to ask if I was doin' it."

"I was just surprised. You haven't flirted with me yet," I told him.

"No?"

My brow furrowed, and I leaned back. "Have you?"

Sean's mouth decided to blow my mind with this part smirk, part mischievous grin thing I had yet to experience.

It was pure magic, let me tell you.

"Stop it. I need focus," I scolded, feeling his body quake beneath me with a soundless chuckle. Then I shifted back a little to allow me some space to write. Looking at his chest, I uncapped the marker.

"What are you doin'?" he asked.

I didn't speak yet.

I leaned in and carefully pressed the blunt tip to his skin where there wasn't any ink, and wrote my first word in a slant up his right pec.

Beautiful.

"I have to apologize for something," I said as I continued writing words on Sean's skin. I dragged the tip up the side of his neck and in scripted print wrote *Deserving*. "I lied to you the other night when I slept over. I wasn't crying because I'd been throwing up. I wasn't even throwing up at all."

"What?"

I met his eyes and nodded, then I wrote the word *Important* curling over his left shoulder. "I was looking at your tattoos while you slept because I hadn't really gotten a chance to study them yet, and I saw those words, Sean. This one," I stopped writing, and with my other hand I rubbed my thumb over the word *Nothing*.

His grip on my body changed. It became severe. It nearly hurt.

"And this one," I touched the word *Loser*, then our gazes met.

There was fear in his eyes. And they were suddenly wet with tears. My heart sank.

I sat the marker down and cupped his face. "Sean, why? Why do you have those words on you? Did she put them there?"

He tried looking down and away, he tried to hide his tears from me, but I wouldn't let him.

"Sweetie, it's okay," I said. I could feel my own eyes watering now. "You can tell me anything. It won't change how I feel. I promise." I kept my one hand on his cheek and touched his chest with the other. "You are not these words, Sean. You aren't, and not just to me. You matter to so many."

"What are you writing on me?" he whispered. His eyes jumped between mine in panic.

"I'm writing what's true."

His chest shuddered, and he subtly shook his head.

I let go of him to pick up the marker again, and when I did, Sean wiped his forearm across his eyes and cursed.

I wanted to find that woman and slowly kill her. I'd drag it out for days. She would have an entirely new definition of pain when I was finished.

Just as I was lowering the marker to his skin again, Sean caught my wrist and stopped me.

We looked at each other. He was breathing raggedly out of his mouth, and his eyes were red.

I almost tugged my arm back to toss the marker. I almost began to sob—I shouldn't have done this. Sean crying was the saddest thing I'd ever seen and probably would ever see, and I was to blame for it. His grief was unbearable.

But then I felt my arm moving closer to his body as he slowly pulled, and when the marker touched his skin, he trembled.

"I don't have to," I whispered. "I'll stop."

"No," he rasped. He dropped his head back and squeezed his eyes shut. His hands were no longer on my body. They were curled into fists on the bed. "*Fuck*, just do it . . . hurry," he begged. "Hurry before I can't."

My breath caught.

Not days. Years—I'd make sure she suffered forever.

I blinked tears from my eyes and carefully wrote *Worthy* on his rib. I moved to his bicep and penned his value there, the other side of his neck, on his hand where *Space* was inked. I wrote the word *Loved* over top of it in heavy outline so it covered.

I had to be slow because Sean trembled, and I worried my hand would slip and the words would be too messy to read, and I couldn't have that. Even though I wanted to rush and finish so he'd relax and let me hold him, I couldn't.

I took my time, and it killed me.

"Okay," I rushed out when I'd covered everything and painted his skin with words good enough to touch it. I capped the marker and tossed it on the bed.

Sean opened his eyes. His chest shook as he breathed.

"Do you want to see it?" I asked softly.

He didn't say a word. He didn't move. I wondered if he even could.

"You don't have to get up. I can show you," I told him, swinging my leg over and sliding off the bed. I darted into the living room and pulled a compact out of my purse, then I rushed back to the bedroom and climbed on top of him again. "Here. See?" I opened the compact.

Sean lowered his eyes to the mirror when I angled it at his body.

When he read the word *Beautiful*, his gaze shot to mine.

I smiled. "You are. Not just on the outside, Sean. You have the most beautiful heart. Despite everything." I moved the mirror lower, over the word *Worthy*.

Sean's hands flew to my hips and squeezed.

"It's okay," I soothed, because I interpreted his embrace as that reactional battle he was ready to put up at any moment. Sean was gearing to contest me. I just knew he was.

But then he sat forward and dropped his head to my chest. His body sagged.

"She didn't write them," he mumbled.

I stroked my fingers through his hair. "Who did then?"

"Me."

I tensed. "*What?*"

Oh, my God, no. No. No. No.

"I'd write them all the time when I lived with her. I got good at it. Standing in front of a mirror, I could see what I was doing. It was easy."

"And you got them tattooed on you?"

He nodded. "When I was sixteen. Found a guy who didn't give a fuck about me bein' underage. He liked cash. I had some." His shoulder jerked. "Words have been there ever since."

I hadn't even considered the possibility of Sean doing this to himself, but it made sense. That woman broke him. She poisoned his mind. She might not have been the person who put those words all over Sean's skin, but she'd been holding the pen.

"Do you think they still belong there?" I asked.

Sean paused, then peered up at me when I leaned back to see him. "Don't know," he answered.

My heart stopped and startled to a pace again.

"Before . . . yeah, I did," he continued. "Met Val. Started thinking different. She was good to me. Good *for me*. I didn't deserve her."

"Yes you did," I cut in.

Sean's eyes lowered to a spot on my neck. "I was in the dark all the time, then she followed me in and got me out. I had her light. Had it tenfold when I was given my girls. I still fucked up, but I had them so it didn't matter. I slowly got a lot of those words covered but not all 'cause I couldn't. I'd still hear that bitch telling me I was nothin'. I heard it all the time. Then I fucked up all that good I had and lost it. Went back to knowin' I ain't ever gonna deserve another decent thing again, 'til you were in my ear and filling my head with shit." He looked up at me. "I still hear her telling me I'm nothin', but I hear you, and you're fuckin' loud. I don't know what I deserve anymore. I got my girls. I keep catchin' breaks. I don't fuckin' get it. I just know I don't wanna be nothin'." Tears filled his eyes again. "I'm so fuckin' sick of bein' nothin', Shayla."

"You're not nothing," I said, pulling him into a hug. His tears wet my chest. "You're not nothing, Sean. Not even close."

"Don't quit talkin' to me," he begged.

"I won't. Ever."

"I want you fillin' my head. I want it so fuckin' bad."

God, his pain—it became my own—I felt it. And I knew I'd feel it for as long as he did.

"You'll never feel alone again. I promise," I whispered.

His whole body shook.

Sean clung to me while I stroked his back and pressed kisses to his neck and shoulder. I spoke soothing words against his skin and into his ear.

I'd never been held so tight.

Eventually, we slid down and lay side by side on his pillow, watching each other.

Sean's eyes stayed red, but his tears were gone now. I studied his face while he seemed to study every inch of me. He stared like he couldn't believe I was real and here, beside him. We touched and we kissed like we'd done after sex. I asked him to tell me more about his girls, and he lit up. We talked for hours. The steaks and chips went forgotten.

After I showed him the other words I'd written, we dozed off, and I woke with his hands lightly stroking me.

I expected another repeat of chaos and hard kisses after the flirting, and because we'd come together so savagely before, but his touch was feather soft on my breasts and the flare of my hips. Even when Sean nuzzled his mouth between my legs and I bowed off the bed, he was gentle with his tongue.

But I couldn't be tender or quiet. I couldn't contain the cry that tore out of my throat when I came with my hands in his hair and my heels digging into his back. And when I crawled over his legs and explored him with my mouth and hands with determination to spend hours touching Sean until I knew his body better than he did, I took my time.

I stretched every second.

When I tasted cum, Sean gave up his restraint and pumped into my mouth. We both moaned when he coated the back of my throat. I swallowed and lapped at his cock, then I gazed up at him and smiled.

He looked delirious with pleasure, and nowhere near his fill.

Our noises filled the house after that.

Sweating, breathless, we panted beside each other on Sean's bare mattress. The fabric itched my back. I had no idea where the sheet had gone.

I became irritated with myself. If anyone deserved proper bedding, it was Sean.

"Get dressed," I told him, sitting up and searching the floor for my clothes.

"Why?"

"We're going to Target." I looked back at him.

He was pushed up on his elbows, brow furrowed, his cock softening on his thigh. He looked edible as fuck.

Putting on clothes was a challenge, but I managed.

Sean held onto that perplexed expression until I made a beeline for the home section at Target with my cart and stocked up on bedding supplies for his and the girls' bedrooms.

Later that night, we made love on satin sheets.

Sean was amazing on a floor and a bare mattress. But on high-quality fabric, he was magical.

"Fi! Straighten your legs, baby! Why are you standing like a flamingo?"

I giggled as Val struggled to get Fiona into her tights.

The girls' recital was tonight, and they'd shown up at my apartment roughly thirty minutes ago to get ready.

I'd already fixed Fiona's hair into a bun with braided sections, making her look like a Disney princess. Now I was working on Caroline, who was so excited she was barely keeping still.

"When are you putting the pink in my hair?" she asked me for the twentieth time since she sat down.

"Soon."

She threw her arms in the air in celebration, and I noticed the same thread bracelets on her wrist like Sean wore, only Caroline's were all pink.

I smiled at her in the mirror.

"These are too tight, Momma!" Fiona cried.

"The joys of being a woman, baby. Get used to it." Val blew out a breath. "*There.* Okay, one thing down."

I moved around to the side of the chair and looked over at Fiona.

She only had her tights on so far, so she didn't have anything covering her stomach.

I noticed a long scar running down the center of her abdomen, about three inches long, but before I could study it any more than a glance, Caroline was bouncing in the salon chair again and whipping her head around.

"You're not excited one bit about tonight, are you?" I teased as I gathered up the strands again I'd been braiding that had pulled out of my fingers the second she started quaking about.

"Yes, I am!" she shrieked. "I'm *so* excited!"

"Oh, okay. I wasn't sure. You're just so calm."

"You should've seen her earlier," Val said. "She kept taking my keys and going out to sit in the car."

I eyed Caroline in the mirror. She started giggling.

"*Is it time for the pink now?*" she shrieked.

"Almost." I wrapped the braid around her bun and secured it with a few bobby pins. Then I told Caroline to cover her face so I could set the bun with some hair spray. When I was finished, I capped the bottle and spun her around so when she stopped, she was facing the mirror again. "Ready?" I asked.

She nodded quickly and covered her mouth with her hands.

"Me too!" Fiona yelled. "Mommy, hurry up!"

"I still need to zip you up. Hold still."

I shook up the can of pink hair color and gestured at Caroline's hair. "How about we do some on this side, and a little bit over here, around the bun."

"Can't I get my whole head?" she asked.

"Caroline," Val warned.

The little girl sulked and sank in the chair.

I bent down and whispered, "Maybe we throw in some glitter too. What do you say?"

She perked right up hearing that.

Both girls got dolled up with bubblegum streaks of shimmer in their pretty blonde hair. They couldn't stop looking at themselves in the mirror when I was finished, and they kept fighting over the chair.

"Okay, time to go!" Val exclaimed, purse dangling from one elbow and bag of clothes hanging from the other. Her eyes cut to me, and for a moment, she seemed startled. "Oh, my God, I almost forgot. I have an extra ticket tonight. Would you like to go to the recital?"

"Really?" *Wow. That was unexpected.* I paused mid-OCD-organization of my hair clip drawer and smiled at her. "Sure. I'd love to go."

And only ninety percent of that reason had to do with Sean being there tonight. I also really wanted to watch the girls. They were so excited about their recital. It was infectious.

"Awesome!" Val dug the ticket out of her purse and handed it to me, then she pulled me into a quick hug and thanked me again for helping her out. "All right, girls, let's go. Did you thank Shay?"

"They did," I said.

"Thanks, Shay!" both girls hollered as they chased each other around the salon room in their tutus, squealing and giggling.

My ears were ringing when I walked them to the door.

After a quick shower since I'd worked a shift at Whitecaps today, I fixed my hair in loose waves and dressed in leggings and a flannel tunic. I applied a powder foundation and kept the focus on my eyes with a winged liner and the mascara I had that made my lashes look too thick to be real. Then I shot out a quick text, letting Sean know I'd see him tonight at the recital before I left my apartment. His text back to me came as I was backing out.

Glad you're going.

I smiled the entire drive there.

Val had saved four seats in the auditorium, which didn't make sense to me until her sister showed up five minutes after I'd arrived.

Apparently hood rats went to recitals. Go figure.

"Shay, this is my sister, Bridgett," Val introduced. "Bridgett, this is Shay. She's the girl who's been doing my hair. She works with Sean too."

Bridgett claimed the seat next to Val at the end of the row and leaned forward, waving and smiling at me like the giant ho-bag she was.

It was possible I was still holding a minor grudge about the other night.

"Hey, girl," I whispered, waving back and grinning like we were besties.

I wasn't just good at being fake nice. I was great at it. Years of experience waiting tables and dealing with rude clients helped me perfect that painted-on smile and pleasant demeanor. It was a talent, really.

And I had to play it up. I wouldn't cause a scene at the recital.

People filed into the auditorium and took their seats, chatting with one another. The room was packed. Val had mentioned something about the entire company dancing tonight, and to be prepared for this to last a couple hours.

That didn't bother me. I was just excited to watch the girls. They were the youngest class performing tonight.

"Where is he?" Val sat forward and whipped her head around to look toward the auditorium doors. "It's going to start soon."

I glanced at the empty seat between us, then I reached down and slipped my phone out of my bag. I checked the time.

Sean had one minute to get here.

"Traffic was crappy," Bridgett said. "I'm sure he's on his way."

Whoa. Did she just stick up for Sean? I was not expecting that.

I sat forward and gestured across the aisle, getting Bridgett's attention.

"I don't know if Val mentioned it, but if you're looking for a new stylist, your first haircut with me is free. And I'll give you a discount on color."

Funny how quickly you could have a change of heart about a person. I wasn't expecting those words to fly out of my mouth, *ever*, but anyone who looked out for Sean was good enough to sit in my salon chair.

"She's the best," Val chimed in, reaching across the seat and squeezing my arm.

I gave her a warm smile.

"Wow. That's awesome, thanks!" Bridgett grinned at me. She looked young. I'd guess her age to be around twenty, tops. "I'll definitely take you up on that."

"Looking forward to it."

That wasn't me being fake nice either. I meant it. I was genuinely anticipating adding Bridgett as a client.

Strippers needed good hair care too.

The lights dimmed, and the room hushed to a silence.

"*Shoot*," Val whispered.

I watched her mess with her phone and wondered if she was sending Sean a text. I almost sent one myself, but figured he'd probably be coming on his bike and wouldn't hear the alert.

I said a silent prayer everything was okay and he'd get here soon.

A spotlight turned on and focused on the stage, then a woman walked out and stood in front of the curtain holding a microphone. She welcomed everyone and spoke about the company for a minute, then she asked the audience to stay in their seats while recording so they wouldn't distract the dancers.

When she moved off the stage, the curtain lifted, and I smiled as Caroline and Fiona's class walked out, holding hands. They were all so little and sweet-looking, all big smiles and eyes full of excitement. They stood in a line that stretched across the stage.

Val sat forward and waved, and when the girls spotted us they stood on their toes and waved back, then I watched them search around where we were sitting, frown, and slump back onto their heels.

They were looking for Sean.

I turned in my seat and squinted in the dark, hoping to see him enter, but he didn't. I was sad for the girls and for him. I knew how badly he wanted to be here.

Where was he?

The music started—a slower piano number—and I spun around

and pulled up the video mode on my phone. At least he'd be able to watch it later.

I smiled videoing the girls—they looked seriously freaking adorable in their little tutus as they danced around, twirling and pointing their toes in front of them—and they stood out too, considering the pink in their hair and the way the spotlight hit them.

Val leaned over the seat and whispered what a good idea that was. I couldn't have agreed more.

The girls were focused and in sync with the rest of their class. They didn't miss a beat. Then Caroline stepped forward and pointed toward the back of the auditorium, jumping up and down and yelling, "Daddy! Daddy!" in the middle of the number.

Everyone turned in their seats.

"Oh, thank God," Val exclaimed, taking the words right out of my mouth.

Sean stalked down the aisle with his attention focused solely on his girls. His steps were heavy and purposeful.

Hair down and tucked behind his ears, he was dressed in jeans and a tight dark T-shirt that was showing off his chest in a crazy good way, even in the dim lighting. He grinned at the stage as he moved toward it.

"Daddy! Watch!" Fiona yelled.

Everyone started laughing quietly as Caroline and Fiona dashed to the front of the stage and kept up with the routine, dancing right in front of Sean, who hadn't even glanced at the seat Val had saved for him. He was too busy focusing on them.

Sean stood directly in front of that stage, arms crossed over his chest, grinning, looking proud while he watched his girls dance, smile, and wave at him between steps—they were too excited to simply go through the routine.

It wasn't just sweet. It was a beautiful moment I knew they'd all remember forever.

And because it was both of those things, nobody seemed to mind, and I swore, most of the women in the audience were too busy watching Sean rather than their own child if they were up there. I really couldn't blame them. Did I mention the tight shirt? Well, his jeans were a little tight too, right around his ass, so just add that to the mix.

The number ended, and the girls, along with the rest of the class behind them, all curtsied, then Caroline and Fiona both gave Sean a big hug and a kiss before running off stage.

"Sean!" Val whispered, waving and getting his attention when he finally turned and glanced around at the seats.

He squeezed down the aisle and sat down between Val and me. He smiled at me and winked.

I smiled at him, and added *Sean winking* to the kryptonite list. *Holy wow.*

The show went on, and the next number the girls performed was a tap dance to the tune of "I Just Can't Wait to Be King." I'm positive it was adorable, though I wasn't watching them at all.

I was watching Sean.

"There was a pile-up on Route Seven. Tractor-trailer overturned. That's why I was late."

The show had finished, and once Val had grabbed the girls from backstage, Sean gave his explanation so everyone, including the girls, could know he'd wanted to be here on time and would've been, had circumstances allowed.

"See? I told you," Bridgett said, looking at Val.

"Well, we're just happy you made it. Right, girls?"

"Right!" Caroline shrieked, while Fiona stayed on task and kept playing with the ends of Sean's hair.

She'd claimed his arms the moment she came running out into the auditorium.

"Daddy, can we have a sleepover tonight?" Caroline asked.

Sean's face tightened like he was uncertain about that idea, but before he could say anything, Val chimed in.

"Oh, um...I'm not sure about that, baby." Val bit her lip and looked to Bridgett, who merely shrugged in response.

Sean wasn't the only one unsure. It seemed everyone was. Well, everyone except me.

"*Please*," Caroline begged.

"Yeah, Daddy, *please*? Please with a cherry on top?" Fiona pleaded.

"I think that's a great idea."

All heads turned to me after I spoke.

"You do?" Val questioned.

"Absolutely." I grinned at Sean, who was looking shocked as shit and a bit terrified, which I found to be completely adorable and totally unnecessary—he'd be just fine—then I gave that grin to Val. "I bet they'd have a blast," I told her.

Her brows lifted, then she seemed to warm up to the idea, and slowly nodded her head. "Yeah. Yeah, I bet they would."

"Plus, a little birdie told me someone has new princess bedding..." I added in a singsong voice.

Caroline stared at me like she'd just tried swallowing a watermelon.

"*Princess bedding?* Daddy, is it mine? Is it!" she shrieked, tugging on his shirt. "I'm gonna die if it's mine!"

Val, Bridgett, and I all started laughing.

Sean rubbed at his mouth, thinking. He still seemed hesitant, until Fiona grabbed his face with both her little hands and forced him to look at her. She pressed closer until their foreheads touched.

"Daddy?"

"Yeah, baby girl."

Okay, Sean saying "baby girl" was now at the top of my kryptonite list. My GOD. Could he say that to me? Would that be a weird thing to request? Probably. I didn't care.

Fiona stayed serious when she spoke. "We really want to spend the night. Really bad. This is a big deal."

Bridgett and Val both made an "aw" sound. I was smiling behind my fingertips.

Sean's eyes were filling with emotion. I knew there was no way he'd say no to this now, and I was right.

"If it's a big deal, then you got it," he told her.

Fiona threw her arms around his neck and hugged him while Caroline jumped around in a circle, chanting, "Yes, yes, yes!"

"We'll need to get your sleepover bags packed," Val directed at the girls, then she looked at Sean. "I can drop them off. Shouldn't be more than an hour."

"Works for me," he said.

"Wow. I'm going to have a free Saturday night." Val pulled her hair over one shoulder and fidgeted with it. She laughed a little. "I haven't had one of those in forever."

"Let's go out!" Bridgett suggested, grabbing Val's hand so she quit twirling and twisting strands.

"That sounds like fun," I said, encouraging her. "Everyone needs a girls' night."

Bridgett pointed at me. "Yes, sister! You get it!"

"Shay, you should come with us," Val proposed, smiling, looking eager for me to join in.

"Oh, uh." I looked to Sean and saw him watching me with interest.

I had planned on spending time with him after the recital, and going by the way Sean was looking at me, he'd been banking on that too, but hey, I could still do that. It would just be later than I'd originally hoped for. This would allow Sean and his girls some alone time, and that could never be a bad thing.

Decision made, I smiled at Val and nodded firmly, telling her, "I'm in."

Val hugged me. Bridgett gave me a high-five. Caroline was still jumping around and chanting.

Sean stared at me like I'd just agreed to commit a double murder or something, until I winked at him.

Then I knew he had his own list going inside his head of things I did that drove him absolutely wild, based on the way his eyes heated and his body grew taut.

I had plans on exploring that list thoroughly very, very soon.

But first, girls' night with Sean's ex and her stripper sister.

You couldn't make this shit up.

Chapter Sixteen

SEAN

How's it going over there?

I read Shayla's text while Caroline tied another bracelet around my wrist, this one yellow. The one before that had been purple.

You need more colors, Daddy, she'd explained.

Using my left hand, I typed out a response.

Good. Girls are having fun. U?

I still thought it was weird the three of them were hanging out, but as long as I wasn't getting a call to bust Shayla out of jail for assaulting Bridgett, I didn't care.

Still would've preferred her here, though.

I just rode a mechanical bull and DIDN'T fall off. So, I'm kind of a big deal now. Spread the word.

Not surprised.

No?

Didn't fall off me the other night.

A bunch of cartoon faces with open mouths came through.

Are you flirting with me again? I LOVE THIS. Keep going.

Get over here and I will.

We're almost done. I think we're leaving soon.

"Daddy, can you paint my toes?" Fiona asked, climbing up onto the couch and holding out a tiny bottle of pink polish.

The girls' sleepover bags included a duffle stuffed full of makeup, jewelry, dress-up dresses, and other shit I now had spread out all over my house. Caroline's bracelet-making kit was shoved in the duffle too.

I was beginning to think Val let the girls bring over every fucking thing they owned.

"In a minute," I told her, then I glanced back at the phone when it vibrated.

I'm on video duty. See you soon! xoxo

"How about a blue one next, Daddy." Caroline rummaged in her kit on the cushion next to me. "Or red. Which one do you want?"

"Whatever you wanna give me, baby girl."

"I think blue."

She got to work on sizing the string and cutting it the length she needed while Fiona knelt in front of the couch and colored a design on my knee with markers.

She always drew on me, and anything she put on my skin, she thought I'd get permanent.

Fiona had reason to think that, considering the designs I'd gotten made permanent over the years.

Since the girls were both occupied, I opened that stupid fucking snap app and checked it for pictures of Shayla, wanting to see her.

She'd changed her username to *HairByShayla* a couple weeks back. Changed the sign hanging on that door too.

Every time I saw it, I grinned.

Clicking on her name, I got into what she'd posted.

I shook my head at the images of her with that weird shit on her face that made her look different, and the ones she took with Val and Bridgett, posing together, looking friendly like they'd all known each other for years...I didn't know what the fuck to think about those.

Then I smiled because that was just her—Shayla being Shayla. She could push her way into any group, onto any person, and make them want to hold on to her. Even a group including my ex and her sometimes pain-in-the-ass sister, someone Shayla did not have a good first impression of. But that was just how Shayla was. She had a light that people wanted to be around, and once she found something good about you, you didn't have to work at getting her to be on your side. She was already on it.

Looks like what I told her about Bridgett finally penetrated.

"Daddy, you got Snapchat?" Caroline asked, putting her weight on my chest and trying to grab my phone.

I looked at her while keeping my arm outstretched. "You know what that is?"

How the fuck?

"Mommy has that," Fiona explained, getting up onto the couch now too and trying to get at my phone. "Can we play it?"

"Daddy, we wanna see the filters!" Caroline cried.

"I wanna be a cat!" Fiona yelled.

"I wanna be the princess first, then the puppy, and *then* the cat!" Caroline informed me, planting her knees in my lap and reaching out while holding on to her sister for balance.

"Ow, Care!" Fiona hollered when Caroline pushed into her too hard. "Stop!"

"Jesus, here." I handed Caroline the phone and then grabbed Fiona, scooting over with her to make room. Then I planted her next to Caroline on the couch.

After pulling the leg of my jeans down, since Fiona was clearly finished drawing on me, I threw my arm behind the girls and leaned over, watching Caroline work that app like she messed around with it every day. She gave me the run-down on how to work the filters—something I did not give one fuck about—then she took pictures of herself and Fiona while the two of them giggled.

"Daddy, my toes," Fiona said, wiggling her bare feet while she made faces at the phone.

I snatched up the pink polish she'd showed me before, then I knelt in front of her and carefully painted the color on her tiny nails. While she dried, I moved on to Caroline after she requested I paint hers next.

An hour later, the girls were in bed after a bath where I was forbidden to get water anywhere near their heads.

Apparently, that pink color Shayla had put in washed out, and Caroline looked close to tears just thinking about losing it.

I got them as clean as I could.

Once the girls were asleep, I snuck out of their room, grabbed my phone, which I had to charge since they drained the battery messing around on that app, and called up Shayla.

"Hey, I just pulled onto your street. I'll be there in a sec," she answered.

"Thought you'd be here already," I said, yanking the front door open and stepping out onto the porch.

The April air was warm with a slight breeze.

"So did I. We got caught up kicking ass at trivia night."

I saw headlights approaching. "Yeah? You win?"

"Second."

"First-place loser."

"Oh!" She giggled. "Look at you cracking jokes. I forgot how funny you can be."

Shayla slowed in front of the house and turned into the driveway.

"I see you," she purred, waving through the windshield.

I smiled and disconnected the call, tucking my phone into my pocket as an energy moved beneath my skin.

My hands shook. I itched to touch her.

"Are the little princesses still awake?" Shayla asked, stepping up onto the porch and stopping in front of me.

She was grinning, excited to see my girls and just happy being here, because she always was.

And *fuck* if I didn't feel the exact same way.

"They're out cold." I grabbed Shayla's tiny hips and pulled her body into mine, bending to kiss her.

Her lips were soft, so fucking soft, just like the rest of her. She was little and smooth everywhere. I wanted to keep her and keep doing this for hours.

And it felt fucking good not fighting that anymore.

"I bet they had so much fun with you," Shayla said, staring up at me with nothing but truth in her eyes, like she knew that information for a *fact*, like there was no way my girls wouldn't enjoy being here.

"Yeah." I wrapped my arms around her shoulders and just fucking held her, my nose in her hair so I could breathe her in.

"Aw." She burrowed closer. "You missed me."

I didn't say anything, but when Shayla tried leaning back I squeezed her tighter so she couldn't pull away.

She giggled into my chest, then her body seemed to melt into mine, and she sighed and held me back with all the strength she had.

"I got some good news tonight."

I leaned away then to peer down at her, brows lifting. "Yeah?"

Shayla nodded. "My dad started this new medicine, and it seems to really be helping him."

"Fuck. That's awesome."

"It is." She grinned. "Lately, everything is."

Knowing she was including me in that everything, I bent and kissed her once more, lingering there, my tongue pushing inside her mouth and stroking against hers.

Eventually, and only because I knew I'd be kissing her again inside the house, I released her and we made it inside.

"Wow." Hands on her hips, Shayla glanced around the living

room while I locked the door. "It's like a princess party bomb went off in here." She looked over at me and smiled. "What all did you guys do?"

"What the fuck *didn't* we do?" I returned. "They brought every toy they own. Didn't need to, though. Once the girls got into those stupid fuckin' filters, that was it."

Shayla cocked her head. "Filters? You mean like, on Snapchat?"

Oh, fuck.

I gripped the back of my neck and looked at the floor.

"Oh, my God." She giggled. "Sean, do you have Snapchat?" Shayla stepped closer, getting right in front of me, and tilted her head so she could see my face.

Might as well confess, dumbass. You brought this on yourself.

I dropped my arm. "It's fuckin' dumb, but yeah, I have it," I said.

Her eyes brightened. "Really? What's your username?"

"Username."

Shayla giggled. "What?"

"I don't fuckin' know," I grumbled. "I just picked one. I didn't care. I just wanted to see you."

Her face lost all hint of amusement. "You watch me on there?"

I nodded.

"How long? Since we started—"

I shook my head, halting her. "Before that," I confessed.

An emotion passed over her face. Then Shayla grabbed my hands and slid her fingers between mine, looking almost relieved to be hearing that from me. She smiled.

I smiled.

Fuck, I smiled a lot around this girl.

Then her gaze lowered to my neck. "That's new," she said, running the tip of her finger just above the collar of my shirt, where Fiona had dragged a marker earlier.

"Fiona," I explained, watching Shayla's eyes grow wider.

"Those lines you have tattooed... she did them?"

I nodded.

"Did she draw that little stick figure on your arm?"

"Nah, that was Caroline. Fi likes patterns. That's her thing."

Shayla grabbed my face and rolled up onto her toes to kiss me. "You're sweet."

I wasn't, but I told her to say that again, because I wanted her speaking inside my mouth.

She smiled, then whispered, "You're sweet. I always knew it too," before licking my bottom lip.

I slid my hand through her hair to the back of her head and held her still while I kissed her. I pushed my tongue inside her mouth and made her moan. I sucked and I licked, until my lips burned and hers begged my name on a whisper. Then I kissed her cheek, her jaw, down to her neck where I growled and cursed, because I wanted her, right there in that spot on the floor again, and that couldn't happen.

"What?" Shayla leaned back to study me. Her mouth twitched. "Ohhh, you want to get freaky all over the house, don't you?"

"I'd settle for right here, but yeah."

She grinned and slid her arms around my neck. "This is when you realize during all that fixing up you did, that you should've soundproof insulated your bedroom and reinforced it with a steel door."

"That wouldn't stop my girls. They'd find a way in. Trust me."

Knowing Caroline, she'd figure out how to tunnel through the floor.

I brushed a strand of hair off Shayla's cheek and tucked it behind her ear while she kept grinning, most likely picturing my girls busting in on us. "You hungry?"

"Nope. I ate bar food."

"Want somethin' to drink?"

"Sure. A water would be good."

I gestured at the TV with my head. "Got cable installed. You wanna watch one of your dumbass shows?"

"Hey." She softly punched my chest, laughing, then she slipped out of my hold and rounded the couch. She dug her phone and keys out of her back pockets and dropped the items on the end table. "Just for that, I'm putting on the most obnoxious reality show I can find," she warned.

"Like I give a fuck. I'll be watchin' you anyway."

Shayla whipped her head around and blushed. "*Mad* flirting skills," she said, lifting her hand to her face and pointing at me. "Look at you."

Grinning, I padded to the kitchen and got her a water, grabbing a Coke for me, while she flipped through the channels.

"I talked to Dominic tonight," Shayla called out. "He wanted to know if there was anything else around here you needed help with. I told him I'd ask you."

"I wanna get started on the basement soon. Could use his help with that."

"Awesome. I'll let him know."

"How's he doin'?" I stepped out into the living room and walked around the couch.

Shayla smiled at me as I claimed the seat beside her. "Good, thanks to you. My mom says he's not nearly as angry anymore."

"That's good, babe. But if he does go back to that place, the offer stands whether I got shit here that needs demolishing or not. I don't mind talkin' to the kid."

Her smile reached her eyes. "I'll pass that message along."

"What about the other one? He doin' all right?"

"Yes." She leaned over and kissed my shoulder. "Thanks for asking."

"You don't gotta thank me."

"Yes, I do." Sitting back, Shayla reached over and touched the new threads around my wrist as I cracked open the can. She was back to smiling.

I stared at her, ignoring the TV like I'd said I would. I didn't give a fuck what was on.

"Does Fiona make you anything?" Shayla asked, toeing off her boots. She twisted to face me, swung her legs up and tucked her feet under her hip, getting comfortable. Then she took the glass of water I held out.

I shook my head. "Just likes to draw on me. That's her thing. Caroline's only done the stick person on my arm. The rest is Fiona, and shit I put on there." I took a swig of Coke and sat the can on the end table.

"I saw their names, and the footprints. That's so sweet."

I shrugged.

"Do you have anything for Val?"

Shayla looked hopeful, like she wanted something representing my ex inked on me, which I did not fucking get. Still, I brought my left arm across my body and dropped my hand to her thigh.

"The roses are her," I said. "Got those added after we got married."

Her fingers, which were cold from the glass, traced the skull that spanned across my knuckles. Then her eyes came up. "I love that."

"Yeah?"

"Yeah." She grinned. "I really, really love that. She lit up that darkness you were living in. Roses can't bloom in the dark. I think this is perfect."

I stared at her. *Jesus.* She was serious.

"You like me havin' somethin' I gotta look at the rest of my life, knowin' it reminds me of my ex?"

"Was your ex good to you?"

"Yeah."

"Then there you go." Shayla dropped her head to the side and smiled. "I will never have any problem with anyone, Sean, as long as they are good to you. Val gave you love and kindness when no one else did. Plus, those beautiful girls sleeping in there. I like her having a tattoo. I like that she meant something important enough to get one."

"What about you then?"

She lost her smile. "What about me?"

"Going off that checklist, aside from the kid thing, shouldn't you have somethin' on me?"

Her mouth fell open. "Are you serious?"

"Do I *look* serious?"

"You always look like *that*." She gestured at my face. "I don't know. You tell me, *are you*?" Her voice jumped.

I grinned, liking how flustered she'd gotten.

Shayla leaned back. "Okay, now you're smiling, and I have no idea what to think." She shook her head, then laughed nervously. "If you're being serious... Wow, uh, are you, though? I still can't get a read."

I threw my head back and laughed.

"Sean!"

My hand on her thigh flew to her mouth. "You wanna wake up my girls?" I asked.

She blinked with wide eyes.

I yanked my hand away when I felt her tongue, grimacing, and seeing that, she giggled and fell over into me, spilling some of her water on my leg.

"Oops."

"You're not gettin' a fuckin' tattoo now," I said as I wiped at my jeans, but I was laughing with her. I couldn't fucking help it.

Fuck, I loved being around her.

Shayla's giggle shook her entire body.

"Come here." I took her drink and sat it on the end table next to mine, then I threw my arm around her, and getting the invite, Shayla burrowed herself against my side, draping her leg over top of mine and wrapping her arm around my waist.

She sighed and blinked at the TV.

I kept my head down and watched her and nothing else, like I said I would.

"The day you got arrested," Shayla began, only letting a minute of silence pass. "Did that have something to do with the scar on Fiona's stomach?"

"How'd you know about that?"

"I saw it when Val was getting the girls ready for their recital." Shayla shifted back a little, tilted her head up, and looked at me. "And Val mentioned something about some medical bill, and that you were doing something to help pay for it."

I jerked my chin in answer.

"What were you doing?"

"Stealin' a car."

"Really?" Her eyes flickered wider.

"I needed close to eight grand to cover that surgery," I explained. "I knew how much I'd get if I boosted one. I told Val I was done with that, but I didn't know what else to fuckin' do. We couldn't get the money."

"What about insurance? They didn't cover it?"

"Probably would've if we had any."

Shayla frowned.

"I kept fuckin' up," I told her. "Couldn't keep a job, plus Val was in school. Any money we had went to that and what the girls needed after paying rent. We couldn't afford insurance. That bill came, and Val was stressin' out about it. She thought we'd lose our apartment. I had to do somethin'."

"And the girls were in the car with you?"

My jaw clenched as I nodded.

I hated thinking about that.

"Val had a class. I was watchin' the girls. Bridgett was doing whatever the fuck. She wasn't home. It was fuckin' ridiculous—I don't know what I was thinkin'. It took me thirty fuckin' minutes putting those damn car seats in. The girls were screaming—the alarm bothered them and I had trouble cuttin' it 'cause I was dealin' with the two of them climbin' all over the place and shit. By the time I got on the road, I made it two fuckin' miles before I got stopped."

Shayla placed her hand on my leg and pushed up. "You put their car seats in the vehicle you stole?"

"I wasn't drivin' anywhere without them strapped in," I replied. "What if I got into an accident or somethin'? They could get hurt."

"*Sean.*" Shayla grabbed my face and pouted. "Jesus. Even doing something illegal, you're still only thinking about your girls."

I brusquely shook my head, which dropped her hands away. "I wasn't. If I would've been thinkin' about them, I wouldn't have done it," I argued. "Now they got that memory of me plus all that time I missed out on, and Val still had to take a loan out to cover that bill, so a lot of fuckin' good it did. I'll never make up for that."

"Yes, you will. You're making up for it now." She pushed my hair out of my face and tucked it behind my ear. "And I believe down in my bones that if you would've had a different life growing up, none of this would've happened."

I didn't believe that.

"No one's to blame but me. I did it."

"We're not arguing about this. Agree to disagree."

My face tightened. "Christ, *again*? This isn't one of those *leave it at that* moments. My girls were screamin' 'cause of me. They went a long fuckin' time without a dad 'cause of *me*, Shayla. No one else."

What the fuck? How was she seeing this any different? I didn't get it.

"You didn't have anyone guiding you, Sean. Nobody teaching you right from wrong, or showing you how to treat others. That is not your fault. I understand feeling guilty and regretting what you did, but I'm talking about carrying that blame yourself. No one is putting that night solely on you. Not even Val—I believe that."

She spoke softly, which was calming me down, but it was also her touch—the way her hands kept pushing through my hair and stroking my cheek. It was gentle. It felt good. Better than good. I couldn't help but lean into it and will her to keep going. I had gone most of my life without someone touching me like this.

I had gone all my life wanting it.

"You're sorry," she went on. "Everyone can see that. And you're doing right by those girls now, and you're going to keep doing right by them. Focus on where you are right now, Sean—fuck the rest. Just keep going forward. You're going to give them a beautiful life."

"You think my girls are gonna forgive me for that shit?" I asked.

Shayla shifted closer so she was practically in my lap and stared deep into my eyes. "I don't think they ever needed to," she said quietly. "They didn't hold a grudge or hate you, Sean. They couldn't do that. They just missed you. And when those girls get older and you explain to them what happened, if that's something they need to hear, just like everyone else—they will understand why you did it and why you had to. They will understand—I promise."

I wanted to believe that. I wanted her to be right.

Dropping my head against hers, I closed my eyes and breathed deep while she kept soothing me with her touch and her voice, telling me how good I was and how much love I had around me.

"Let yourself feel that love, Sean," she whispered. "Take it in. Let it fill you."

I fell asleep with her voice in my ear. I wanted it to stay there forever.

But it never did.

Chapter Seventeen

SHAYLA

I startled awake when I felt Sean's body jerk beneath me.

"No," he murmured, voice heavy with sleep. "No. No, stop. Stop!"

"Sean?" I whispered. I rubbed sleep from my eyes and sat up as best I could, putting my weight on my hip.

I was trapped between Sean and the couch, our legs interwoven. I peered down at him.

He was on his back, head on the armrest, body sprawled out. His skin glistened with sweat. The shirt he was wearing clung to him.

"Hey." I placed my hand on his chest. "Sean, hey, wake up." His body began to twitch spastically. He mumbled incoherent words. He was stuck in a nightmare. "Sean!"

Teeth clenched, a scream tore out of his throat.

Panic filled me.

"Sean!" I yelled again, getting to my knees with some difficulty and looming over him. I grabbed his shoulders and shook him, hard. "Wake up! Wake up, Sean!"

With a gasp, his eyes flew open and he shot up, knocking me into the back of the couch. He stared like he was seeing right through me.

"Hey," I whispered, cautiously reaching out to him. There was so much fear in his eyes. "H-Hey, are you okay?"

Sean's body retched, and I watched in horror as he rolled to his side, hung his head off the couch, and vomited onto the floor.

"Oh, my God." *Shit. Shit! What do I do?* I started rubbing his back, trying to soothe him while he continued to gag and expel the contents of his stomach. I held his hair out of his face. "It's okay. It's okay, Sean."

I repeated those words like a mantra.

I thought about running to grab the bucket, but I didn't want to leave him. What if he started choking? Was he even fully awake yet? I didn't know. I could feel his heart pounding through his back. And when I grabbed more pieces of his hair as it dangled into his face, I touched his skin. It was soaked. He couldn't stop sweating.

I listened as the vomiting ceased, and just as I was climbing over Sean's legs to get to my feet and help him up, he began to sob.

"Oh, baby," I whispered, kneeling behind him again. I wrapped my arms around his chest and hugged him from behind. I tried not to crush him. "It's okay. You're here, Sean. You're here. She can't hurt you anymore." I kissed his shoulder and the back of his neck as tears stung my eyes.

My poor man. I was heartbroken for him and so unbelievably angry at that bitch. This was what his nightmares were like? How often did he have them? How long? My God, he went through this alone? I couldn't bear it.

Sean kept trying to pull away from me and duck his head. He wanted to hide.

"Come on." I climbed over his legs and got to my feet, careful of the vomit that spread out in a spatter. Then I leaned down and grabbed his arm, helping him sit up. "Let's get you cleaned up in the shower, okay? I bet a shower will feel really good."

Sean hung his head and swiped his forearm across his mouth. He was staring at the floor where he'd puked. His hair was matted.

"I'll clean that up," I told him, drawing his head up then. He shook it. "It doesn't bother me. I'll do it. Come on." I got him to his feet, brought his arm over my shoulders, and held him around his waist as we walked around the couch. He was still shaking. "Do you think you're going to be sick again?" I asked.

Sean was staring blankly ahead, like he was in a trance. His cheeks were wet with tears.

"No," he rasped.

"That's good." I tried smiling at him, but my lips were quivering too much.

Pull yourself together. Be strong for him. He needs you.

When we got inside the bathroom, I flicked on the light and helped Sean out of his clothes. He brushed his teeth. I was fighting back tears. Then I got the water running and tested it with my hand while Sean held onto the sink. When the water was warm, I moved behind him and kissed his back.

"It's ready. Do you need my help?"

I was prepared to take care of Sean—to do anything he needed me to do. I'd wash him. Dress him. Clean him up if he got sick again. Anything.

But Sean shook his head. "My girls," he began, looking back at the door.

"I'll check on them. I think they're still asleep."

Sean nodded his head lifelessly, then he stepped inside the shower and drew the curtain closed. He was silent.

I scooped up his clothes and carried them to the laundry room that was just off the kitchen. I dropped them in the washer and started the load. Then I checked on the girls.

Their room was dark and still. They were covered up in pink, fluffy bedding and breathing in steady rhythms.

I closed the door on my way out.

"They're still asleep," I called out into the bathroom, listening for Sean's response.

I heard water running and nothing else.

There were rubber gloves and cleaner under the kitchen sink. I loaded up on supplies and dragged the trash can over to the couch. Then I cut the TV off, since it was still on, and knelt beside the vomit, pushing up my sleeves.

The cleanup wasn't too bad. And the floor hadn't stained, which I was happy about. I knew how hard Sean had worked on it after he'd pulled up the carpet, and I didn't want him looking at that spot and reliving the memory of that nightmare.

I'd been prepared to rearrange furniture, though, if the floor had been damaged.

After I tied off the bag and carried the trash outside to the can, I washed up and returned to the bathroom.

The shower was still running.

"Sean?" I stepped up to the curtain and pulled it back slightly so I could peer inside. "You okay?"

He had his hands braced on the wall and was letting the water run over his head and down his strong back.

He didn't have any ink there, and I could see every groove of muscle as he trembled. I fought the urge to climb inside the shower and hold him while he tried to wash.

"Do you need anything?" I asked.

"Towel," he mumbled.

I turned and went to the small linen closet opposite the sink and frantically felt around for the softest cloth.

I'm not sure why I did that or why I thought it might help. I was running on this strange energy. I wasn't typically an anxious person, but I felt like something was pushing me around and forcing me to move at a much faster pace.

"Here you go," I said. I held the white cotton against my chest and shifted on my feet while Sean cut the water off and pulled back the curtain. I braced myself for his tears.

When he stepped out onto the mat, he kept his gaze on the tiled floor. I couldn't tell if he was crying or not. His hair was dripping. Drops of water slid off his skin.

"Let's go lie down," I told him, stroking his back as he secured the towel around his waist.

"The floor?" he croaked.

"Everything's cleaned up. The floor is fine. No damage."

He turned his head and peered down at me then, but only briefly. Then his gaze returned to the tile.

I gave him a soft smile even though he couldn't see it and took hold of his hand, knowing he was probably embarrassed about the cleanup. "It wasn't a big deal, Sean. Not at all, okay? Come on."

He let me lead him out of the bathroom.

We kept the overhead light off and turned on the small lamp. Sean pulled a pair of boxers out of his dresser and slipped them on, letting the towel drop to the floor. His movements were stiff.

I scooped up the damp towel, then helped him over to the bed. Once he was lying back, I turned to leave the room.

Sean shot up and caught my arm, halting me. "Stay," he pleaded.

A piece of my heart broke off. *God, he was terrified I was leaving.*

"I'm staying," I told him, smiling. "I just want to put this towel in the bathroom and make sure all the lights are off. I'll be right back."

Sean nodded rigidly, then released me and collapsed onto the bed. He was breathing fast through his nose.

I ran through the house. I made sure the door was locked and grabbed my phone off the end table. After shutting off all the lights, I returned to the bedroom.

Sean was on his side facing the wall. His head came up, and he peered back at me when I entered.

"Hey," I whispered. "I'm just setting my alarm. I have a client coming at eight."

I kept to myself how I thought the girls waking up to me being here might confuse them, and it was probably best I slip out before they woke, figuring we could save that conversation for another time.

We had enough to talk about.

After setting my phone down on the trunk, I climbed over Sean and sat on the bed, facing him. I touched his face, and his eyes slowly slipped opened.

"Are you okay?" I asked softly.

His breathing had slowed a little. He was no longer panting, but he didn't look any better. Even in the dim light, I could see his fear. His sadness. His gaze was anxious. It wouldn't settle on me; it darted from my face to different spots on the bed.

"Sean, what are your nightmares about? What happened to you?"

I wanted so badly to take away his pain, but I couldn't unless he shared his past with me. I had to know all of it.

He gritted his teeth. He wouldn't look at me.

"Let me in." I stroked his cheek and shifted closer. "It's okay, you can tell me anything. It won't change us. I won't leave."

His gaze shot to mine, and his nostrils flared as he sucked in a breath.

"What did she do to you?"

Sean pinched his eyes shut, then shook his head with a short jerk. He wasn't going to tell me.

"Baby, please, I want to help you," I said, bending down and kissing his head. I rubbed his shoulder. "Please, tell me. I won't leave. I promise, I won't..."

"Not her," he mumbled.

I leaned back a little to peer into his face. *Not her?* "What do you mean? Your nightmare wasn't about her?" I asked.

I felt something move through his body where I was touching him. A wave of fear. It left his muscles rigid.

"Tell me," I begged. I was crying now. I couldn't help it. "Sean, *please*."

"I just wanted somethin' to eat," he whispered, staring at me with wild panic in his eyes.

I nodded, encouraging him to keep going. *Please keep going.*

"I was so fuckin' hungry. They had food and they wouldn't give me any...I could smell it."

"Who had food?"

"That fuckin' *cunt* and the men she'd bring over. Whoever. It was someone different all the time."

"Okay." I brushed his hair back. "Okay, what happened? How old were you?"

"Don't know...nine, I think. I waited 'til I couldn't hear them, then I snuck out of my room. If they saw me, I'd get beat. She was passed out on the couch. I thought...I thought he was in the bedroom. I didn't check. I should've *checked*! I knew better! I knew—"

"Shh," I soothed and pressed kisses all over his face. *God, what happened to him?*

Sean began to cry. "I got to the kitchen, and he was at the fridge. I tried sneaking out but he saw me. I was scared. I didn't want to get hit. My head was still hurtin' so bad from when I got hit earlier, so when he told me to get over to him, I did. *What the fuck you doin'? What the fuck you doin'!* he screamed at me. I told him I was hungry. Then I watched him pull this bucket of chicken out of the fridge and set it on the counter. I thought he was gonna give it to me. I smiled. I remember fuckin' smiling at him. *Jesus*." Sean shook his head as his tears wet the pillowcase, then he looked at me. "I hadn't eaten anything in days. And it smelled so good and I just...*fuck*, I had to. I had to do it, Shayla. I had to fuckin' do it!"

"Do what, baby?"

"Touch him. I had to touch that motherfucker so I could get somethin' to eat!"

The air drained out of my lungs. I trapped a whimper inside my mouth and grabbed at Sean, pulling his upper body into my lap as he began to sob and curse. He clung to me.

I willed my own tears to dry up. I had to stay strong for him. But God, I had never wanted to break down and scream so badly before in my life. How could this happen to him? How could no one protect this boy?

What the fuck was wrong with people?

"Shh, it's okay. It's okay, you're safe now," I whispered, stroking his hair, his face.

His arms around me flexed and held tighter.

I kept rubbing his back. Kept kissing him. Kept telling him it would be okay. This went on for minutes, until Sean eventually fell asleep, and even then, I kept repeating the same thing over and over while I stared off into the bedroom.

Hours passed. I couldn't sleep. I couldn't relax or lay back, and it didn't matter anyway. I was no longer tired.

I thought about that woman. About Sean as a boy. So sad and scared. About all the pain he lived and was still living.

I had to do something. I had to help him.

When the alarm on my phone went off, I climbed over Sean's legs and slid out of bed. His head was back on the pillow now.

I felt his hand on my hip as I turned off my alarm.

"Hey." I smiled at his sleepy face, half covered by his hair. He was sprawled out on his stomach.

Sean slid his hand up to my arm and pulled me as he rolled, allowing me room to sit on the edge of the mattress.

"You sleep any?" he asked.

"A little."

I hated lying, but I didn't want Sean feeling any guilt or regretting sharing with me the thing I was betting he had never wanted to share. He'd warned me before about stuff happening to him we'd never talk about. And even though it killed him to say it and me to hear it, we *had* talked about it.

I didn't want him ever feeling sorry for telling me.

"Are you hanging out with your girls today?" I asked, pushing his hair back and running my fingers through it, discovering how much he seemed to like me doing that last night.

His eyes closed briefly in bliss, then he nodded and opened them again. "Val's picking them up later. Not sure how that's gonna go. The girls said last night they were movin' in."

I laughed. "Well, it is pretty awesome here. Can't say I blame them." I bent down and kissed his mouth, feeling his goatee tickle and the fullness of his lips and wanting to stay there, kissing him, but there was something bothering me, and I couldn't leave here until I got it off my chest.

I sat back and gently stroked his face. "Was it just the one time? With that man…did it happen again or with anyone else?"

My stomach tightened as I braced. *God, what if it happened all the time?*

Sean stared at me, released a tight breath, then shook his head.

Relief sagged my shoulders.

"Did she know what was going on? That woman—did she do anything?"

"Walked in on me jackin' him. She laughed and walked out."

My teeth clenched. *My God*, I was going to torture her like nobody's business. I just had to find her.

"Hey."

I blinked the bed into focus and looked down at Sean after he spoke.

He was studying me. "You're thinkin' somethin'. What is it?"

"Nothing," I lied.

"What is it?" he pressed.

"I'm wondering if that horrible woman is still living here, and how difficult it would be for me to find her," I admitted. "I'm hoping not too difficult, so I can get on with the torture sooner rather than later. I have a lot planned."

Sean stared at me, his expression unreadable, then he sat up and moved beside me so we sat shoulder to shoulder. He grabbed my face. His hold was gentle.

"Leave it alone," he said, and just the thought of letting that bitch get off, it made my blood boil.

"I can't do that," I told him. "She hurt you. And she did worse than that. She didn't protect you at all, Sean. She doesn't deserve to be breathing..."

"Leave it alone, Shayla," he repeated, his voice firm and final. "You don't need to be diggin' on this. I ain't worried about her."

"*I am.* What if she finds you? What if she's *here*? God, she could come into Whitecaps or try and see your girls. I won't let her."

"She ain't gonna do shit."

"You don't know that."

"Yeah, I do."

"How? How do you know?"

He curtly shook his head.

"How, Sean?"

"*Shayla*," he growled, bringing his face so close to mine our noses almost touched. His tone was severe. "Remember before when I said pick another topic?"

I blinked, asking in a quiet voice, "You aren't going to tell me about this?"

"No."

"Never?"

"Never."

I pulled out of his hold as this strange hurt filled me. "You told me all that stuff last night, and you won't tell me this? Is it worse?"

Sean cursed, looking away, then he stood up and stalked out of the room with heavy steps. The bathroom door closed behind him.

I stared off into his bedroom.

I didn't want to let this bother me, but God, it did. I didn't want any secrets between us. Even ones too difficult to talk about. I wanted Sean open and honest with me.

How could we be together if he couldn't be?

I pushed that worrying thought aside and decided I wouldn't lessen what *was* shared and how difficult that must have been for Sean. He was trusting me with it. He'd told me so much already.

Don't dig, Shayla. Do not dig.

I stood from the bed and searched my bag for something to write on. I found an old market receipt and dug around in a pocket for a pen. Finding one, I smoothed out the soft, crumpled paper on the edge of the trunk, then I flattened it on the top and wrote out my note.

Sean,

Thank you for letting me in. I'm not leaving. (I won't) I'm just going to work.

xoxo,

Shayla

I left the note on the bed, then I slung my bag over my shoulder, tugged on my boots, and slipped out just as sweet little voices filled the hallway.

How I managed to get through four clients that day without dropping on the spot was a miracle.

By two o'clock, I was dead. But I knew taking a nap would only mess up my sleep that evening, so I was fully committed to powering through and staying up.

I was also extremely motivated.

I had work to do. Sean needed help. And I'd give up sleep for the rest of my life if it meant making sure he got it.

After cleaning up after my last client, I grabbed my laptop and plopped down on the couch with my second Red Bull of the day and some trail mix—the good kind with M&M's. Not that shitty kind that only had dried fruit and unsalted peanuts. I was not a squirrel, and in my opinion, the only reason to purchase trail mix like that was for some sort of feeder out in your yard.

Red Bull cracked open and search engine ready, I got my snack on while looking up local therapists who specialized in childhood traumas.

I hadn't asked Sean if he'd ever spoken to anyone before about what had happened to him, but I was guessing he hadn't, considering how closed off he was about the topic. Maybe he didn't want to talk to anyone, and if that was the case, I wouldn't push it, but I needed him knowing there were people out there who could help him.

I spent the rest of the afternoon reading bios and client reviews. I looked up addresses and calculated the distance from Sean's house. I Googled, eliminated, and narrowed down the choices. I was picky. I had to be. Nothing short of the best. Then I made my list of potentials and split them up by gender, in case Sean had a preference.

I was anxious to give it to him. I was prepared to drive over to his house and show him the second I was finished, but I didn't need to.

Headed over. You home?

I smiled as I read Sean's text and quit pulling on my boots.

Yep.

Be there in 20.

Can't wait. xoxo

I sat on the arm of my couch and watched the door.

Even though I might've pulled an all-nighter, you couldn't tell by looking at me, and not just because I was buzzing and wide-eyed from all the caffeine I'd consumed.

I'd showered when I got home this morning and curled my hair with a flat iron, so it looked beachy. I was wearing makeup—which I kept to a minimum except for my lipstick choice, going with a deep ruby shade that looked amazing against my pale complexion—and instead of bumming it in sweats or slipping right into my PJs, I was in black jeggings and my favorite oversize sweater that looked expensive but wasn't, meaning it looked nice and not frumpy like some oversize sweaters tended to look on me.

So, running on Red Bull and zero sleep, I felt pretty.

Nearly twenty minutes later, a knock sounded, and I dashed across the living room and threw open the door.

Sean stood there in the dim light, looking all kinds of sexy in his white T-shirt and tattered jeans. His hair was tucked behind his ear on one side and hanging freely on the other. His hands were shoved into his front pockets, and his head had been lowered, but he lifted it when he saw me and was currently doing that amazing thing with his mouth where I couldn't tell if he was smirking or smiling and I didn't care, because the combination looked incredible.

"Hey." I grinned and moved to step back, but Sean reached out and took my face between his hands, backing me inside himself. He blindly kicked the door closed and pressed a kiss to my mouth, barely giving any tongue but giving enough that I felt that kiss all the way from top to toes.

"Mm," I hummed when we were finished and swayed a little. Probably didn't even need the Red Bull. I was wide awake now.

Sean stared at my lips and tugged at my bottom one with his thumb. "You look really fuckin' pretty," he said.

I swayed a little more.

Damn. Sean giving compliments—major kryptonite.

"You do this a lot?"

I quirked a brow, but going off the way he was concentrating on exactly one part of my face, I took a guess. "Wear lipstick? Yeah, but not always this dark."

"You should. *Jesus.*" His eyes came up and I saw how heated they were. "I like this. Like the other shit too, but I *like* this."

I grinned. "Well, excuse me while I go throw out every other color I own. Won't be needing them anymore."

He stared at me, his eyes going intense but only holding that emotion for a breath before he lowered them, dropped his hands, and stepped back.

"You okay?" I asked.

"I gotta tell you shit, and I don't know how you're gonna react," he began, and I held my breath because I knew, oh, God, I *knew*, he was talking about the stuff he was never planning on telling me.

But now he was here, ready to share it all with me, and even though I wanted to know everything about this man, even the dirty stuff he was ashamed of, I worried he wasn't ready.

I stepped closer. "Sean, you don't need to tell me—"

"Yeah, I do," he cut me off. "You're tossing out every color except the one I want, you need to know it." He looked up at me then. He was breathing heavily through his nose. "I decided earlier I was gonna tell you. Worried about it the whole way here. Saw you, kissed you, forgot what the fuck I was doin' here 'cause kissin' you makes me forget shit, especially shit that's weighin' heavy on my mind. Then you say you're only gonna wear that color on your mouth 'cause I want it and hearin' that, *feelin' that*, I'm rememberin' why I'm here. I gotta tell you this. I want you knowin' it and I don't. I'm scared how you'll look at me after. I like how you look at me now, I don't wanna lose that."

Okay. Wow.

Okay, okay, okay.

That. Was. HUGE.

"Uh." I wet my lips. I was breathing heavily now too. "Can I just say firstly, that was probably the greatest compliment of my *life*. I'm glad you like the way I look at you and that kissing me takes you out of that dark place. That's all I could hope for. I want you surrounded in nothing but light, Sean. I want that more than anything. You deserve it."

He shook his head and cursed. "Now I really gotta fuckin' tell you," he growled, then he turned away and stalked over to the couch, taking a seat on one end. He braced his elbows on his knees. His legs were bouncing.

God, he was really worried about this. About how I'd react.

I sat down beside him and placed my hand on his thigh. "I won't leave," I said quietly.

Sean froze. He was staring straight ahead at a spot on the carpet.

"I won't," I repeated, just as softly.

His head slowly turned, and our eyes met. "I told you not to go diggin' around about that cunt, yeah?"

I nodded. "Yes, and even though I wanted to, I didn't. I busied myself with other things today we'll get to in a minute."

Sean blinked. "What other things?"

"You first."

"They gotta do with me?"

"Oh, yeah."

"Then share."

"I will after you, since I'm still going to be sitting here and looking at you the way I always look at you. Nothing you could ever say to me would stop me from doing that."

Sean narrowed his eyes, then muttered a "fuck," before he resumed staring off blankly at the carpet. His hands were clasped in front of him.

I kept my hand on his bouncing thigh exactly how it had been. I didn't brace with light pressure. I did not move. I wouldn't.

React on the inside. Do not show it.

Sean blew out a breath. "A lot of the shit I've done—I regret," he began. "Most of it. I wish I could take it back, but I can't. *This*...this I do not wish I could take back. I don't regret it."

"Okay."

He turned to look at me. "Last time I saw that bitch, she was dying. I'm talkin' minutes away from takin' her last breath, and I didn't do shit to keep her alive. I didn't do a damn thing. I killed her."

I blinked and nodded slowly, encouraging him to keep going while willing my body and pulse to stay unreactive.

"Could've helped. Could've called the cops or whatever. I walked in to get out of the cold, found her lying on the floor with a needle stuck in her arm, lips blue, barely breathing. She was covered in puke. I felt her neck—there was a pulse—she was lookin' right at me, starin', I could've done somethin', Shayla, and I didn't. I stood there until that bitch died, then I took any money she had stashed in that house and left. I never went back."

Again, I blinked and nodded slowly.

"That's it," he said; then he released a tense breath and looked away. "I didn't want you diggin' around 'cause I knew you'd find out she was dead and ask me about it, and I didn't wanna tell you. Not 'cause I didn't want you knowin' she can't hurt me anymore. I didn't want you knowin' who I am. Now you know—I let that cunt die. I killed her. A better person would regret it. I don't. I'd do it again."

I was processing Sean's words and waiting for that rush of shock or fear to fill me. But all I felt was relief.

Sean was safe now. He never had to worry about that woman hurting him ever again.

And even though this act could've defined Sean as a person, it didn't. I didn't judge him any differently now. I didn't look at him in a new way. I couldn't.

I got it. I got *him*. This was Sean protecting himself. And I didn't see it as murder or Sean assisting in someone's death by not stepping in to help. I didn't see it that way at all.

"Okay," I said; then, before Sean could look over at me, I quickly slid onto the floor, moved in front of him, and knelt between his legs. I grabbed his face. "You see me looking at you?" I asked.

Sean's beautiful copper eyes were dilated and jumping with worry. "Yeah."

"Am I looking at you any different than I've always looked at you, aside from that time we weren't talking anymore and I avoided looking at you because it killed me to do it when I didn't think you wanted me looking?"

His brows pinched. "You didn't think I wanted you lookin'?"

"You turned me down and quit speaking to me so no, I didn't."

Why were we talking about this now? This was not important, Shay. Stay on track.

"Anyway, am I—"

"I always wanted it," he rushed out, halting my speech. "At the time, I knew I didn't deserve it. That's why I pushed you off. I wasn't good enough for you. Not even you lookin' at me, no matter how much I liked it."

I shook my head. "Sean..."

"I know different now. I'm just sayin', that's how it was before."

That made me smile. *Finally*, he understood his worth. He was getting it.

"I didn't think you were interested," I told him.

"That was never the fuckin' problem."

I smiled bigger.

Sean watched my mouth, his jaw ticked, then he repeated in that low, gravelly voice that made my skin tingle, "Never the fuckin' problem."

Holy crap, the flirting skills.

Stay on point, Shay. Keep focus.

"Okay, so you know how I've always looked at you," I prompted.

He met my gaze and jerked his chin.

"Am I looking at you any different right now?"

Sean stared into my eyes, breathing fast and heavy, studying me, searching for the slightest change—I could tell—and God, it was worrying him. I wanted so badly to tell him with words, but I knew he needed the proof, so I was staying silent and giving it to him. Then he reached out, slid his hands to the back of my neck, held there, and pressed our foreheads together. He kept staring, but his breathing was slowing, still just as heavy, but he was calmer now. He was seeing what I knew was there.

"Val got it too," he shared, and hearing he'd told his ex what had happened, and she didn't look at him any different after the fact, made me like Val a hundred times more, and I already liked her a lot. "Thought she'd run. She didn't. Thought you'd leave..."

"I won't," I cut in, finishing his sentence.

"She was wrong."

I blinked, curious whom he was referring to. "Val?"

Sean shook his head lightly since we were still touching. "That bitch," he answered. "Val didn't run. My girls forgave me. The way you look at me...I ain't nothin'."

My heart swelled. *God*...thank God, thank God.

"Not even close," I whispered, smiling, crying a little—I couldn't help it. I was just so happy for him.

Sean's thumb caught my tears, then he leaned in and kissed me, murmuring inside my mouth. "*Baby...baby.*"

Not the *baby girl* I'd been wanting before, and I was glad because this was better. This was mine.

"I want you," he said, kissing the corner of my mouth and then my cheek. "Share what you got for me, and then I'm taking you here. I wanna touch you. Feel you touch me."

Couch sex. *Hell, yes to all of that.*

I pressed one more kiss to his stubbled jaw, then I got to my feet and grabbed the list I'd made, returning to the couch with it.

I sat cross-legged facing Sean and held it out.

"What's this?" he asked, looking at the paper.

"People you can talk to, if you want, and I think you should," I told him, getting his eyes then. "They can help you, Sean. That nightmare... I don't want you having them ever again. I told you I'd get you to a place where you'd never need that bucket. This is me getting you there."

"I don't like talkin' about that shit," he said, which was something I already knew.

"I know, and I know it'll be hard, and if you don't want to do this, I'll understand. But I really think you should at least give this a try. These people are trained to heal. And you're still hurting."

He looked back at the list, read it again, rubbed at his mouth harshly, then kept reading.

I leaned in and placed my hand on top of one of his. "I can go with you if you want," I said, getting his eyes again. "Or pick one and I'll check them out first. I don't care. But no one will see you unless you want them to, Sean. No one gets to you without going through me, and even though I've spent the afternoon checking references and studying backgrounds, I didn't get the opportunity to meet anyone on that list face-to-face. I will be doing that. They don't just need to be good, Sean. They need to be the best. You just give me a name, and I'll make sure of that. I promise."

Sean's eyes got intense, then he looked at that list one last time before folding that piece of paper in half, getting to his feet, and stuffing the list inside his back pocket.

I smiled watching that happen because I knew it meant Sean was going to give me a name, possibly more than one, I'd scope them out in person, and then we'd get started on healing him.

I couldn't have been happier in that moment.

Until I watched Sean pull his shirt off, toss it, and then get to work on his belt.

"I've never had sex on a couch before," I admitted, getting to my feet now too so I could strip myself of clothing.

Sean unzipped his jeans. "Glad I get to cross that off your list."

"Me too. I'm glad it's you."

He'd just sat down on the couch to work at his boots when he froze and looked up at me. Our eyes met. His flashed with lust, hunger, and so much meaning, I began to ache in a way I knew meant there was a good chance I'd hold a world record for orgasms tonight, the first one building already.

How crazy was that?

"Gonna cross it off a lot," he promised.

I pulled my sweater off and grinned. "Awesome."

He grinned back.

We resumed stripping, both of us holding on to our grins, then I got on my back, Sean got on top of me, we started kissing, touching, stroking, our moans coming soft and then building when Sean guided my legs around his waist and slid inside me.

Floor sex was amazing.

Couch sex was equally incredible, especially since Sean hadn't lied about crossing this location off my list multiple times.

I came once on my back. Once on my knees with Sean taking me from behind while I gripped the armrest. Once with Sean's fingers sliding inside me when I thought we were taking a break, but Sean's break included exploring my body the way he always did when we'd lie naked together, and when Sean explored, he explored thoroughly.

Last, I came grinding my hips down on top of Sean while he

licked and sucked on my breasts. That orgasm surprised me because I thought it would take a while, but it didn't, thanks to Sean's tongue and the words he spoke against my flesh while he went to town there. Sean talking dirty was possibly at the top of my kryptonite list.

I didn't stand a chance.

Though, I had a feeling if it did hold top billing, it wouldn't hold that title forever. Sean was always surprising me with something that made my heart ache or beat so, so wildly, and before the night was up and he went home, he did it again.

We were standing at the door kissing, Sean dressed and me in nothing but my oversized sweater and panties. I didn't want him to leave, but we'd see each other at Whitecaps tomorrow morning, so I didn't protest.

Still, I kept attacking his mouth every time he pulled away, so I had a feeling he knew where I stood on him leaving.

Finally getting enough (not really), I kept my arms around his neck and rocked back onto my heels.

Sean smiled down at me. Then he topped the dirty talking, giving me compliments, going shirtless, and everything else he'd ever done.

He topped it all.

"I'm sellin' the trailer."

My lungs ceased working for a beat, then I pulled in a breath and grinned the biggest grin of my life. I rolled up onto my toes again and went in—I had to.

Sean was the one who attacked my mouth when I pulled away that time, which led to longer, harder kisses.

He eventually went home. It just took him a while.

Chapter Eighteen

SEAN

Eight Days Later

I got five hundred bucks for my trailer, exactly half of what I paid for it. I was expecting less than that, so I felt good about what I got.

Shayla was beaming as she stood there watching that transaction happen.

Now I had an extra five hundred dollars, which wasn't a ton of money, but it was still extra, and I wanted to do something with it, or at least something with the two-fifty I'd have after giving Val her cut.

She'd paid for enough on her own while I was away.

I wanted to give her the full amount, but she suggested I treat the girls to something with the rest.

I liked that idea.

Shayla did too when I told her.

"What are you thinking for them?" she'd asked me when I picked her up later that afternoon after speaking to Val about it. "We're going to get something, aren't we? I know we are."

"Why's that?"

"We never take your truck anywhere."

She had a point.

My truck was a piece of shit that served the purpose of a truck, nothing more, which was why I kept it. I liked my bike better and went for that unless I needed to haul something.

I'd choose my bike and Shayla holding on to me and pressing close any day.

I pulled away from her apartment, sharing, "Found a playground in the paper this guy is selling 'cause his kids don't use it anymore. It's nice. Small, but has swings and a slide. My girls will love it."

Shayla smiled over at me, then she unlatched her seat belt and slid across the bench seat, burrowing against my side. "Good choice," she said. "Can't think of a better way to spend that money."

I wrapped my arm around her shoulder, liking the feel of her against my side almost as much as I liked the feel of her at my back.

Maybe my truck wasn't so bad.

Once I paid the guy and we got the playground broken down and loaded, Shayla and I spent the afternoon putting it together at the house.

We talked like we always did. We laughed too, especially when Shayla joked about being an expert at heavy lifting, referencing my cock and how well she manages with that.

It was a good fucking day.

I was having a lot of those lately with Shayla by my side.

Then later that night after we got cleaned up, we headed over to Syd and Brian's place for family dinner.

I didn't know what to expect going over there. I never got invited to shit like this unless it was dinner over at Bridgett's house when Val and I were together. I figured I'd talk to Shayla most of the night and field questions from the other girls who showed up, since they didn't know how *not* to talk to me, and truth be told, I didn't mind it. What I hadn't anticipated was getting pulled into conversation by everyone there.

And it started the second we walked in.

The girls latched on to me first—Tori and Jenna, Brian's sister I'd met the other night. They pulled me into the kitchen, where everyone was standing around, talking and waiting for the food to be ready. Syd was in there cooking, and once she saw me, she got in on it too. Brian and Jamie, who I met when Shayla brought all that furniture over last month, got a few words in when their women quit talking long enough to take a breath. They welcomed me and told everyone to ease off, which didn't happen. Even Jenna's kids, Oliver and Olivia, stayed close and fired questions at me. I wasn't used to attention like that.

I didn't mind it, though. It felt good—everyone wanting me there and not being shy about making sure I knew it. I understood real fast why they called it family dinner.

This was family.

The conversations carried throughout the meal, which was damn good. I hadn't been expecting that.

I found out the guys owned a surf shop together—this place called Wax. Cole, their friend and the guy Kali was seeing, worked there as well. He couldn't make dinner, and Kali was working with the new girl Lauren whom Tori kept complaining about, and once it was clear she was gearing up to complain for a good while, the guys stepped out on the deck and asked me to join them.

Each of us took a seat around the glass patio table, drinks in hand, while Oliver and Olivia, Jenna's kids, chased Sir, Syd and Brian's dog, around the yard.

"Sean, you surf?"

I was gazing at the sliding door listening to Shayla's loud, pretty laugh when Jamie spoke, grabbing my attention.

I looked at him. "I have. Wouldn't say it's somethin' I do, though. Fucked around with it when I was younger."

"You got a board?" Brian asked.

I shook my head.

"That's a problem." Brian looked to Jamie after he spoke, who was taking a pull of his beer. "You care?"

"Nope," Jamie answered, then he directed at me, "Come by the shop. We'll fix that."

The slider opened as I was replying, "Doubt I can afford one. Thanks, though. I appreciate the offer."

"Ain't nothin' to afford when it's free," Jamie shot back.

I blinked. "You're not chargin' me?"

For a fucking surfboard? Was he serious?

"Have you *met* my woman?" Jamie gestured at Tori as the girls filed outside. "She'll shut me out for a solid month if I take your money."

"Longer than that," Tori cut in, getting everyone's attention.

She had a bunch of foil in her hair you'd typically wrap food in, which Shayla was examining as she stood on her toes behind Tori.

"Jesus. You bring that shit with you everywhere?" Jamie directed at Shayla.

"Of course," she replied, looking at him like he was crazy to think she wouldn't. Then she went back to examining Tori's head. "I want to add a few more. Hold on," she said, dashing back inside. "You're next, Jenna!"

Jenna grinned over her shoulder as she made her way to the end of the deck. She peered out into the yard.

"What's that shit on your head?" Brian asked Tori as Syd walked over to him and took a seat on his lap.

"It's foil for my color. What's it look like?" Tori shot back.

"It looks like you're tryin' to pick up a signal out here."

Everyone started laughing, except Tori.

"Ha ha." She rolled her eyes to Jamie, then she plastered on a smile, all beauty. "You giving him a board?"

"You think I could go longer than a month without you?"

"Nope."

"Then I'm givin' him a board."

Her smile turned into a grin.

Shayla rushed back outside carrying a bowl and more foil, and directed Tori to the chair, then ended up standing next to the one Jamie was occupying since Tori took his lap instead. Shayla got to work painting more pieces of hair.

"Swing by whenever, man. We'll get you set up," Jamie told me.

I was geared up to protest. I didn't need a board. I especially didn't need one for free.

What the fuck did I do to deserve it? I barely knew these guys.

Then, looking from Jamie to Shayla and seeing the smile take up her face while she worked, knowing she was responsible for all the kindness being put on me lately, including what I'd felt tonight, and feeling that, remembering why I deserved people treating me this way, I nodded, meeting his gaze.

"Thanks. Appreciate it."

"No problem."

I watched the smile Shayla was wearing amp up a bit, though she kept on working and didn't make a big deal.

I appreciated that too.

"All right, guys. We need to talk carnival details," Syd announced, then looking to Tori, she added, "You want to take this? You know more about it than I do."

"Sure thing," Tori answered with a grin. Then she gave us the rundown of the idea she and Syd had come up with to help kick off the summer season at Whitecaps.

We'd put on a carnival over Memorial Day weekend, offering food, games, and prizes. The menu would be simple—hamburgers and hot dogs—plus sodas and water. There would be a DJ and booths set up the girls would be in charge of, with help from

Brian, Jamie, and Cole, considering how many booths Tori wanted to get.

"We want this to be *huge*," she said. "I've already talked to Nate about it, and he's down with closing Whitecaps for the day and throwing a kickass party in the parking lot. He knows we'll make a killing with how many people typically flock to the beach that weekend. And we'll draw the crowd with good tunes, great food, awesome prizes, and fun games for kids."

"You can definitely count us in," Jenna said. She'd walked over during the conversation and took a seat between Jamie and me. "The twins will love it."

Tori smiled. "I think it'll really kick off an awesome summer for Whitecaps. Nobody else does anything like this. They just open for the day. We'll be throwing a kickass party. Everyone will want to come back."

"You got three weeks before that weekend," Brian said. "Is that enough time to get shit lined up? You're talking about locking in booths and a DJ. You might be cuttin' it close."

I'd been wondering the same thing.

Tori cocked her head and grinned. "Well, *two of us* have connections to the best surf shop in Dogwood...I was thinking you boys could pull a few strings."

"I'm feelin' used," Jamie mumbled.

Tori elbowed him.

He wrapped his arms around her and buried his face in her neck, making her giggle.

"We'll let you advertise for free," Syd informed Jamie. "You can put your stickers on everything and bring a few boards. It's a win-win for you too."

Brian chuckled. "Is it, Wild?"

Brian called his girl Wild. I didn't understand why. Didn't ask either. That was their business.

"*Yes*," she said with emphasis, laughing. "And we already got the booths locked in. Tori called about them weeks ago. We just need you to help us get the DJ."

"I think we can handle that," Brian replied. He jerked his chin at Jamie. "We'll make a few calls next week."

"Won't be a problem," Jamie assured, earning himself a kiss from Tori.

"The only thing is, we'd have to work that day without getting paid." Tori glanced around the table, saying, "I'm fine with that."

"Me too," Shayla put out.

"Anything for Nate," Syd announced.

"Stitch, what do you think?" Tori asked.

There was nothing to think about. "Guy's done a lot for me, shit he didn't need to do... No question—I'm in."

Tori beamed. "God, I am so glad you're here!" she declared.

"No shit," Jamie grumbled. "Between the four of you, that phrase has been uttered tonight every other fuckin' minute."

Everyone started laughing.

I looked at Shayla and saw she wasn't laughing, but she was grinning while she worked on Jenna's hair, no doubt agreeing with Tori's statement.

The girls kept talking and throwing out more ideas for the carnival. Brian and Jamie listened and chimed in. I listened and stayed quiet, watching them interact, but mainly watching Shayla work because I liked doing that, until my phone vibrated in my pocket, and I was forced to quit watching her.

It was a text from Val. I read it.

Caroline fell at the park and split her lip. She's okay but she needs stitches. We're at PromptCare. She's asking for you. U busy?

I stood from the chair and shoved my phone away.

"What's up?" Shayla asked.

"Caroline fell and needs stitches in her lip. She's fine, but she wants me there," I said.

"Oh, that poor thing," Shayla whispered.

All the women muttered something similar.

"Do you…uh…" Shayla looked at Jenna's head, then peered over her shoulder at Tori before returning her gaze to mine. It was anxious.

I read it.

"Stay," I told her, walking over to her side. My hand went to her neck and I bent down, pressing my mouth to her hair as I spoke. "Don't rush what you're doin'. I'll go, text or call and let you know what's goin' on. Then you'll see me later, yeah?"

Shayla had one hand in Jenna's hair but with her other she squeezed my side. "Yeah. That's perfect."

"Good." I leaned back, my hand on her neck tensed, and when it did, Shayla tipped her chin way up to look at me, granting access to her mouth. Getting that, I kissed her.

Someone gasped.

Someone shushed.

Jenna started laughing, and I knew that only because she was closest to me, and there was no mistaking it.

Brian commented with, "Jesus, babe, you cryin' 'cause they're kissing?"

Jamie threw out, "Big fuckin' surprise there," which got Shayla giggling against my mouth.

I pulled back and smiled at her. "Later."

She winked. "Later."

Then I said my goodbyes and thanked everyone for the invite, stood there while Syd, Tori, and Jenna took turns hugging me (I guess that was becoming a thing), shook Brian and Jamie's hands while promising I'd stop by soon to get a board, and finally, I took off.

PromptCare wasn't far from the house. I got there in fifteen minutes and was immediately taken back to the exam room once I showed my ID.

"Daddy!" Caroline was lying on the table with a rag on her mouth, and seeing me, she burst into tears.

I went to her.

"Oh, Caroline, you were fine until Daddy walked in the room," Val shared. She was holding a sleeping Fiona, who began to stir, hearing her sister.

"Let me see, baby girl." I pulled the rag away and examined Caroline's mouth.

There was a tiny cut in the corner of her bottom lip she was bleeding from.

"The doctor will be in soon to stitch it up. I asked him to wait for you."

I smiled at Caroline, then looked over at Val. "Thanks for lettin' me know."

Val frowned. "Of course. Thank you for coming." She moved over to stand beside me. "I would've sent that text whether Caroline insisted you be here or not, Sean. I hope you know that."

I stared at her, wondering what I had done to deserve the good she was showing me, but then I shut that thought down.

Thanks to Shayla, I knew.

"*Daddy*," Caroline whined again.

I put my attention on my oldest, bending down and speaking to her gently, trying to calm her, and staying there even after the doctor came in and informed everyone on what he'd be doing.

Caroline tensed up and started kicking when the doctor approached her.

It took three nurses to hold my baby girl down, but once I moved to the head of the table so she could look up and see nothing but me, Caroline went calm and let the doctor stitch her up. She kept crying, but it was silent. Nothing but little sniffles escaping her. It took two stitches to get the wound closed, and the doctor was quick.

He was also a plastic surgeon, so there wouldn't be a scar.

That had been a worry, but I kept that to myself, not wanting to put it on Val and add to her concern.

While things were getting settled at the reception desk, I pulled out my phone.

Caroline is good. Got 2 stitches. Should be leaving soon. You still there or home?

Shayla's text back was quick.

Just got home. Glad she's ok!

Same. Heading over soon.

Can't wait. xoxo

Exactly twelve minutes after saying goodbye to Val and the girls, I was knocking on Shayla's door, and exactly thirteen seconds after that, I was grabbing her up, guiding her legs around me, and kissing her hard and hurried while kicking the door closed.

Her hands were in my hair. She was tugging, moaning. "She's okay?" she asked breathlessly inside our kiss.

"Yeah. Cried, but she calmed enough for them to stitch her up."

I carried Shayla through her apartment and into the bedroom.

"She wanted you there. You went. You got her calm," Shayla said, smiling up at me when I laid her on the bed.

The shirt she was wearing was unbuttoned at the top, revealing enough skin I'd have to be a fucking god to keep my mouth from it.

Shayla arched her neck and gave me access, then she moaned, "Sean," when I sucked and licked her cleavage.

"We go fast a lot, a little rough," I said, pulling back but looming over her still. "Every time, it's like that."

I was talking about how we fucked, and she picked up on that right away.

Shayla started nodding before I finished, her fingers staying in my hair. "I can only speak for myself, but I think it's that way because I've wanted this for so long," she confessed. "I feel like this has been building forever, and when something builds up that much, there is no easy release. It's chaos."

"I feel the same. Couldn't get over here fast enough just now. I never can."

Hearing that, she smiled. "Okay. Then it's 'cause we're both crazy and hard up, and coming together after waiting for so long . . . I think it'll always be like this. At least for a while."

"You good with that?"

"I'm good with any sex involving you," she answered. "Fast or slow. Although slow might be fun . . . " She wiggled her brows.

I grinned, then bent lower and kissed her jaw, her lips. "I'm gonna drag it out then," I promised, feeling her body shudder. "Start with your taste filling my mouth, then I'll work you up with my cock. Might go between the two. I don't know." I straightened up and got to work on her jeans, unbuttoning them and getting at the zipper. I ran my thumb over the small scissor tattoo she had on her hip bone when it came into view.

"Go to town. I won't stop you," she said.

I looked at her.

She was grinning now too, and she giggled when she had my eyes. "I'm excited for slowed-down Sean," she revealed. "Taking-me-on-the-floor Sean is amazing. Banging-my-back-out-on-the-couch Sean—fantastic. Slowed-down Sean might top the list. You're always giving me better than the last time, and I'm not just talking about sex, so I wouldn't be surprised."

I'd gotten her jeans off but paused at her panties. "You're not just talkin' about sex?" I questioned.

"Nope."

"Explain that."

She cocked her head cutely. "Mm? I'm sorry, are explanations a part of this slowed-down Sean? Less talking, more stripping." She wiggled her butt against the bed.

Shayla was trying to hurry me along and keep that shit to herself. She forgot who controlled what was happening here. I was prepared to take this shit *slow*.

Tugging her panties down her legs and tossing them, I kneeled beside the bed and bent her legs up, pushing her thighs open. My head lowered, I got as close as I could get to her bare pussy without burying my face in it.

That was a fucking challenge, but I was getting this out of her. I needed to know.

Because I knew it was something big, something that held meaning, and something I'd feel for fuckin' ever.

I wanted that.

"Um…is everything okay?" she asked shyly, pushing up to her elbows when I didn't move.

Our eyes locked across her body. "Got your pussy in my face—everything's great on my end. You?"

She frowned. "Considering your tongue is still in your mouth, I'm not doing too hot."

I smirked.

Her stare became intense, then she gestured with it between her legs, urging me on.

"You want my tongue? Explain," I ordered.

Her mouth dropped open. "You're willing to keep your head that close to me and *not* taste until I share?"

"Yep."

"That could be minutes."

"So?"

"Hours."

"I'm comfortable."

Steel determination flared in her eyes, and she tried wiggling out of my hold and scooting back, but I kept my grip on her legs and held her captive.

She grunted in frustration and flattened on the bed. "Fine. It's not even that big of a deal, I'm just really wanting your mouth on me."

"You'll get it," I promised. "Pretty sure I want it more than you do."

Her head came up again and a second later, she was back on her elbows. "That's impossible," she spat.

"Mouth is waterin', baby, you got no idea." I bent lower so my lips brushed against her flesh.

Fuck, did I want a taste.

Shayla gasped. "Okay…okay, you win. God, that's so fucking sexy. This is my new favorite game."

I chuckled.

Then Shayla smiled at me, all soft and sweet, and gave me what I wanted.

"I refer to certain things about you as my kryptonite," she began. "All of this happening in my head, obviously. I don't tell people. That would be weird. But, like, for example, your chest—the first time I saw it when my brothers and I brought you dinner, I nearly passed out. The list I have is huge. It's physical things and it's things you do you don't realize you do, like the way you flirt. I don't think you do it on purpose—it's so subtle and surprising. How you listen to me when I speak… that got me last year. It was one of the reasons I liked sticking my head in that window and talking to you so much. You listened like I was telling you stuff you needed to hear."

"'Cause I did," I said.

She shook her head, disagreeing. "How could you need to know about my dad getting diagnosed with Parkinson's? Or about how much I wanted my own salon?"

"Wasn't what you said, it was you putting it on me. Sharin' it. Like I was deservin' of the stuff you thought about."

Her eyes softened. "Holy shit, *see*! Right there, prime example. You just topped the list again!"

I grinned. "Just tellin' you how it is."

"Well, this is why I have a list in the first place," she said, laughing. "You say stuff like that, Sean, or you squeeze my neck or do something sweet with your girls, just you being you, and I'm weak."

I pulled in a breath. *Just me being me.* I was someone to her, and fuck, did that mean everything.

I was right. That was worth the torturous wait having my mouth this close to her was.

"And I—oh...*oh*, God," Shayla groaned when I dove in, eating her roughly because I was a starving man at this point, but going at her slowly because I'd promised I would.

"Your cunt is so fuckin' good," I said between licks and sucks on her clit that made the fingers in my hair pull.

She tasted hot and sweet. She was so wet, I could open my mouth and drink her.

And I did. I took my time and drank my fill.

"*Fuck*," she panted, her body writhing and trembling.

I moaned into her pussy.

"*Sean.*" Shayla's heels were pressed to the tops of my shoulders. She dug them in and began to grind against my face. "I'm close," she warned.

I pushed my tongue inside her and brought my hand off her leg. I rubbed my thumb against her clit. I was slow with that too.

"I need to come. I need to come."

"Do it," I growled. "Do it, let me see."

Shayla arched off the bed with a cry and sat up to watch me fuck her with my tongue, gripping my head and holding me against her. Her body jerked. Her hand in my hair tugged so hard, my eyes watered.

She was pretty here too—how eager she got when her orgasm hit. A little greedy. I fucking loved it.

When I lapped at her pussy like I was licking her clean, her mouth fell open, and she fell back with a sigh.

"Shit," she breathed. "So good . . . slow is *so good*." She giggled.

I stood and got undressed, smiling down at her. I could taste her arousal on my lips.

Shayla watched shyly as I licked them.

Shirt off, I sat on the bed and worked at my boots, getting those off while she dug her toes into my thigh. Then I stood and got out of my jeans, watching her peel her top off. I crawled on the bed.

"Hey," she said, opening her legs so I could fit between them.

I slid inside on a slow drag, no warning. We moaned together.

Then I put my weight on my elbows and kissed her. "Hey."

She smiled. Her legs around me. Her fingers pushing through my hair. "Go slow," she urged.

"Plannin' on it."

I dropped my head, buried my face in her neck, and started to move.

We touched everywhere, like we did when we were hurried, but we spent time. I memorized Shayla's body and the way it moved beneath me and with me. I took her breasts into my mouth. They were small, and her nipples were so hard against my tongue. Her skin tasted like honey. Her ass filled my hands. She was perfect.

I fucked her with her legs on my shoulders and pressed against her chest. I kept it slow even when her second orgasm took her and she begged, "Please please please," fighting the urge to buck my hips. I wanted to pound us both into tomorrow. I wanted to fuck this girl so she felt me next week. I wanted her voice in my ear and her hands guiding me and her mouth against mine, every fucking second of every day. I wanted her knowing how I felt, and being scared shitless didn't stop me. I came inside her and I said it.

"I wanna be yours," I panted, watching her eyes dilate and blink wider as she took in what I was saying. "You at my back, stickin' up for me, and there when I'm fuckin' terrified . . . I wanna go to you and I want you tellin' me I can. I wanna be yours, Shayla."

Our hearts pounded together.

I wanted that every day too.

"I want that so bad," she whispered. "And I will stay at your back and stick up for you always, Sean. I won't leave."

"Promise that."

"Sweetie..." She tenderly stroked my face.

"Promise that," I repeated, staring into her eyes. "You won't leave, ever. Say it."

"I won't leave, ever," she vowed.

I buried my face in her neck and held her, and Shayla clung to me, stroking her fingers softly up and down my back.

We shifted so I was under her and her body was lying across mine, her leg draped over my hip, her cheek on my chest.

I had Shayla in my arms, I just came hard—my eyes closed the second my head touched the pillow. I couldn't fight it.

Her voice filled my head as I drifted off.

"I want you to have all the love in the world, Sean. You deserve that. And I won't stop until you get it."

Chapter Nineteen

SHAYLA

Thirteen Days Later

It was Saturday, I was working a shift at Whitecaps with both Kali *and* Tori. Sean was here. The weather was gorgeous, meaning people were out and about, leading to a steady lunch rush that had just ended. Everyone stopping in seemed to be in the mood to tip.

It was a good day.

If I was being honest, though, it would've been a good day running the floor by myself with gross weather keeping patrons at bay, except for the stragglers coming in dealing out shitty tips.

As long as Sean was in that kitchen, nothing was corrupting my mood.

We'd been together for several weeks now, and things were fantastic. *More* than fantastic. Not only with us, but Sean was getting to spend time with his girls at least a couple times a week.

I loved hearing about those visits.

As much as I wanted to experience them with him, I said no each time I was invited. It was more important to me for Sean to get that alone time with Caroline and Fiona. Besides, hearing about it was possibly better than being there anyway. He gushed on his girls. It was both sweet and sexy.

The other thing making life fantastic lately was the steps we were taking toward healing him.

Sean had taken that list of names I'd given him and handed it back to me a week later, telling me he'd see whoever I cleared. He was trusting me with something that important. Possibly the *most* important.

Sean wanted me at his back. I was standing at his front, too. Nobody got to him without getting through me.

I told him that after securing the list I had plans to nitpick as soon as possible. Then I watched Sean gesture at his back seat instead of getting out of his truck.

He did not have to gesture twice.

Back-seat-of-his-truck Sean was *insane*. Hot. Sexy. Slow. Fogged windows. His moans amplified.

Mother of God, it was awesome.

I was happy for a lot of reasons lately; stellar sex and a hopping business will do that to a person, but deep down in my heart, I was happiest because Sean was getting what he deserved out of this life.

Kindness. Love. Friendship. Respect. Compassion. All of it given freely.

So, even though I was having a good day today, it wasn't out of the ordinary. I had a lot of good days lately.

"Guess what?"

Tori, dashing out of the employee lounge, slid up beside me at the register and nudged my hip.

I looked over at her grinning face. "You're engaged? *I knowww*," I teased.

She playfully shoved my shoulder, then held up her hand and studied the new sparkler decorating her finger.

I wasn't the only one having good days around here. I was crazy happy for her and Jamie.

"We got the DJ locked in," Tori shared after she was finished beaming.

"Hell, yes!" I held my hand up and she high-fived me.

"Whoo! I am *pumped*!" Tori exclaimed.

Kali came hurrying over carrying a tray. "DJ?" she asked Tori.

Tori gave her a thumbs-up as she backed away.

"*Yes.*" Kali shimmied her hips while sitting her tray down on the counter.

Now with the DJ, we were all set.

"Cole and I are working the kissing booth," Kali shared, looking all kinds of happy about that.

I'd been assigned face painting.

It seemed appropriate, considering my skills with a brush.

"Not sure what kind of money we're gonna drum up if you two are only kissing each other," I joked.

Kali blushed, then quickly replied, "Hey, I'd pay to see that."

"Oooh, nice!" I winked at her and she giggled.

After collecting the paid tabs that were waiting for me on the two remaining tables I had left, I decided a break was in order.

I had yet to take one today and couldn't earlier, thanks to the rush, and now, as I swung myself up on the counter and peered through the kitchen window, enjoying my current view of Sean's ass in those sexy, ratty jeans he wore, I was craving a breather.

J.R. stepped up in front of me.

"You're blocking my view," I murmured.

He paused chopping up some garnish and peered up at me, smiling. "My bad."

"Hey," I whispered, leaning closer and getting his eyes again. "Can you cover things so Sean can take a break?"

"Yeah. He need one?"

"Probably not, but I do."

J.R. grinned. "If the lounge is a rocking . . . " he started.

I slid off the counter, laughing.

I was not planning on banging Sean at work, at least not during business hours. But a little private make-out session? *That* I was down for.

I walked around the corner so I could peek inside the kitchen. "Psst."

Sean glanced over at me, his brows lifting in question.

I gave him a tease of my tongue, slowly licking my upper lip. His eyes lowered to my mouth, and when they met mine again, they were heated.

Break time.

J.R. stepped up beside Sean and slapped his shoulder. "I got this," I heard him say as I turned and headed for the lounge.

Door swinging closed behind me, I straddled the bench seat and waited.

I did not wait long.

Sean came rushing inside that lounge within seconds, and had the door locked, me straddling his lap instead of the bench, and his tongue inside my mouth before you could say *inappropriate workplace conduct*.

Typical breaks lasted fifteen minutes, unless you were a smoker, and then you got ten.

Since Sean had given up smoking for the most part once he got his girls back, we both had fifteen minutes to use, and I wasted no time suggesting we combine those fifteen minutes and stay in the lounge for a solid thirty.

Sean mentioned something about us getting fired.

I pretended I didn't hear him and, in my head, I split the difference. Relationships were about compromise.

We made out for twenty minutes in that lounge like two teenagers who hadn't done more than kiss yet but wanted to do so much more than kiss.

There was quiet moaning, roaming hands, and hidden marks left from sucking.

It was the best break ever.

Three days later, I was working from home, a full day of clients keeping me busy, and currently enjoying the hell out of one of my favorites who was coming in to get her color touched up.

"Is it weird that I'm using a professional day to get my hair done?" Val asked.

"No way. What's more professional than kickass hair?"

She laughed and held her hair off her neck while I buttoned the cape around her.

"Are we touching up the pink too?" I asked.

Val met my eyes in the mirror and grinned.

"Rock on." I gave her shoulders a squeeze, then got to work mixing the color.

"So, what's new? School's out soon, right?" I asked.

"June eleventh."

"I bet the girls are excited." I sectioned off Val's hair and began applying the color.

"Right now, the only thing they care about is us going to the beach this weekend."

"Oh, that's fun. Which one?"

"Outer Banks."

"Nice." I met her eyes and smiled. "Are you staying through the holiday?"

Val gently nodded since I was holding pieces of her hair. "We have to come home Monday because of school on Tuesday, but it'll be late. I want to get as much time at the beach with them as I can."

I pictured Caroline and Fiona building sand castles and jumping waves.

"Well, your hair will look super pretty while you're sunbathing, that's for sure."

Val's smile turned shy, and she lowered her eyes in the mirror and bit her lip.

"What?" I giggled at her reaction. "Okay, no sunbathing then."

"No. Not that." She covered her face and groaned.

"Oh, my God, *what?*"

Lowering her hands, Val blushed in the mirror. "I'd like to look super pretty for *another reason*..."

My brows lifted.

"I'm sort of crushing on my ex."

Air left my lungs in a whoosh. "O-Oh!" I stammered. "That's...cool. I had no idea."

Oh, shit. Shitshitshitshit.

This was awkward.

"Yeah, it's been slowly becoming something I can't ignore," she said timidly, but I knew it wasn't because of who she was sharing this with.

Val had no idea about Sean and me. Neither did his girls. We hadn't gotten around to saying anything because we were too busy enjoying it ourselves. We were letting go and letting things happen. And anyway, we were still pretty new. Unless you saw us together, you wouldn't know, and the only time Val had seen Sean and me together was at the girls' dance recital, and that night had been all about them.

Maybe we should've said something.

"I mean, I don't know, to say I'm crushing on Sean is weird when I've been in love with him since I was seventeen, but that's what it feels like."

My heart began to pound.

I kept my focus on my work—section, paint, fold foil, repeat. Section, paint, fold foil, repeat.

Val was still in love with Sean. Nobody knew Sean and I were together—fold foil, repeat.

"I hated him while he was away," she said. "I thought I was done, but then I look at him now, and I watch him with our girls... and I'm *so* proud of him. He's really stepped up and gotten his shit together."

"Yeah," I agreed, not knowing what else to say.

"He's not just an amazing dad, he's an amazing human being. He always was," she added.

That drew my head up. We locked eyes. Hers were holding so much emotion it gripped at my chest.

"Sean has been through so much, way more than any person ever should," she continued. "I remember when we were younger and hearing about some of the horrible things he went through... It made sense—how he acted, the things he did, the things he kept doing. I would look at him and think, *God, you are a miracle.* How he survived, I'll never understand, but I was so happy he did. I was so in love with him."

Tears stung my eyes. I bit the tremble in my lip and looked away, sniffling.

"Hey, are you okay?" Val asked.

I nodded, playing it off, and wiped under my lashes so my makeup wouldn't smear. "Yeah, sorry... I'm just super sensitive to stuff right now. I'm about to get my period. And that was just... so sweet."

One of those things was a lie.

Val smiled gently.

I regained my focus and resumed my work. "Do the, uh, girls say anything?"

"About us?"

Us. Another piece of my heart chipped away. I nodded tightly.

"Fiona asks all the time why Sean lives in a different house," Val revealed. "Caroline thinks it's cool having two bedrooms."

I smiled. It felt strange, like I'd never done it before.

"I don't really talk about it much with them. I don't want to get their hopes up."

God, she was such a good mom.

"Do you think I'm being crazy? Please be honest with me... I know I probably sound insane considering how angry I was at Sean when you first met me, but it's just so hard to stay angry when you see someone you care about finally getting the life they deserve, you know?"

God... not just a good mom, Val was a good person, which I already knew but now, I *knew*—she got it.

Val saw Sean exactly how I did, and how everyone should see him.

"I don't think you're being crazy," I answered honestly, my hand holding the brush still as I looked in the mirror. "Making sure someone gets the happiness they deserve is not crazy. And I can't think of anything better than a life with those girls."

Val nodded in agreement. "I watch them together, and I remember our family... I miss it. I miss him."

Section, paint, fold foil, repeat.

"I was thinking about heading over to Whitecaps after picking up the girls at Bridgett's and asking if he wanted to go on vacation with us. What do you think? Good idea?"

She wanted my opinion, and despite my suffering, I had one, and it was honest.

"Great idea," I told her.

Val grinned. "I thought maybe while we were there, I'd make my move..." She laughed nervously, then blushed hard and covered it with her hands. "God, I'm terrified. I feel like I'm seventeen again. You gotta make my hair look so amazing, he won't be able to turn me down."

I watched Val lower her eyes and gnaw at her bottom lip. She looked lost inside her head, daydreaming about the man I was secretly in love with.

I never told a soul.

I never would.

After Val left with amazing hair and wearing the smile of a giddy teenager, I took the fifteen minutes I had before my next client arrived and spent them crying the tears I'd been holding back.

I needed longer than fifteen minutes, but a knock sounded, and I wouldn't ever shove my personal shit onto clients. I dried up my tears, checked my makeup situation, and knocked out the rest of my day, keeping myself composed.

And on the drive over to Sean's house later that night, I remained composed.

When his headlight shined in my rearview, I got out of my car, locked it up, and walked across the grass, reaching the driveway as he swung off his bike.

He bent down and kissed me, murmuring a tired "Hey," against my mouth.

"Hey," I said back. "Good day?"

"Yeah. Long, but good."

Sean threw his arm around my shoulders and led me inside.

"I gotta shower," he informed me. "Give me five, yeah?"

I nodded, leaning into the kiss he pressed to the side of my head before he released me.

Sean stepped inside the bathroom and closed the door.

I began to pace.

I felt like I was on autopilot. There was no rhythm or reason to my stride. I walked everywhere, throughout every room, as my anxiety began to claw at my skin. My feet dragged, but they moved me, and before I knew it, I was standing in Sean's bedroom in front of his dresser, examining the collection of items he had scattered there.

Aside from loose change and one of the ties he kept for his hair, there was a framed picture of him and the girls taken outside in front of the playground. Next to the frame was one of those clay molds you can bake and harden. It was a misshapen blob painted rainbow colors. There was also a drawing done by one of the girls—Caroline, if I had to guess—of a stick-figure family, resembling the one on the fridge, but this one had a beach background. Next to the drawing was a small wooden box you'd keep little trinkets in. I flipped back the lid, expecting to see little tokens. Maybe a few crayons, since they seemed to be hidden throughout the house.

I laughed when Chuck E Cheese tickets popped out. Rolls of them.

As I folded them up to put them back inside, I saw something else in the box.

Created from the same thread adorning Sean's wrist was a tiny ring.

Breath quaking inside my chest, I picked it up to examine.

It matched the colors Sean wore, the threads tightly braided together into a pattern. The design was flawless. It had taken time, and maybe Caroline could've spent the hours, but I knew this was all Sean. He made this.

Tears filled my eyes. I dried them up when I heard the bathroom door open, and popped the ring and tickets back inside the box, closing it up quickly.

Sean entered the bedroom with a towel wrapped around his waist.

I moved away from the dresser so he could get to it and took a seat on the bed.

"Your day good?" he asked as he dressed. "Val said she saw you."

"Yeah. Did you talk to her?"

He pulled jeans on over his boxers. "She stopped by work," he shared. "Asked if I wanted to go to the beach with her and the girls this weekend."

"You should go," I blurted out.

Sean's head came up as he finished buttoning his jeans. "What about the carnival?"

Shit, I'd forgotten about that.

But it didn't matter anyway. That wouldn't be a reason for him to miss this opportunity.

"J.R. can handle it," I said. "I'm sure he'd be fine. Go to the beach with them."

Sean's head popped through the neckhole of his shirt. With hard eyes filled with confusion, he stared at me as he pushed his arms through the sleeves. "You want me goin' on a vacation with my ex," he stated in disbelief.

I stood from the bed. "With your *family*, yes, I do," I told him.

"Why?"

"Because they're your family."

"And what the fuck are you?"

I shrugged and, in the steadiest voice I could manage, replied, "I'm someone who wants you to be happy."

Sean's chest began to rise and fall rapidly. We stared at each other, seconds passing before he asked, "What the fuck are you sayin'?"

"I just told you—I think you should go on vacation with them."

"You're not just talkin' about me going on some fuckin' beach trip," he growled, approaching me. "So I'm gonna ask again. What the *fuck* are you sayin' to me?"

I stared up into Sean's face as my hands stayed glued at my side.

I wanted so badly to touch him, and it killed me not to. It killed me being here, letting these words fall out of my mouth while keeping others to myself. All of it, *this* was killing me.

I tried looking away when tears built on my lashes, but Sean caught my chin and guided me back.

"Explain," he ordered.

"I want you to have what you lost," I whispered.

His eyes softened, and the tightness in his jaw released. He no longer looked pissed.

"Your family...life with your girls every day, I want you to have that, Sean," I said. "I think you should go on vacation with Val. Spend some time with them. Love them. Be a family…You deserve to have everything. *Everything.* Even things I can't give you because they aren't mine to give."

"You're leavin' me?" he asked, and God, there was so much ache and shocking hurt in his voice. It cried into my heart. "Tellin' me to go, but you're leavin' me. That's what this is. You're fuckin' endin' this?"

I couldn't nod or tell him yes. I couldn't utter the words I promised I'd never say. I could only stand there and weep.

Sean released my face and lowered his arm.

"I love you," he said.

More tears flooded my eyes. They wet my trembling lips.

I was dying. This was pain unlike I'd ever felt. It was crushing. Not only what I'd said, but staying silent when the only words I wanted to speak were trapped inside my heart and would stay there. He would never hear them.

Sean pulled in a breath through his nose and jerked his chin. His mouth hardened.

"I'm sorry," I whispered, moving around him. I made it to the door.

"I tell you that, and you leave," he declared at my back.

I peered over my shoulder.

I could barely see him through my tears, but Sean's devastation was clear and written all over his face. He looked shattered.

"I'm sorry," I repeated.

Then I walked out of his room, out of the home he deserved, and away from the life he'd worked so hard for.

I got in my car and left, when I'd promised I never would.

Chapter Twenty

SEAN

When I was a kid, I did a lot of dreaming.

I dreamed about a different life, one where I had parents who wanted me around, who liked me. I tried picturing it, but it was a hard thing to imagine when I didn't know what it looked like.

Then my girls were born, and I didn't need to dream anymore. I didn't have a hard time imagining what a family was, what they did, how they loved each other, because I had it. I had them. And even though I didn't understand the why, I was grateful.

When I got locked up, I did a lot of dreaming too.

I dreamed about my girls, about the life they were living without me. I imagined them with Val and knew they were getting love, but I also knew they deserved to get it from me. I didn't want my girls growing up needing to dream like I did. I didn't want them wondering what it would've been like having a dad around, one who cared, one who didn't hurt them. I made a promise to myself—I'd do whatever it took to give them that life I always wanted. We'd be a family. And unlike me, they wouldn't ever need to wonder what the fuck that was.

Meeting Val changed my life. She was the first person to ever look at me like I was worth something. And from that love came my girls.

Meeting Shayla changed my life for the second time. She kept it going.

And without her, I wouldn't understand the why.

I deserved that life. I deserved those dreams.

I deserved it all.

I met Val and the girls at the beach on Saturday morning.

I got coverage for the weekend, but getting Friday off wasn't happening, so I couldn't go down with them the day they left.

The girls didn't seem to care. Neither did Val. They were all happy to see me when I showed up, and excited to spend the day together.

Once Caroline and Fiona saw the board I brought down with me, having picked one out from Wax the other day, they couldn't contain their excitement.

My girls always loved riding the waves.

We spent the day in the water, the girls taking turns riding out with me on the board while Val stood with the other and took pictures. Then we switched. This went on through the afternoon, neither one of them tiring of it. While I ate one of the sandwiches Val had made, the girls built sandcastles and hunted for seashells.

It was a great day. One of the best I could ever remember having.

My girls were smiling nonstop. I'd never seen them this happy before. They loved all of us being together. They missed it. *I* missed it.

We looked like a family—just like we used to.

Fiona giggled as she chased away seagulls, and Val helped Caroline write our names in the sand in front of the castle.

"Look, Daddy," she said. "It's our home."

My chest tightened. *I could give them this*, I thought, watching Caroline take off running after Fiona with Val staying close behind. I could give them our family, *us*, every day. It would be better than it was before. It would be what my girls deserved all along. I would do anything for them.

I would do *this* for them.

No question.

We posed for more pictures after the girls cleared the seagulls off the beach, then it was time to head inside to make dinner.

Val bathed the girls while I handled that, then we sat and ate together on the patio so the girls could watch the waves.

"Daddy, you're quiet," Caroline said, poking my hand with her fork.

I was being quiet. Mainly, I was listening to everything the girls were saying, but I was also stuck inside my head.

I stroked Caroline's cheeks, reassuring her, "It's been a long day, baby girl. Daddy's tired."

"Not me!" she shrieked.

"Not me either!" Fiona copied.

Val and I shared a laugh when the girls both yawned around their next bites.

"Let's put them to bed," Val whispered.

She was sitting beside me in a lawn chair, Caroline passed out in her arms.

I was cradling a sleeping Fiona. I had no idea when she'd fallen asleep, but I got to my feet and followed Val inside to put the girls to bed. I kissed and tucked them in while Val waited at the door. When I stepped out into the hallway, she placed her hand on my chest and smiled up at me.

Her hair was lighter and curled from the ocean, and her face was suntanned. She looked like she did when we first met.

"Can we sit outside and talk?" she asked.

"Yeah, sure."

I followed her out onto the patio and went to move around her so I could take a seat, but Val grabbed my face, preventing that, and tried to kiss me.

Body stiff, I pulled back so she couldn't. It was a reflex. Instinctual. It didn't matter how badly I wanted this life for my girls...

I couldn't do this.

Not without Shayla.

"Oh, uh..." Val sank onto her heels and quickly dropped her hands. "Sorry," she whispered, her face flushing with embarrassment. "Sorry...God, I just totally went for it, didn't I? That sucked."

My mouth twitched. "You wanna sit?" I asked.

"Yeah. Yeah, I do." Val plopped down in a lawn chair and I took the seat beside her. She looked over at me and winced. "You're not here because of me, are you?" she guessed.

I shook my head.

"I'm not mad," she quickly shared. "Disappointed, maybe." We both smiled. "But you're here for the girls, and that means a lot to me, Sean. It means a lot to them."

"I'm sorry it ain't that way for me anymore," I said.

She reached out and squeezed my hand. "Don't be."

"I want to give them everything." My leg began to bounce. "I want them havin' the life they deserve, but—"

"They have a *great life* the way it is now, with you back in it," Val interrupted.

I nodded, appreciating her for saying that to me.

"Maybe we make better friends," she suggested. "We've been getting along better these past couple months than we ever did."

She was right about that.

"I was a dick to you back then. I should've been better."

"You weren't healed yet. I understand that now." She released my hand. "And I'm happy. I'm happy for you and our girls. It's really okay. I promise."

Sitting forward, I turned my seat so I was facing Val. It was time she knew. "I've been seein' Shayla."

Her mouth dropped open. "*What?* Are you serious?"

I nodded.

"Oh, my God..." Her voice was hushed and hurried. "Oh, my God. *Oh, my God!*" She covered her face with her hands.

"Val."

"I'm not mad. I'm not," she said, letting her hands fall away and gaping at me. "An idiot, *yes*. I am definitely that." Val began to laugh.

I stared at her, confused as fuck.

"Shay helped me decide to give you another chance," Val revealed. "Back when she first did my hair, she talked you up—telling me how good you were doing at your job, and the house—she told me you were really fixing it up nice for the girls. I didn't believe it until she told me. I thought you were lying."

Given our history, I understood why Val would think that, so I didn't react. But hearing what Shayla had done got a reaction. Heat spread out from the center of my chest and filled my limbs.

"I didn't think anything of it," Val continued. "She said you guys were work friends."

"Back then, that's all we were."

"Even if it wasn't, I don't think I would've picked up on her motive. She was genuine. She *is* genuine. What she said, that wasn't for her."

"Yeah," I mumbled. That was Shayla.

"You selling the trailer, was that her?" Val asked.

I nodded.

"And the therapy?"

"She thinks it'll help."

Val sat back. "She got to you."

I stared at her for a breath, then shook my head, not understanding.

"For as long as I've known you, Sean, I've been trying to get you to understand how worthy you are of a good life, and Shayla did that. I never could."

My lips pressed together tightly.

Val was right. Not only about Shayla, but about how hard she'd worked at trying to get me to hear her back then.

I fought it. I fought it so much, *we* fought. In the end, that was all we ever did.

"You did a lot for me," I said, not wanting her to feel ashamed or disappointed in herself. "Gave me the best two gifts sleepin' in that room, and I'll have love for you forever 'cause of that."

She smiled softly.

"I'm sorry you couldn't get me there," I added.

"At least someone did. How, is the question."

"She's stubborn," I said. "She never would've let me ignore her."

"*You're* stubborn."

"Not like her." I laughed. "She stands up to me. All five foot nothin' of her, she won't back down."

"Good." Val grinned.

"I love her."

I waited for Val to lose the smile, for it to fade, but she held it.

"The girls really like her," she said. "*I* really like her. And I like her for you. She did what I couldn't, and that's why you belong with her and not me."

I stared at Val for a breath, thinking about Shayla standing in my room, cutting me loose then leaving me. I squeezed my eyes shut and rubbed at my face.

"What?" Val asked.

Elbows resting on my knees, I looked at her. "Shayla told me to come here," I shared. "She pushed for it, said she couldn't give me this and wanted me to have it."

Lips parted, Val slowly closed her eyes and made a face like she was in pain. "Oh, my God, Sean." She caught her head with her hand when it dropped to the side, her arm bent and braced on the chair. "I told her the other day that I still loved you and wanted to try and get back together, and she *supported me*. She had tears in her eyes, but she told me I should go for it. I even told her I was going to invite you to come along with us this weekend, and she said it was a good idea." Val sat up straight and grimaced. "I am an *idiot*. I can't believe I didn't see why she was really crying."

I stared at Val, thinking on everything she'd just shared.

She had seen Shayla on Tuesday, right before I saw Val. Shayla left me on Tuesday.

"That girl cares about you *so much*, she gave you up so you could get us back, and I sat there like a moron and watched her cry over you, believing she was just having PMS. What is wrong with me?"

I shook my head, because yeah, Shayla was the type of person to do something like that, considering everything else she's done for me, but this shit still didn't make sense.

"She told me she'd never leave," I shared. "Fuckin' *promised me*, Val. I said I loved her, and she walked."

Val scooted forward in her chair and stared into my face. "She walked *because* she loves you."

I looked away. I didn't believe that.

"Love is sacrifice, Sean," Val continued. "It's putting your own happiness second. When you really care about someone, you do what is best for that person before you even *think* about yourself. You will suffer for love. If it's true, you'll do anything for it."

Her words rang out in my ears. I cracked my knuckles. *Fuck, was she right?*

"You think she did this shit for me?" I asked Val. "Her leaving, that was so I'd come here?"

"Did she look happy about it?"

"No."

"Did she look even *remotely okay* with walking away from you? Or pissed at you for something, which might explain her breaking it off?"

My teeth ground together. "She was cryin'," I mumbled, picturing Shayla standing in my room and then leaving it, the tears still in her eyes. "Kept sayin' she was sorry, but that sorry wasn't 'cause she was leavin', was it?"

Val cocked her head. "Now you're getting it."

My chest shuddered with a breath. "*Fuck*," I growled, pissed at myself.

I sat on that beach thinking about what my life would be like going back to Val. But I didn't just think about it. I considered it, knowing what I'd be sacrificing if I made that choice.

Or *who* I'd be sacrificing.

And Shayla had been doing the exact same fucking thing. Only difference was, she went through with it. She gave up her happiness for *me*.

And I hadn't seen it.

"You were hurt and angry, Sean," Val said, touching my arm. Her eyes were kind. "Anyone would've reacted the way you did and thought the same thing."

"No, I know her," I argued. "I fuckin' *know her*. I should've seen what she was doin'. I should've stopped it. She left—I let her leave. That's on me."

"Don't beat yourself up about it. Just fix the damn thing."

My brow furrowed. "I fuckin' am. *Jesus*, you think I wouldn't?"

Val sat back and giggled.

I shook my head, laughing. "This is weird."

"Both of us wanting you to be happy? Knowing you deserve it?" She smiled. "Not weird at all. I'm just glad you're *finally* on board."

I slumped back in the chair and linked my hands behind my head, looking through the glass and peering inside the condo. "I'll stay through tomorrow so I can get more time with the girls, but then I gotta head back," I told Val.

She nodded, then her eyes got soft. "Look at you," she said quietly.

"What?"

"You're getting it all, Sean. Everything good you always should've had."

"A lot of that is 'cause of you."

She slowly shook her head before putting her gaze on the ocean.

"No," she said. "It's you. You were never nothing. You're finally seeing that."

I was never nothing.

Those words didn't surprise me anymore or piss me off. I carried them with me now. They were mine. Shayla had given them to me.

Shayla.

Fuck, I couldn't wait to get her back.

Hearing her voice inside my head, I stared out at the ocean, wishing it was a different beach.

Chapter Twenty-one

SHAYLA

It was Memorial Day, the official kickoff of summer.

For beach lovers, this was it—the best time of the year. The start of everything.

For me?

It was a day I just wanted to sleep through.

Air conditioning on full blast, I sat parked behind Whitecaps with my head resting against the back of my seat and my eyes closed.

I felt exhausted. I knew I could fall asleep right now if I let myself.

But what use would that be? Someone would find me.

I was parked sandwiched between my closest friends. Tori and Sydney were expecting me to show up today. I hadn't just volunteered my time. I had committed.

Minutes ticked by as I tried holding tight to my procrastination, but the better person in me fought back.

I couldn't just sit here any longer. The carnival had started twenty minutes ago. I needed to move.

I cut the air down and tried rousing to a more alert state, but my limbs felt heavy against the seat. In the distance, I could hear music playing, children squealing with excitement. Commotion from the crowd. People gathering at Whitecaps for the excitement today would bring.

But none of it, not one thing was perking me up.

I missed Sean. Plain and simple.

Not even a beautiful, fun-filled day with my friends was taking that pain away.

Before anyone came looking for me and started asking questions, I locked up my car, slid my sunglasses on, and padded around the side of the building.

The gravel popped and crackled beneath my sneakers as my eyes scanned the crowd, searching for the one person I needed to quit searching for.

It was something I did out of habit and hope, and thinking today would be the day I would break routine was almost laughable. How could I not look for him here? I always did—when we were nothing and when we were everything, it didn't matter. I always looked.

Love was the killer of sanity.

"Shay!"

I turned my head toward the far corner of the parking lot.

Tori was standing with Jamie in front of the dunk tank. He was dripping wet in his swim trunks and tugging her against him when she tried getting away, wrapping his arms around her and soaking her clothes. She squealed and playfully pushed against his chest as Brian climbed up in the chair and waited his turn.

"Hey, babe." Tori stopped in front of me and smiled with sympathy in her eyes. She squeezed my hand. "How are you?"

"I'm here," I replied, shrugging. "I don't know. Maybe this will be a nice distraction. I can paint ladybugs and rainbows on fat, sunburned cheeks and pretend I'm not completely miserable and on the verge of crying every other breath I take. This could be like, art therapy, or something. I might actually leave here not wanting to kill myself."

Tori frowned and held me tighter.

I immediately regretted speaking.

"I didn't mean that last part. I don't know why I said that," I quickly threw out, shaking my head and blinking back tears behind my glasses. "Sorry. Put me to work. Seriously. Is my booth ready, or do I need to set it up?" I glanced around the lot.

"Actually, I wanted to run something by you." Tori released my hand to tie her long, blonde hair back out of her face. "Kali had to stay home with Cameron 'cause he has that foot and hand disease or whatever it's called, so Cole is flying solo at the kissing booth, which would be fine, but we have a lot of guys here with potentially thick wallets."

My brows lifted.

I knew exactly what she was getting at. She really didn't need to say any more, but she did.

"I'm just saying," Tori continued on. "This could be beneficial to both Whitecaps *and* yourself. They say the first step is the most difficult. This could make it a little easier, you know?"

"What could make it easier? If I made out with random guys all day?"

I wasn't convinced this was the best move for me. Even though Tori knew everything that had gone down six days ago, and always had my back, meaning she would never set me up for something she didn't think was in my best interest, still, I wasn't so sure.

"You don't have to kiss them on the mouth," Tori informed me. "Cole isn't. He's just offering up his cheek or kissing theirs. And just look at them. They don't mind that. Those women are practically trampling over each other to get to the front of the line."

I looked over my shoulder in the direction of the kissing booth.

Tori was right. The line was at least twenty bodies deep, and the women all looked eager, pushing closer every chance they got, clapping their hands, high-fiving each other and counting their cash.

And poor Cole, he did look a little overwhelmed all by himself as he flinched while some grandma planted a big, wet one on his cheek.

"I don't know," I said, turning back around.

"Is there any reason why you shouldn't do this?" Tori asked.

I released a tight breath, then shook my head.

She tilted hers with a soft, sympathetic smile, took hold of my hand again, and tugged me toward the restaurant. "It'll be good. I promise. But if it is too much, you can always back out. No one will say anything."

Tori and I walked up the stairs to Whitecaps and pulled the door open to step inside. I pushed my glasses on top of my head.

The brightly colored, beach-themed restaurant was empty, except for J.R., who was in charge of all the cooking today. And I guessed Nate, who was probably back in his office.

If Nate had a choice between being in his office and being out of it, no matter the circumstance, he chose the former.

"But if I don't do it, who will help Cole?" I asked, following Tori to the kitchen window where trays held stacks of burgers and hot dogs, ready to be served.

"I don't know. No one, I guess," she answered. "I can't. Jamie would blow a gasket and go on a killing spree. Brian too, so Syd's out. I'm going to have her do the face-painting since Lauren called dibs on games and is refusing to move her ass to another booth, even if it means sacrificing her own selfishness for once and doing something in the best interest of the team." She rolled her eyes and slid a tray off the ledge. "Help me carry these out, will you?" Tori asked, tipping her chin at the other tray.

I grabbed the tray of hot dogs and smiled through the window at J.R. when he looked up from the cutting board.

He smiled back, immediately, and, like always, wasn't shy to initiate conversation with a friendly "Hey you."

Which only made me think about the man he shared that kitchen with, who was the exact opposite when it came to workplace pleasantries and prompting conversations.

My smile disappeared as quickly as it came on. "Hey," I returned faintly.

"Keep them coming, Jay. We got a big crowd out there," Tori said. "Lots of mouths to feed."

"Roger that." J.R. passed his smile between the two of us before he resumed slicing onions and heads of lettuce. "Why the pouty face?" he asked me. "You and Sean get into a fight or something? Is that why he isn't here and I'm having to feed the whole fucking town all by myself?"

I let out a small noise that sounded like a squeak, my eyes so wide I was sure I had zero forehead space left.

Damn, J.R. was way more perceptive than I gave him credit for.

Shit.

"Do we look like we have time to chat?" Tori asked, stepping up to the window and saving me from having to answer. "I've already been asked twice about the food situation. People are starving, Jay. And considering this is an event hosted by a restaurant where food is *supposed* to be served, I'm thinking we need to feed them sooner rather than later. What do you think?"

"All right, damn," he muttered, suddenly looking uncomfortable, which was a common reaction to being on the receiving end of Tori's signature sass. "Jesus. Sorry I asked."

J.R. went back to focusing fully on his vegetable chopping.

I sort of felt bad, but apologizing might lead to that explanation I was avoiding, so I kept my mouth shut and followed behind Tori in the direction of the doors.

"Thanks," I whispered, falling in a step behind her.

She turned her head and winked. "Any time, babe."

Jenna came rushing inside with her kids, Oliver and Olivia.

She smiled at us. "Hey! Can we use the bathroom? Is that allowed?"

Olivia pinched her legs together. "I'm gonna bust!" she shrieked.

"Gross, Livy." Oliver grimaced and leaned away from his twin.

Tori laughed. "Only you three. Everyone else has to take it down the beach to the porta pots," she said.

Jenna looked relieved. "Thank you," she rushed out, then the three of them hurried past us.

Tori and I headed outside, carefully carrying our trays down the steps, and slid them onto the tables set up beside the railing. There were already condiments put out and aluminum pans filled with burger toppings and utensils.

"Okay, so, are you good?" Tori asked, moving to stand inside her booth and tying on her work apron.

The sunlight caught her square-cut diamond ring, making it sparkle.

I'd seen Tori's ring a handful of times already. I knew it was stunning. Probably worth a fortune. And it fit her delicate hand perfectly. Until six days ago, I'd never seen a prettier ring.

Until I did see a prettier ring.

Sadness flooded me, along with this strange hurt I'd never felt before. The pain felt hollow and heavy at the same time, like it scooped out all my insides, taking bone and blood and replacing it with *nothing*, leaving me an empty, gaping wound.

A hole so deep, it would never see any sunlight.

God, why did I come here today? I never should've left my bed.

"Shay?"

My head snapped up at the sound of my name, and I locked on to Tori's curious expression.

Shit.

I cleared my throat. "Yeah, I'm good," I lied, quickly dropping my glasses down when agony stung and made my eyes water. I bit the inside of my cheek and prayed for a pain I could get angry at instead.

A blistered mouth felt promising.

Tori looked momentarily unsure, but quickly covered it with a pageant-winning smile as she turned her display sign toward the crowd, showing food prices and choices. "You got this, Shay. Just have fun with it," she told me, waving at the line quickly forming behind where I stood.

I didn't think there was a chance in hell I'd be having fun at anything any time soon, but I kept that to myself, and with sagging shoulders, I turned and crossed the parking lot.

I passed the face-painting booth and waved meekly at Syd, who was cleaning off her brushes in a cup of water while a little girl sat waiting in a chair, swinging her legs excitedly.

Like Tori, Syd also knew what all had gone down six days ago. But I couldn't talk about it with her yet either.

And I communicated that by not pausing or slowing in my steps when she appeared eager for conversation.

The smile she was wearing changed from encouraging to subtle and understanding.

Reaching the far end of the lot, I slid into the booth beside Cole, who had his back to the line and was discreetly scrubbing a rag over his suntanned cheek.

"Rough start?" I asked, pushing my glasses on top of my head again, since we were shaded inside the booth.

"Nah, I'm just doing this every tenth person or so," he said. "Or if someone uses tongue."

My back straightened. "What?"

Gross! People were using tongue?

Cole chuckled and tucked his rag into his pocket. "It's not that bad. I am grateful for a break, though." He turned back around and flattened his hands on the booth, informing the crowd, "It's time for the guys to pony up some cash! We got Shay up now. Ladies, I'll be back in thirty."

Collective groans filled the air before the women in the line dispersed.

I felt panic tickle my spine. Crossing my arms over my chest, I stepped closer to Cole.

"You could keep going, you know? We could do this together. I lure the crowd, you do the kissing. It's a win-win for everyone, really."

"Even the dudes?"

"Sure, why not?"

Cole smirked as he grabbed the can of soda off the ledge of the booth and took a quick drink. "I gotta take a piss," he explained, checking the time on his watch. "And I wanna call Kali and see how Cameron's doing. I shouldn't be too long."

I felt a slow-moving warmth fill my chest—contentment for Kali and her quiet romance with Cole. And even though it should've surprised me, appreciating someone else's union when I had so recently severed my own, it didn't.

I was happy for my friend.

"Okay." I took a deep breath and stepped up to the front of the booth, my fingers tangling together on the ledge next to the jar labeled *$5 for a Smooch*. "I'm not sure how well this is going to go... I'm really just planning on talking to people."

No fucking way was I kissing anyone.

Cole stepped out of the booth and stood in front of it, stuck two fingers in his mouth, and cut a sharp whistle through the air that had heads turning and eyes focusing on me.

The DJ turned down the music.

Oh, crap.

"The kissing booth is open!" Cole hollered. "And five dollars to kiss Shay seems like highway robbery if you ask me. She's hot."

"*Cole*," I snapped, my face heating up as the men in the crowd clapped and cheered in response.

"Yeah, Shay!" Tori yelled, whooping at the top of her lungs.

I met her eyes as Cole stepped away, laughing, and silently pleaded with Tori for her to stop making a commotion, which only seemed to egg her on even more.

She leaned out her booth and pointed at me, yelling, "Go get her, boys!"

Great.

Looking away with an enormous amount of apprehension tightening and twisting my stomach up in knots, I swept my eyes over the sea of men (where did all the women go?), hoping none of them were paying attention to me or my loudmouthed friends.

Unfortunately, the men were paying attention. All of them, to be specific. Especially one in particular.

With dark, short, styled hair and even darker eyes, the eager gentleman smiled at me as he pushed his way through the crowd.

Maybe he was simply eager for conversation?

Yeah, right. *Look where you're standing, Shay!*

I shifted nervously on my feet.

The young guy was attractive enough. Totally someone I'd normally go for.

No, I argued with myself. *His hair isn't long enough and his arms are bare. I like tattoos. I like a male body that tells a story. I bet this guy doesn't even have any scars. Plus, he's wearing a polo shirt. Total preppy. I bet he drives something expensive. A two-door sports car, most likely. Which could only mean one thing—perpetual bachelor. Everyone knows fitting multiple car seats in the back of a two-door vehicle is a giant pain in the...*

I blinked and shook my head. *What the hell was I doing?*

God, I was losing it. Was I really going to stand here silently judging this guy as if he even had a chance right now? I wasn't on the market. Single, yes. But no way was I ready for anything involving a guy. What was wrong with me? Why did I care if he had tattoos, or what his views were on kids? Was it the sun? Heat stroke? I hadn't been outside that long, had I?

My breathing accelerated, quick puffs of air began pushing past my lips. And my panic only escalated further the closer Preppy got, because now I could see the cute little lift in his brow as he tugged out his wallet. And before I knew it, as if he'd possibly bribed people on his way through the crowd to make sure he had top spot, he was right there at the front of the line, and right in front of me.

Oh, God. This was not good. This was not good at all.

Smiling, *interested*, the guy pulled a five-dollar bill out of his wallet before tucking it back away and dropped the cash in the jar, keeping his eyes on me the entire time as a steady line of eager donors formed behind him.

"That dude was right," Preppy started, spreading his large hands out on the ledge, head tilting. "I'd pay a lot more than five bucks for this kiss. You should change your sign."

A nervous laugh caught in my throat. Then, because I didn't want this guy thinking for *another second* he was about to get a kiss from me, I prepared in my head the explanation I needed to give him, one that would hopefully keep his money in that jar, only to have my thoughts abruptly cut off.

"You wanna explain to me what you're doin'?"

I sucked in a breath and stood up straighter, feeling panic shock me like every part of my body was touching a live wire.

That low, rough, and achingly beautiful voice filtered through my ears and reached some deep part of me that hadn't been scraped out and tossed away. And then it reached deeper still and spread, filling that giant hole inside me, replacing everything I lost with something better, because of who that voice belonged to.

My eyes focused and moved first, then my head turned.

We locked eyes.

Sean stood off to the side of the line that had formed, and I knew just from hearing his beaten tone how he'd look standing there, but I wasn't prepared to see it. Even if he hadn't spoken first and I had seen his approach, I still wouldn't be prepared for that broken, empty look on his face.

Breath shuddered inside my chest. I suddenly felt dizzy.

It was too much.

It was all too much—being here in this stupid booth promoting something I was absolutely *not* participating in, seeing the one person I was hoping to see, who was never supposed to be here. Those eyes—those beautiful copper eyes that were now black and void of life, when they should've been filled with all the love in the world. Nothing but love.

I didn't understand it. Why did he look like that? He shouldn't look like that. He shouldn't look exactly like I felt. I gave him everything. I gave up everything so he could have the life he deserved.

But the man staring back at me didn't look like a man who had it all.

He looked like a man who deserved nothing.

"You left," he growled.

A stabbing pain shot through my chest.

God...

Hearing his voice, knowing I broke my promise to Sean, and seeing what it did to him...It was crippling.

I didn't think I had the words to explain myself, because they were locked inside my heart. I wouldn't speak them.

What could I say?

"I-I—" My mouth snapped closed when Sean approached.

Glaring, he got up beside Preppy while reaching for his back pocket, his other hand fishing the five dollars out of the jar. "Take a walk," Sean ordered, pressing the bill against the guy's chest.

The man backed up, muttering, "No problem, man. Sorry," under his breath before he slinked away.

Sean turned back to me, then held my eyes as he dropped his wallet into the jar.

My brain short-circuited.

The crowd reacted with interest and went quiet.

I quickly glanced around.

Everyone was staring at us, looking curious. Tori and Syd were grinning, most likely because it appeared Sean was purchasing the kissing booth and declaring my mouth his, which I wanted to grin about myself, but I couldn't because he shouldn't be declaring something like that anymore.

What the fuck was happening? Why was he even here?

Wide-eyed and heart racing, I watched Sean flatten his hands on the ledge and lean forward.

"I fucked up," he said.

"What?" I whispered.

Oh, God, his girls...

"What happened? Is everything okay?" I asked.

"You got my back, I should've had yours," Sean replied, ignoring my questions. "I should've protected us and I didn't. I let you walk. All your hurt, it's on me, Shayla. I should've known what you were doin'. I was too fucked up to see it."

Blinking, I shook my head. I was so confused right now.

So nothing had happened with his girls?

Sean read that and continued explaining himself.

"Hearin' you tell me you were leavin'... You were puttin' me first and thinkin' I wanted my old life back. The life I had with Val before I fucked it all up. And it's my fault for not informin' you—that shit with Val? That was over before I got put away. We both know that now. Feelin's are always gonna be there 'cause she gave me my girls, and she cares for me, knowin' what all I've been through, but we're better as friends. She agrees."

She agrees?

"You talked to Val?" I asked.

"Yeah."

"And you didn't get your old life back?"

Sean cocked his head. "Did you *not* hear me just say I don't want it?"

"I don't understand... Your girls. Your family. You want that. I know you do."

That was *everything* he wanted.

Sean leaned closer. "I got my girls. I got Val as a friend. What I *don't got* is my family, 'cause you're here standin' in a fuckin' kissing booth instead of at my back where you're supposed to be. How the fuck can I have my family when the woman I love more than my own fuckin' *life* isn't with me? You wanna explain that?"

My lips parted. I got it then. I understood why Sean was here and why he looked the way he did.

I understood everything.

Sean didn't have it all because he didn't have *me*. And he didn't have me because I left when I said I wouldn't. I had given him that broken, beaten down look. I took away his chance at getting all the happiness the world had to offer him, when I'd promised to make sure he got it.

I left him.

I did this.

"I'm so sorry," I whispered.

"You've said that enough."

"I haven't," I argued. "I promised you I wouldn't leave, and I did. You gotta know how much that killed me, Sean."

"I know how much, baby. I saw you."

I pulled my lips between my teeth as my eyes stung.

God, I love him.

"You stood there wantin' me, wantin' us, as much as I did, and you buried that want so I could get it all."

He knew. He knew everything.

"Yes," I whimpered.

"But you didn't know, I already had it," he shared.

Oh, God.

"I should've told you," he said, leaning closer. "I am so fuckin' sorry I didn't."

I wiped the tears from my cheeks. "It's okay."

"It ain't, but you know it now."

"I do."

He stared longingly into my face. "Am I yours?"

I nodded immediately.

"You love me?"

My shoulders dropped. "Oh, my God, you have no idea," I cried, my heart splitting open and letting those words spill out. "I've been in love with you since last summer. Maybe even before that. I don't know. I don't remember the time between meeting you and loving you. I just know I love you and I can't stop. That's it."

Sean's eyes warmed to that beautiful copper shade again as his face got soft, then he glanced down between us, met my eyes again, and asked. "You gonna get the fuck outta this booth so I can get at you?"

I stopped breathing.

Holy yes, please get at me.

"I didn't want to be in here in the first place," I informed Sean as I stepped out of the booth and met him around the side. "And I wasn't going to kiss anyone. I swear."

"So what, you were just gonna take their money and chat?"

"That's exactly what I was going to do. And don't act like people wouldn't pay. I'm a good fucking time."

Sean chuckled, his mouth stretching into a grin, as he took my face between his hands. He bent lower.

Arms around his waist, I rolled up onto my toes, head tilting back to give him access, and as his lips slid against mine and pressed, a round of applause surrounded us, along with sharp whistling and cheers from Tori and Syd.

We laughed inside our kiss, but we kept it up.

It was a kiss worthy of applause, in my opinion.

When we finally pulled away, I planted my chin on Sean's chest and smiled up at him as his arms circled my back.

"Told my girls about us," he said.

Us. "You did?"

"Yeah," he murmured, brushing strands of hair off my cheek and staring into my eyes. "Val and I talked to them about it. They like you. They were excited."

I grinned. That felt nice. Almost as nice as this.

"We're splittin' custody fifty-fifty."

My entire body jerked. "Oh, my God, Sean, that's *great*!" I yelled. "I'm so happy for you."

He smiled, then he pulled me tighter against him and dropped his head so his mouth was in my hair. "Wouldn't be happenin' if it wasn't for you. You gotta know how much you mean to me."

"Sean," I whispered, leaning away so I could see his face. "It happened because of *you*..."

He cut me off. "Meetin' you, gettin' your voice in my head and feelin' what you'd say in my heart, I was able to get it knowin' it was mine," he shared. "I might've gotten it without you, but I wouldn't know I'm worth it. That was you."

A tear slid out of my eye. "Okay," I whispered.

His brows shot up. "Yeah? You ain't gonna argue that?"

He sounded shocked.

"I'm too happy to argue right now," I returned. "I'm in your arms, you just kissed me stupid..."

"Shit, baby, if that's all it takes." Sean bent down, gripped me under my butt, and lifted me in the air while he pressed kisses all over my face. "I would've been doin' this since we first fuckin' met."

"Sean!" I screamed, holding on to him.

It was not a scream of protest.

I was laughing, shrieking, crying tears of joy, and waving at the crowd as they cheered us on.

I said my happiness came from being in Sean's arms and feeling his mouth against mine, and that was true, but it wasn't all of it, and because Sean knew his worth now and was well on his way to living life in all its beauty, I knew I didn't need to list the rest.

But I was prepared to.

For him, I always would be.

Epilogue

SHAYLA

One Month Later

I stood in front of the mirror in Sean's bathroom as I popped in my silver hoop earrings, this pair the classiest I owned since they were studded in diamonds.

The necklace I was wearing was classy too—a halo pendant, also encrusted in diamonds.

Sean and I were going out tonight and eating at a restaurant that required reservations, and in my opinion, reservations called for classy jewelry.

Aside from my earrings and necklace, I was wearing a blue sapphire ring my late nana had left for me. It was an antique, more than a hundred years old according to my mother, and if that didn't scream class, I didn't know what did.

And on my left hand, I wore the threaded ring Sean had given me when we got to his house after working the Memorial Day carnival together, and after a round of hot and heavy hallway sex, not being able to make it to the bedroom.

Classy was the best of the best, and the ring I never took off was just that.

I loved it more than any piece of jewelry I owned.

Sean didn't propose to me that day, and I didn't need him to. The ring was something he'd made thinking of me, hoping I'd wear it like he wore the threads around his wrist, and knowing how much those threads meant to him and the gesture he was making by giving me that ring, that was enough.

It was more than enough.

I didn't need a proposal. I didn't need Sean getting down on one knee. We were together, letting go and letting things happen like we always did, and because we were doing that, Sean and I both knew we would eventually get married and make things official.

But right now? We were just enjoying the ride.

And like all rides that included Sean, it was continually getting better and better.

Life was truly amazing.

Sean and I spent a lot of time with his girls, splitting weekends with Val and alternating weekdays, based on everyone's schedules. Hair by Shayla was picking up thanks to word-of-mouth, leaving me to cut back on my hours at Whitecaps.

I was still able to pick up a shift once or twice a week, which kept me happy. I loved that job, and not only because I had a mad crush on the cook.

Working with my friends-turned-family was always part of my dream. And now with Sean, his girls, *and* my salon, I felt like I had it all.

I was applying my lipstick—the deep ruby color Sean liked so much—when I heard the front door open and close, and then Sean's heavy booted feet getting closer until he filled the doorway of the bathroom.

"There you are. You better hurry up and get ready," I told him.

"Reservations are in thirty minutes." I pushed my nail along the edge of my lower lip to sharpen up the line, then I capped the lipstick and looked over at him. "Where you been anyway?"

Sean had his shoulder pressed to the door frame, leaning into it, as his eyes slowly canvassed the little black dress I had on. "You wore that the night you couldn't spell for shit," he murmured. "Didn't get to tell you then 'cause I didn't know if I could, but that dress." His eyes lifted and met mine. "*Fuck*," he growled.

My skin tingled. Best compliment yet.

"You like?" I teased.

"Oh, yeah."

I grinned. "Wouldn't look half as good without this going with it." I held up my left hand and showed him the ring.

That got a grin out of Sean to beat all grins, equal parts beautiful and breathtaking.

And holy Lord, was it sexy.

"Shit. Go get dressed before we miss these reservations altogether." I laughed, guiding him out of the bathroom with me. His arm draped over my shoulders, and I looked up at him as we entered the bedroom. "Where were you? I thought you got off two hours ago?"

"I did," he answered. "You look at that stupid snap app today?"

"Not recently. I did this morning. Why?"

"Go look at it."

I tilted my head. "Did you do something on Snapchat?"

No fucking way. He hated that app.

Sean didn't answer me, and when he *still* didn't answer me after I narrowed my eyes and inched closer, I squealed, spinning around and snatching my phone off the trunk he used as a night table.

I ignored his breathy chuckle as I unlocked the screen and clicked on the app. When I pulled up my friends, my mouth dropped open.

Sean had a story.

"No way," I whispered, smiling now as I made sure my volume was turned up before clicking on Sean's icon, which didn't give any hints to what his story was about. I could barely make out the tiny image, even when I raised the screen closer to my face.

I didn't need volume for Sean's story after all. It was a still image of his ribs, and a tattoo-gun pressing into his skin. I gasped and looked up.

Sean had pulled his T-shirt off. His chest and arms had bandages on them. The kind of bandages that obviously covered tattoos.

I dropped my phone on the bed and walked over. "Sean," I said, taking hold of his hand when he reached out for me.

Staying silent, he pulled me in front of him and slowly peeled away one of the bandages, revealing the design underneath that hid the word I could no longer make out, even upon close inspection.

"You got them covered up?" I asked, looking into his face.

He nodded, smiling a little, then kept peeling away bandages and revealing more designs that were beautiful because of the way they looked—roses with soft shadows around them—and because of how well they concealed what had been there before.

Sean would never see those words again.

"Oh, my God, I'm so happy," I whispered, not even caring about the tears in my eyes ruining my makeup job.

Who the fuck needed reservations anyway? We could just go eat at Frank's.

The last bandage remained on his rib, and Sean left it there.

"You do that one. That's yours," he said.

My breath caught in my throat. *Oh, my God.*

"You... that's my tattoo? You got one for me?" I asked.

"Told you I would." Sean grinned and took in a deep breath, then he pushed his hair out of his face and held it back, keeping his fingers interlocked behind his head. "Fuck, I hope you like it. I like it."

"I'm sure I'll love it if you like it," I said.

"Go ahead. Take it off."

"Okay." I gave him a smile, and with excitement warming my blood, I reached forward and gently peeled away the bandage on Sean's rib, revealing the word I'd written there all those weeks ago in black marker, but now, that word blended with another, so there were two words mirroring each other, and depending on where you focused determined which word you'd see.

Worthy or *Shayla*.

"Sean," I whispered, blinking tears from my eyes.

"You like it?" he asked.

"It's the most beautiful thing I've ever seen, and I've done some amazing updos in my time. Let me tell you."

He chuckled. "I'm gonna assume that's some fuckin' hair shit you're talkin' about."

I nodded, peering up at him then. "I love it. I love it so much."

His thumb caught a tear on my cheek. Then he dropped his arm and looked down at himself.

"Couldn't get one without the other," he shared. "Wouldn't be able to get *worthy* if it wasn't for you, and your name... now I know I'm good enough to have that on my skin for fuckin' ever."

My stomach flipped and dropped out. *Oh, my God, did he just say that?*

Fuck you, reservations. We were not making those.

"You're goddamned right, for fuckin' ever," I cried, sniffling, letting the tears fall. I didn't care.

Sean lifted his head to look at me, then broke into laughter. "I am so fuckin' insane for you, you know that?"

I nodded quickly and wiped off my face, because I could not be crying while asking the next thing I needed an answer to.

This was serious.

"The question is, though, are you insane enough to skip out on a fancy steak dinner and make love to me on the floor instead, followed by some takeout from Frank's? Because I can't see myself leaving out of here before *both* of us orgasm at least once, and I really want you banging me where we first did it. I love that memory. I want to relive it."

Sean's grin faded to a smile that was equally beautiful, then he reached out and took my face between his hands, bent down, and pressed his forehead against mine.

"Frank's does have good crust," he uttered softly.

My heart warmed and melted into a pile of Sean-loving goo.

"You're the best," I whispered.

"Say that while I'm fuckin' you on the floor."

"You got it."

Sean grinned.

I grinned right on back until we started kissing, then I just held on, let go of the dinner plans we'd made, and let what needed to happen happen.

For Sean, with Sean, I always would.

Look for Nate and Jenna's story in

DOWN TOO DEEP.

AVAILABLE IN SUMMER 2019.

ABOUT THE AUTHOR

J. Daniels is the *New York Times* and *USA Today* best-selling author of the Sweet Addiction series, the Alabama Summer series, and the Dirty Deeds series. She loves curling up with a good book, drinking a ridiculous amount of coffee, and writing stories her children will never be allowed to read. Daniels grew up in Baltimore and resides in Maryland with her family.

You can learn more at:

AuthorJDaniels.com

Twitter @JDanielsBooks

Facebook.com/JDanielsAuthor